THE BONNIE ROAD

Suzanne d'Corsey

ThunderPoint Publishing Ltd.

First Published in Great Britain in 2015 by
ThunderPoint Publishing Limited
Summit House
4-5 Mitchell Street
Edinburgh
Scotland EH6 7BD

Copyright © Suzanne d'Corsey 2015
The moral right of the author has been asserted.
All rights reserved.

Without limiting the rights under copyright reserved above, no part of this publication may be reproduced, stored in or introduced into a retrieval system, or transmitted in any form or by any means (electronic, mechanical, photocopying, recording or otherwise), without the prior written permission of both the copyright owner and the above publisher of the work.

Extracts from The Book of Common Prayer, the rights of which are vested in the Crown, are reproduced by permission of the Crown's Patentee, Cambridge University Press.

This book is a work of fiction.
Names, places, characters and locations are used fictitiously and any resemblance to actual persons, living or dead, is purely coincidental and a product of the authors creativity.

Illustrations: © Pat Vestal
Back Cover: © Pat Vestal
Front Cover: © aleksandarvelasevic
ISBN (Paperback): 978-0-9929768-6-6
ISBN (ebook): 978-1-910946-01-5

www.thunderpoint.scot

Dedication

To my beloved daughter
Jules

Acknowledgements

I would like to thank those who assisted with The Bonnie Road's creation: from the start, encouragement from Jim Thomson, and valuable editorial work by John Paine. Thank you, Kier Salmon and Dolores Klaich, for your vision and advice. Deep gratitude goes to Beth Clary, who has journeyed with me as the best of writing companions from the novel's inception to its publication; to Lisa Wilson, one of those truly rare collaborators in a lifetime; and to Jules Thomson, who kept me right with her keen knowledge of developments in archaeology and folklore, for her lively intellect and assistance with everything from regional accents to Gaelic phrases.

And as ever, I cannot thank my dear parents, Pat and Ted Vestal, enough, for their loving support and belief in me, and for being excellent examples of the artistic and writing discipline necessary to create the finished product, and the vision to follow one's vocation through thick and thin.

Special thanks go to my mother for the remarkable painting she created for the cover art of this edition of The Bonnie Road, and for her illustrations and maps that enhance the book far beyond my solo efforts.

To ThunderPoint Publishing: Seonaid Francis for her enthusiastic support and keen editing, and to Huw Francis for his many talents in the evolution of manuscript to book.

And, always, for Bride.

And see not ye that bonny road,
Which winds about the fernie brae?
That is the road to fair Elfland,
Where you and I this night maun gae.

St Andrews

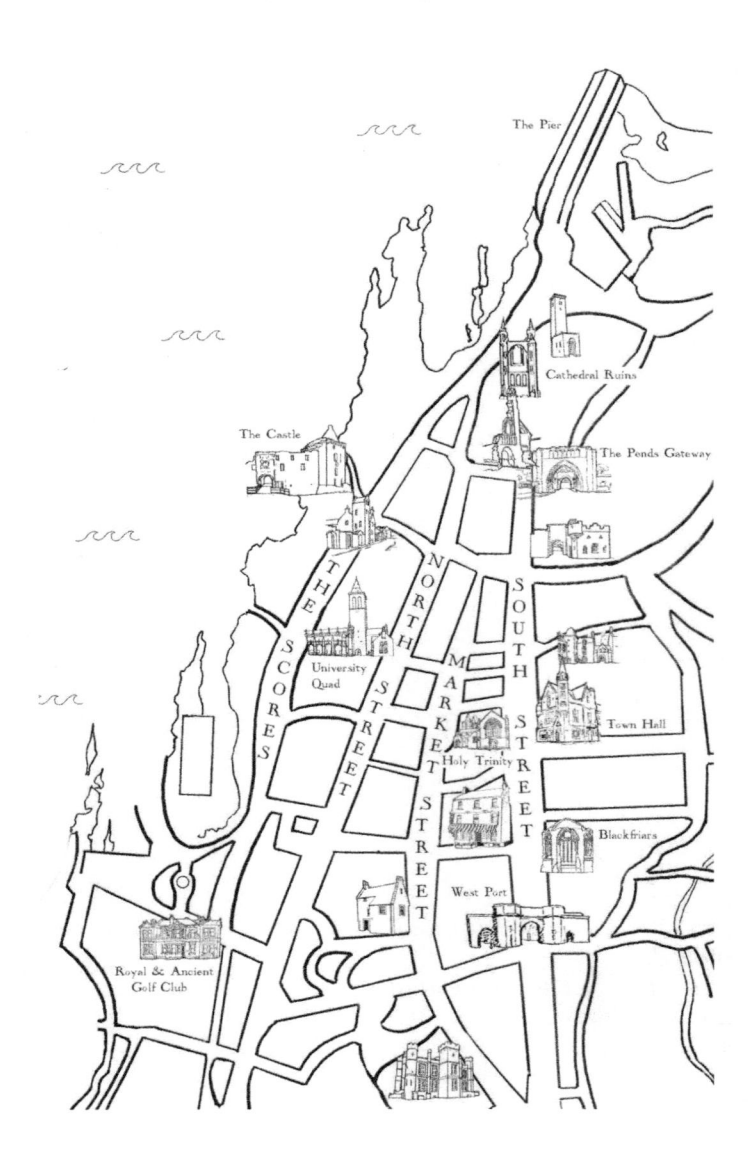

PROLOGUE

Morag's Quair of Light and Shadows
My grandmother passed me in transit. She was leaving, I was coming into this world, our spirits meeting at the door to my mother's womb, as she bent over the bed to close the thin crinkled lids of her own mother's eyes. The same bed I sleep in now, where sometimes my dead Gran still visits, standing at my feet when she has a message to impart, or sometimes just for the hell of it. I've lost three lovers very abruptly when she's shown up in this manner, aye, one through the window and down the old rowan tree, the same route by which access had been gained, right enough, and twice as fast.

Some lovers are excited by the idea of sharing a witch's bed. The magical thrill draws them in, the power of the witch's green eyes, the unabashed desire directed at them, rumors of ritual sex-magic and occult practices, a dangerous edge to the passions already ignited. All is well until they discover she really is a witch. In the heat of passion the spirits visit, the cat has a knowing wink, the sighs and whispers are joined by others unseen. A chuckle in the ear from an invisible throat, a presence at the bedside, a transformation of the witch-lover into some indefinable creature, no longer human. Then is the safe boundary of their fantasy dashed, and away they flee, leaving me to sigh or curse in my rumpled sheets.

Then there are the others, the brave few who seek the awakening of an innate wisdom, who know that those who can offer this ancient gift with skill and knowledge are rare indeed.

It's true, time is an estuary river flowing back on itself, and we Gilbrides have only to ease a hand into the stream to see the spirals of history rippling about us.

My grandmother kissed me as she went by. There may have been enough vestige of the physical world in her yet to create a bit of heartbreak, both at leaving her own daughter, as magnificent a witch as ever traipsed over the ancient cobbles of the town streets, and at not having the opportunity to dandle this new bairn on her knee. And she gave me the gift in that interchange. Not only her Highland name, Morag, to be mine. She kissed to life a double spirit. A duality that can see the past and sense the future. And the irrepressible desire to manifest divinity in the act of lovemaking.

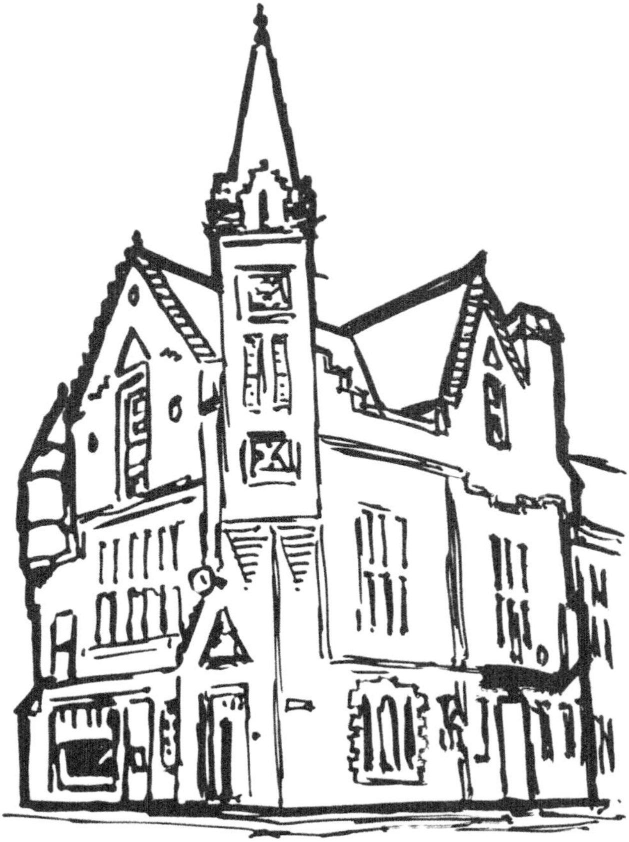

PART ONE

Chapter 1

September 1979

This is how it appeared to Morag. In a rustling of feathers, in the sideways glance of a black shining eye. The shadow crow, little herald to the Dark Goddess, hovered about Captain Ogilvy's creased forehead, its phantom beak tugging at his sparse hair as if testing for signs of life. Taking possession even as Morag scribbled his half-coherent words on the page.

"Will my sister come, Morag?" he asked.

She stilled herself for a moment to be sure. "No."

His eyes half closed as the feathers caressed his brow.

"She won't, but another will come in her place." And as she said it, a sharp tingling swept across her shoulders and breast to herald a premonition. "What's this?" she said, half to herself. "What's this?" But Captain Ogilvy had drifted back into a morphine-induced haze. The tingling increased to a painful shock, and Morag stood, surprised. The phantom hoodie craw opened its wings in a ghostly whisper and flew away to find someone else in the hospital. The captain would have a few weeks yet to live.

Morag went outside and straightaway opened the quair – the book – of divination. Which is to say, she dissolved into the elements and tripped over into the second sight. And by the stars and moon, there she saw the one who would be coming for the Captain. A foreigner, yet not a foreigner. All in the instant, out of time, Morag knew it would be someone who would test her sorely. A catalyst. Harbinger. Innocent of her own power to alter fate. Morag could discern nothing beyond this, which was equally distressing.

Into the cold air she plunged, and down the lane bordered by the old priory walls. The rooks went silent in the stilled breeze, element and birds caught together in the golden-leafed branches of the beeches. Then they burst out, wheeled and swooped in the thickened air, and old Mrs. Mackenzie, walking her wee dog up the lane, crossed over and stood with her back pressed hard against the opposite wall, Westie quaking in fear, a little stream of piss running down the pavement, until Morag and the company of rooks had passed by. At the bottom of the lane, and up to the old city gate called the East Port, the birds dispersed like smoke swirling and rising, and she looked down to see the plovers in the harbor, where the pongy mud of the burn meets the incoming tide. It's in the way the birds move that portents are divined, and even a slight twist in the airts offers insight, and this is how she sees through the fabric of creation. In this instance, it was a lone figure standing on a train platform. She had already arrived.

*

The suitcase slipped from her tired fingers and fell to its side under a large station sign, which read, 'Leuchars alight here for St. Andrews.' But nothing more than soggy pastures surrounded the platform, their far boundaries erased in the misting rain. Frayed, downtrodden hay stubbled the field on one side of the tracks, and from the other a herd of damp sheep, tongues protruding in the effort, bleated what sounded like deep belches.

Nobody else stepped onto the deserted platform. No other doors along the sleek length of the Intercity opened. An unseen hand from inside pulled her door to with a crash. The engine roared, the train moved away, gathering speed, until it slid around the bend of a hill and was gone.

She shrugged her carry-on bag higher to her shoulder. There was no movement inside the station building, nor in the gloomy waiting room. No cars on the road. She wondered if perhaps she'd made a mistake, got off at the wrong station. She pulled her coat tighter against the steady cold wind that had a tarry smell to it. The sign beside her creaked mournfully. In her tired mind, she went over the travel instructions again, fighting down despair.

She sensed a presence on the platform, and looked over her shoulder, but nobody was there. Nor anyone to be seen through the window of the ticket office. Only the dark shape of a large crow perched on the top of a lamppost.

A deep roar came from beyond the field. She thought it was another train coming through, but the tracks stretched away empty in either direction. The sound grew louder and louder. She glanced all around, bewildered. Nothing. The sheep raised their heads and looked at her, as if she were to blame. The terrible noise quickly reached an incomprehensible threshold, a thunderclap suspended at its peak. The sheep scattered, heavy wool bunching and stretching like muddy accordions.

She slapped her palms to her ears. The platform, the very air vibrated. Her whole body filled with sound till it felt as if it poured in harsh waves out her mouth and eyes. Then she saw it.

Heading straight at the station, low over the field, came a dark aircraft. It skimmed directly over, so close the air followed, and she saw a tunnel of fire clinging to its tail, saw the very detail of colors in the flame.

She spun to see it rise and bank sharply to the left, a shooting star arcing over distant hills.

"Rosalind? Pardon me. Wretched jets! Rosalind Ehrhart?"

An earnest, narrow face tilted over her shoulder, straight brown hair disordered by the wind, anxious eyes searching through wire-rim glasses. "I'm so sorry I'm late. I'm Helen Forbes. Were you waiting long? I do hope not. Oh dear, are you all right?"

She's English, Rosalind's mother had said with the last minute instructions. But she can't help that.

"That jet," said Rosalind. "I didn't know what it was."

"RAF Leuchars. They make a dreadful noise. This way. Oh, your bag! Allow me." Helen grabbed the suitcase and took the stairs over the tracks at a trot, her calves pumping up and down below her tweed skirt. "Sorry I'm in such a frightful rush!"

Rosalind shouldered her bag and ran to keep up. Their mothers had been close friends before either she or Helen had been born, and though the mothers kept one another up with news and the proud progress of their daughters, Rosalind had never actually interacted with Helen before this trip.

"I hope," Rosalind said, "it wasn't inconvenient to come get me."

"Heavens, not at all. Such a shame about your uncle."

Helen led the way to a small red car. "This side." She hoisted Rosalind's suitcase into the trunk. "Unless you want to drive. Ha ha."

When they settled in, Helen forced the gearshift forward, pulled hard on the steering wheel and sped off down the narrow lane.

A red double-decker bus turned at the top of the hill and came at them, filling the narrow road. Helen never slowed.

Rosalind braced her hand against the dashboard, and shut her eyes as the bus thundered by with inches to spare. Helen drove hunched over, her chin almost touching the wheel she gripped so fiercely.

"I've never met my uncle," Rosalind said, voice higher than normal.

"I'm afraid the doctor didn't offer much hope when we phoned this morning. We don't really know Captain Ogilvy, aside from an occasional hello on the street, and he may or may not reply." Helen gave a sympathetic smile, then yanked the car back to the center of the road. "But how fortunate you made it before... yes."

Glimpses of velvety greens and fairways bordered by dense rough, and beyond that, the sea, gray and choppy, opened to view, then snapped out of sight behind pine forests or stone walls. The low clouds and diffused but sharp light gave an unreal, intimate quality to the landscape. A rain shower passed over, and through it a brilliant double rainbow emerged.

Helen pointed through the thrashing windscreen wipers. "There's St. Andrews now."

Church spires and towers appeared to tear rents in the clouds, exposing ribbons of blue over the sea. They passed a huge modern hotel, banners flapping, which dominated the golf links on their left. As they entered the town, the street ascended past stone buildings and broad sidewalks suddenly filled with people. Helen stopped at a bleeping, flashing pedestrian crossing, where upbeat Scottish accordion music spilled out the open doorway of the 'St. Andrews Woollen Mill.' She drummed her fingers against the steering wheel as a young woman pushed a plastic-encased baby stroller across the road. After the deserted train station, St. Andrews bustled with activity.

"These new pedestrian crossings are dreadful. You've to sit

and wait when there's nobody there." Helen pointed to a regal row of town houses. "I live just there. You'll find nothing's too far away from anything else." The car leaped forward, swayed around a small roundabout, and skidded to a halt to avoid hitting four nuns in purple habits and billowing violet veils crossing the street.

"Come on, come on, come on," Helen muttered.

Above the surge of shoppers, store signs proclaimed their goods: fishmonger, butcher, bakery, gift shops, realtors, banks and B&Bs. There was hardly a view without a church or pub in it. Walkways cut between the buildings, secret passages to distant centuries. Flower pots hung from white lampposts standing by cheerful blue and red awnings. "It's beautiful," said Rosalind.

"That's what kept me back," Helen said. "See by the big church there, where it's roped off? We're doing an excavation. This is the last day, and it's all hands on deck."

Filthy fingers tapped on the car window. A bearded man in a muddy jacket stood in the middle of the busy street, trying to get their attention. Rosalind leaned away from him, her hand moving to lock the door when Helen reached across and rolled down the window. "What is it, Angus?"

"Helen, we need you desperately." Despite the unkempt beard, closer inspection revealed an unusually handsome face, an attractive mouth hesitating in its speech as he glanced at Rosalind. His eyes lit up. "Hello," he said.

"I'm just taking Rosalind here to her cottage." The car inched forward.

"It'll be dark soon. There's a parking place." He hurried back to the torn-up earth.

"Do you mind terribly?" Helen asked. A car beeped its horn behind them. "We could actually walk from here. It won't take but a moment. You can come to the dig if you like. I'm afraid we're a bit frantic."

Despite Rosalind's considerable fatigue, this was too good an opportunity to miss. "I'd love to see what you're doing."

Helen steered into the parking space after the bearded man aggressively waved on another car trying to pull in. He impatiently waited for Helen, stealing glances at Rosalind at the same time. It had been years since a man had appraised her with such unabashed interest.

"Movie-star good looks," Rosalind mused.

8

"Sorry? Oh, Angus, gosh, do you really think so? I only see 'beleaguered colleague' I'm afraid."

Rosalind got out, stiff and grimy from overnight travel, and followed them over a rope separating the excavation from the street. Helen bent beside the bearded man as he pointed out something in the earth. Rosalind lagged behind, taking in the sight of the old church tower above the dig, its gargoyles straining far out from the walls as if trying to break their stony tethers. She lifted her foot to step over a ridge of dirt, and stopped short. In a shallow pit at her feet lay a brown skull and bones.

"Rosalind? Over here. Rosalind?"

Helen hurried back, forehead creased with concern.

"There are human remains here." The loose earth moved under Rosalind's shoe, and a clod fell to the bones.

"What?"

She pointed at the skull.

"Oh, it's a medieval graveyard. This was a parking lot and they're making it into a pedestrian courtyard. We've been excavating the graves. Bit of a rush job. A matter of priorities, you understand, ha ha, economics and all. I think that's the last one, isn't it, Angus?"

"They're so shallow," Rosalind said.

"Rosalind, may I introduce Angus MacLeod, archaeologist?"

"Delighted." He reached over the grave, took Rosalind's hand, and to her surprise lifted it to a bristly kiss.

"Rosalind has come from California. Our mothers were friends, long ago. Isn't that lovely?"

"I hope you'll be staying for a bit?"

She pretended to be unconcerned about the bones. "Less than a week, I'm afraid."

"Angus is my houseguest just now," Helen said. "He actually lives in Edinburgh."

"This," Angus opened his muddy palm to reveal a dull gold cross, about four inches long, "is what I wanted to ask you about. Pectoral?"

Helen peered over her glasses at it. "Oh, gorgeous! Yes. For a bishop. Fourteenth century."

"Thirteenth. Bet you a dinner at the Chinky."

"Angus, you cheapskate. The Indian restaurant or no deal. Let me get this poor soul to her cottage."

"You'll be visiting Helen, won't you?" he called. "Then I'll say *au revoir*."

Helen pulled Rosalind's suitcase from the car and led the way at a fast clip.

"I can carry it," Rosalind protested.

"Not at all."

"Is there any reason why the graves stop where it's roped off?"

"No. That's simply where the road's been torn up. The medieval cemetery will extend farther out."

"So, like under this sidewalk, there might be more graves?"

"We call it a pavement. Yes, very likely."

"But they're right below our feet."

"St. Andrews has a long ecclesiastical history. Angus is really here to excavate a Culdee foundation not far away, but we needed everyone we could get for this rush job."

"Culdee?" Rosalind dodged a group of French-speaking youngsters loaded with backpacks. Helen was already yards ahead.

"This was the medieval marketplace," called Helen, "desecrated in its heart by that hideous Victorian fountain that supplanted the old market cross."

Booksellers' stalls were set up around the large stone fountain. Marigolds festooned the wide basin where water had once run. It looked beautiful to Rosalind, an indiscriminate focal point of a two-thousand-year timeline, deposited there in a swirl of history. The vendors were in the process of peeling back the tarps covering their tables.

"How big is the town?" she asked.

"Excluding tourists and students, small enough that everyone knows everyone's business if they've a mind to. But really, large enough not to be too oppressive. I do love living here," Helen concluded mournfully.

"My mother said you were a professor at the university."

"No, that title goes to the chairman of the department. I'm merely a lecturer. Medieval history. My office is one street over from your uncle's cottage. I'll show you when you've settled in."

The marketplace narrowed into a lane fronted by smaller houses, their joined walls creating a smooth facade all the way to the end of the lane.

"Here we are," said Helen. They stopped at a dark oak

door. A brass plaque on the wall, green with neglect, read 'Morning Star.' She tapped it with a slender finger. "Some of the fishing community named their cottages after their boats. Isn't that lovely?"

"I'm supposed to ask for the key from the neighbor on the left." Rosalind put down her bag and stepped to the adjacent house's door.

Before she could knock, the door opened and a girl of about sixteen emerged, eyes red and puffy with weeping. She glanced at them, uninterested.

"Excuse me," Rosalind said, but the girl kept her face averted and walked away, sniffling.

"Oh," Helen began. "Don't I know you?"

The girl gave one frightened glance back and increased her pace to a trot. From within the house, a woman shouted, her voice edged by concern.

"Catriona!"

Helen looked after the departing figure. "Not a student." She shrugged. "Try again?"

The door had not shut. Rosalind raised a hand to knock, when it opened wider. A cloud of incense rolled out. In the thick of it stood a scraggly creature in a tattered sweater and wrinkled full skirt, dark hair loose and tangled. She put a hand to either door jamb and, eyes closed, took a deep breath before opening them to look directly at Rosalind.

"Did a young lassie just leave?" she asked.

"Yes," said Helen.

The woman ignored Helen, all attention on Rosalind, gazing intently, as if looking through her with unfocused eyes.

"Hi." Rosalind hesitated. "Do I know you?"

She didn't answer.

"I needed to...I mean," she stumbled along, "I'm Rosalind Ehrhart."

The woman looked even more intently.

Helen cleared her throat.

Rosalind tried again. "Are you Captain Ogilvy's neighbor?"

"Aye," she murmured.

"Yes. You. I mean, you are?"

"Aye," she said again, smiling.

"Your name is Morag?"

"Aye."

"I think what she means..." said Helen.

"Do you have the key?" Rosalind asked.

"Piseag Dhubh!" the neighbor cried, as a black cat shot between her legs and out the door.

"I beg your pardon?" said Helen.

"Lusty wee fiend," Morag said by way of explanation.

Helen gave up on Rosalind, and stepped in to take charge. "Sorry to be a nuisance, but would you happen to have the key to Morning Star Cottage?"

"Aye, aye, I do." She reached over and plucked a stray hair from Rosalind's coat in so intimate a manner that Rosalind stepped back and bumped into Helen.

"Would you mind terribly...?" Helen said a little forcefully.

The woman, with the same odd smile, drew back in beside the door, lifted a large key from its hook, held it up before Rosalind's eyes, took Rosalind's limp hand, the long strand of hair still pinched between her fingers, eyes half-closed. "You are Sheila Ogilvy's daughter," she stated. Then she slapped the key into Rosalind's palm. "Now fair, fairest of every fair, welcome of Scotland to be Queen!" she cried, as she shouldered by to chase the errant cat.

They watched her go down the lane and disappear into the white air. She was there, and then she wasn't.

Helen unexpectedly burst into a laugh. "How funny. Quoting William Dunbar." She sobered. "She's quite mad. I know her. I mean I know of her. Morag Gilbride, one of our unusually odd town eccentrics." Helen peered up at the windows of Morag's cottage. "Funny, I didn't recognize her at all at first. She's not usually so scraggly. Let's try the key, shall we?"

"Helen," said Rosalind, "that woman just disappeared."

"The sea mist is coming in. We call it a haar."

"Ah-hah?"

"That's right."

One thing at a time, decided Rosalind. "What a strange person."

"St. Andrews," Helen observed, "could never be accused of a lack of colorful characters. The problem is having to deal with them. Oh dear, here comes another. Quick, try the door."

A small plainly-dressed woman, bonnet scrunching her curly dark hair, clopped down the cobbles, making a beeline for them.

"The key," said Helen. "Do hurry."

Before Rosalind could fumble the key into the strange lock, the woman stopped next to her, very close, gray eyes on a level with Rosalind's chin.

She held out a pamphlet. "Are you going to heaven?" she asked coyly.

Her face looked familiar. The paper showed Jesus ascending on clouds and rays of light.

"No thanks." Rosalind smiled politely, trying to twist the key in its ancient lock.

"Are you going to heaven?" The riveting gaze of her unblinking eyes never wavered.

The key turned and the door creaked open. Helen pushed Rosalind into the hallway. They stumbled and almost fell over a mass of clutter on the floor as the heavy door boomed shut.

"Thank God," Helen gasped.

"Is there a light switch there? I can't see a thing. Oh, what a stink!"

"Got it. Behind the door."

A bare bulb illuminated a short hallway in which all kinds of household items had been dumped. Rosalind tripped over a box of old books. She pulled one out and laughed. "*St. Andrews Ghost Stories.*"

Helen put her delicate fingers to her forehead. "Oh gosh, we left your suitcase outside."

"I'll get it."

"No, wait. Give that creature time to accost someone else."

"She looks like the Queen," Rosalind said. Helen was silent and Rosalind feared she'd blundered into an unintentional offense. "I mean her face. A little."

"You're right." Helen's lips twitched in a stifled smile. "I'd never have thought it, but you're right. Her name is Mrs. Pearse. The town evangelist. She has a built-in radar for heathens like me."

Rosalind peeked out the door. "Coast is clear." She pulled the suitcase in. They turned to see the hallway in the daylight of the open door.

"Oh, dear," said Helen. "Oh, dear."

A doorway on the left revealed a low-ceilinged room from which most of the clutter spilled. A glacier made of junk, of pieces of furniture, lamps, electrical appliances, cushions, a bicycle with no wheels, clothing and tools, spilled into a moraine of trash in the hallway, with a narrow path meandering through it to the stairway at the far end. Rosalind hauled her suitcase through, trying not to touch the damp walls. The stairs made a turn halfway up at a small landing. On the back wall Rosalind came face to face with herself. A large old sepia photograph as she might have looked in period costume. It was so uncanny she stood and stared; all the years looking in a mirror, now cast upon the wall in this ancestor's cottage. It was the pleasant round face similar to that of her Scottish mother that Rosalind had inherited, so like her it took a moment to figure out the difference. The photograph was missing the edge of facial structure defined by her American father's more rugged Scandinavian looks. It suggested a similar hair color, light brown perhaps, the same gentle eyes, all familiar yet assembled slightly differently.

"Gosh, look," said Helen. "What an astonishing likeness. Even her hair in a bun like yours. Isn't that lovely? An ancestor, I assume?"

A flicker of movement broke the spell. Rosalind turned and looked up to the first landing. Four rooms radiated off a small central hall.

"Hello?" said Rosalind. "Is anyone there? Uncle Rab?"

"Did you see someone?"

"I thought so, a shadow. There shouldn't be. Did you hear anything?"

"No." Helen appeared a little agitated. "Hate to say, I must get back to the dig. Let's have a quick look 'round."

The kitchen stank of rancid butter and sour milk. Dirty dishes lay heaped in the sink and on the small stained table. Whorls of dried mold decorated a limp gray dishrag hanging over the back of a chair. The sitting room was the least cluttered, but the furniture was soiled beyond redemption. Rosalind, with Helen peeking over her shoulder, glanced at the other rooms on the landing. Dirty laundry sprawled across the bedroom floor. Sheets with suspicious stains draped off the lumpy mattress as if someone had been pulled forcibly from the bed.

"You can't stay here," said Helen. "Angus is in the guest room, but we could figure out some arrangement."

"Let me think for a minute." Rosalind opened the window to let in the fresh cold sea air.

Helen, giving little exclamations of disgust, returned from inspecting the bathroom. "There's another landing." Her shoes clicked up the steep stair. "Here's another bedroom," she called down, "not half so bad, and a bathroom that looks actually functional."

Rosalind went up the narrow second flight to find Helen trying to open the bedroom window.

"Perhaps he didn't use this floor." Helen clapped the dust from her hands. "It's actually rather nice, in an old sea-captain-cottage sort of way." She turned back to face Rosalind. "Whatever is it?"

Rosalind stood still in a dawning realization, trying to encompass the cozy space, to find any hint of memory. "This must be the room where I was born."

"Gosh, fancy that. In that very bed do you suppose?"

Rosalind touched the smooth wooden footboard of a simple oak frame. "I think so. I'll have to ask my mother." She went to a corner of the room where one of the ceiling beams, dark old wood, met the plastered wall. Behind the lowest part of the beam her questing fingers found the cuts in the wood. "Yes, she carved my initials here. 'R', 'O'."

"How lovely."

From downstairs a door slammed shut. They both jumped.

"The draught," said Helen. "But isn't the 'O' for Ogilvy? How could that be?"

"A family skeleton. My mother wasn't married yet when she had me. He was an American soldier who left for France, and who knew if he'd return? But he did, and took us to California, where we've been since."

"Ah. A war bride."

Rosalind pulled open the door of a tall wardrobe, to the soft chime of hangers within. "This is actually pretty clean. And look, some old photographs."

She held up one of a group of four adults and two children, all standing in front of a harbor wall. The two women, in distinctive full-skirted dresses, mended fishing nets, and the men smoked pipes. "I wonder if the children are my mother and Uncle Rab." She handed it to Helen.

The floorboards outside the bedroom creaked. They both looked up, but nothing appeared in the doorway.

Helen meandered to a small sitting room on the same floor. "Rosalind," she called, "would you rather come stay with us? Even a bed-and-breakfast would be preferable, if it's just for a few nights. I doubt there's hot water."

Rosalind put the photos back, unwilling to explain that she could not afford a B&B. "Thank you, Helen, but how could I pass up the chance to stay in this room?"

"Of course."

"What I think I'll do is clean this bedroom and the kitchen, and that'll be enough for the short time I'm here. I'll see my uncle as soon as I can, find out what he needs."

Helen pulled back the coarse wool blanket on the bed. "Damp. Look, if you're set on staying here, why don't you light that fire? There likely will be coal in a garden shed." She nodded at a small ash-filled fireplace. "I can bring you anything else you need, a duvet perhaps? Clean sheets. I'm afraid I really must dash back to the excavation before Angus has apoplexy. How about I look back in on you later tonight?"

When Helen had gone, Rosalind sat in a wooden chair by the window overlooking the back of the cottage. Down below, each property had a garden the width of the house, contained within high stone walls, back to back with the garden wall of the houses the next street over, divided by a narrow alley. Under the thickening sea mist, the outline of neglected flower beds was just visible in Uncle Rab's garden. It was like looking into a strange sea, the eddies of mist flowing over a few pieces of garden junk and overgrown shrubs.

Rosalind tossed her suitcase to the old bed and clicked open the latches. She opened the lid and took out the creased letter which had traveled with her across the Atlantic, back to its place of origin. She unfolded it and read. It was addressed to her mother.

>Morning Star Cottage
>Market Street
>St. Andrews
>Fife
>Bonnie Scotland
>
>15 September, 1979
>
>Dear Sheila,
>
>Aye, it's me. Don't keel over. My neighbor

> Morag is writing this. You'll remember her mother, Fiona, and her aunt, Meg. I'm in hospital. I'm not well. I'm dying. It's about the house, the things in it. I can't cope. I couldn't be bothered before anyway. Forget the past. Bygones, eh? Can you come across? Help sort this estate business out? I'm making a right mess of it. Will you come quick, before I'm dead? What a guddle. Are you wanting the old spindle? Photies? I'm sorry for some things but there's nothing to be done.
>
> Your brother, Robert Ogilvy
>
> P.S. Stay in the cottage. Morag will keep the key if I'm still in hospital or worse.

That her uncle did not know how infirm her mother had become was obvious. Rosalind remembered a picture of Rab from many years past, but some sort of disagreement that her mother refused to elaborate on kept communication to a minimum. Rosalind had no idea what sort of man she would encounter, nor what state his health would be, nor how he'd accept the niece he'd never met in place of his sister at what appeared to be his deathbed. Uncle Rab had been on the high seas at Rosalind's birth, and in a persistent huff in any event for his sister's mysterious transgression.

Rosalind returned to the window. In the neighbor's garden, as prolific as Uncle Rab's was barren, rosy apples weighed down branches trained along the high walls.

The scruffy neighbor, Morag, glided out, parting the mist, to stand in the center of her neat lawn. She stayed still a long time, hands on hips, head bent as if in thought.

Suddenly she raised her arms to shoulder height, hands bent back at the wrists, and spun around three times, her flaring skirt creating a vortex in the mist. Then she stopped and held her hands high, fingers spread wide.

A lithe black shadow, the little cat, bounded across the grass. Her hand moved as if to collect invisible strands from the air, then grasped and pulled them to her breast, with a piercing whistle. A black bird plummeted out of the fog and landed on her shoulder.

Rosalind blinked and sat back, and as she did so, a figure in a long skirt passed the door. Or she thought it might have. She shook her head. She was very tired, almost asleep.

*

Morag took the strand of Rosalind's auburn hair from her desk. She pinched it taut from either end, spinning it around the tip of her index finger, until it formed a ring. She held up her hand, fingers spread, turning her palm one way then the other.

"This should work nicely," she said to her black imps, the one watching from beneath indolent lids, the other, head turned to rest on its feathered shoulder. "What?" she asked Piseag Dhubh. "You don't approve? Don't give me that look, ye wee fiend, or I'll give you to the minister's wife as a substitute for the bairns she's been unable to bear." Puss blinked ever-so slowly in pure adulation. "Do you feel it, my darlings? The very elements are stilled in expectation."

Morag stood to pull the leather-bound notebook from the bookshelf, feeling an unaccustomed ache in her knee, sign of aging, wondering all the while if the American could hear her movements through the wall. She held the leather to her nostrils and snuffed in the earthy scent, then parted the pages and ran her hand down the book's smooth inner spine to coax it to open. "A new time, a new magic. A new book that I have been saving for a decade. What say you, Macha, Piseag Dhubh?" She took up the fountain pen and scratched:

The Quair of Light and Shadows
Being a Grimoire of the Deepest Mysteries

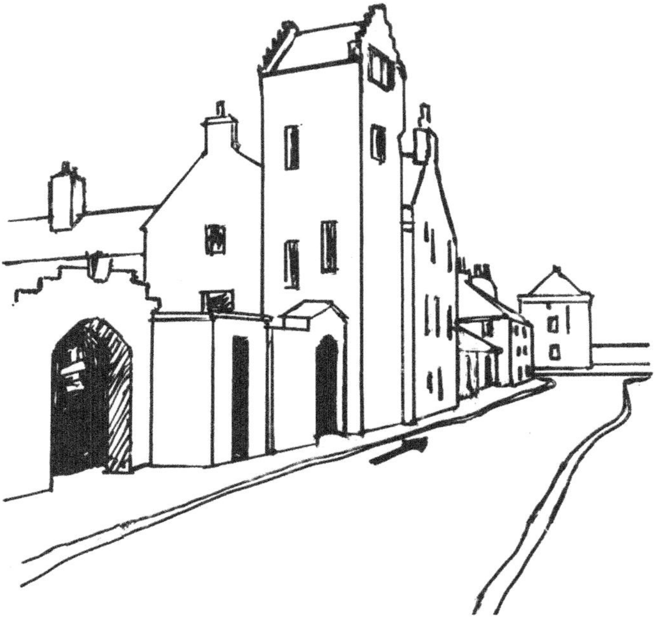

Chapter 2

It should have come as no surprise that the hospital would be an older building, with the date 1903 engraved on a corner stone. The hallways, through fire doors, were clean but drab. A nurse in a spotless white uniform and little half hat greeted Rosalind with cheerful efficiency and led her to her uncle's bed in a room with three others.

The framed photograph of Captain Ogilvy on her mother's piano back in California, never removed despite long silences or quarrels, showed a young, hawk-nosed sailor, booted feet planted wide on the deck of his fishing boat, pipe in hand, cap at a jaunty angle over a tangle of curls. But seeing him now, Uncle Rab looked remarkably like an ugly exaggerated version of her mother. He lay on his back, mouth open, snoring through worn and missing teeth. His long face, despite his illness, glowed very ruddy, the red veins along his high-ridged nose splintering across sunken cheeks.

The nurse leaned over. "Captain Ogilvy? You have a visitor."

He snorted and blinked open yellow eyes. The nurse left, with a nod for Rosalind to sit on a chair by the little side table.

"Uncle Rab?"

"Sheila?" His bristling eyebrows pulled together.

"I'm Rosalind," she said. "Sheila's daughter. Your niece, Rosalind Ehrhart."

"Ehrhart?" His voice was scratchy, like an old gramophone. "What the bloody hell kind of name's Ehrhart? Sprechen Sie Deutsch?"

"I'm American."

"You were a fool. Going off with that young pup of a G.I. Have you come back to apologize?" Uncle Rab's breath betrayed his body's corruption. "It'll take more than words, I can tell ye."

"I'm your niece, Rosalind. We've never met. My mother, Sheila, asked me to give you her love. She couldn't come, and I've come instead. Remember you wrote?"

He stared blankly a moment longer, mouth open, then grunted. "She never could find it in her to return. Cared nothing for the family. She'd rather live in that violent place. It's a wonder she's no been shot."

Rosalind thought longingly of her mother's tidy little frame house in Palo Alto, its year-round flowers and orange tree, its abundant hot water and appliances, none of which she'd found in Uncle Rab's filthy cottage that morning. "I'm sure she's very safe. She sent a letter with me, for you, since I got here sooner than the mail would have. Would you like me to read it to you?"

"Sheila's bairn. Aye." His ears and nostrils were stuffed with protruding beige bristles, and he pushed a gnarled finger into one ear and twisted it, then wiped the wax on the sheet.

Rosalind took the letter from her purse. "'Dear Rabbie,'" she read, "'you old tattie-heid.'"

"Eh?"

She hesitated. "Oh. I haven't actually read it, since it was for you."

"Go on," he scowled.

"'Why did you never send a telegram? And have you not heard about this marvelous new invention called a telephone? Well, I suppose it doesn't matter. You've left it years, decades, too late. Were you thinking nobody but you ages? Did it never penetrate your thick head...'"

"Thick head?" The color flooded across his face.

"Maybe this isn't the best time to read this."

"You've started," he said ominously. "Carry on."

"'...and all the letters I faithfully wrote, that I'm failing as well, hobbling about on a stick? Rosalind will go in my stead, though it's difficult for her, with her job and recent loss. They've had to move in with me, I'm certain I told you. It's a bit difficult, but we'll manage just now. Ros is a capable lass and will be far more help to you than I. She won't be able to stay long, just a few days. I've warned her nobody gets on with you.'"

Uncle Rab's face had locked into an expression of dour anger. "It surely doesn't end there."

"'Shame we must draw our last breaths so far apart. Maybe I'll ask Ros to carry my ashes back when I'm gone, scatter them on Loch Morlich. Remember our wee holidays? Heather has a scent, doesn't it, sweet and musky, and the bog myrtle perfumed the air.'"

"Aye, aye, right enough."

"'Or maybe I should just rest beside my husband here. California has been good to us, though I never could make you understand, ya neep.'"

"Neep?"

"A turnip?" Rosalind suggested helpfully.

He glared with renewed vigor. Rosalind hastened to finish. "'There's nothing I want. Possessions pull me back now. Try to be civil to Rosalind. In sisterly love, Sheila.'"

"Possessions, is it? Some things have far more worth than possessions. Do you ken how many generations have stayed in Morning Star cottage? It was built by an Ogilvy, a skipper with more fucking brains than I've got anyway. Now," he sank deeper into his pillow, "what will become of it? Just tell me that."

The other patient across the room had a fit of coughing. The nurse came in and pulled a curtain around his bed.

Rosalind shuddered at the memory of what she'd awoken to that morning, after the most bizarre night of intense sexual dreams, the like of which she'd not had since she'd been pregnant with Chris almost two decades ago. And after she'd arisen and made her breakfast, delighting in the fresh bread from the bakery just around the corner, the inexplicable feelings had not dissipated, banked like a smoldering fire in her belly. She ascribed it to either being in a new place, freed from the daily worries back home, or the culmination of years of abstinence. A bizarre comparison, the strange new lustiness at odds with the filthy, cold cottage. "Are you interested in selling it?"

Spots of red surfaced on his already ruddy cheeks. "Sell it! Over my dead body! Eh, that's true enough," he chuckled, then coughed. "Sell it! Rah ... Roh..."

"Rosalind. Your niece."

"I ken that! I'm no as stupid as I look."

The nurse passed by, forefinger to her lips.

"Don't you hush me, woman!" He glared after her like a fierce bird of prey. Then to Rosalind, "Is yer man here?"

"You mean my husband?"

"How the hell many have ye got?"

"Haven't you been reading Mom's letters?"

"Mom?"

"Sheila. Your sister."

"Fucking Christ! Do you think I dinnae ken my ain sister?"

"My husband," Rosalind said quickly, eyes stinging from an angry moistness, "Henry, died a year ago. He was just fifty. I have a son named Chris. He's in college. Do you remember in your letter you said you needed help with your estate? The thing is, I've got to return in a few days. My job. Do you think that will be enough time to get done what you need?"

"You're hoping I'll have died by then?"

Rosalind's mouth opened, then shut.

"Did you bring me cigarettes?" He glared at her. "Are you deaf? Ci-ga-rettes."

Her mother's warnings had not prepared her for the real thing. She put her hands over her eyes.

He stared at her in wonder. "Here, you're a bit of a timid wee mouse. What about whisky then?"

"No."

"Pity. Next time, eh?" With a groan he reached over to his side table, opened a little drawer and took out a worn wallet, from which he extracted two ten-pound notes. He thrust them at Rosalind.

"What's that for?"

"Grouse."

She took the money and frowned at its depiction of a castle, as if it could enlighten her.

"There's a good lass. Away ye go now for my messages." The stubble on his cheek rasped against the pillow. "Get yourself to the hairdresser," he murmured. "Ye look like a frumpy auld Scots wifie." One hand, fingers bent under swollen knuckles, rose and fell on his chest as his eyes closed.

She sat and studied him for a minute, perplexed by his demeanor. When it was obvious he had sunk deep into sleep, Rosalind walked the labyrinth of fire-doors, stairs, and hallways back to the main entrance, thinking she should have left crumbs to follow. For a long time she watched the car park swimming in and out of focus through her tears. At least she knew some of his terms from her mother. Messages meant groceries, but grouse was a mystery. And worst of all, he was right. How could she just leave him to die without one family member present?

A couple burst out the hospital door, almost at a run, a girl in a brown school uniform followed by a man in a dark business suit. He reached out a hand to stop her.

"I can't," she said. "I can't, it's wrong."

"It's not wrong," he said. "It's the only choice."

"If my mother knew…"

"Of course she's not going to know, Catriona. Stop, just stop, and listen." He took her in his arms, and she wept against his shoulder. "There, there. You've nothing to worry about, it will all be taken care of."

The girl pulled away, face grief-stricken, hand raised to keep him at arm's length. "You don't understand, you never did. It's too late now, there's nothing can be done to put it right."

She ran out the car park and was lost to sight behind the high stone wall. The man shook his head, made a sound of exasperation, and walked away to the parked cars. "Fucking bloody Calvinists," he mumbled.

"Rosalind Ehrhart?" said a voice just behind her. "I'm Doctor MacKay. Could I have a word? My office is just here."

"Sure." She followed him back inside.

"Good of you to come all this way. I'm sure Captain Ogilvy appreciates it." He indicated a chair in his office for her to sit on, while he perched on his desk.

"How is he doing?" She was so exhausted and bewildered by Uncle Rab's demands, the tears came. She couldn't help it. "Sorry."

"Not well. He has lung cancer, and it's too far gone to do anything. He never came in, until a neighbor found him unconscious in his garden." As if well used to weeping visitors, the doctor offered her a box of "man-sized" Kleenex. "By then he'd been lying in the cold rain for hours. Not surprisingly he's got pneumonia. Plus a few more degenerative problems, result of too much drink and smoking primarily. I'm afraid it's a matter of days."

"When's the best time to talk to him?"

"He's most lucid late morning. Why don't you try again tomorrow?"

"Do you know if he's made any funeral arrangements?"

"Not that I'm aware of. You'll have to speak to him."

"Is there anything I can bring him?"

"Not cigarettes, please, and not whisky. Someone's been sneaking him things he oughtn't to have, and we're having a bit of a bother. He's been passing round drinks in the middle of the night, that sort of thing, you understand. It's simply got to stop."

*

"What business this is of yours I cannot imagine."

Pompous ass. Morag gritted her teeth and against her savage impulse, tried to reason with him. "All I'm asking you to do is give her some small word of comfort. You don't realize, she's fragile, she takes things hard. She's just a lass."

Rosalind, from the window above the street in Morning Star's cottage, heard them and peeked out. She recognized Morag. The man looked familiar, and she realized, despite her own whirling emotions, it was the man she'd seen at the hospital. A few pedestrians hurried by, duly embarrassed in good British manner by the exchange.

"Then let her see a bloody counselor. You're the one who's put her into a panic, with your ridiculous nonsense."

"Oh, it's my fault is it? You used her and threw her away when you got bored."

"As if you could reprimand me when it's common knowledge you'll fuck anything that moves."

That made her laugh. "Except you, it seems. And in any case, I love my lovers, but by the stars, I think you hate yours."

"I'd appreciate being able to walk down the street without being accosted by the likes of you," the man said. "You can damned well leave me alone, or I'll see to it you stop your interfering." He lifted a warning finger as he stomped off down the lane.

"I'm asking you do to the decent thing for once in your life," Morag called after him. "Just speak to her!" When he ignored her, she spun around and put a hand to the wall, snarling like a dog. "You'll pay dearly for this," she said with such quiet vehemence, Rosalind quickly stepped back from the window before she could be seen.

*

Auntie Meg peered out the front window in the direction of Clive Forbes's departing figure as Morag came back in. One of her eyes was clouded over with cataracts, and she had a habit of tilting her head like a bird to see better. "Curse him!"

cried Auntie Meg. "Curse him!"

"Were you eavesdropping, Auntie? Anyway, he's cursing himself. Let him make enough rope and then I'll hang him, but not yet."

"Bah! Then I'll curse him!" She scuttled off to the kitchen and pulled out the drawer with all the candle stubs, collecting the black ones together into a wee pile on the counter.

"Catriona said no."

"Ach! Foolish girl." She clutched Morag's sleeve. "You do it. I can't do it like you can. It'll take if you do it."

"It's not necessary, Auntie. I've told you. Much as I would love to. I promised Catriona. Later. Later."

"I'll do it then. I'll go now and point the cursing bone at him."

"You're not going to their house, Auntie. They're respectable people. They'll call the police if they see you hanging about."

"Respectable!" She spat on the floor.

"You'll clean that now, auld woman." Morag held out a rag and stared Auntie Meg down to her knees, where she wiped at the spittle like a child having to tidy its own mess.

"I will, I will, I will!"

"Now, listen." Morag knelt beside her and gathered up her knobby old hands. Auntie Meg became very still and waited, her single eye bright as a flame, tongue protruding a little in her excitement. The images came.

"What do you see?"

"I see the Cailleach. At Samhuinn. It's yourself. Think of that."

"Hah! Me, the Cailleach. That's grand! This man, will I be cursing him?" She paused for a moment. "But how can this be?"

"Sheila Ogilvy's daughter has come home, Auntie Meg."

Meg drew in a sharp breath. "Has she?"

Morag smoothed the bumpy knuckles and veiny skin on the back of Meg's hand. Dark forest and the sleek sides of the stones, fire so hot it burned the inner nostrils, leaping shadows across the breast of the hills. Turmoil. Lust. Destruction. Some sense of violence that made the pit of her stomach tighten. These same old hands on a man's cringing flesh, but who was he? And there, the central force around which all the rest spiraled, the American.

It was true then. This sealed the divination decisively. No mere coincidence in the fact of Rosalind's arrival.

"You have that smile, Morag."

"Have you ever noticed, Auntie," Morag said, "how our Goddess loves sex and death above all else? None of this birth and rebirth nonsense, flowers and tinkly music. Sex and death. And all the secrets of creation between them."

Meg yanked her hands away and gathered up the black wax stubs again, muttering to herself. Then she stopped and peered closely at Morag's face. "It's death."

"Aye, it's death."

"Then, hasten it," she hissed. "For Catriona's sake."

*

Archaeologists outside Holy Trinity Church had been replaced by workmen carting off the last of the old asphalt. Rosalind stood and watched for a time, until a man coming out of the bookshop behind her, thinking she wanted to go in, held the door open. As much to oblige him as for a lack of anything else to do, she entered. There were magazine racks by the door, maps and notepads, numerous postcards and pens, and displays of envelopes arranged in tiers under the cash register. She picked up a copy of a St. Andrews guidebook for walkers, and was about to pay for it with the heavy British coins when an artist's sketchpad close to the register caught her eye. A modest size, not so large as to denote a serious interest, and not so small as to inhibit a hand's movement across the page. On an impulse, she bought it and an artist's eraser, plus four drawing pencils and a small metal sharpener.

"Are you an artist?" asked the woman behind the counter, punching in numbers.

She hesitated. "No, not really. I mean..."

The woman waited with a polite tilt to her head.

"I'm sorry," said Rosalind. "How much did you say?"

"Three pounds, ten pence, please. There's a good show of local watercolorists at the Crawford Arts Center just now."

The innocent question stung as she made her way to the high spires of the cathedral ruins, the sketchpad clamped like a rebuke under her arm. It had all been wasted, futile, the excited start twenty-five years ago. The hard-won scholarship to the Rhode Island School of Design, her mother's cautious pride, the good teachers, the first prize for her work in a city-wide festival. All the doors opening nicely, something she and most of her student peers took as their due back then.

Then, love, the trump card, the one thing most devoutly to be wished for by all, it seemed, descended, heralding marriage, new responsibilities and a change of course. First through the unexpectedly forceful opinions of her new husband, Henry, who had his own notions of a domestic partnership. But he was older by ten years, and she was grateful for his seasoned knowledge. While Henry prided himself on being able to support his talented wife, he made it clear a joint income would be necessary at some near future date if her profession could not elevate itself above the tax category of 'hobby.' Fair enough. And so she had set up a studio in the guest bedroom in the hope of realizing both their plans. In short order the studio became the nursery and the artist became the doting Mom, and eventually an archivist at the Junior College with a meager but steady supplemental paycheck. Order and security ruled the day. Her son was the light of her life. She had no regrets. Of course not.

Rosalind's feet crunched over the pea gravel of the cathedral ruins walkway. Of course not.

The sea mist flowed in, enveloping the ruins, advancing even as she watched, to roll over the houses and down the streets. The breeze pushed against her jacket, slackened, then pushed again, harder. Rather than dissipate the mist, the wind became an avenue for its travel.

The soft thunder of the sea came from beyond the ghostly ruins. High above, thick clouds of fog sped through the empty windows of the cathedral's east tower. Something coalesced, coming ever closer to clarity as the fog dissolved the boundaries of reality. It was her artist's eye, her visual way of perceiving, rising like a liberated ghost from its grave.

Behind the cathedral, amongst the large tombstones, a gnarled tree spread a remarkable canopy of corkscrewed branches over the graves. Rosalind flipped open the notebook to the grainy paper, and studied the pencil's point. Between one and the other, nothing but the visible air. The blank creamy page filled her senses, the old forgotten measure of success or failure. But what of it? Nobody here knew her, nobody cared. She could dabble and play, mess up and start all over, and it didn't matter to anyone. She could even step back into drawing and maybe painting from a new perspective, if she could figure out how to birth it and convey it.

"Stop thinking," she muttered, "and just draw." She considered the placing of the high stone wall behind the tree, paced this way and that until she found an angle where the diffused light fell over the stone and grass in a pleasing symmetrical pattern. The mist dropped a sheen of moisture on the thick dark lawn between the tombstones, leaving ghostly footprints wherever she went.

Rosalind began to sketch, hoping to capture the mist in the eerie boughs, or more specifically, the boughs' dissolving, with the gravestones below and the high peaked wall behind. But it was as if her hand was encased in iron. It slowed and stuck in meticulous detail of branch and stone, outlining forms rather than freely finding their substance. Rosalind cursed and flipped the page over, and took a deep breath. She knew she should have bought the larger sized pad. She shook out her hand to loosen it, and began again with more abandon, sketchpad braced in left forearm, an extra pencil in her teeth, drawing to the steady roar of the sea. It pulled her in like a lost friend, the joy of creating, even as she recognized how horribly rusty she was. It would take a lot of hard work to catch up to where she had left off all those years ago, but there it was, the echo of excitement.

Then she heard another sound, a rhythmic scraping, almost matching the sound of her pencils darkening the paper, a sound which had been occurring intermittently before she was aware it was not natural.

What little she could see of the graveyard was empty but for tombstones moving slowly in and out of sight as the mist curtained and withdrew. Hers were the only imprints in the grass.

To her left was a square tower, incorporated into the high cathedral wall. One of its doorways opened at the top of a small stair that ascended the wall, the iron gate swung wide. It was from this upper chamber the strange noise came.

Rosalind stepped closer. Something moved in the gloomy vault. She held the sketchpad under her arm, and consulted the guidebook, gripping the pages tight in the wind. It identified the tower as having been used as a mausoleum for a family killed by a plague in the early sixteen hundreds. It was famous for having a resident ghost, the 'White Lady,' who, naturally, resembled one of the bodies interred there.

The mist parted. In the gloom of the upper chamber stood an old woman, hunched over, her face close to the wall. Her wild hair, as tangled a skein as the corkscrew tree branches, fell over a ragged sweater from which her bare elbows protruded. She intently scraped at the stone with a kitchen knife, collecting the dust into a small jar. Strange words became a chant, incomprehensible syllables punctuated by the knife's movement.

Signs at the entrance to the ruins warned against defacing the cathedral monument.

The old creature sneezed.

"Bless you," Rosalind said.

The woman spun around and glared with a face like Medea. Then she relaxed and flashed her teeth. It wasn't an old woman, it was her neighbor, Morag. A gust of wind knocked Rosalind back a step. The spires above twirled. One hand clutched the air for support, the other gripped the jumble of sketchbook, guide and pencils. The guidebook was torn away by the wind, cartwheeling and flapping its pages across the lawn. Rosalind's free hand found solid stone. It was difficult to breathe, to catch the harsh wind into her lungs, as her elbows clamped the sketchpad to her ribs.

Morag emerged from the dark vault, preceded by an unruly, billowing skirt. She pulled a large iron key from her skirt's pocket, turned, and locked the gate that served as a door, as Rosalind wondered how such an unlikely person would be allowed access. Strands of Morag's dark hair lifted in the leeward wind as she skipped lightly down the steps on bare feet.

"I knew you were an artist," she boldly observed, coming directly up to Rosalind. "May I see?"

Rosalind clutched the sketchpad to her chest. "No," she said, surprised by her own bluntness.

"Just a peek?"

"There's nothing to see."

"All right then. Here." Morag untwisted a carved piece of wood, about four inches long, from the shoulder of her raggedy sweater. It was whittled to a point at one end, and a little

T-shape at the other. "The auld yins used these for buckles or buttons. It's a poor-man's pin, you see?" She held it up. "They cut them from specific wood for the powers in the tree, asking the sidhe draoi's permission, of course."

"Oh." Rosalind re-entered the now familiar state of utter incomprehension.

"This one is oak, which will give you courage and steadfastness, something artists need, correct me if I'm wrong." She gently pulled back the lapel of Rosalind's jacket, and pinned it into the weave of her sweater. "Here, it will bring you good fortune in your creative endeavors, mark my words."

Rosalind cautiously touched it. "Thank you."

Morag twiddled her fingers in parting, hurried away past the gravestones, and disappeared again into the mist.

Another gust of wind hit. Rosalind reached out again to steady herself, then realized she was hanging onto the shoulder of a tombstone. She jerked her hand away. A worn skull and crossbones, under the date 1789, adorned the stone's face. Such images would never be used back home. She was overwhelmed by a strong memory of sanitized, modern stones set flush in the grass for ease of maintenance. It made her feel a little sick, the memory of that place where death was hidden behind a play, a masque, so that the only thing remaining was the worst part, the pain of loss, left to wander like the ghosts, with no tangible focus. She did not realize until then how she hated the hot sun on the stones, hated Henry's manicured, false grave in California.

Something gritty irritated her hand, the same sort of grainy dust her neighbor had been collecting in the jam jar. No matter how she clapped or tried to rub it off on her jacket, it remained between her fingers, under her rings, in the very lines of her palms.

The tombstones crowded closer. High above in the sinister cloud someone chuckled. Rosalind craned her head back to find the source. There was nowhere in the sheer face of the wall a human could be. It was impossible, but it was happening. A small white rounded object began to solidify in the transparent whiteness of the mist. It was a seabird nesting in a niche of the ruined east chancel, ducking its smooth head and crying *ah-ahahah*.

Rosalind shook her head. Every way she turned, something perplexing manifested. The details of everything around her, the feathers and plastic-looking beak on the bird, each blade of grass on the shadowless lawn, minute particles of mist passing over the gravestones all contained the same strange vividness she'd experienced coming into the town with Helen, yet she might have been moving through a dream.

Not far from the haunted tower, a smaller gate along the high wall exited to a lane outside the cathedral grounds. Her guidebook was there, pinned against the wall by the wind. She folded its pages back and crossed to a railing at the top of the cliffs. Tendrils of mist came streaming past. Far below the waves roared steadily, revealing glimpses of rolling breakers. The North Sea, which should have filled the horizon, tantalizing with its sound and smell and spray, was almost completely hidden.

Something bobbed on the surface, riding the waves. A few round objects. Rosalind dismissed them as buoys until she saw black eyes glistening above whiskered snouts. She drew in her breath, a sigh of delight, and reached a hand to them, the seals, but they pulled their heads under and were gone. Rosalind gripped the railing, grateful for the seals and waves and the bracing air, and the cold hard iron in a world that seemed bent on dissolving away.

Very faintly through the mist, a clock tower chimed four times, calling her back. Helen was due to drop by that afternoon. Rosalind headed off in what she hoped was the right direction, and eventually came to an indented section of the wall she recognized, close to the cathedral entrance.

With a brief glance to the left, she began to re-cross the street. She didn't see the car until it skidded to a stop inches away. She stumbled with its sudden presence, slapped her hands to the hood, and went to her knees. The car's fog lights were on, but it had rounded the bend so quickly it seemed to materialize from nothing. The driver got out, hazard lights flashing, and peered around the front of the car at her.

"Good Lord!" he cried.

Rosalind's heart thudded, filling her chest and throat. "God. Close call. It's all right, I'm okay."

The man picked up her sketchpad and book and scattered pencils from the road and thrust them at her. "What on earth did you think you were playing at, stepping in front of me like that?" His lifted chin revealed a clerical collar. Another car, its lights glowing, slowly rounded the bend. "For heaven's sake, get out of the street before you cause an accident."

She had misunderstood his concern. She backed away. "I'm sorry, I looked the wrong way."

"I can't stop, I have an emergency." He quickly got back into his car and drove on, shaking his head angrily. The red taillights of his car dimmed in the mist, then disappeared down an arced cathedral gateway over the road.

Rosalind leaned against the wall till her heart slowed. Her throat constricted as she fought back tears. Grit from the graveyard remained between her fingers. It seemed the more she rubbed, the closer it stuck, mixing with the sweat of her fear, absorbed into her very skin. Morning Star cottage was just around the corner. Without taking off her jacket, she ran upstairs to the kitchen and washed the gravestone dust off with soap and a fingernail brush, dragging it across her palm until it hurt.

She finally let herself weep as she filled the old kettle, and wished she were home in the predictable, unexciting routine of her life. Back to something she disliked intensely but knew how to deal with.

*

Captain Ogilvy's bedroom in Morning Star cottage needed cleaned and aired out to overcome the elusive scent of mold, and worse, the sickly sweet smell of an old man who did not keep himself or his surroundings clean. Hoping she was not making a costly mistake, Rosalind dragged out the filthy, tattered rug to be heaped on the yellow stained mattress by the back garden gate.

Old paperbacks of western pulp fiction, as well as a couple of Tarzan books, with lurid covers depicting heroes rescuing damsels in distress, and yellowed copies of the 'St Andrews Citizen' newspaper, perched precariously on the small mantel above the coal fireplace. As Rosalind collected them together, she found half a dozen wooden carvings hidden under the newspapers. These were of sea mammals and whimsical human figures dressed in old fashioned clothing of long skirts and bonnets, or vests and caps, all remarkably well done, each about six inches tall. Rosalind arranged them on the cleaned mantel, a little parade of sculptures, smiling at her handiwork.

She wiped down the walls with disinfectant, carefully hand-washed the curtains, which had begun to fall apart with age, and waxed the floor. Oddly enough, cleaning supplies were stored neatly, and were abundant. It appeared they simply had never been used. But once cleaned, the furniture and room itself – the plastered stone walls, the wooden beams and lintels – came into their simple beauty. If she ended up selling the cottage, the work was necessary, however much she resented having to do it.

She hoisted up the window sill, and had turned to dust the old wardrobe, when she heard voices in the street directly below. A couple was walking to her front door, Helen, in her tweed skirt and overcoat, and a man whose pipe smoke trailed behind in the mist. He looked familiar, but she couldn't place him. They stopped out of sight, and before Rosalind could pick her way through the hallway, the doorbell gave a buzzing rattle.

"Hullo, Rosalind." Cold mist drifted into the entrance from behind the two figures. "May I introduce my husband, Clive?"

"Delighted." He held his pipe in one hand and took hers in the other, raising it to a kiss. He looked very dapper in a tweed jacket and bow tie, his dark moustache and goatee and hair neatly groomed. A handsome devil.

It was the man she'd seen at the hospital, and then heard outside in the lane, arguing with her neighbor Morag. Rosalind immediately knew discretion to be the better part. "Nice to meet you," she smiled. "Come in if you can." She led the way through the clutter.

"What's this?" Clive pushed on the door into the little room off the hallway. "Look at that. A vaulted ceiling. Why, it's beautiful."

"It is?" Rosalind came back to look.

"There's a gramophone with a squashed trumpet," Clive said. "And look at that old bike. I'll bet you it's pre-war."

"I just hurry through here and don't look at anything," Rosalind said. "That stone floor reminds me too much of the excavation Helen showed me. Who knows what might be under it?"

"No, but really," Clive insisted. "Look beyond the clutter. See the ceiling? It's original. This would make a really lovely room."

"It would?"

"Ask Helen to show you the one in the Medieval Department. I think there's a fireplace back there, see? Good heavens, with a Victorian iron facing. Rosalind, may I call you Rosalind? What a treasure you have here. And look at that old wooden spindle. A treadle wheel it's called."

"Did you sleep all right?" Helen asked.

"I feel much better, thank you, though by the time I get over the jet lag, I'll have to go home again."

She led them to the stairs. Clive looked out the small window panes set in the back door. "And what a nice little garden. Gone a bit to seed. Do you mind if I look around? I love to explore these old buildings." He was already headed up the stairs before she could reply.

"Have you seen your uncle?" asked Helen.

"This morning. The doctor says it's a matter of days."

"Oh, I'm terribly sorry."

There was an awkward pause. "Would you like some tea?"

"That would be lovely."

Clive spun through the four doors radiating off the central landing. "Want my advice?" He joined them in the kitchen, where Helen was eyeing the stained metal teapot with distaste. "Get the old boy's permission to refurbish the cottage. Toss out all the dreadful carpet, wallpaper, furniture, except for the antiques, and start from scratch. You're sitting on a gold mine, you know. Property values in St. Andrews are high just now, especially for something like this."

"But I can't. It's my uncle's home. And I won't even be here this time next week."

"Not be here?" Helen asked.

"My job back home..." She suddenly saw herself through Helen's eyes, sweet Helen who was too polite to ask why she was abandoning her uncle at his death, yet still giving her the benefit of the doubt.

"Do you think he'd sell it?" Clive was oblivious.

"Clive," said Helen.

"He says he won't, but what else could he do?"

"We'd help, wouldn't we? I've contacts, you see, through my office. I'm an architect, did Helen tell you? Imagine putting Swedish cabinets in here. Think of it! And reviving that old Aga stove. Those are wonderful, they heat everything with no fuss, the water, the house, the cooking. Bare, sanded wainscoting below white walls. I've not seen such potential in years."

"Well," Rosalind said, "you have a point. I'll try again to speak to Uncle Rab about it." She opened the box of tea bags. "These decisions have to be made."

"A Danish table, simple, placed just there, with matching chairs for the kitchen," Clive said, then sneezed.

"Where on earth do you pick up these colds?" Helen asked mournfully. "Rosalind, we've actually come to invite you to a dinner party tomorrow night. Short notice, I know, but could you?"

"I'd love to. That would be great."

"It's turning into too many men, and I need another woman for moral support. You remember Angus MacLeod, our houseguest, at the excavation? He's good fun. Plus Niall and Mary Paterson. He's a minister. An interim for a short spell. We want to be sure he feels welcome, nominal parishioner that Clive is."

"He's a bit of a stuffed shirt," said Clive. "But not as bad as his wife."

"Clive, really. Mary's a good soul. In her own way."

"We'll also have a friend named Alastair Comyn. He lives in a castle," said Clive. "We owe him a dinner."

Rosalind dipped the tea bags in the mugs and handed them around. Helen and Clive exchanged a glance.

"Alastair's castle is reputed to be one of the most haunted places in Scotland," Clive said. "All those ancestors floating about. I saw a ghost, only last week. A coach-and-four going down South Street. Thing is, only the top half was visible. Took me a moment to figure out what it was."

"The top half?" asked Rosalind.

"Clive," said Helen.

"Probably Archbishop Sharp's coach. He was murdered at Magus Muir, just up the road, by a band of Covenanters in the sixteen hundreds. Of course the coach would be traveling the road of its time."

"Of course," said Helen.

"Which is lower than the modern street. They get built up over the centuries, you see. Sharp's monument is in Holy Trinity Church, where the coach was headed. Where the excavation was. Maybe somebody didn't like having his bones disturbed. It's a famous ghost. I'm lucky to have seen it."

"Clive," Rosalind looked hard into his twinkling eyes. "You're not serious." Despite the disturbing impressions she had been left with after her unintended eavesdropping on Clive and Morag, it couldn't be denied that he had an attractive charisma. A cologne with which she was not familiar – European perhaps – added to his allure.

"Come to think of it, I'm not lucky. Helen, isn't it a bad omen? Does it mean I shall die?"

"I'd have thought it would be odd if you didn't."

"I must regrettably leave you ladies to it," Clive said. "I'm off to the club."

"And I to my office," said Helen.

"Lovely to meet you, Rosalind. Do consider what I've said about the cottage."

They left their cups of tea untasted on the kitchen counter. The sight triggered her mother's voice in her head. "You never would learn to make a decent cuppa." The persnickety ritual of British tea-making was too ponderous to take seriously. Now, for the first time, she regretted not learning from her mother.

"Club?" Rosalind asked as she escorted them down the stairs.

"The R&A. Royal and Ancient Golf Club," said Clive.

"No women allowed, I'm afraid," Helen added.

"Why not?"

"It's a men's club," said Clive.

"Because, that's the way it's always been, I suppose," said Helen. "You'll find a venerable tradition of institutionalized misogyny in Britain. I'm afraid that women who don't fit into it find themselves rather on the outside."

Clive opened the heavy front door. "Methinks you protest too much," he said.

"Do you?" stated Helen. There was no humor in their bantering.

As Helen and Clive started down the lane, a young dark-haired woman hurried past them to pound on the neighbor's door. Everyone stopped at the sight of her distress. She hesitated when she saw Clive and Helen, then resumed her knocking. The neighbor Morag opened the door as Clive turned his back to them, to cross the lane.

"Come along," he said curtly to Helen, who was hanging back by Rosalind.

"Morag, Morag," the young woman said. "Come quickly! It's Catriona."

"What's happened, Kirsteen?"

She pulled Morag by the arm. "That awful minister is already there."

Morag stepped out and saw the little group. She spoke quietly to the young woman, but she was looking daggers at Clive as he impatiently gave up waiting for Helen and walked quickly away. "If anything's happened to the lass," she said, "there will be such retribution as this town has never known before in its bloody history."

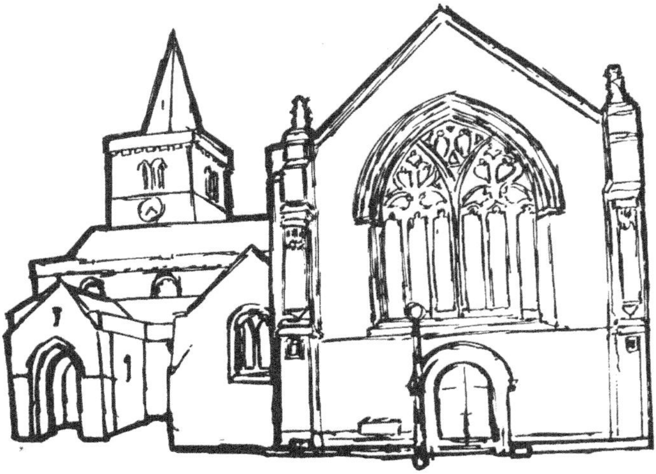

Chapter 3

The following morning Rosalind peeked into the hospital room to see Uncle Rab on his bed, half-propped up with pillows, his grizzled chin on his chest. He appeared to be lost in thought, but his eyes, as Rosalind approached, were clear.

"Did you bring me cigarettes?"

"Sorry."

"Christ."

"What are you doing?"

Uncle Rab held a penknife in one hand and a wooden carving of a seal pup in the other. Small chips and slivers of wood were mostly caught on a tea towel across his lap. He held it up for Rosalind to take.

"That's really good."

"I wasnae bad in my day."

"Those figures of people and animals around the cottage, you did all those?"

"Aye."

Rosalind turned the seal over. "This is so sweet." The seal pup was carved to lie on its side, its head turned to look past its tail, raised slightly on one shoulder, fore-flippers relaxed along its rounded body.

"It's for you, but gie it back, it's no quite finished."

"Are you in a lot of pain?" Rosalind perched again on the chair by his bed.

"You're very like your mother, but bonnier, if you look hard."

"You seem a little better than yesterday."

"I'm no drugged. I'm in fucking bloody pain I can tell you. Bastartin doctor tried to dose me but I'm having none of it. I'm needing a clear head. There's not much time. Now." He struggled to sit up, setting off a long episode of gentle coughing. Rosalind handed him a glass of water from the bedside table.

"What's Sheila tellt ye about the cottage?"

"That I was born there. That it's been in the family a long time."

"A damned long time. Since it was built four hundred years

past. The fisher folk have had their share of disasters, it's true. We Ogilvys have aye had hard luck, my father and his father lost at sea, aye, no the first either. And no the last." He knit his brows till the white bristles met. "Why did the sea no take me, eh? Tell me that? Better that than this." He screwed up his face into an expression of black distaste at the hospital room.

"Do you really believe that?"

"One of your ancestors was kidnapped by the press gang, what do you think of that? Aye, and Sheila had her own version of it, that G.I."

"He was a decent enough father. And husband, as far as I know."

"I wouldnae ken. He disgraced the family. Broke the line. When I die, the family that's kept the house all this time will be gone, and the idea of strangers in it, ach! So, now you've come, what do you intend to do about it?"

"Me? The incarnate disgrace?"

"I take it Sheila's no coming back. So that leaves you." Rab resumed his whittling on the seal, pressing the back of the blade against the white wood with his thumb to carefully hollow out a section above the tail.

"I'm not sure what you mean."

"What do I mean?" He rolled his eyes.

"Well," Rosalind said, "I'll do whatever you want me to do. That's why I came."

"Good. Then you'll stay."

"Stay?"

"God save us, woman! Do they no speak English where you come frae?"

"You don't understand. I've got a job in California, a son at college. I can't just move here. I'm supposed to be back at work Monday."

His eyes narrowed. "Is that how family treat one another over there? Would you leave a man to die alone?"

Rosalind bowed her head. "Well, look. Have you thought about selling the cottage?"

"Don't be daft."

"The reason I'm asking is because I've started cleaning it, but I can't do a whole lot more until I know what you want to happen. What about all the things in it?"

He stared at her, then shook his head in disbelief. "Things?

It's folk tossing things out that have nothing when they need them." He put his huge hands over his face and sighed. The tips of his swollen fingers were stained yellow. Scars crisscrossed the back of his hands. "Sheila's right. They become burdens, tangled nets, no use and a damned nuisance. I'm sick of it all, sick of life. Aye, clear the decks, then. Have you any money?"

"I have a little from my husband's insurance, but Chris's university payments are taking it all."

"Payments? For university?"

"I'm afraid that's how it is in the States."

"Who the bloody blue blazes is Chris?"

"My son."

"I suppose his name is Rhinehart."

"Ehrhart."

"Ogilvy's a good old Scots name. You couldn't do better than Ogilvy."

"I changed my name when I got married."

"Is he no deid?"

Rosalind pondered a moment what 'ezzeenodeed' meant. Either something about a legal document or the status of Henry's existence.

"Deed?"

"Dead. Dead!"

"Yes." She refused to allow the tears to surface. "He's dead."

"Then what's tae stop ye changing your name back? Rhinehart indeed."

"But then it would be Smith. That's my parents' name."

"Not your mother's name!"

"But they got married."

"Did they? Oh, did they then? I wouldnae ken. I must have misplaced my wedding invitation." Rab vigorously cut out small chunks of wood above the seal's shoulder. The chips went flying to the floor. It seemed they were coming to grips with the family quarrel, when Uncle Rab changed the subject.

"How did your man die?"

"Henry? He had gone to a conference in Florida and was on the golf course, and he was struck by lightning."

Uncle Rab took a slack-jawed moment to comprehend, then laughed, then coughed again.

"What's so funny?"

"You're no serious!"

"Yes, I am."

"Raise your club tae curse the wee ball, and blam!"

This time Rosalind did burst into tears.

He rolled his eyes again. "There, there, I'm sorry, I'm very sorry."

Mercurial changes of emotion crossed her uncle's face with such exaggeration, that the blinking fierce scowl accompanying his last comment pulled her out of her self-pity. She dabbed at her eyes with a Kleenex. "We don't seem to be connecting very well. Are there any things you need me to do? Valuables? Messages? People to contact? Should I get in touch with a realtor?"

His face bunched on the verge of an outburst, but he kept his voice low. "You can be hard when ye want tae be. Is that what life in America does? I've tellt ye, yer tae have it. Aye, aye, flinging back a gift like that. I've never heard the like."

"Me, hard? I'm in the little league compared to you."

"Aye, well." Suddenly he chuckled. "Maybe she's no a wee mouse after all." He leaned towards her. "Wee sleekit, cow'rin, tim'rous beastie, oh, what a panic's in thy breastie! Eh? Who wrote that, then?"

"Robert Burns," she sighed. Her mother had often recited Burns's poetry to her whether she welcomed it or not.

"Ey, aye, this must be the burns unit, eh? The hospital burns unit!" He burst again into laughter, ending with mighty spluttering coughs. "Oh, dear, I'm plocherin' and clocherin'!"

"I'm sorry, Uncle Rab, I don't understand. What exactly do you mean, I'm to have it?"

"It's in my will. There will be nae difficulties." He waved any problems away. "I've little else. Give your mother a keepsake of my Mum's, a brooch I should have posted her a long time ago, and anything else she's wanting. The photies. There's an auld spindle your mother and her mother used to use. And the few pounds I've squirreled away, that's for Sheila. But the cottage needs a strong young life in it. It's yours."

"The cottage."

"Aye, good, that's that then. A load off my mind. You're a good lass, and bonny enough, if you'd make an effort. Ye'll get another husband, nae bother. Here, tak this wee seal." He finished touching up the face, giving it a sweet smile and big, soulful eyes.

"Thank you, Uncle Rab, it's really nice. I'll treasure it."

Rosalind decided against raising the specter of funeral arrangements until later. She touched a worn cord dangling off his small side table. Three knots were spaced evenly along its length. "What's this for?"

"Eh? Och, just an old sailor's toy. I practice my knots on it. Come back tomorrow. We'll hae another wee chat."

She stood. "Anything else?"

"What the hell have I been telling you, woman? Cigarettes. Whisky!"

*

"Where have you been?" Helen demanded, apron on and bowl and wooden spoon in hand.

"I went for a walk." Clive hung his coat on the hook in the dim hallway.

"Have you forgotten we're hosting a dinner tonight?"

"No."

"For heaven's sake, Clive. You've left me to do it all again."

"Not at all. What needs done?"

"It's all been done."

"I'll go have a shower then." He turned on his heel.

"Yes, wash her scent off, why don't you?"

He paused. "Why do you inevitably feel it necessary to bring up differences just before guests arrive?"

"Differences? Not only do you not help with a dinner that you yourself requested, with that pompous minister and his silly wife, but you use your latest whore as an excuse. This really is too much."

"Oh, just shut it, why don't you?"

"It's that Catriona, isn't it? What's happened? Finally get caught by someone who can hold you accountable?"

"Actually, I'm not seeing Catriona, if that's what you mean." His mouth twitched but he hid the smile. Not seeing Catriona anymore; to be precise, not seeing the needy, clinging bitch of a girl. Even at a tender age it was possible to detect behaviors that would someday blossom into feminine neuroses, as apparently proved by her feeble attempt at attention-getting by doing whatever it was she'd just done to create such a fuss. Clive pulled his sleeve back and looked at his watch. "Look, I'm not going to argue with you. The guests will be here in half an hour. And Angus..."

At that moment the front door opened, and Angus's hearty greeting boomed out. "Hullo, Clan Forbes! Who needs a drink before we are besieged by God's Frozen Chosen? And, dare I mention it, one lovely American?"

"I, for one," said Clive, leaving Helen to stare into the melted chocolate in the bowl.

*

Morag's Quair of Light and Shadows
Under cover of darkness in the wee hours, over what was once known as the Witches' Hill, down the path to the Step Rock tidal pool, the Witches' Lake, I dropped my clothes over a sandy rock, and felt my way into the slippery stones and cold, cold sea water. Soft tendrils gripped my ankles, seaweed becoming clutching fingers of the dead. Small waves lapped, tide caught at its apex. My feet sank into soft cold sand or sometimes painfully slid across a hidden rock. Down into the cleansing sea, past the creatures darting underfoot, past the dim phantoms of the women hurled over the cliff or tied to stakes, desperate mouth and nostrils sucking in the last air between the final waves, the rejoicing Presbyters above. Letting the rising tide do the dirty work for them, the self-righteous cowards. Their descendants take great pride in the big, phallic Martyr's Monument on the green above, but who remembers the women they killed?

And in the cruel sea, a reprieve, another wave, a choking sputtering minute of life, again and again, what satisfaction did the brutes watching gain, a perverted thrill in vanquishing these creatures with a horrible, lingering death? Until the heads were under water, eyes turned up, mouths agape, lungs burst, spirits wrenched untimely from the bodies, but not from the tidal pool. The ghosts' agony bound them in time to a perpetual imprint in the eternal tide.

The cold knocked the breath from me as I went under with them. My hair swirled in the current, mingled with the bladderwrack. I drifted in the sinewy water and let it take the residue of expectations and hopes away. Dissolved into the pool of death, I lost myself among the sorrowful forgotten.

A change of fortune, a new destiny was slowly forming. Something quite grave. I was woefully out of practice in the deeper magic, caught up with trying to help Catriona, poor lamb, take care of her mother and Auntie Meg and young Kirsteen, who has recently come to live here. And now with the crisis finally broached, things were shifting in a confusing pattern. I don't usually turn to the cards. Much easier to go directly to the source, but the doors would not open. And still and yet the cards proved to be no use, nor the runes, nor even scrying. Something was on the verge of change, here, too, even in these forms of divination. I'd caught an intimation through Auntie Meg, a hint of what would unfold through the channel of her old eyes – eye, I should say – but only enough to cause me great concern.

Catriona was dead. She'd been found two days after she'd gone missing from home, at a pal's house in Leuchars. She was unconscious when they transported her to hospital, and died within hours. An accidental overdose, so it was reported.

And yet it didn't ring true. Aye, there were problems in her home, her mother was no great example of strength in hard times, and secretly turned to the bottle often enough, leaving the young lassie to pester me or her own wee pals for company. How easy a target she was for a cunning older man who could provide both fatherly support and a sophisticated lover's irresistible flattery. Until he tired of her and tossed her over for the next victim.

Now, too late, too late, I could see Catriona quite clearly in my mind's eye, the last moments of gathering courage in her loneliness, her desperation, the hurt and hopelessness. And the mistaken belief, all too common in young lassies, that she was to blame for his cruelty.

My tender and innocent wee niece. Auntie Meg was right, I should have hastened things with Clive, and I might have been able to stay her hand. She'd still be alive. I will never forgive myself, never.

The minister Niall Paterson had been at her deathbed in the hospital, insufferable with his infuriating platitudes. Did he feel the need to spout his rubbish over her body? Perhaps so, given that she had had enough sense to avoid him in life, unlike her mother Margaret, a weak soul. 'Aye, meenester, no, meenester, whatever you say, meenester.' But he made himself scarce right enough when I showed up, and Margaret in such a state she didn't know what was worse, his leaving or my arriving. No doubt he'd make her pay next time they conversed. My idiotic half-sister, on my father's side, a Highland family of Wee Frees, so scared by the second sight in the family, she went over completely into the enemy camp. St. Margaret we call her. Is it any wonder her husband left her all those years ago? Which only fanned the fires of her martyrdom.

I put it all out of my head. My back and thighs slid over sand and stone as the sea's motion rocked me, until I was utterly empty. Erased. Creature of the sea and earth, floating free between water and rock.

Occasionally, discernment of future events will not unfold until all the strands are come together to dictate the movement of fate, and this was such a time. I could see nothing beyond what was already revealed, of indecipherable sex and death, embroiled with an ancient magic from beyond my kenning.

My head lifted from the ritual bath. I took air into my lungs and felt my body fill. My feet searched for solid rock, and, slowly, step by step I emerged from the sea. The ghosts watched with hollow eyes from their watery tomb.

Some of the townsfolk say I am immoral. I say truth makes a mockery of human concepts of morality, as witnessed by the spirits of the slain innocents around me. Did they deserve to die, and the wicked to go unpunished? For that is most certainly what happened. There is no good or evil in creation, but for the thoughts and deeds of men. There is no right or wrong in the Goddess, only that everything becomes as one in the spirals of time.

Which of course gives me free rein in the present. An instrument to redress the balance in whatever form it takes. I stood in the air, warm after the cold sea, and let the water spill off my vengeful body. I raised my arms and swore by the stars and moon that Clive Forbes would rue the day he'd been born, and that such pleasure as I'd never known would be mine in the execution of his fate.

*

In the upstairs bedroom, the wardrobe's left-hand door opened to little shelves, labeled with metal plates to indicate which men's clothing went where – shirts, trousers, handkerchiefs, and so on. The few feminine contents of Rosalind's suitcase looked incongruous in its staid depths.

Sleeping in the room had given it an intimacy previously lacking, despite the fact that the bedroom door was always open when she awoke, no matter how carefully she made sure the latch caught. After a bout of worry was replaced by curiosity, it became a game. She would shut the door for a night's sleep, tugging on it to be sure it was truly closed. Inevitably, it was ajar when she awoke, offering a glimpse into the dark sitting room opposite. She never caught it in the act of opening. Of course the floorboards creaked, that was to be expected in such an old house. Sometimes the sounds came rhythmically, like a slow shuffle up the stairs, but it happened so often for no apparent reason, she'd become accustomed to it.

A far stranger thing was the flowering of sexual arousal. It came strongest when she was relaxed, mind quiet from all the pressing concerns of the cottage and Uncle Rab. Then it was like a smoldering heat that had taken possession. It simply existed and refused to depart. There was no aspect of fantasy to it, it was purely physical, but she had to admit, after the novelty had faded, it was a lively spark of life that she welcomed.

She had lain in bed that afternoon following a brief nap, door duly open, and studying the white cottage walls, the wooden sills handmade to contain the windows' distorted, thick glass, the small room cozy and warm with its fireplace. The sexual heat, unabated, had become a companion, sometimes amusing, sometimes annoying, but always present. Had it not been for the heavy sea air and the amount of work and cleaning needing done, sleep would have been almost impossible in the face of this new restlessness, this raw energy.

In the stillness, Rosalind mulled over finding a solution to Uncle Rab's assumption that she would stay on in the cottage. She wondered how much could be made by refurbishing and selling. Maybe enough to buy a small house in California. Property prices had leveled off when she was forced to sell their house in Palo Alto at Henry's untimely death, creating a major loss at the worst possible time. She had never once seriously considered moving to Scotland, leaving behind family and familiarity, but Uncle Rab was forcing the issue. She recalled again the safe stability, impoverished though it was, of her grim steady life back home, and weighed it against this constant barrage of new impressions. Nor did she have the common American romantic notions of Scotland. Her immigrant mother had made sure of that.

"The devil you know," she said to the wardrobe.

From the choice of her two simple dresses, she decided on the dark blue knit. Flat black shoes, good for travel, if not very fashionable, were all she had. On a whim she tried tying a white scarf around her waist, and was pleased enough with the improvised outfit.

Dusk had descended with as thick a mist as on the previous evening. Rosalind locked the front door, headed off down the lane, and almost bumped into an elderly woman standing at the threshold of the neighbor's house. Rosalind feared it was the eccentric Morag again. But no. The old woman was what she appeared to be. Two tusky eyeteeth glowed in the streetlight. Her head turned to peer up like a bird's sideways glance from a bent back twisted into a hump. One eye was cloudy. She clutched neatly folded linen sheets.

Rosalind apologized and was just stepping aside to head up the lane, when the old woman gave a rasping laugh.

"Mind I don't catch you in it!" With surprising sprightliness, the old woman shook out the sheets. They billowed round, blinding Rosalind, catching her in a deeper whiteness than the mist. Quick words hissed close to her tingling ear. "Six feet of earth makes us all of one size."

Rosalind was afraid to move lest she topple the old woman. "Hey, what are you doing?"

The woman pulled the sheet tighter. Its edge dragged over the cobbles. She circled Rosalind, singing in a quavering voice. "To Brig o' Dread thou com'st at last."

"I'm late for a dinner." Rosalind tugged at the cloth. "Your sheets will get dirty. Let me fold them up for you."

"We warned her," the old woman said as if Rosalind were her closest confidant. "The young ones these days, they won't listen."

Rosalind tried to pull the sheet over her head, but her skirt rode up with it, and her hair came loose and fell over her eyes.

And that was how Morag found her when she came to the door, wondering why the chest of drawers had been left open and the winding sheets gone. This was a combustible mix, Auntie Meg in her current state, and the innocent American.

"Auntie, you really are naughty." Morag tried to disguise her amusement as she eased Aunty Meg out of the way. She pulled the sheet from Rosalind's body, walking sunwise around her, breathing in her scent, and if her fingers trailed over Rosalind's shoulders, it was done so lightly she never noticed.

"The fire shall burn thee to the bare bane," Auntie Meg sang, then cackled.

Rosalind caught the tail of the linen off her shoulder and pushed it into Morag's arms, feeling as if the old woman had literally cast a pall over her. She shuddered violently. "Ah, God!"

"Forgive her," Morag said. "My Aunty Meg. She gets a little confused. Someone close to us has just died, you see."

"Catriona, Catriona, hardly cold." Auntie Meg's mouth opened wide in an exhalation, like a serpent's hiss, but her eye was a black pool of sorrow.

Rosalind froze in shock as she suddenly realized that this must be the person she'd heard Morag and Clive arguing over in the street.

"I'm so sorry to hear that, I truly am." Rosalind backed down the lane, gathering her spilled hair with her fingers. "Please excuse me? I'm late."

"Tell me your name again," Morag said, holding out a hand, knowing perfectly well. "I am Morag Gilbride."

She was reluctant to stay, reluctant to touch Morag. Her eyes pleaded in a mix of confusion and fear, but she put her palm into Morag's. "Rosalind."

The spell had taken. A magical tweak which breaks a dam and lets the connection flow between the two. Morag's eyes lit up, piercing. Rosalind did a double-take and looked more closely at her.

"Oh, ho ho ho," Auntie Meg cackled. "Sheila's bairn. Does she ken?"

"Wheesht, Auntie."

Rosalind backed away, then turned and fled, through the haar, through the white darkness, as the two women whispered behind her. All along the lane, mocked by the swirling mist, she imagined the sheets tightening around her. Her hand tingled with a strange warmth. Her feet thudded over the bones of the dead, jarring them, disturbing them, till she feared they would awaken from an ancient sleep, even as the sound of her own name on Morag's lips echoed in her mind.

Rosalind.

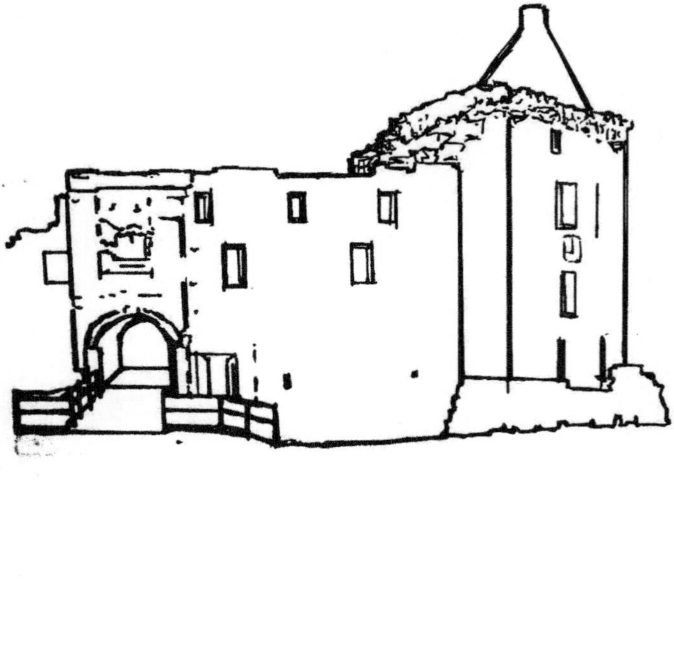

Chapter 4

All the guests politely kept their heads bowed through the interminable grace, except for Clive who studied his own Scottish prints hanging on the wall behind Rosalind with a newfound interest, and winked at her when he saw that she was watching.

"And heavenly Father, help us to understand the need for the sacrifice of life for the sustenance of life. Make sacred the use of these your plants and animals so that we might have life not only in the flesh but also in spirit." The top of Niall's balding head gleamed in the candle light.

Rosalind wondered if he recognized her from the near-miss car accident, but if he did, he'd given no sign upon being introduced.

"And we thank you, heavenly Father for that sacrifice of life to sustain us, and keep us ever aware of the need for our own sacrifices in turn, and of our debts and of our sins, which are manifold."

"Amen," said Helen.

"And," he carried on, "we give you thanks, heavenly Father..."

"Oh," said Helen. "Sorry."

"...for our coming together this evening, for this food we are about to share, and we ask your blessing on this company, in Christ's name, amen."

"But Helen," said Alastair, "I could have sworn you were an atheist."

"Even atheists can be considerate of others. And anyway, I'm not. Not really. I attend the Scottish Episcopal church from time to time."

"Then you didn't ask this man to say grace simply for his own sake?"

"Oh, Alastair," said Helen. "Don't be contentious this early on."

"I hope we are not offending you, Niall," said Angus. "Reverend Paterson, I should say!"

Niall smiled faintly. "I don't take all my meals with saints."

Rosalind had been seated between Angus MacLeod and

Clive. Helen and Clive were strategically placed, she by the serving counters at one corner of the table, and he at the opposite, to manage the wine, which he did with generosity. Niall Paterson sat at the far end, with his wife Mary on his right. The double glass doors at his back appeared to make him uncomfortable. He frequently glanced over his shoulder into the night beyond.

Elderly Alastair Comyn, cravatted and perfumed, sat directly across from Rosalind, next to Mary, bending the force of his florid personality to her flustered attention. Mary's straight dark hair was cut in a jagged fringe across her forehead, which did not flatter the plumpness of her face or figure. With some squirming necessary because of the tightness of her skirt, her chair moved a little away from Alastair every time she shifted, which occurred more and more frequently as the dinner progressed.

"Ah," Alastair said. "Helen makes a point of mixing volatile guests."

"I do not!" Helen said. "No thanks to you, Alastair. But I will admit to enjoying a certain intellectual level. And Niall has just had his book published. He deserves to be fêted."

"Fated?" Alastair feigned surprise. "Our wills and fates do so contrary run."

"No fools in my house, if you please!" Clive flapped a rumpled handkerchief and blew his nose with a loud honk, then hiccupped. He looked at Rosalind, as delighted with himself as a little boy, and laughed.

"Which book would that be?" asked Angus.

"Better warn you, Niall," said Clive. "Angus is the son of a minister."

Niall sat back and made steeples with his fingers. "Then you might appreciate my work. *God's Warriors, The Early Celtic Saints.*"

"Sounds interesting," said Angus.

"It's a very exciting premise," said Mary.

Niall needed no encouragement. "There is so much rubbish written these days about the Celtic saints, which paints them as tree-hugging, nature-loving milksops out in their little coracles..."

"Honestly," said Mary, "they've become the equivalent of the New Age fad of Christianity, and everybody claims them for their own..."

"Everybody," Niall echoed, "Church of Scotland, Anglican, Roman Catholic…"

"True enough," said Clive. "Part of this absurd Celtic fad."

"Even non-Christians," said Mary, "for heaven's sake."

"And you are redressing the misrepresentation?" asked Alastair.

"They were adamant evangelists." Niall banged the table with his open hand. "Nothing irresolute about them, whatsoever."

"Quite right. Perhaps I could have you sign a copy for me," said Alistair.

"Be glad to." Niall sat back.

"Why, I happen to have one here." With some difficult, Mary leaned over to pull a slim volume from her handbag.

"Call it a conservative view if you like," said Niall, taking the book and waiting with hand held out for her to find a pen. "But we've lost our way in this maze of… what do they call it?"

"Liberal leanings," Mary said.

"High time people understood what the Celtic Saints were really about," said Niall.

"Hear, hear," said Alastair. "And I suspect you're just the man to do so!"

Rosalind couldn't tell if he was egging the oblivious minister on.

"Thank you." Niall inclined his head in humble acknowledgment.

A voice whispered in Rosalind's ear. "How do you find St. Andrews?" Angus's breath confirmed Rosalind's suspicions that he and Clive had been drinking before the guests arrived. His boyish good looks were made all the more appealing by being a little rough at the edges, face etched by frequent exposure to the elements, but she guessed him to be slightly older than herself, in his late forties. His full head of unkempt hair was the same gray brown as his beard. He smelled good, of wool and fresh air. "Is it what you expected?"

"It's an enchanting place," Rosalind said, "with lots of interesting characters."

The sound of distant thunder rose and persisted, a familiar roar of the RAF jets across the estuary.

"Yes, but I must say not what I expected," Niall broke in. "Given the rich heritage, even unto John Knox himself gracing the pulpits here, the martyrs, so many of God's chosen, yet I find cynicism running rampant."

"Do you mean the unchurched?" asked Alastair.

"Not only that, but the church itself is...progressive."

Mary made a little 'hm' of support.

"They'll be having those classes... those..."

"Yoga," offered Mary.

"Yoga classes next." They laughed.

"We are cursed with an overabundance of eccentrics," said Clive. "Like the retired brigadier next door. When those jets fly out of Leuchars, he goes to the garden to watch. Leers like a goat and says he finds the noise so *virile*."

Mary shifted slightly.

Rosalind had an impulse to engage the obviously uncomfortable Mary. "Do you have children?" she enquired.

Mary's eyes widened and she sat back. "We have not been blessed in that regard."

"Potatoes, Rosalind?" Helen passed a large bowl.

Rosalind appeared to have stumbled into a *faux pas*, and quickly took the potatoes.

"The salmon is perfect," said Alastair. A tilt to his bulbous-nosed face revealed a line of rouge under his chin, though it might have been the dancing reflection from the brass pots hanging above the stove behind him.

"You rub the fillets with ginger and *sauté* three minutes each side, and Bob's your uncle." Helen glanced at Rosalind. "Oh, that means..."

"Hey, presto," suggested Angus.

"All systems go, bub," said Clive.

"So what eccentrics have you encountered, Rosalind?" said Angus. "Mrs. Pearse perhaps?"

"The religious lady?" she asked, at which everyone laughed. "And there's an unusual woman who lives next door to my uncle's cottage. This evening, for instance, when I was coming here, her aunt, I think, was out in the street, shaking out some sheets, outside, you understand. Something to do with someone dying."

Clive stood to reach the bottle from the counter.

"And the old woman wrapped me in the sheets, I mean literally wound them around me."

The only sound was the wine tinkling into Mary's glass. Then Clive, bent over her shoulder, said, "She what?"

"How very odd," Helen said.

Clive moved to Alastair's glass. "Perhaps she thought you were cold." He laughed loudly.

"This pushes the boundaries of credulity," said Niall.

Surely he didn't think she was making it up? Rosalind gave a bewildered glance at Angus who beamed her an encouraging smile.

"What did you do?" asked Helen.

"The younger woman, the one next door, rescued me. But she's the one who makes me uncomfortable. I can't quite put my finger on it. Is it possible for people to have pet ravens?"

"I've never known ravens to be pets, but some people have jackdaws," Helen said. "They're like rooks, or crows. Cheeky little devils."

"Is the cottage about halfway up Market Street, after the lane narrows?" asked Alastair. "Do all sorts of people come to her door at odd hours?"

"Why, yes, now that you mention it."

"Of course," said Helen. "That girl who came out when you asked for the key, Rosalind. Catriona. Did the woman ever tell you her name? She did look odd, like a hippie."

Angus frowned. "Morag Gilbride, our famous witch."

Clive's hand jumped over Rosalind's glass. The wine splashed on the table.

"I don't think I envy you," Angus continued, "having her for a neighbor."

"Tsk," said Alastair.

"Witch?" Rosalind took the sponge Helen handed her and mopped up the wine. "Are you serious? What do you mean?"

"She's quite well known," said Alastair. "Have you met her yet, Reverend?"

"I regret to say I do know someone by that name," Niall said ominously. "One of these muddle-headed do-good environmentalists who just cause worse problems for everybody."

"There is only one Morag Gilbride," said Alastair. "She's a shape-shifter, like the old Celtic gods. Can go anywhere and blend right in."

"Famous?" Clive banged the empty bottle on the counter and sat down. "She's a damned nuisance. A menace. I'm sorry, Rosalind, that she's next door to you, but there you are."

"Peddling pagan superstition," added Niall.

"Tut, what nonsense," said Alastair.

"Does she have a big hook nose?" Mary giggled. "And warts?"

"She happens to be one of the most beautiful women I have ever seen," said Alastair.

"Well!" Helen arched her thin eyebrows. "Did you notice this small detail, Rosalind?"

She hesitated. "It's weird, like she gives off conflicting images. But yes, she does have a lovely face. What do you mean," Rosalind asked Angus, "when you say she's a witch?" He was studying her in a warm, dreamy way. He opened his mouth to answer when Clive interrupted.

"Bitch."

"Clive!" Helen glanced at Mary, who had pursed her lips as she glanced at her husband. "Really."

"She's a bloody charlatan, duping idiots foolish enough to want their vanity groomed. I'm sorry, but that sort of thing annoys the hell out of me."

"It's more than an annoyance," said Niall. "It's a danger, preying on the credulity of those who need spiritual nourishment from legitimate sources."

"What does she do?" Rosalind asked.

"Lots of things," said Alastair. "But if you mean what do all those people see her for, probably psychic counseling."

Clive snorted. "Psychic bloody counseling! Let's call a spade a spade. They go to have their fortunes told. Tarot cards and all that tripe."

"It was for good reason such persons were condemned through the centuries," said Niall.

"I'd be happy to strike the match," said Clive.

"Oh, stop," said Alistair. "Our American guest will think she's landed in the midst of religious fanatics."

"There are worse things to be called," Niall said. "She was," he started to chuckle, "she was one of those Findhorn lunatics in that glorified caravan site they're now calling a spiritual community."

"Can you imagine," Mary laughed. "Seeing goblins and whatnot squatting under mushrooms."

"How do you know this witch person?" Helen asked the scowling Alastair.

"You university types, with your noses to the grindstone of your little world's concerns do not catch all the goings on which occur in other circles. Fishing. Farming. Tradesmen.

Morag Gilbride is well known to us."

Clive mopped at his nose. "Is the Laird of Carlin Castle singing an anthem to the common man?"

"Don't mock. Dear Clive. You really don't look well."

"Morag the witch has hexed me."

"I shouldn't wonder," Alastair said mildly.

"I don't feel some sort of interloper," said Helen. "The University is the backbone of St. Andrews."

"A few vertebrae, maybe," said Angus. "The church is the real backbone."

"There speaks a minister's son," said Helen. "Of an elitist institution."

"The University isn't?" Angus said.

"But the church is not elitist," said Niall. "It is the potential salvation of every soul."

"You can't argue that the hierarchy is not an elite brotherhood," Angus said, "educated, elevated..."

"The first shall be last, and the last first." Niall bowed his head.

"Very noble of you to say so, but I think," Helen said, "it speaks more of your honesty than a real interest by any congregation I am aware of, in more a kind of moral guideline; a buttressing up, if you will, of the status quo, sanctioned by the institution."

"Oh, dear me, no," said Mary.

The phone trilled. "Pardon me," said Clive. He jumped up to lift the portable receiver from its place by the door. "Helen's right in that the church reflects society," he said over his shoulder. "And a conservative society at that. Hullo?"

"Perhaps," Alastair said, "church politics boil down to what people are accustomed to. Will all the so-called spiritual justifications over certain issues appear rather mean in hindsight? Homosexuality for instance. Role of women. Don't you think, Reverend Paterson?"

"No, actually, I don't. There is a sound theological basis for these issues."

With the receiver pressed to his ear, the upturned lines on Clive's face sagged. He carried the phone into the hallway.

"Not for me?" Helen called. The door shut. "Apparently not."

"I'm afraid," Angus said, "I can't find it in me to raise much interest in the subject. I'm not a religious person, despite, or maybe because of my upbringing. Unless you want to look at it as a study of trends in British society."

"You've traveled enough," Helen said, "to be able to look back from a different perspective. Most don't have that luxury. Sometimes I think we're like rats in a maze, barely coping with a life that really has little meaning."

Rosalind pulled her attention from Angus's enticing proximity to look more closely at Helen. But if Helen was hinting at her own life, she quickly carried on, the good hostess making conversation.

"No, a question I'd like to see answered is, what has happened to our society? We are disintegrating into little islands of frightened, selfish humans. Niall, from a moral standpoint, what do you think?"

He put down his wine glass. "It's quite simple. And twofold. One, individual desires have supplanted the will of God. We do not subjugate our sinful natures any longer, we glorify them. And two, respect has been lost for the authority of the Word, and for the ministers of the Word."

Mary made a deferential bow toward her husband. "Well said, dear."

"Isn't it likely, though, that economics and an increased awareness of global trends play a part in what Helen was talking about?" asked Angus.

The door slowly opened. Clive stood in the dark of the hallway. His eyes were vacant, and his lower lip hung moist. Then he raised his head, and rejoined them, squeezing round the table to open another bottle of wine. "It's drugs. It's the easiest thing in the world to bring drugs into Britain. You can unload them anywhere on the coast."

Alastair said softly, "One may smile, and smile, and be a villain."

"Is this Morag Gilbride threatening because she is outwith social strictures?" Helen ignored the baleful glare between the two men. "I mean, has that not been the common denominator for so-called witches down through the centuries?"

"God," Clive moaned. "Are we still on about her?"

"Precisely, my dear," said Alastair. "Morag Gilbride will not play the games we spend all our lives setting the rules to, and so she is often perceived as a threat to the order, which she is. We know, we whose roots are sunk deep into the pagan earth, that there are some people gifted with the second sight."

"Oh, come on, Alastair!" said Clive. "This is becoming tedious."

"Now, now, let's be considerate. You may not realize we have a guest in our midst whose family has dabbled in the occult arts."

Curious glances went round the table. Helen's expression began to change from a slightly puzzled affability to a dawning realization.

"Oh good heavens," she said. "I'd quite forgotten all about that."

"Well, don't keep us in suspense," Angus said as Alastair chuckled.

"Your mother," said Helen to Rosalind. "Sheila. The story is, she put a curse on the Gilbrides which remains to this day."

"My mother? No way," said Rosalind in surprise.

"Here's the interesting thing," said Alastair. "It apparently worked."

Clive snorted. "If only."

"I've never heard about this," said Rosalind.

Niall gave an impatient huff.

"Of course, I don't know that much about it, I mean I wasn't even born yet," Helen explained, "but there was a romantic rivalry between your mother and Meg Gilbride over your father."

"That old woman with one eye?" Rosalind said in disbelief.

"We were all young and beautiful once, dearie," said Alastair.

"But what did my Mom do?"

"There are rumors," said Alastair, "but nobody really knows. You'll have to ask her. All I can say is it must have been quite the hex to halt a Gilbride witch's ambitions."

Niall's irritation at the unworthy topic had been plainly growing with perturbed exhalations and tongue-clicking. "You make it sound as if these Gilbrides had some real power, Alastair. What utter nonsense."

"They are like the old druids, shamans, quite a different breed from the priestly cast, don't you think, Reverend?"

"I would rather see a little of this 'second sight' in action before I made any judgment," Niall said. "Believing because you like the idea is as bad as pooh-poohing something because you can't see the sense in it, trying to perceive the spiritual in a logical or secular manner. Experience of the divine should undergird our beliefs."

Rosalind sat back, mouth half open in amazement at her mother's secret life, relieved that the conversation had resumed in a different direction.

"I quite agree," said Alastair. "But how can you preach this idea from the pulpit, then ask them to recite the Westminster Creed? Pre-ordination, resurrection, and all that?"

Angus cleared his throat.

Mary, looking extremely puzzled, squashed a potato with her fork. "People need to be educated in what to believe."

Niall shot her an irritated look, and Mary dropped her gaze. He returned his attention to Alastair. "I'm sorry, but I don't understand your point. The Word is the experience."

An awkward pause followed as everyone made a conspicuous effort to say nothing. Rosalind felt out of her depth again, ignorant of theology in general and British manners in particular.

"I'm afraid," Helen stepped in, "that some of the most fascinating history boils down to the antics of popular religion, such as the oozing saints business, collecting samples from bodies and graves to mix into potions, you know, remarkably horrible, superstitious stuff. I'm quite certain it's still going on today, in its own way."

A vivid memory filled Rosalind's mind, of Morag Gilbride scraping dust from the tower vault into a jar. "Did you say 'oozing saints'?"

"Oh, yes, not a particularly pleasant dinner topic; the believers took relics from bodies that were still decomposing."

Angus's beard tickled her ear. "Your serviette, Rosalind. It fell."

Helen was still speaking. "There has always been a segment of the population more than ready to burn people who don't believe their way."

"Yes, but they've all gone into politics, now," Mary said. Everybody laughed. A tension Rosalind had not been aware of until then broke. Mary beamed in her unexpected turn of wit.

"The potatoes are delicious," Rosalind said. "Did you do them with mint?"

"Yes, it's a trick my mother taught me."

"Lovely dinner," Mary said.

"About the sheets you mentioned," Angus said. "There is an old custom, which I thought obsolete, of a special set of linen sheets being kept for a person's deathbed. The sheets were sometimes taken outside. I'm not sure why, perhaps because of the cramped spaces in the old houses, perhaps to let the villagers know someone had died. They were shaken out," his large hands flapped an imaginary sheet over the table, "then placed on the bed where the corpse was laid out."

"Oh, great," said Rosalind. "Do you mean that old woman put sheets around me that were for someone's death bed?"

"I am telling you, Gilbride ought to be locked up," said Clive.

"But why did she do it?" Rosalind said.

"Trying to pull a tasteless joke," said Clive. "Just sell that house. Forget the improvements."

"She's only just arrived, dear." Helen stood to collect the plates.

"I doubt you were singled out in particular," said Niall. "You just happened to be passing at the wrong time. It's traffic you should be more concerned about. It's difficult, I'm sure, to remember which side we drive on."

So he did remember, and had completely fooled her with his poker face and icy blue eyes. She made an attempt at humor. "You had an emergency and I hurled myself in front of your car."

"Didn't make in time, I'm afraid."

Rosalind wondered if he was hinting that it was her fault.

"Catriona Hamilton," Clive stated gloomily.

Niall's pale eyebrows lifted. "How on earth did you know, Clive?"

"That phone call."

Everyone turned to see Clive sink lower in his chair and cross his arms.

"Clive," said Helen, "what's going on? Who phoned?"

"What am I supposed to do about this girl? I mean, bloody hell, what can I do? Why won't that damned *witch* leave me alone? She's mentally ill, one of these people who fixates on some poor unlucky bastard." Helen tried to speak, but Clive cut her off. "Do you see what I mean, now? She's a nuisance. To lots of people, not just me. I'm fed up! If she calls again, I'll get the police."

"Clive," Helen said to the stunned silence, "that was her, this Gilbride person? Why? What could she possibly...?"

"I really don't feel well. Will you pardon me?" Clive perceptively calmed himself. "You lot carry on. Sorry. I'll be back in a moment." He disappeared down the hallway.

"Curiouser and curiouser," Alastair said.

"Was this person who died a parishioner of yours?" Helen asked Niall.

"Yes, of the church, though a very poor attendance record from what I understand. The poor girl accidentally overdosed in Leuchars and died here soon after. I'm sorry to say but I'm not surprised. Her mother is a good soul. Faithful. Very devout woman. I expect she'll ask me to do the funeral."

"You do know that the young lass is – was – Morag Gilbride's niece?" asked Alastair.

"No," said Niall. "I didn't. Oh, Lord help us."

Alastair sat back and took a packet of cigarettes from his jacket pocket. "Ciggy anyone?"

"I don't understand why…" Helen began. "I don't…" She faltered and stopped.

Everyone seemed uncomfortable as if some unspoken thought hung in the air. Alastair kept his eyes lowered as he scraped a match over the box and lit his cigarette. "I assume that if the women brought out the winding sheets to be used in the old manner, the body will be laid out for the wake. It's good to keep the old ways. I approve."

"You mean the body stays at home?" Rosalind said. "A corpse is in their house?"

"One you tested the sheets for, my angel," Alastair said, eyes twinkling at her over his cigarette.

"But don't you use funeral homes?"

"Oh, heavens, darling, given a choice, what would you rather?"

"I remember now," Angus said. "My grandmother had them. I was just a wee boy, but I recall my mother shaking out the sheets."

"Then what happens?" Rosalind asked. "I mean, to the sheets. Are they buried with the body?"

Angus thought for a moment. "If I remember right, they're washed and used as ordinary bed linens after the wake." He looked into his wine glass, then took a sip. "I must have them at home."

"That's so morbid!" Rosalind said. The unbidden image came of herself and Angus, lovers, in his bed with the corpse's sheets around them. But what of it, she suddenly thought recklessly. It would be worth it. As he gazed at her with unmistakable fondness, she sat back, amazed at herself.

"That's so Scottish," laughed Helen.

Rosalind realized it was one of the very few times she'd seen Helen laugh or even smile.

Angus's bright eyes watched Rosalind closely. "We can't seem to waste anything."

With an exaggerated gesture, Niall stretched out his arm to pull the sleeve back from his watch. "I regret to say we must be going soon."

"Oh, but Niall," said Mary. "I'm sure Helen's made a lovely pudding."

"Oh, here," said Helen. "It's ready." She jumped up and turned to the counter to retrieve the dessert.

Clive, looking a little chastened, rejoined them. He sniffed and tugged at his nostrils, sniffed again, and sat down with a weak smile. Alistair exhaled a long stream of smoke and watched, eyes keen under his shaggy white brows.

"Hullo, dear," Helen said. "I'm just serving dessert." She placed a dark chocolate torte on the table. Everyone watched as she sliced and served. Mary licked her lips.

"How's business, Clive?" Alistair suddenly asked.

Clive looked wary. "Why do you ask?"

"No specific reason beyond a polite query."

Clive again composed himself and answered in as mild a manner. "Not bad." He thought for a moment. "Except that our librarian ran off with the manager of a marmalade factory in Dundee. You can't imagine the trouble we've had finding a replacement. You'd think countless people would jump at it, but my God, if they show up at all for an appointment, they're hopeless! The time I've wasted. How is it possible that with so much unemployment, I can't get one librarian?"

"Quite simple," said Mary. "They'd rather stay on the dole. They can even buy quite a nice house with subsidies. They get more money on the dole than from many jobs, and spend their days in utter self-indulgence. It's contributing to the moral decline in Britain. But mark my words, Margaret Thatcher will have things sorted out in double quick time!"

"What needs to be done?" asked Rosalind.

"Religious education," Niall began.

"Our archives..." Clive said at the same time.

"I mean at the office," said Rosalind with an apologetic smile to Niall.

"The archives need organized. I'm getting desperate. We can't continue to function with this chaos."

"Do you mean like trade literature?"

"Plans, books, codes, fiche, magazines, building samples."

"Oh, I could do that," said Rosalind. "Except that I won't have time."

"Hold on. You can?"

"I'm an archivist. At a junior college. Pretty basic stuff, but I'm leaving to go home in a few days."

"But that's splendid!" said Clive. "You must come in, just for a morning or two, please. Would you have a look, advise us what to do?"

"Well . . . " Rosalind made a quick calculation of her time away from work, then considered the pressing unknowns of dealing with Uncle Rab. Then she met Angus's bright eyes, gazing with endearing hope.

"I'll be eternally in your debt," said Clive.

"Let me see what I can do. To be honest, I'd like to stay longer, if I can."

"Angus," Niall interrupted. "Have you turned up any interesting finds in the Culdee church?"

"Em, well..." Angus appeared to be reluctant to answer, then smiled at Rosalind. "There are some fields by Tentsmuir forest where we suspect a medieval community was located. I thought it was going to be a fairly small project, but – and this is pure coincidence – a farmer in an adjacent field pulled a lintel stone off the entrance to a Neolithic cairn with his plow."

He was interrupted by a collective moan of appreciation as the torte was tasted around the table.

"Divine," said Alastair.

"Absolutely delicious," said Mary.

"Would it be possible to borrow some students?" Angus asked Helen. "One week from today?"

"Oh, yes, I should think so. I'll round up a few eager beavers, if you like. But why the delay?"

"I've a few things to put right first."

"But Angus," said Niall. "What about the Culdee church?" He leaned slightly towards Rosalind. "The Culdees, a true reformed church, embodied a very exciting time in ecclesiastical history."

"I see," said Rosalind.

"The cairn takes precedence in the eyes of this archaeologist," said Angus.

"Cairn?" asked Helen. "What sort of cairn?"

"I'm not sure yet, but it looks like it might be a chambered cairn."

"In Fife? That would be quite remarkable, Angus."

"In the meantime," he glanced at the guests scraping their plates, "would all of you be good enough to keep this business about the cairn quiet just now? Perhaps I shouldn't have spoken."

Rosalind looked up at him. He was fidgeting with his napkin, eyes on his half-eaten dessert.

"Angus. What have you found?" Helen asked. "You've found something, I can tell."

"I'm not sure, yet. I don't want any rumors to start."

"But Angus. It's important, isn't it? You can tell me," said Helen.

"When I know what I'm dealing with. Promise. If word got out... I mean I'm not sure yet, but if the press got wind of it... but I simply don't know. I mean it could be absolutely nothing, and there are, well, to be blunt, thieves and grave robbers."

*

Angus offered to escort her home, but Rosalind declined after a mighty internal struggle, wanting the short walk alone. There was so much to process. With the dinner, the scales had tipped from the barrage of disconcerting impressions she wanted to flee, to a glowing pleasure she wanted to experience again. Best of all was the excitement generated by being among such lively conversationalists after the countless years of lacking engaging social circles back home. Henry had been a homebody, who insisted on being left alone in the evenings after his work, viewing social visits to what had once been mutual friends a chore to be endured. After a time Rosalind had given up and took to reading in the long evenings.

She couldn't recall having enjoyed a dinner so much in her life. She hoped very much she would see the handsome Scot again.

*

Kirsteen hung back like a petulant child.

"What's wrong?" Morag asked.

Kirsteen clutched the winding sheets tightly to her breast and rolled her eyes like a spooked cow. "Must we do this?"

Morag unlocked the door to the council house and entered. Kirsteen hesitated, till Morag reached back and pulled her in.

"I'm not pleased being a part of this," she said. "I'm supposed to be meeting Calum, he's taking me tae the pictures."

"We can't do it ourselves," Morag said. "And you were friends, were you not?" She quietly closed the door in the hush of mourning. "Margaret?" she called. "Auntie Meg?"

"Here," said a feeble voice. "Just coming."

"Do you smell that?" Kirsteen cautiously sniffed the air.

"Oh, you'll make a fine nurse," Morag said.

Auntie Meg came into the room. "Wheesht," she hissed at Kirsteen. Her *wheesht* came out a whistle because of her lack of teeth. "Don't distress Margaret."

"And that's all we're going to do, right?" Kirsteen nodded at the sheets. "I don't trust you. I know what you get up to."

"I very much doubt that," Morag said.

Catriona's mother appeared like a silent wraith. Morag studied her half-sister for signs of grief that could trip over into madness. Margaret's pale cheeks were sunken, her eyes rimmed with red. Morag held her arms open to her. Margaret stood, too weary to protest, arms dangling at her sides, but melted slightly into the embrace, something she normally would never have allowed.

"All right?"

Margaret sighed. "This was not meant to be, Morag," she said.

"No."

"I'll just go out, I don't know where, maybe for a wee walk. Otherwise I sit there and watch her and slowly go mad."

"Will I come with you?"

"I want to be alone."

"Away you go then, we'll get the sheets changed."

"Why, why did she do it? Do you know?"

They all hesitated. "No," said Morag. "I don't know."

"She was a bonnie, happy lass. I don't understand."

They all waited respectfully as Margaret slipped into her coat and left the house. Then Auntie Meg made a shuffling beeline for the bedroom, detouring slightly to the clock on the mantel. "Here, Kirsteen." She pointed a gnarled finger at it. "Stop that clock ticking."

"Why?"

"Because she's dead, ye wee besom! Her time has stopped."

Kirsteen scrutinized the clock. "How?"

"Take out the blasted batteries," Morag said.

Kirsteen heaved a dramatic sigh but did as she was asked. Auntie Meg and Morag went to the bedroom. The body was laid out on the bed, white and cold, like a porcelain doll. Despite knowing what they would find, the sight came as a shock, and Morag leaned against the door, caught in the profound weariness that comes in the face of a senseless death. Auntie Meg tut-tutted.

"Catriona." Morag passed her hand over her eyes as the tears came afresh. "Why didn't you let me help?"

Kirsteen peered over their shoulders and made a sound of despair.

Still at the door, Morag took a deep breath and opened to the second sight. Auntie Meg knew. She clacked her dentures and patiently waited.

"She's still here," Morag said. The spirit was luminous, hovering by the large mirror above the chest-of-drawers.

"God," said Kirsteen.

"Come on then," said Auntie Meg.

"God," she said again.

"Can you sense Catriona's spirit?" Morag asked. "Our family has the gift."

"Even if I could, I wouldn't want to," said Kirsteen. "Thank you very much."

"Kirsteen," said Auntie Meg, "find something to cover the mirror before it draws her in."

"I'm no goen in that room."

They both turned to glare at her. "You most certainly are," Morag said. "Cover the mirror!"

Kirsteen pushed by, hugging the wall to be away from the corpse, and rummaged around reluctantly in one of the creaky drawers. She pulled out a blanket and tossed it over the large mirror, arranging it to cover every part.

The body was a pallid, dense object. Morag lifted the heavy feet of the corpse off the bed. "Kirsteen, pull that bottom sheet away. Put on the one Auntie Meg gives you."

"Kirsteen this, Kirsteen that. What difference does it make which sheets are on the bed?" Kirsteen whined, but she did as she was told.

"It's the old way," said Auntie Meg.

"The Goddess knows her life was ended before its time." Morag slipped her hands under the corpse's upper body and lifted it, to let the other two remove the old sheet and smooth on the new linen. Only days before Morag had embraced the same body, warm, vibrant, agitated in its agony of struggling with a lover's betrayal that shouldn't have been in the young lassie's mind at all. Now she was heavy and cold, an incomprehensible waste. Red rage flared and Morag's arms trembled so that she almost let go. "Catriona," she whispered to the cold ear, "I promise you the one who caused this will pay."

Auntie Meg spoke mournfully. "Baith rich and poor can bring me no more, and what I tak I cannae gie back."

"What?" Kirsteen asked.

"It's a riddle," Morag said. "The answer is death."

"Aye, aye, he'll be finding out soon enough. What's the English blackguard's name? Oh, aye. Forbes."

Kirsteen paused in her bed-making. "What are you talking about?" But Auntie Meg was oblivious, chuntering away to herself. "Morag, what is she talking about?"

It was no place for lies, standing over the body of young Catriona. "Clive Forbes was responsible for Catriona's death."

Kirsteen looked at the corpse. "Oh, what bullshit is this?"

Morag tucked in the sheet on the far side. "He did not treat her well. To say the least."

"What happened? Why have you not told me?"

Morag sat on the edge of the bed. Auntie Meg continued to smooth the sheets, humming and champing her loose teeth. The spirit's light hovered in Morag's peripheral vision, waiting. "I've tried to warn you, how many times?"

"Tell me," Kirsteen insisted.

"I never thought this could happen. I'm to blame. It's a tragedy we will never recover from. I should have stepped in and stopped it while I could."

"Ach!" Auntie Meg waved a dismissive hand.

"Stopped what?" Kirsteen asked.

"He has a penchant for young lasses," Morag said.

Kirsteen scowled, but did not speak.

"She came to me," Morag said. "She was desperate, but she couldn't bring herself to speak of all that had actually happened."

"Well, she can hardly have been mentally stable if she did hersel' in."

"Did herself in? Is that what you think?"

"I don't know! How should I know?"

"Perhaps there was depression there," Morag admitted. "And desperation. But that's no excuse for what he did."

"She must have led him on. She was desperate, aye, but no in the way you mean."

"Don't speak ill of the dead." Auntie Meg waved a thrice-bent finger at Kirsteen.

"We must stop," Morag said. "This is not the time or place."

"No," Kirsteen conceded. "I'm sorry."

"Morag," said Auntie Meg in an ominous voice. "Somethin's no right."

Kirsteen started to speak till Morag lifted a hand for silence.

"What is it?" Morag asked.

"Ah cannae say."

Morag stilled herself again. Her attention was wanted by Catriona's ghost. She let herself be led into the parallel realm, and saw a thing she'd never seen before. Within Catriona's spirit, a second entity was revealed, at first difficult to distinguish, but once seen, obvious.

"There's the spirit of a child with her."

"What do you mean?" demanded Kirsteen, eyes wide.

It was a lovely wee boy, its only existence in this life within his mother's womb, which must have been why they appeared as one.

"She was pregnant."

"And she knew? How could she...?"

"Kirsteen," Morag spoke in anger. "Just what do you think would have happened when word got out? Bad enough she was seeing Clive, which you are not to say a word about to

Margaret, do you hear? Her pious mother would have kicked her out into the street for disgracing the family. An unforgivable sin." The spirits stood in silent lamentation. "Now I understand."

"Och, the poor wee lassie," said Auntie Meg.

Morag lifted the corpse's upper body slightly to allow Auntie Meg to pull the sheet tight. As she let the body lie back on the bed, it exhaled in a long, slow breath. All three women froze. Morag reared back and covered her nostrils and mouth, holding in a retch.

Kirsteen bolted from the room. The front door slammed.

The sorrowful spirits had flown with the exhalation. "Catriona was waiting," Morag said. "That was the full circle of the last breath with her first, completed. The circle of her short life, one with no summer or autumn to it."

"The mist, the dew," Auntie Meg sang. "The dew, the mist. Thou who didst open the young eye, close it in the sleep of death, in the sleep of death."

"Be at peace, Catriona," Morag said. "Be at peace, you and your wee bairn. Sorrow nor grief can live in that beauteous land."

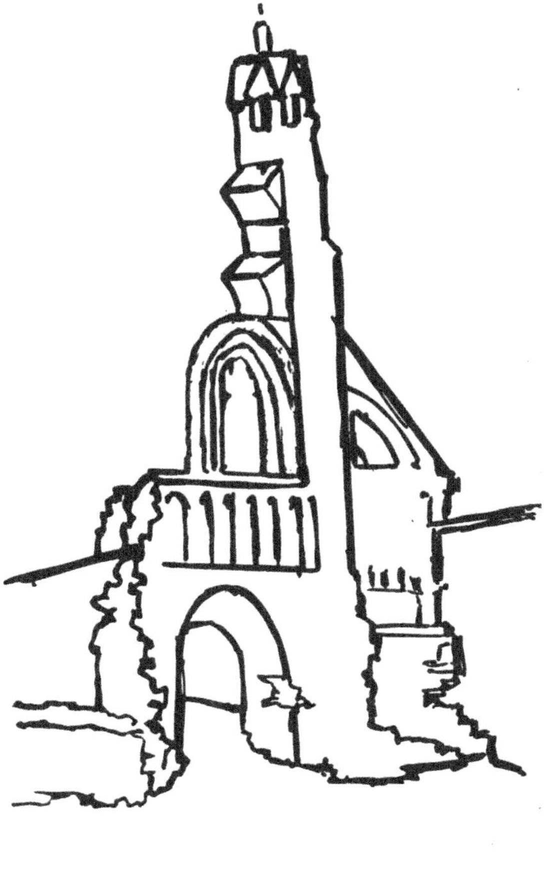

Chapter 5

"What do you think of the place?" her mother asked.

"It's a charming little town, Mom. And it's just amazing to be in the same room as where I was born. But I'm afraid the cottage is in a horrible mess." A full second later Rosalind's words echoed in the receiver, disembodied along the transatlantic cable: 'horrible mess.'

"How's Rabbie doing?"

"Not well. He's on morphine round the clock and sometimes it makes him hallucinate. You're right, he's difficult to deal with, but I think we're starting to communicate okay. But there's a problem."

'A problem,' repeated the phone.

Helen put her head around the kitchen door. When she saw Rosalind speaking, she gave a thumbs up, withdrew and quietly shut the door.

"He insists first of all I stay here till his death, and secondly to live in the cottage. Permanently."

'Permanently.'

"Oh, dear," said Sheila. "Of course he's attached to the old place. But we all need to let go at some point."

"What do you think about the idea of my cleaning the cottage as best I can, then selling it when he's..."

"Past caring," her mother said.

"I don't see any alternative, do you?"

"The library phoned this morning. They're getting antsy."

Rosalind put her elbows on the kitchen table and massaged her forehead with her free hand. "Helen's husband thinks I'll make a lot of money refurbishing the cottage, but then what? It's not his job on the line, is it? I've been cleaning, that needs to be done whatever happens. It's awful, you have no idea. How can someone live like that?"

"Aye, he always was a messy wee boy. But he kept his boats ship-shape. Housework was women's work. No woman, no housework. And what about your plane ticket?"

"I don't think I'm going to make that flight."

"I've heard of cases of bereavement for which the airlines give some reimbursement."

"And there's Chris."

"He's a young man now. Perhaps he needs a wee bit less of his mother."

She sat up. "What do you mean?"

"Well, I've been thinking. Henry's death set us all back, more than we might have admitted to ourselves. Just trying to survive is a good way to get stuck in situations you wouldn't have chosen otherwise. I mean, perhaps it's time for a new start."

"But Mom, that job's all we've got. It would be irresponsible..." She sounded like Henry, as if his ghost was speaking through her.

"Hold on. Here's Chris back from his class."

"Hi, Mom." His voice was deeper than she remembered. "How's it going?"

"Hi, Sweetheart. Okay, I guess. I'm kind of stuck here for a little while. What time is it there?"

"Ten."

"It's six p.m. here, dark and cold. You're just starting your day while I fix my dinner."

"Cool."

Rosalind scratched at some candle wax on the table, the only sign of last night's dinner party. "I'm phoning from a friend's house. Do you know Uncle Rab never had a phone? Or a TV? Or a washing machine? And the hot water! Oh, don't get me started. How are classes going?"

"Well – kind of hard. They're trying to weed out a lot of the class. And with football practice..."

"Try to keep your grades up, that's the main thing. Is everything else," they both knew what she meant, "all right?"

'All right?' How tentative and fearful the echo sounded, the voice shooting through cables under the Atlantic.

She imagined him shrugging. "Yeah. No problem. I've applied for a loan to stay in the dorm. Gran wants another word."

"Ros? Listen, you might as well turn this into a wee holiday. I know it's not under the best of circumstances, but you've had no break since Henry passed away, and little enough before that."

"I'm trying to do a little sketching when the weather isn't too bad."

"Are you? Well, that's a good sign if you ask me. Why don't

you just stay on for two or three weeks? I'll mention it to the library staff, explain your predicament, maybe it will help, who knows? Here, we'd better say goodbye. This must be an expensive call."

"Wait, there's something I want to ask you about, that came up at dinner last night, about a quarrel you had with the neighbors, the Gilbrides."

"Are folk still on about that? From almost forty years ago? That's small town life for you."

"Anything I should know about?"

Her mother gave an uncharacteristically wicked low laugh. "I'll just say this, 'all's fair in love and war.' It's all water under the bridge now. Give Rabbie my love, whether he wants it or not. Don't worry about us, we're fine. 'Bye now."

"Bye."

'Bye,' echoed a plaintive stranger's voice from the other world.

*

Floor to ceiling bookshelves leaned a little off kilter, filled haphazardly with binders and books, and loose pages stuck between them, or let fall to the floor. Any obvious attempt at categorizing the material had created a worse muddle. Rosalind squatted beside a sprawling pile of blue architectural plans tossed into a corner of the library, and riffled through the corners.

She jumped when something soft brushed her thigh and trilled. Elsie, the receptionist, bent double to see into the library from her desk in the adjoining entrance room, shrieked a laugh.

"His name's Whisky," Elsie called. "Because he's black and white. Like the whisky label."

Rosalind lifted the cat off the plans, but it insisted on returning to the pile. She was about to take it out when she heard Elsie speaking in lowered tones to someone else.

"But you've an appointment at half-one, Mr. Forbes."

"I won't be long. Make him a cup of tea or something. Work your considerable charm on him till I get back." Clive came to the library door, wearing a black suit and tie instead of his usual tweed. "Rosalind, all right?"

"This isn't so bad. It just needs a little organizing."

"If you could do as much as possible while you're here, at least issue some sort of guidelines, we could work out some suitable reimbursement. I'd be ever so grateful."

"Well, how about the next few mornings? That would put a good dent in it. I'm going to stay for a little while, as long as my uncle needs me."

"Perfect." He rubbed his hands together. "You may find the architects start calling on you. They're rather helpless when it comes to research, but you can see why. If you decide to refurbish the cottage I could get whatever you need at cost. Tiles, fixtures, carpet. Sorry, I must dash."

The front door banged shut, but for a minute the sound of Clive's whistling carried over the traffic. Rosalind sat in a chair jammed into a corner of the room where a little office space had been carved out. Papers and pamphlets lay strewn across every surface. She lifted a stack to uncover an old electric typewriter on the small desk, and tried the switch. It hummed and clacked into life. Beyond the bookcases and through the door, she saw Elsie poke her tongue out at Clive's departing figure.

Elsie wailed happily. "You weren't supposed to see that! You won't tell, will you? Are you from North America?"

"California."

"I never ask if anyone's from America, because if they're Canadian, they get miffed, but if they're Yanks, they don't care. A bit like the Scots and English. If England is used to mean Britain, it puts the Scots into convulsions."

"Where are you from?"

"Auchtermuchty. But I'd to acquire a posh Morningside accent before anyone would hire me."

"What's that manic tune Clive always whistles?" Rosalind picked up her handbag and sketchpad, and stopped at Elsie's desk.

"Funny you should ask." Her phone bleeped. "Gillespie and Forbes. I'm sorry, he's just gone out. Would you care to... well sod you, you silly bitch." She put the phone down, then snorted at Rosalind's expression. "She'd hung up. This mystery woman, she's been calling often, won't leave her name, and if she can't get Mr. Forbes she's rude. Nothing to do with architecture, I'll wager, but I'm not saying anything. Jobs are hard to find. Even with a posh accent."

"I'll be back in the morning."

"That tune – it's been driving everyone batty. The engineer says it's Britten's ' Simple Symphony.' He whistles it when he's nervous. I prefer Sting myself."

Rosalind stepped out and was blinded by a silver sun which, at noon, paralleled the ridge of the hills to the south. Although dazzling, the sunlight was distant and cold compared to the golden California sun. It spread a hazy brilliance through the atmosphere, mixing silver edged shadows on the lintels of the town houses opposite with the glancing rays of the sun itself.

She bumped into someone's ample bottom. "Oh, excuse me!"

A storekeeper looked up from her fruit stand, apples in both hands. "Yes?"

Rosalind heard Helen's distinctive laugh, a sharp 'ah!' from behind them. She was walking towards them with a brisk step from her office in the Medieval Department, a few doors down from Gillespie & Forbes. "'Excuse me' means you want to ask something."

"That's all right, dearie." The fruiterer returned to her pippins and jaffas.

"What's going on there?" Rosalind pointed down the street.

"No idea. A church service? Where are you going?"

"To see my uncle, but I want to buy a little gift for him first."

"I'll walk with you. I'm going home for a bit."

"Thanks for a great dinner last night, Helen."

"Oh, pleasure. What did you think of Angus?"

"I really enjoyed his company."

"Well, good. I expect he'll be calling on you at some point."

Rosalind tried to hide the leap of excitement the offhand sentence produced.

A police car, 'Fife Constabulary' emblazoned on its sides, blocked traffic from continuing down South Street past the church. Rosalind hugged her sketchpad and handbag close as they wove into an increasing crowd.

"Something's certainly on," said Helen.

About fifty people in dark clothing stood silently in the new courtyard beside Holy Trinity Kirk. It had already been turned into a pedestrian precinct, linking a wynd and two streets, with new park benches under transplanted trees. There were still roped-off sections not yet cobbled, but the work had proceeded rapidly. Shoppers seemed reluctant to cut through the strange gathering. The crowd waited patiently, with little talk, many sucking on cigarettes.

"Do you think," Rosalind looked at her feet, "there are more graves under this sidewalk?"

"Oh, the pavement." Helen craned her head this way and that, searching the crowd. "Probably."

A man in a cassock and Geneva collar strode out the church porch with the air of striking self-confidence his black clericals bestowed. Reverend Niall Paterson. Rosalind and Helen made a vain attempt to cross the courtyard. A police woman was there.

"Would you step back, please?" She held her hands out as if shooing cattle.

"Oh, heavens," said Helen. "It's a funeral. I can't stand here all day."

Niall rounded the church and hurried to the west door under the tower. A black hearse was backed up to the entrance. Clive was there, on the far side of the crowd. Even Mrs. Pearse, sliding between the people to offer him a pamphlet, could not distract him.

Helen fixed a narrow-eyed stare on her husband. Ridges of lean muscle tightened and slackened along her jaw.

Below the fifteenth century tower, an old horse-drawn hearse would have seemed more appropriate, the casket elevated behind big glass windows. It should have been noisy, horses stamping their hooves and huffing, harness jingling, and a low roar from the iron-rimmed wheels putting paid to the riveting hush of death. Instead, what resembled a black American station wagon slunk away from the church on silent tires, stealing away the flower-veiled coffin.

The hearse moved toward them. Rosalind was about to ask if this might be Catriona's funeral when she noticed a speck of blood on Helen's lower lip.

As soon as the hearse turned down South Street, a surge of shoppers, mothers with prams, students recently arrived in the town, some in scarlet academic gowns, a few tourists with cameras and new Argyle sweaters, and all the harried locals, filled the spaces. Clive was lost in the crowd.

"I'm going this way," Helen said curtly.

"Okay." Rosalind watched her stiff back and fragile ankles as she walked quickly up the wynd. Funeral-goers lingered, talking in subdued voices. Without knowing why, only that something was dreadfully wrong, Rosalind's heart went out to Helen.

Angus appeared from the crowd, bustling down the street, struggling to close a briefcase over a mess of paper, unaware of the funeral. At the sight of him Rosalind's heart leapt in a swirling mix of foolishness and raw-edged joy that she was still capable of the almost juvenile delight. She smiled in anticipation, and stepped across his path. He looked up and his face softened into the same, crinkly-eyed happiness. She helped him tuck the papers – archaeological drawings – into his briefcase and close it.

"Hullo," he said.

"Hi," she said.

They gazed at each other in shared stillness, the town bustling around them, she hugging her sketchpad, he his briefcase.

"Don't suppose," he said, "you'd care to go out for a coffee tomorrow?"

"I'd love to."

"Right then." He beamed. "I'll come round perhaps five?"

She nodded, watching him reluctantly carry on down the pavement. Something that had bound them in a secret excitement as they came together, stretched and even strengthened when they moved apart. It was delightful to feel a crush on a man after so many lonely years with a distant husband. And at the same time she feared she was overreacting for the same reason. But so what? What could happen in such a short time?

He glanced back to see her watching him. "Soon!"

Rosalind was standing close to the window of an upscale gift shop, where a surprisingly good painting, a watercolor of the harbor, was on display. Pottery plates and mugs had been carefully arranged on Irish linens, all tastefully adorned with sprigs of heather. 'Elizabeth Stratton Interiors,' the shop's name, was scrolled across the top of the large windows, with 'The Gallery Stratton, Object d'Art, Sculpture, Original Contemporary Paintings' along the bottom.

"Rosalind?" said a woman's low voice, close to her ear. "Are these your latest?" Her fingers touched Rosalind's forearm where it cradled the sketchpad. "I've seen you sketching around the city." The woman's dark hair was drawn up in a neat bun, not one strand out of place, and the simple black dress, perfectly tailored, adorned a figure that needed no enhancements. A silver necklace with a charm of a Celtic triple spiral lay on the smooth skin of her breast. Her dress drew in to a trim waist and draped strong thighs. Not a delicate frame, but athletic, uncommonly beautiful, and absolutely unidentifiable.

"City?" Rosalind asked.

"When a community, however small, has a cathedral, it's called a city. I'm not sure what happens if the cathedral falls to ruins, but you still hear St. Andrews called a city. The graveside service starts in ten minutes, so I must be quick. May I?" She gently drew the sketchpad from Rosalind's arm, then opened it to view the work. "Yes. Yes." She raised dark eyes to study Rosalind's face with such searching intimacy that Rosalind felt a blush start. "Lord Comyn *would* be interested. He said he found you charming. But I could have told him that."

"Lord Comyn?" Rosalind hoped that her inability to conceal her utter bewilderment would not offend, but the woman continued, either not noticing or not caring.

"You might fetch a decent price for these drawings. Do you paint?"

"Not really, I mean I hope to, but I'm just getting started again."

"Oils or acrylics?"

"Both maybe."

"May I offer you some advice?" She tapped the sketchpad. "Let this dictate your choices."

Why was this strange woman saying such odd and personal things? And then, thanks to the familiar sense of utter bewilderment, it finally dawned.

It was her neighbor Morag again, in a completely different guise. The *shape-shifter* Alastair Comyn had called her at the dinner party. And then she got the allusion to 'Lord' Alastair Comyn. Apparently there was more to him than met the eye, as well.

"You'll come for tea?" Despite the banter her features were heavy with what Rosalind realized was sadness. "Thursday? Will you still be here? I've been meaning to ask, but it's been impossible until now. A coorse business." She glanced past Rosalind's shoulder. Suddenly her eyes narrowed and her upper lip slid off her teeth in a snarl of naked hatred.

Shocked, Rosalind turned to see Clive Forbes approach, obviously as unaware as Rosalind had been that he was about to encounter the 'famous witch.'

"I'd like that. Thanks." Rosalind took back the sketchpad from Morag's loosened fingers and hurried into the shop before Clive could see her. A young woman behind a desk stood as Rosalind entered. She eyed the artwork, which Morag had left open to a sketch of the cathedral's distinctive spires.

"Oh, have you brought that for Elizabeth to see?"

Rosalind did not want to be distracted from what was about to happen outside. "No, these are just some drawings," she said, "nothing but sketches."

"May I?"

As the shop woman took the sketchpad and carefully studied the pictures, Rosalind moved slightly, standing to the side of the window, and watched the scene unfold.

Morag barked something at Clive, and he stopped. His features twisted into a frightening, almost bestial mask. They exchanged a few terse words, then Clive fished into his jacket pocket and brought out a folded piece of paper, like a check. He lifted it, and she snatched it from his hand. His face screwed up, eyes shut tight, and he put his palm to his forehead. The gesture she mistook at first for grief. It was pure rage.

"Pardon me."

The woman who had been at the desk brought over a slender middle-aged woman, dressed in a stylish English arrangement of scarf, cardigan and calf-length skirt, then left them alone.

"I'm Elizabeth Stratton."

"Rosalind Ehrhart."

"I've just seen your sketches. We don't usually conduct business this way, but would you be interested in selling in my shop? I could frame them – your expense, you understand – and they'd look quite attractive. Sixty forty, does that sound fair?"

"Oh, I'm a visitor. These are just quick sketches. I mean, I didn't intend to sell them."

The earnestness on Stratton's face did not dissipate.

"No, but seriously," Rosalind said. "They're not that good."

"I don't sell anything that isn't. There are one or two that I think are quite nice. What about the cathedral sketch? You could leave your address and I'll send on the money when it's sold. Perhaps around fifty pounds. What do you say?"

"Fifty pounds? For a drawing?"

"Oh, at least. You will? Jolly good. I'd be happy with any local scenes, houses, churches, golf links, whatnot. Tourists buy them all the time, I can't keep good work in the shop. Couldn't you do one more, a church perhaps? Even a drawing of the inside. Parishioners can't resist those, especially for Christmas gifts. There's always a bit of the sentimental driving those sales, but really, there is some nice work here. Come and give my assistant your address."

Rosalind looked over her shoulder, out the window, as Stratton led her away. Clive and Morag were gone. She put her hand into her jacket pocket and absent-mindedly caressed the smooth wooden charm Morag had given her in the cathedral graveyard.

"Do you do watercolors? Pastels? Oh, this is an interesting drawing of the castle. An unusual angle. That's so important, you know, unusual angles. May I take this one as well? That's two. Same price?"

Rosalind laughed. "Sure, why not?"

As she left the shop, the last of the funeral party was dividing up and getting into cars. One of the cars slowed and stopped. Its window lowered and a familiar man's voice called, "Kirsteen!"

It was Clive again, waving at someone. A young dark – haired woman skipped over to the car, put her hands on the door, and smiled in at him.

"Can I offer you a lift?" he asked.

It was the same woman she'd seen outside Morag's house when Helen and Clive were leaving. Rosalind backed away and turned to look again at the shop window, knowing that if she continued on, he'd recognize her.

"Why are you goen' to the cemetery?" the young woman asked.

His voice was wary. "Now, you know better than to listen to rumors."

"Why are you goen' then?"

"It's a terrible tragedy that affects many people I know. I feel obliged. So am I giving you a lift?"

"Sorry," she teased. "I already have a ride."

"Pity," he said, lingering over the word.

"Aye, pity."

The young woman walked away, turning her head to give a smiling glance over her shoulder. Clive, with the same half-smile, drove on.

"Kirsteen!" called another voice. A hundred yards down the pavement a young man in an ill-fitting dark blue suit waved his burly arms to catch her attention. She gave a look back at the car as it inched along the crowded street, then allowed the young man to give her a quick embrace and kiss. She ruffled his hair.

"Calum," she said. "You kept me waiting, my daft lad."

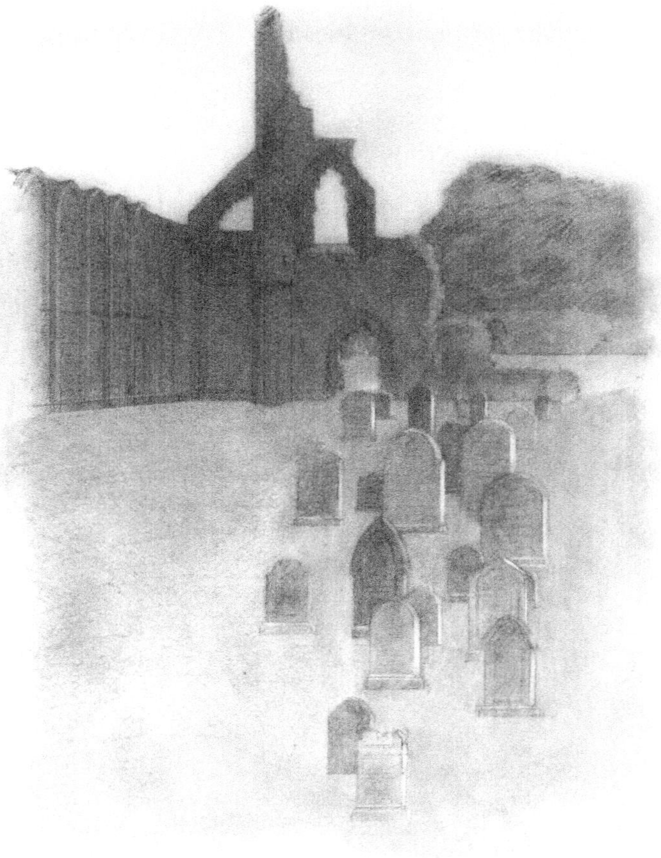

Chapter 6

Reverend Niall Paterson stood with head bowed at the final prayer, encircled by a small group of mourners. Margaret, Catriona's mother, numb and drugged, stood wherever she was directed.

The cemetery, contained within a high stone wall, was strewn with fallen leaves of festive red and gold. It was the newer cemetery, outwith the town's boundaries, surrounded by farmland.

"Come on, Margaret," Morag whispered in her ear. "Let's get you home." Calum took Margaret's arm and gently led her to the gate. Margaret leaned heavily on Calum, hardly aware of where her feet trod. Morag followed, guiding Auntie Meg away from the graveside. Some of the people fell back to let them pass. Niall watched from under his brows.

"Ye pious wee shite," Auntie Meg muttered under her breath. She'd been ill at ease during the entire service.

"Pardon? Did you speak?" Niall raised his head.

"Wheesht, Auntie," Morag whispered. "Catriona's there."

A pale figure stood alone among the gravestones. The baby's spirit was gone, nothing to bind it still to that unborn life. Catriona's ghost stood ashen faced, expressionless, in the beautiful, full-skirted dress her callous lover had bought her. One she'd proudly modeled for Morag a month ago, twirling and laughing in her joy.

"Is she?" Aunty Meg looked away to the side. Sometimes, as when it's possible to see a faint star in the night sky by looking to the side of it rather than straight on, something at the threshold of the next world can be better seen in the same way. "Oh, aye," said Auntie Meg. "So she is." She lifted a claw-like hand in farewell. "Catriona, dearie!"

Niall's face reddened. "Catriona Hamilton is gone to her just reward. As must we all."

"Bollocks," said Auntie Meg. "She's there, can't you see?" She pointed a crooked finger, and the people in her line of fire quickly stepped aside. Because of the curse Sheila Ogilvy had placed on her long ago, Meg was relatively harmless in the way of spells and magic, but guilty by association.

Niall clapped shut his black book. "We are not a barbaric people. We do not jest in death's shadow." He strode away. "We are not barbarians."

It was an ugly look he shot Morag, and not lost on the Righteous. Unfortunately, young Catriona moved in varied circles, her work, her friends, her church, and some knew Morag only as the Christians cried her, wicked and perverse and unnatural. Satanic. She could tell them by the way they glanced her way with sneaky looks, and wagged their gossipy heads. Oh, for a dram and an end to all this. Morag rubbed her tired eyes.

Clive Forbes had been hanging a little distance away, close enough to the funeral party to be a part of it, but very discreet. It infuriated her to see him there, his audacity, especially given what she now knew. More, she feared he was up to no good.

To get to the gate and car parked along the road, Morag would have to walk Auntie Meg past him. There was no help for it. She looked for Kirsteen, and found her safe with some girlfriends, all smoking cigarettes on the far side of the grave.

As Morag and Auntie Meg approached, Clive held his ground. It did not bode well.

"Why, Morag," he said rather loudly. "Why would you be here for Catriona's funeral?"

"I could ask the same of you," she shot back.

"Making sure you finished the job properly?"

Auntie Meg sucked in her breath. That explained his presence. To test the waters of his revenge. And to redirect any suspicions. Clive was a wily and charming man, a man of importance in the community, accustomed to getting whatever he wanted. If people needed a push in the right direction, he was clever enough to make it appear it was what they wanted all along.

Clive spoke to one of the small group that had gathered closer. "What were we just saying?"

"Yes," one of the women said. "We were discussing how often Catriona went to visit you before she died."

"Odd, that," said a man standing with her.

A glance at the gate revealed Margaret being helped into the car by Calum. Thank the Goddess she was unaware of the little scene unfolding over the grave of her daughter.

"I can only imagine why she'd want to see the likes of you."

One woman in the back wouldn't meet Morag's eye, only shooting quick glances from under the brim of her dreadful hat, and no wonder. She'd been in to see Morag the day before last for advice with her love life and was now fearful of being exposed. And she was not the only one in the group. Hypocrites.

Auntie Meg was lost in her own world, mumbling vituperations as she continued her slow shuffle. "Reward, reward, just rewards, aye, that'll be right ye wee jobbie."

"What's she saying, the old crone?" asked another, her face dark with suspicion.

Clive, his mischief done, quietly slipped away. Into the atmosphere of dark glances and murmured questions, Niall appeared.

"Your presence is not wanted here, Morag Gilbride," he said.

"She is my niece..."

"I'm perfectly well aware of your family tie to the deceased, and also perfectly aware that your presence here is causing a great deal of distress for the mourners. I would ask you to leave now."

Auntie Meg, her one eye watching a small flock of rooks in the pine trees at the cemetery's edge, started to count the birds on her bent fingers, muttering a rhyme all the while. Normal behavior for the old one, but bad timing.

The hateful looks all around crowded closer, pushing in, a little mob creating waves of fear and loathing directed at an outsider who was as integral to the village as any other. History repeating itself.

Without warning, the fabric of time rent. As it tore with a blinding flash, Morag's second sight kicked in. It was now a succession of generations standing before her, their faces made ugly by the same base cruelty and fear. She struggled to stay in the dangerous present, but lost it to the power of her own magic. The centuries of kindred passions crowded in and Morag swooned, lifted out of herself.

"Leave immediately, this minute," she heard Niall say from far away.

Other voices cut through. "Wicked. Unrighteous. Not wanted here. Shame."

Her hand moved through the air to stop the flow of impressions. She shut her eyes and stepped back, and the tide of history became her thoughts, and she was helpless to stop it.

Oh, my country, oh, my Scotland, do you remember? Do you remember how it was? Do you remember the blood and the fire and the cracked bones and the tears spilled from ancient eyes, eyes that could see the wind? Do you remember the thumbscrew and the breaking irons? The screams? The weeping? Do you remember tears lost in a sea of tears? The stones smashed on their bodies, the wagons driven over the crunching limbs, the rapes, the indignities, the purest evil born of domination and self-loathing inflicted on the helpless? Do you remember?

It's still here. And it will aye be here.

"You. Gilbride." The boldest townswoman jabbed a finger at Morag. "Did you no hear the minister? How dare you set foot in this consecrated place? Among decent folk."

It was impossible to disengage completely from the second sight, and she could say nothing, for what could be said in the face of such hatred as sparked from the kirk woman's eyes, and from the eyes of the eight or so others around her? Aye, rest assured, it takes a gang to raise this kind of courage.

"God-fearing folk."

"What did Catriona want of you?"

"What did you do to her? Give her potions for an abortion?"

Auntie Meg finally clued into the danger. She quieted her murmurings and shook Morag's arm, hard, as she glanced from face to face like a cornered fox. Morag took a deep breath and made a mighty effort to pull herself back through Auntie Meg's fear.

"Do ye ken whit was done tae women like yoursel'?"

All too well, you bastard. By bigots like you.

The woman spat in Morag's face.

She wiped it away with the back of her hand. "Let us pass."

"Far too long we've been putting up with you and your wickedness."

"Let them go, let them go," Niall ordered.

The townsfolk parted, and Morag dragged Auntie Meg through the gauntlet of harsh stares.

Hanging back slightly, a couple of young men, dressed in grimy jeans, heavy boots, and jackets, held their ground as the two women approached. One made as if to walk by, but ducked in sideways and hit Morag hard with his shoulder.

Had she not been a strong woman, it would have felled her. But Morag held her anger in check, and said nothing. They would have disintegrated into an absurd melee, local bored thugs and two women.

"Is there a problem here?" Calum stepped between them, solid and scarred from his rugby playing. He must have seen what was happening from the car and returned to escort them back.

"Wit the fuck ye daen standing with that bitch?"

"She's my girlfriend." Calum put a brawny arm lightly around Morag's shoulder. "Did you no ken? Aye, we're getting married next month."

Flickers of bewilderment moved over the heavy, stupid faces before them.

"Come on, you," Calum poked a strong finger against the man's chest. "Give me a good reason to smash your ugly face. Come on!"

The two young men made themselves scarce quick enough, slinking away with many a 'fuck this and fuck that.' Cowards. It pained Morag to see that Kirsteen had stayed back, unwilling to be associated with them, even with her own boyfriend risking much.

Calum took Morag's hand in his big paws. "Are ye a' right?"

"Married, is it?"

He blushed. Auntie Meg still clutched Morag's arm, eye going from the two neds to the huffy funeral goers as they dispersed, all giving the women a wide berth, their funeral finery an odd adornment to their head-wagging and clucking. Margaret waited in her car where Calum had left her, head back, eyes shut, beyond tears, beyond caring.

"Clever lad." Though he and Kirsteen sometimes came to Morag's cottage for a cuppa, she'd never stood so close to him, felt his familiar good, honest masculine energy. The seriousness of what could easily have occurred had her heart thumping, and his solid strength was a balm.

"Calum, thank you. I dare not think what might have just happened were it not for you."

"I hate them and their smug faces and a'."

"Aye, well, come along, Auntie Meg, let's away hame."

They walked slowly to the gate, Morag and Calum on either side of Meg, who still glanced anxiously side to side.

"Morag," Calum started, then hesitated.

"What is it? Tell me."

He couldn't hold her gaze, and stared instead at the ground. "Morag," he said. "You know my dearest wish."

"Sorry?"

"Kirsteen," he said.

"Aye," she said, relieved that it was only about love. "What about the lass?"

"Will you put in a good word to her mother? She respects you, your opinion. If you spoke for me…"

It was almost too much there in the cemetery of spirits and destiny weaving in moving filaments, to add another strand to the tapestry, but Morag refrained from smiling at his fearful plea for a thing already written in the stars, and what courage it took to ask for it. And yet, still half in the Otherworld, she knew there was far more to it than that. It wouldn't be easy for either of them.

Kirsteen stood with her girlfriends, all sobered eyes on them. They knew fine what had happened, and Morag hoped they had the decency for a bit of shame. "If that is her desire, you will have my blessing, and aye, I'll speak to her Mum."

He said nothing but gripped her hand tightly, lips pressed together, eyes blinking. Innocent and good-hearted Calum. He walked quickly away to join Kirsteen. There's a lot to be said for Scotland's lads. Courage where it's most wanted, and shyness where it's most attractive.

But still and all, it was difficult to fit the key into the car's ignition, for the trembling of her hand. Auntie Meg perched on her seat, still silent. Only a short time past and that wee mob would have dragged them away after a good beating, and tortured and killed them with the minister's blessing, and suffered no consequences. And at the least, the neds might have put Morag in hospital. She had not foreseen the danger of this situation. It was as if she were relinquishing control to something beyond her, whether she wanted to or not, for an unknown purpose. She did not care for this new development at all.

As they pulled out onto the road, the fields and pastures radiant in their early autumn color, Morag glanced back. Catriona's ghost was no longer to be seen.

An illustration in a Scottish history book on loan from Helen depicted a Celtic warrior from pagan times. And there he was in the flesh, albeit clothed, in the person of her uncle. His coarse hair jutted out in stiff spikes, like that of the ancient warriors who mixed wet lime in their hair to achieve the same bristling effect before hurling themselves into battle.

"I ken what you're thinking." He wagged a thick scaly finger, speaking through a series of coughs. Some spittle landed on her face. "You'll wait till I'm dead and sell the cottage. Eh? It's wrong. You'll be under a curse for the rest of your life! Going against the wishes of a dying man."

Rosalind wearily rubbed her eyes. "All my life nothing, I mean *nothing* happens, except drudgery and hard work for tiny gains I don't even want, and nothing to tell one year from another, until Henry's death, and since then it just got worse. Maybe I grew used to it. You know, I think I like routine. I like boredom. I can't cope with all this."

"You've Scots blood in you, all right," he sneered. "A nation of girners, pissing and moaning in the face of hardship, doing fuck-all to lift ourselves up, whining about England all the time. Gies me the boak."

"You sound like my mother when she's angry. Anyway, things are good enough back home."

"Good enough? Since when is good enough, good enough? Your soul has died. It's risk you want, something to make your heart beat fast."

"I admit it, life didn't turn out the way I thought it was going to. Whose does?"

Uncle Rab vigorously tapped his sunken chest. "Mine did. Mine bloody well did."

"And anyway, people can't just change personalities. Chuck it all and start over. Unless they're highly irresponsible. I have others depending on me."

"You're young yet. You could pull up the nets and find a shoal you've only dreamt of. Or maybe you don't dream."

"You learn pretty quickly not to create expectations that are bound to fail." She studied the odd earnestness in his yellow eyes. "Why are you saying all this?"

Uncle Rab grasped her hand. The skin of his palm was hard and callused. "Can you no see I'm trying to help? I'm a wee bit uncouth. I ken that. What I'm saying is, you've never lived. It's no great crime. That's how most folk pass their time. But you're an Ogilvy, like it or not."

"Can we stop talking about me? Can't you understand that everything's fine?"

He snorted. "That'll be right."

Tears welled up, unexpected and unwelcome. She turned her head until they were blinked away. "I won't go if you tell me more about yourself."

"Well, it is good of you to stay by my side. I'm no picture of beauty. You're a good lass, I can see that. I'm a good judge of character, and I don't take back what I said!" He jabbed a gnarled finger again at her. "Hand me that tumbler." He made a face and drank. "Uch, water." The loose skin of his neck was permanently tanned, speckled with dark spots. "I was an engineer on a freighter before I came back for the fishing. It was a man's life." He sank back into his pillow and his eyes grew dim.

She grabbed his water glass from his forgetful hands before it spilled.

"Aye, there'll be a few Ogilvy bairns who've never seen the East Neuk. They'll have their ain bairns now." He chuckled, then wheezed, lost in happy memories.

"Bairns?"

"Aye, weans."

"You mean you got someone pregnant?"

"God save us!" He sputtered with coughing laughter. "Got someone pregnant!"

"You mean, I've got bastard cousins around the world?"

He stopped laughing and eyed Rosalind warily.

"You mean...I don't believe this...you gave my mother a hard time about having me when my father was fighting in France. When he could have been killed? The big disgrace to the family name, while you were off having your fun in foreign cities?"

"Of *course,* it's different for a woman."

"And you've been giving my mother the cold shoulder because of me?"

"I'm telling you, it's different. That's enough! There's things you don't understand."

"I understand, all right. We call it double standards."

"Shut your gob, woman, speaking to me like that!" He

rocked with coughs, bringing up thick pink phlegm.

A nurse peered over Rosalind's shoulder. "Please calm down, the both of you, or I'll have to ask you to leave, Mrs. Ehrhart."

"Go away," shouted Uncle Rab. "Fuck off! Ehrhart my bloody arse." He fumbled with his soiled handkerchief. "Not you, for Christ's sake," he clutched at Rosalind.

They sat in silence as his coughing slowed and Rosalind tried to think up a safer subject. It appeared that funeral arrangements were going to have to be put off again. "Mum said you used to catch fish at the pier when you were a boy."

"Eh, oh, aye." He coughed. "Crabs and a'. Sometimes the fishermen would bring in a monkfish. They're all head. Ugly buggers. They've a fin here," he touched his spiky hair, "like a big thorn, and we'd stick a cork on it and put them back and they'd shoot off like a torpedo, out to sea. Couldn't dive under with the cork."

"But that's so cruel!"

"The sea is cruel. Or maybe it's kind, clean and uncomplicated." Uncle Rab gently coughed again, cheeks puffed.

"Were you on good terms with your neighbor Morag Gilbride?"

Dr. Mackay and the nurse looked in from the hallway at Uncle Rab and watched him for a moment. He glared back at them till they withdrew.

"Bastartin doctors," he muttered. "Eh, Morag. I still am on good terms, far as I know. She comes to visit me. Sometimes she brings her aunty, too. Auld Meg." He chuckled at a memory. "Our family and theirs have a very long history."

"I'm not sure how to read Morag. People seem to either love her or hate her."

"No, she's a canny lass." His voice was softer and deeper after the outburst. "She sees things the rest of us can't. I've kent many unexplained things, but Scotland has its own magic, closer to the surface than other places. You could do worse than having her for a friend..." Uncle Rab stopped and smiled.

"What?"

"Ach, nothing. She's not a part of the common folk, but gie her a chance and you'll never regret it."

"Did Mom and Meg have some kind of a falling out?"

"Aye, indeed they did, young women fighting over a man. But you'll have to ask your mother about all that. Have you seen my wee boat?" he abruptly changed the subject. *"The Reiver.* She'll be rocking in the harbor this very minute, wondering where the hell I am. The most beautiful wee boat of them all."

"A fishing boat?"

"No, no. Sailboat. Pure pleasure in my old age. Take her out if you like."

"I'm afraid I never learned how to sail. If you don't mind my asking, what do you want done with it?"

He sighed, then coughed. "I've no made up my mind yet." He stilled himself and put his hands over his belly. "Get the nurse, Rosalind."

His face had gone ashen, eyes beseeching. She immediately stood, but again he took her hand. "Promise. Promise you'll stay and see to the cottage. You'll not leave it to the care of strangers."

His strained features sank into sharp detail even as Rosalind watched. He bit back a retch. "Promise," he pleaded.

"I promise," she said.

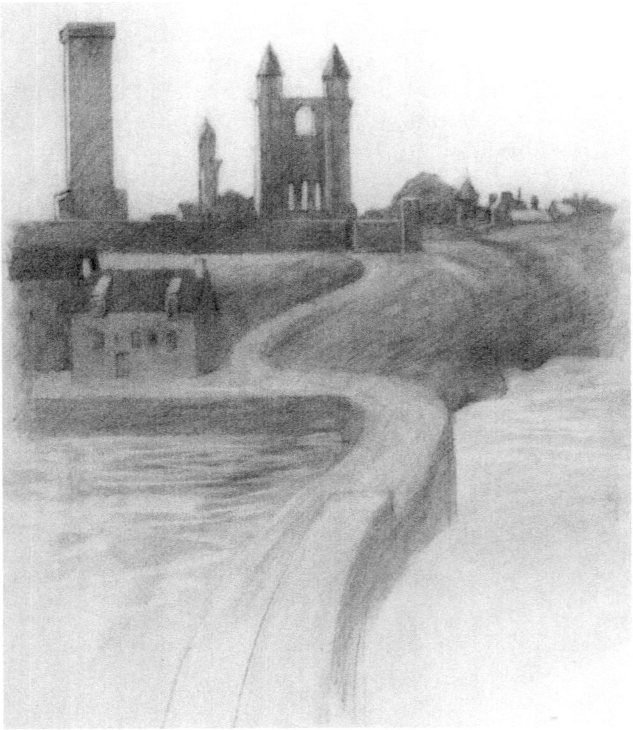

Chapter 7

Angus MacLeod stood at the door in the early dusk, rocking from foot to foot in a dance of unconcealed hope. "Up for a coffee then?"

"Come in for a minute," Rosalind said. "I'll be right with you."

"What a lovely old cottage."

"You should have seen it a week ago." She led him up to the first floor. "Look in the bathroom, and you'll see what I mean." She found her black shoes under the kitchen table and put them on.

"Is this what you've been up to all day? Are you going to paint these walls?"

"Yes. This bathroom is what the whole house was like." She pulled at the corner of the garish floral wallpaper. A small piece came away. "I've had to soak and scrape for every inch."

"Has Helen been round to help?"

"She's busy with the term starting next month, what do they call it, Martinmas?"

"Oh, of course. Ready?"

She preceded him down the stairs. A whiff of damp cold stone came from the vaulted cellar in the hallway.

"I don't like that room." Rosalind hurried by. "Gives me the creeps."

He pushed open the cellar door. "Ach no, it's a lovely wee room. When these cottages were built by the fishing community, something like forty people lived in just one of them. Imagine a whole family in here."

"Probably my ancestors. Clive hired some men to haul away the junk in there, thank God."

"My Granny had a spindle like that, a muckle wheel she called it, without that foot pedal. I'd forgotten about that. I can still see her pulling the wool into yarn from the wheel." Angus began singing as he opened the door and held it for her. "For I'll sell my rock, an' I'll sell my reel, I'll sell my granny's spinning wheel..."

They set off down the pedestrian lane and within two minutes arrived at the coffee shop. Angus pulled open the door for her, but someone was already coming out. It was Niall Paterson, with a couple of black-gowned divines on his heels.

"Oh, good evening." He raised his hand in the same benedictory way as when he'd almost hit her with his car. "Rather cold tonight."

"I was meaning to ask," Rosalind said. "Would it be possible to do a sketch of your church, maybe inside?"

"For what reason?" He stopped.

"I'm an artist. I mean I'm trying to get back to drawing and painting. The architecture is amazing."

"The church is open from morning devotion at half past eight, to evening devotion at half past five. The only price of admission is that you say a prayer for me."

The students were carrying on a rapid, low-voiced dispute. "Insights," said one, a petite young woman with black hair almost to her waist. "Satisfying insights should form the basis for intellectual proofs. And underlie the liturgy."

"So skip services and meditate on your navel," retorted the pale young man beside her. "Why bother having liturgy at all?"

"Then, tell me," said Niall as they walked away, "how we gain these insights without committing errors of judgment? Is that not what the Church provides?"

Angus said quietly as they entered, "So tedious, theology. And I think that's rather a high price for admission." He ordered coffees while she found a table in the almost empty front room, next to a low window. The lights of the houses up and down the street began to glimmer in the dusk.

He sat and smiled, clearing his throat, and fingering his mug. Then he sniffed and looked out the window.

Again, she felt a mix of surprise and pleasure. Surely as accomplished a man as Angus wasn't tongue-tied on her account? "So," Rosalind encouraged, "how's your work going?"

He nodded. "Quite well. I want to hurry and finish within a couple of weeks, at least do what I can before the bad weather really sets in. Believe me, it's no fun doing field work when it's this cold."

"Your site got a mention at the Forbes's dinner, but I wasn't sure what it was."

Angus glanced furtively around the restaurant. A few people had come in for early suppers, but they were all engaged in their own conversations.

"The Culdee foundation is what brought me here, but it'll have to wait till the Spring."

"Wait," Rosalind held up her hand. "What's a Culdee?"

"Sorry. The name is Celtic, from Céli Dé meaning 'companions of God.' They were a sort of loose-knit community of clergy, harking back to a more Celtic tradition after the Council of Whitby. Non-celibate. Patterned their lives on the desert hermits, Syrian for instance, and eventually evolved into a collegiate church, one of the earliest of which we have here in St. Andrews."

The curls of his slightly graying hair adorned intelligent temples, inviting touch. Even his ears were comely, a perfect size, she recalled from art class in anatomy, fitting in a line from eyebrows to base of nostrils. She wished she could sketch his portrait as they sat there.

"But I'm boring you," he said.

"No, listen, I'm appalled at my ignorance."

"Anyway," he lowered his voice and hunched closer, eyes bright. "The real find is the cairn. Neolithic." He stopped. "Do you know...?"

"Tell me."

"It's absolutely unprecedented, a chambered cairn in Fife. The first that's ever been found. It's about five thousand years old. It might be an older, less sophisticated version of subsequent passage tombs found in the north. It's shaped basically like an igloo." He cupped his hands on the table to show her. "There are often sections within containing cists, and this one has two, side by side..."

"Kissed?"

"Yes, though at this point it's anybody's guess what we'll find."

"I mean, what's cist?"

"Oh, sorry, c-i-s-t, a burial chest, usually stone. What appears to be a side section has collapsed, blocking what would be the only entrance just now, barring some major excavation. That's what I need to sort out before the students arrive."

"It's a thing," she said, "that shapes a culture a lot more than I ever realized. History, I mean, especially when it's all around you. You can see where you've come from, what your roots are, just by walking down the street."

"Aye, well, the past can be a prison, too. There are a lot of damaging legacies we haven't figured out what to do with."

"Like what?"

He waved it away. "Oh, class divisions, religious intolerance. If you really do go to Niall's kirk, ask to see the branks they keep in the session room. The scold's or witch's bridle. They're iron cages that go over the head, sometimes with a spike or blade that fits in the mouth."

"What on earth for?"

"Women, mostly, who said things men didn't want to hear. That shut them up!"

"Oh, my God. How awful."

"*Mulier taceat in ecclesia*; let the woman be silent in church!"

"Yes, that would count as a damaging legacy." They laughed, and Rosalind wanted the evening to go on forever. "Should we have something to eat?"

"Aye! Why not? My treat."

They returned to the table with trays of moussaka, salads, fresh rolls, and glasses of wine.

"This is turning into a festive occasion," he said. "Slainté."

They ate in silence for a while. Two students stopped outside the window, and kissed in a long, lingering embrace. Rosalind felt her ears and cheeks blush red, and Angus stuffed a couple of forkfuls into his mouth in rapid succession.

"In your opinion," she said, "is it worth refurbishing the cottage? I'm putting my job back home in jeopardy by staying here. And my son Chris isn't very happy, either. He still battles depression over the loss of his father, and my being gone is rough on him."

"How did your husband die?"

"He was struck by lightning."

Angus looked quizzically at her.

"No, really. On a golf course."

"I'm very sorry." His eyes belied his words. "I assume there were others with him?"

"Lightning is freakish. The other guys were fine."

"I hope this won't dissuade you from taking a stroll on the Old Course?"

"I think I'd feel fine if I were with you," she blurted out.

"I promise, no lightning," he said. "But about your staying on in Scotland? Don't you need a visa?"

"I have a British passport. I'm half Scottish."

"Opportunity knocks." He pushed the plate aside. "That was lovely. I'm not the person to ask. I'll tell you to stay, for purely selfish reasons."

Rosalind felt herself go a little warm again.

Angus took a sip of his wine and fiddled with the stem. He leaned forward and glanced in either direction. "I would like to confide in you. Do you mind?"

"I'm the soul of discretion. I don't know anybody anyway."

"Helen and Clive are old friends of mine, as you know, but something's wrong. They're having difficulties. I'm getting uncomfortable staying with them. I feel as if I'm intruding. It looks as if I'm going to be here longer than I'd thought. Maybe it's a good excuse to find another place. I thought I'd ask the Medieval chairman. He rattles around in that big house of his. Only, I wouldn't want Helen to take it the wrong way."

Rosalind had noticed an air of fragility about Helen, a tension between the couple, and feared it had to do with Clive's involvement with the young woman she'd seen flirting with him on the street in front of Elizabeth Stratton's shop. She wondered if Angus knew about it. "I've only gotten to know Helen in the last week, but she seems to have a good head on her shoulders."

"It's odd, I'm not aware that she has any close friends. She seems to put all her time into her work." He shrugged. "I'm curious, after all that banter at the dinner, have you seen much of your witchy neighbor?"

"Why yes. Last night. I was up in my bedroom, writing a letter. It was midnight, and I heard this weird singing. Unearthly. So I pulled back the curtain, and there she was in her garden. Stark naked."

Angus's wine went down the wrong way. He coughed, eyes teary. "She's very athletic," he choked. "Can't be denied. Did she know you were watching?"

"Yes, she invited me to join her."

"Did you?"

"Are you kidding? It was way too cold."

Angus knocked on the table with his fingers as he laughed. "What a hoot. But I must say, don't get too involved with Morag. I've had a run-in with her, when she duped my brother Hamish out of some money with her mumbo-jumbo. I may be an eedjit, but I really do believe, as Alastair said, that there's something... unusual about her." He wouldn't meet her eyes, but traced circles on the table.

The cold coming off the window bathed the side of Rosalind's face. She lifted the back of her hand to the glass, surprised at the cold's palpable intensity, as much as by his confession. "That wasn't the first time. I saw her with a knife scraping the wall inside of a tower in the cathedral, that square one by the little gate, and keeping the dust in a jar. What on earth could she have been doing?"

He stroked his beard. "We should report her for defacing the monument."

"Are you serious?"

"No," he laughed. "Far worse goes on there, I'm sure. But the tower is historically interesting. There's a famous ghost, the white lady, who is said to pop up from time to time near the tower, the haunted tower it's called. So, what would essence of haunted, death ridden powder be used for?"

"A potion for death. Now I'll be afraid to eat or drink anything she offers."

"Aye, well, it's common knowledge one should never accept food or drink from a witch, or you'll be in her power. I must say, Rosalind, I haven't had such an enjoyable evening since..." he opened his hands. "Come on, let's go for a pier walk, what do you say?"

"In the dark? In this cold?"

"It's the best time. You can see the lights across the firth."

"But in the dark?"

"Come on, lass. Are you afraid of the ghosts?"

"Yes," she laughed.

*

The delights of the young man's body were, at the time, the only thing on Morag's mind. There was the usual astonishment at what erotic pleasures slept below the surface until wakened, easily enough. Then that the tired old ideas of what sex was could be tossed joyfully away, opening the gate to bliss in extended pleasure. Morag knew from long experience that this young man's life would be forever changed, and so down the line of his lovers. Given that the old

Temples of Isis were no longer in business, someone had to help with sexual emancipation in a cold world of Calvinism.

Although Morag's focus was entirely on the singing flesh her hand and mouth and length of body against body had brought to a much-changed vibrational level, the union was apparently so transporting as to loosen the young man's tongue in ways other than the obvious. He, Robin, confessed, to a well-known witch after all, that he himself was a novice in the Occult Arts. He was not supposed to tell this to anyone, anyone at all, but if anyone in the world would appreciate it, and if Morag could keep a secret...

"Discretion is my middle name," murmured the witch, slowly licking into the top of the sweetly rounded buttocks.

... there was a secret coven, very close by, into which the young man had recently been initiated...

"A coven," marveled Morag. "How exciting for you."

... and that the very next night, it being an auspicious time for waxing moon magic, they would gather at a special place, where Druids used to gather in ancient times...

Which Morag guessed was Dunino Den, but kept her thoughts to herself, and gently bit the delicious white flesh under her lips.

... and, he groaned, that there would be a special ritual, the details of which he was not privy to. They usually met indoors, of course, but the High Priest said this was a special time and place, and everyone was excited...

There was a new style of witchcraft migrating north from the Sassenachs. Morag had been tipped off a few years past when rumors circulated about "the Strathkinness coven." The wee village already boasted a resident witch from a century past, who could gang aboot invisibly, and did all the usual folkish mischief. Her specialty was transferring her neighbor's butter to her own churn. Caught in the act of cantrips on the last night of the year, which is to say, the old Celtic year, in November, she was overheard to make a charm by spinning a cow's hide tether about her head and singing "Hare's milk and Mare's milk, an' a' the beas' that bears milk, come tae me!" She must have been a lazy besom that she couldn't churn her own butter, though Morag would never begrudge the use of spellwork to effect changes. The witch would also gang into a hare, a popular game among the auld Scots witches, emerging with the inevitable gunshot wound from a confused farmer, thus proving the witch's credentials. Considering that Morag often enough flew on the raven's wing, she knew this talent to be entirely feasible.

The new magical group from England was very foreign to her own understanding of Scottish witchcraft, insofar as Morag could ascertain. Secretive coven, a hierarchical High Priest and Priestess, inclusion requiring initiation, magic which seemed to be codified in a process within the context of ritual. She knew how Alastair Crowley did things well enough. Her grandmother Morag had visited him in his house on Loch Ness, called Boleskine, and whilst there had enjoyed some so-called "parties." There was a similar structure to their ritual, what with protective circles and invoking this and banishing that with much brandishing of swords and sticks and all, and being joyfully out of their minds with drugs and trance. Young and beautiful, grandmother Morag had been made welcome right enough, by the Master of Boleskine, who was curious to uncover the auld Scots magic, indeed to test whether it legitimately worked for his own purposes. Which were not at all the same purposes as that of a Scottish witch; the one a clever magus, the other kin to the wild. And so they came together like a hunter and a wild deer, enjoyed the exchange, kissed in kindness, and departed back to their own kind.

But this English group was quite different from Crowley's Boleskine frolics. Staid. Proper. Genteel. At last she might be able to uncover the truth of their existence. As far as spying went, what could possibly be more enjoyable, and effective, than seducing the lovely young initiates of the so-called secret coven? That made everybody happy. A little magic of her own, and the lover, lost in a blissful trance, would barely recall any of his pillow talk. He rolled over with a sigh, as Morag's finger traced the line of the thigh's muscle where it joined the groin and soft edge of dark hair, and she leaned down to draw the young man into a long kiss and bring his attention back to the matter in hand. But her thoughts were circling back to Dunino Den and the coven. A mischievous image flooded her mind, an opportunity for a great practical joke if she could figure out how to pull it off. As the thought occurred, she knew it would happen, and made an effort to avoid bursting into laughter at an inopportune time with her young lover.

*

The tide was coming in. Small waves arrived in ranks, lapped insistently at the harbor and boats, then retreated to gather strength for another assault. The cold was so acute it damped down the sea smell. They simultaneously drew up their coat collars, and hunched their shoulders as they briskly walked, hands clenched deep in pockets.

"My uncle has a boat here, somewhere," Rosalind said.

"Oh, I doubt we'd see it in the dark."

The vessels below rode the rising tide, shifting and jostling like huge beasts in a pen. A retractable metal pedestrian bridge separated the two sections of the harbor. *The Reiver*, her name bold across the bow under the harbor lights, was tied in the second section with other sailing boats and a few tubby fishing vessels.

"There it is. What a beautiful boat," Rosalind said. "Do you sail?"

"I couldn't handle a boat like that," he said wistfully. "She wants a real sailor. You could take her anywhere. Across the Atlantic."

"I'll have to do a sketch of it for Uncle Rab. Maybe he won't feel so bad if he has a picture to look at."

Angus turned the familiar fond gaze to her again. "You're a considerate soul, Rosalind." He took a hip flask from his jacket and offered her a swig. His hand touched hers in the exchange, and she wondered if he felt the same acute awareness of it. When she'd handed it back, eyes squinting and moist from the whisky as it burned down alongside her heart, he tipped it and drank with strong movements of his throat.

They walked past neat rows of stacked lobster pots, coils of rope and orange netting. At the far end of the quay, the main pier jutted far out into the water, its seaward wall paralleled by long fingers of black rock stretching from the cliffs. Some seabirds called out, their plaintive peeps heard over the thud and occasional crash of waves. Looking back at the town from the pier, to the right of the high spires of the ruined cathedral, the castle's distinctive silhouette of broken wall and fallen towers extended beyond the sea cliffs, visible in a strange glow. Rosalind was beginning to think Scotland was lit from within, always some sort of light, silvery or red, infusing the air.

The mysterious light showed the little waves to be deceptive. They adorned the swell, which washed over the rock, lifted and swirled the bladderwrack, then slid off, to string out the seaweed like wet hair over the glistening stone.

"I don't think I'd like to be in a boat and meet those rocks," Rosalind said. The pier had two tiers, a higher wall breasting the sea, and the lower, wider level they walked along. Below, the Kinness Burn flowed through the harbor, to mix with the incoming tide.

"Boats have certainly foundered on these rocks over the centuries. There's a ship under the west sands, the Princess Wilhelmina. A piece of the broken main mast sticks out of the sand at low tide."

"A whole ship? Are you saying that when I walk along that beach, I'm standing above an entire ship? When did this happen?"

"1912."

She laughed. "He remembers dates. Why haven't they dug it up?"

"Don't know. I suppose the tide prevents it."

They strolled over the uneven stone, each step taking them deeper into the darkness above the waves, leaving behind the last meager pools of yellow light from the street lamps.

"I can go one better than the town excavation you saw." Angus took her arm and stopped. He was very close. "Come up here a moment." He led Rosalind up steep steps to the top wall of the pier. There was no railing on the far side. It dropped straight down into the waves.

"See the cliffs under the cathedral wall, how they've been shored up with concrete banks? When I worked here, the cliffs had been eroding for a long time. When the cathedral was built, the land extended much farther out, over the rock below, there. The erosion had reached a point where the cathedral wall itself was in danger. In any event, some boys, climbing there," he pointed, "discovered skulls and bones actually falling from the cliff face."

The swell heaved up the side of the pier. Rosalind felt her body caught by the surge in a mesmerizing pull, at first a curious sensation, then frightening, invited by the wave's sudden proximity to slip over into the water.

"Now, that was some job, excavating that graveyard before they could build the retaining wall. There are many more graves we never touched around the cathedral. A large percentage of women and especially children. To be expected in medieval times."

The wave dropped, thirty feet directly below. Her stomach fell with it. The jagged rocks, alive with undulating seaweed, plunged up, out of the waves. She grabbed Angus's arm.

He seemed pleased, until he saw her face. "What's wrong?"

"The waves." Rosalind felt lifted out of her body, could see as if from above a vision of herself on the wet stones of the pier, accompanied by an incomprehensible sense of terror. "Let's go back down."

He helped her to the bottom step. "Sit here. Put your head down. Are you all right?"

The pier's thick wall muffled the deep sound of the waves, yet she could feel the movement in the stone as the invisible swell pushed. "That's not like me. I'm sorry. I'm fine now." But she was still giddy.

"No, I'm sorry, standing up there, babbling on like an idiot."

She realized he'd been holding her hand since coming down the steps. "It was those waves, a touch of vertigo. I'm all right now."

"Come on, I'll get you home. I've been selfish, thoughtless. You must be frozen."

She saw no reason not to take his arm as they stood. "What is this light? Is it the gloaming?"

"No, it's late in the year for that. Sometimes the city lights reflect back from the clouds, but it's clear, and the moon's not risen."

Rosalind looked skyward. To the north, above the castle and over the distant town lights twinkling across the Firth of Tay, the sky glowed orange.

"Unusual," Angus admitted.

Then the sky shuddered, and a sheet of red flame spread up the backdrop of the orange glow.

Rosalind gasped. "What is that?"

"Ah," Angus said. "The Northern Lights."

The curtain of transparent radiance filled the northern sky, becoming more and more active, as if a fire had been kindled round the earth's crown and leapt to life.

"Oh, wow, look at that one! How can it be silent?" she said to the vast sky, stars twinkling like mad in the curtain of luminosity. "It should be deafening, like tons of crystal shattering."

Every impulse of fiery color flooding up waves of sheeted light tugged at something in Rosalind, just as the sea had done. Bursts of energy tickled the soles of her feet, tensed her thighs, rippled through her belly, seared through her scalp, then shot out, high, into the flaming cold air. Angus stood with his head back. Points of light flashed across his opaque eyes. His teeth glowed red.

"Wow!" she cried at every rippled aurora. "Wow! Look at that one!"

"I've only ever seem them a handful of times," said Angus.

"This isn't right," she shouted. "Look at the town. They're all shut up in their houses, oblivious, while the sky has burst into flames!"

"To light our way home." He offered his elbow and she took it, walking with difficulty along the uneven stones of the pier, head craned back to watch the ripples of light ascend to the zenith.

"I've never seen the Northern Lights before. Amazing!"

He smiled at her. "I'll tell the lads to turn them off when we get back."

The walk to Morning Star cottage did not take but ten minutes, even though they moved slowly up the winding Pends road, along the top of the cathedral ruins, and down the lane with the old fishing community cottages on either side. The dancing sky continued to cast an orange glow over everything. With the handsome and solicitous Angus by her side, it could not have been more romantic. As they walked ever more slowly, unwilling to let the moment end, Rosalind had to wonder if her coming suddenly into his life, and his obvious interest in her, could have to do with the fact of her being an exotic foreigner from sunny California. If she'd been British, would he be as interested? Or, if he were an American, would she be as attracted to him? Whatever his interest stemmed from, the fact was they were here, in the beautiful medieval town, both fast growing enamored of each other, lit by the aurora borealis as if by a cosmic blessing. So when his warm lips tenderly touched hers at the threshold to Morning Star, it seemed entirely appropriate.

*

The telephone intercom in Clive's office buzzed. He punched the button. "Yes?"

"Mr. Forbes," said Elsie. "The police are here wanting to speak to you."

"The police?"

"Shall I bring them back?"

"No, no, I'll come and see what they want."

"Hold on," she said.

He drummed his fingers on the desk, then abruptly stood and looked out his window. "Damn," he whispered. "Surely they...damn."

"They want to see you in your office. I'll just bring them back."

"Right."

Within seconds Elsie gave a little knock, opened the door, and ushered in two uniformed officers, a young woman and man in his fifties. Elsie quietly closed the door behind her. Clive could see the shadow of her feet just under the door.

"Mr. Clive Forbes?" said the man.

"Yes. How may I help you?"

"I am Sergeant Kenneth Malcolm, and this is Constable Menzies. We are making some routine inquiries concerning the recent death of a girl."

He waited, still standing by the window.

"Did you know a girl by the name of Catriona Hamilton?" asked Constable Menzies.

Clive scratched his chin. "Yes, I knew a Catriona Hamilton. Not all that well, really."

"You attended her funeral yesterday."

"Yes, I did."

"Did you know how she died?"

"I hear it was an accidental overdose. Far too much of that happening these days."

"Aye, aye, too true."

The policeman was glancing around the office, studying the architectural drawings on the walls, the book shelf, the few items on Clive's desk.

"Would you happen to know of any reason how or why she

might have got caught up in the drug culture?" he asked.

"Certainly not. As I say, I didn't really know her that well." Clive jingled the coins in his trouser pocket. "Why ask me?"

"Simply protocol, Mr. Forbes," said the policewoman.

"You were seen with her a few times," said the man. "The two of you, alone."

"Yes, well, we did meet once or twice, I suppose, now that you mention it. Just to chat about, what was it now, work options for a secretary-in-training in my firm," he lied, "something like that. She came to me about it, not the first time that's happened with young people looking for work. I try to help, give those in need a leg up, though obviously my options are limited. But I really don't see how I can help you. I have no idea what sort of life she really led with her friends, apparently. What a waste. She would have made a good secretary."

"Did you know she was sixteen?"

"The ages of girls don't much interest me."

The two officers paused as if summoning up their foregone impressions.

"So you have nothing that might help us to understand her motives?" said Constable Menzies.

As if they could even begin to understand the nuances of the situation. He shook his head and smiled politely even as he wanted to take her scrawny throat in his hands and squeeze the insufferable arrogance out of her.

"We won't take up any more of your time, Mr. Forbes," she said. "Thank you very much for speaking to us."

When they had gone, Clive sat heavily in his chair. He pushed the intercom button again. "Elsie."

"Yes?"

"Cancel my last afternoon appointment, would you?"

"Yes, Mr. Forbes."

He sat staring for a few minutes out the window, then abruptly spun about in his chair and dialed Kirsteen's number.

"Hullo?" She sounded eager, and he knew why.

"Kirsteen."

"Hiya!" she squealed.

"Have time for a drink? I'll drive us down to Cellardyke. There's a lovely pub there on the harbor."

"Oh, yes, I'd love to."

"Six, then." He hung up, waited, then dialed the Medieval department. He patiently found his way through the secretary to Helen's office. "I'll be having dinner with a client," he said.

There was a barely perceptible pause. "Thanks for letting me know," said Helen.

*

Morag's Quair of Light and Shadows
Yearning for the face of allegory. How many eyes have looked with wonder and pleasure, and sometimes fear, to the moon's course through the starry lift? My Lady of Silver Magic reveals herself in the moon's face and phase. As she has sained us back countless generations, back through the thread of time and incarnation. When I open my arms to her brilliance, she bathes my face and breast, my body lightens, and she comes into me, meeting my desire with her own. The light clears my muddled head, and chases away trauchled or dark places in me.

Sometimes she is suddenly standing beside me in the form she chooses. If a youngster, she is mischievous, and teases, twining herself around my captive body, kissing me, caressing, laughing softly, here behind me, then there, across the garden, then nipping my shoulder and filling me with a sparkling restless energy. Come and play she whispers, and I happily depart my body to race into the ether, circling round, journeying into the moon's swiftly moving progress.

When the moon is full she comes into a maddening power, a time when things are not as they appear, and insight comes cracking sideways through my shifting perceptions. Here is the secret of my life's passion. I am so in love with her that I find her incarnate in lovers. That's my grandmother's gift, the one I received at birth. Do I manifest divinity in the act of love-making? Aye, certainly. Am I reborn in that cauldron of sexual passion? Yes. Profoundly, every time. A progression of rebirths before the final one. We kiss one another to life. It's the crucible of making, of transformation, a joining of divine souls in the bliss that is her gift to us.

Yet something's amiss. Last night the moon keeked through the bedroom window as it glided across the southern sky. Rather than the usual gentle swoon of pleasure, I was drawn up with a jolt. Strange forces meet and form. I feel them, I smell them, I see the shifting veil over the mundane world that heralds change. Spells or no spells, divination, discernment, I cannot see clearly what is about to happen. As if, beyond the simple yearning in my magic, fortune is coalescing in another realm altogether.

Which brings me to the waning moon, my old Crone of wisdom, my Cailleach. She's terrifying to most, as well she might be. The stuff of men's nightmares, particularly those men who have everything tamed and under their control. And women's dreams too, but in a different way. She is equally terrifying until the woman takes her into herself with fearless recognition. Her wisdom is far beyond mortal's ken, and she feels no need to share what cannot be comprehended. Her cloak brushes our lives and leaves us disconcerted, undone, and then re-knit into something wiser.

It is her time coming. Most ancient of Scotland's deities, even older than her name, she wrests the golden light from the beautiful Goddess we call Bride. She will not be neatly relegated to the dark half of the year, but makes her presence known in bizarre times and places, reminding, always reminding the creatures in her wild realm that nothing can be assumed.

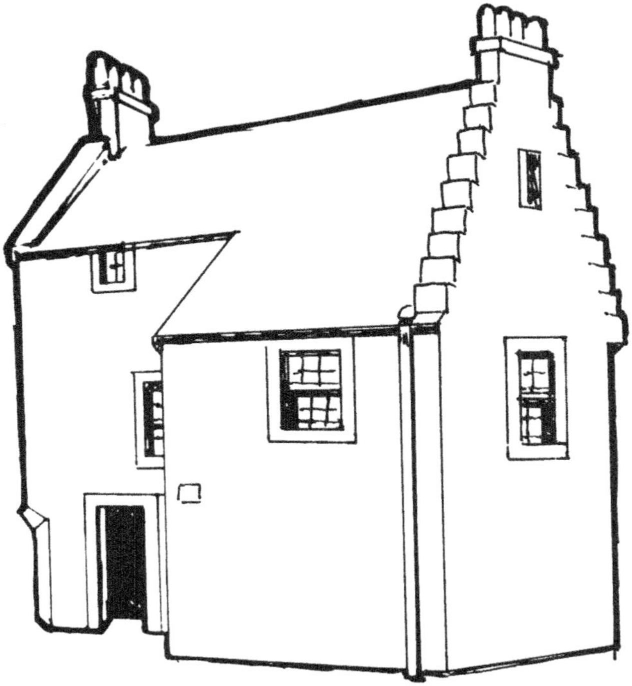

Chapter 8

The cleaning of Morning Star cottage was a tedious, day by day, highly unpleasant task. But as she scrubbed the kitchen cabinets, after throwing out moldy bread and unlabeled jars with hideous clumpy contents, Rosalind found herself humming upbeat tunes. Her thoughts returned over and again to the kiss.

It was the perfect first kiss. Hesitant, shy. She recalled his masculine scent, his warmth, the surprising softness of his lips between the rougher fringe of beard. If it were possible, she'd forgotten what it was like to kiss a man, yet at the same time it was achingly familiar. The kiss was the centerpiece to the evening, forever painted with the glory of the northern lights.

Rosalind pulled the little washing machine from its closet. This old mechanized tub-on-wheels was plugged into the kitchen socket with its giant prongs, the wall socket switched on, its intake hose fitted over the faucet, and its outflow put into the sink. It was almost amusing in its innocence, except that it was small and did not spin well, and it ate up the remarkably expensive electricity, and to top it off, the water heater in the cottage was an absurdly small, uninsulated tank, which needed a couple of hours to be fired up, which also gobbled up the electricity. Bathing required foresight and planning, and speed, as once the small amount of hot water was gone, there would be no more for a long time. The electric kettle provided hot water for washing dishes, and supplemented the tepid bath water. She'd learned by trial and error, and occasional bits of advice from Helen.

The coal fire was the only source of heat in the cottage. Learning how to cope with coal was another new experience. She couldn't get the fire to stay lit until she found that the coals liked to be clumped together, not spread out like wood. It was a filthy job, raking out the cold fireplace every morning and replacing the ash with a bucket of fresh coal taken from a huge sack in a garden shed. This chore was done with trembling fingers and the single-minded intent that the cold seeping through the walls imparted.

Uncle Rab obviously preferred to keep things the way he was used to. Rosalind went into her bedroom and pulled the sheets off the mattress. They were crumpled, since a fitted bottom sheet seemed to be a foreign concept in the household linens. The action triggered a memory of doing the same thing a week ago back home in California, a scene of sunlight, flowers, warmth and stressed haste. It seemed like a faraway dream, yet she had come a full circle to the place of her birth. Incredible to think it had been only days since she'd stripped the sheets off her bed in Palo Alto. Her mother, watching the proceedings, had launched into the inevitable "laundry tale."

"You've got it easy, you young ones," she'd said.

Sheila had been sitting in the bright kitchen, where she could offer advice and sip tea. Girth widened by age and infirmity, knees stiff, but soft face always cheery, her mother told the same tales over and over, triggered by whatever mundane task was at hand.

"I quit feeling young a long time ago, Mom."

"Ach." A hand waved in dismissal. "Young. When I was a lass in St. Andrews, I'd to get up before dawn to light the boiler fire, help my Mum do the wash. The row of houses shared the one wash house. Once the water was hot, I'd to boil and scrub the laundry all by hand. It took the entire day from lighting the fire to bringing in the wet clothes at dusk, and ironing sometimes half the night to get the damp out. One iron on the hob, the other rubbing away." She vigorously imitated the motions. "Tuesday was our day for the wash house. Nobody dared wash on the Sabbath! Life was hard, but we didn't know anything else."

Her mother spoke to her American friends with almost no trace of an accent. To her brother Rab Ogilvy, if she could get him to wait by a pay phone near the town post office since he refused to have one installed in his cottage, for a drunken, nostalgic New Year's Day transatlantic call, she matched his thick Fife accent. Chris, overhearing her, would shake his head and say, "I can't understand a word."

And speaking to Rosalind somewhere between the two, not so much an accent as speech peppered with highly descriptive Scots words, reminiscences of early hardships inevitably gave way to the sentimental.

"Sometimes my father would take us down to the sands for a picnic. He'd build a wee fire and boil a can for tea. He'd find a small bit of wood, and put it in the water. It takes the smoky taste out. And Rabbie, your uncle, he'd be thinking about how to catch crabs in the harbor with a piece of string, or how to knock the limpets off the rock with his heel; you only get one chance or they cling tight."

Rosalind had lifted the sheets from the washing machine and hung them taut on the clothesline in the backyard, where they pressed insistently against her body in the soft breeze. She looked over the small garden with the fresh eye that leave-taking imparts; the old oak trees, the quiet neighborhood, and the hills of yellow-brown grass beyond that always reminded her of a coyote's pelt. The autumn rain would soon be falling, coaxing a green mantle over the rolling hills.

"Why did you never go back?" she asked. "Especially after Dad died?"

"Back to what? Damp and cold and long winters of darkness? Aching arthritis? And don't think the summers made up for it. They could be dreich and dreary as well. Low salaries. High prices. Dreadful taxes, how much of it going to that royal family to keep them in their finery and palaces? We saw Braemar often enough, and once the Queen in her car. She waved to us. There's nowhere as bonnie as the Highlands, if it's not raining buckets. We loved the Cairngorms. A compass is no use in those mountains. Something to do with magnetic rock. I did a lot of hill walking in my day, can you credit that? Rabbie and I walked the Lairig Ghru once, along the shoulder of Ben Macdui. Not for the faint of heart! The ben has a ghost that chases hikers. You can well believe it when the mist comes down."

Chris came through, an armful of books embraced by a thick forearm. "Gran, are you talking about spooks again?"

Rosalind kissed him, surprised as always that her son's soft cheek had been replaced by a man's rough stubble. "You'll be back in time to take me to the airport?"

"No problemo. You coming along for the ride, Gran?"

"Aye, I will."

The door shut. "I told him to see the counselor," Rosalind said.

"I don't think the problem is entirely Chris's."

Rosalind paused with the pillowcase lifted to the line. "What?"

"You've got to let him go, you know. He's a young man now. It might be just as well that you'll be gone for a wee while."

"Mom."

"Don't you be worried. He's a sensible lad. What was I saying? Oh, aye, we'd some grand holidays. They were short, of course. My mother and father both worked themselves into their graves, poor Dad literally. The Ogilvy women are doomed to lose their men to untimely deaths. Like your Henry, aye, like your Henry. Och, what a shame." Her eyes clouded over in the memory. "One minute there, the next gone. Tattooed like a savage by the lightning." She shook her head. "Anyway, I'll always remember our wee holidays. St. Andrews is nice enough, if you like the sea. My mother didn't. Couldn't stand the smell of it. Hated fish. But then, she'd lost her father and husband to it. After that...after that...well, thank God your father came along."

"This is not a good time for me to go," Rosalind said. "The start of the semester is the busiest time. They were not very gracious about it."

"Your uncle has never asked for a thing in his life, so I know it's serious. You'll be able to see where your life began, in Morning Star Cottage. Oh, it's a grand wee cottage!"

*

The first thing had been to overcome her disappointment. She was certainly getting a better idea of what her mother talked about, the hardship of daily chores. Yet beneath the clutter of her uncle's life, Rosalind began to realize how solid and beautiful a building Morning Star was. The fine plaster, the hardwood floors, the hand-carved lintels and stones of the walls had been there all along, and she had not been able to see them until every inch of the house had been fought for and recovered.

She had a phone installed in the kitchen and called Palo Alto. It had been far too long not being in contact with her mother and son, and she was constantly worried that they had no way of reaching her except through Helen, who herself seemed rarely to be home.

Transatlantic miles took none of the petulance from

Chris's voice. "They said they'd give you one more week. Without pay."

Rosalind's reaction came as a surprise even to herself. "I'll be damned! After all the years, all the hard work I've done, and the unpaid overtime." Normally she'd have caved in and quickly tried to figure out how to mend the breach, but some new lion of courage was starting to roar in her gut. "They'll just have to find someone else, then."

"Mom?"

"Tell them I'm sending a letter of resignation. If that's how they want it."

"Mom, this is crazy." Chris was unusually peevish. But then, she'd never left before, and since Henry had died, they'd clung to one another through the forlorn, strange months.

"It is crazy," she admitted. "But there's just no getting around the fact that I can't leave Uncle Rab. He doesn't have anyone else."

"Whose fault is that, if he's as hard to get along with as you say?"

"It doesn't matter, honey. He's still lonely. Maybe he's frightened, I don't know. I can't leave a dying family member."

"But what about our finances?"

"That is the big problem," Rosalind admitted. "Here's the plan. I've been led to believe I can make a profit by fixing up Uncle Rab's old cottage. He wants to bequeath it to me."

"Yeah?" Chris was wary.

"The catch is, in order to refurbish it, I'd have to use what's left of your father's insurance."

"You mean my college money."

Rosalind was stung with annoyance, but kept her patience. "No, sweetheart, I think we can get by. But it's true that if I make a profit, we're fine. I fix the place up, sell it and come home a hero. If I can't, plus losing my job, then we have big problems, and I'll just have to deal with it as it comes. It's a gamble, but I want to try."

Chris groaned. "I hate never having enough money."

"Does this mean you'll switch to law school?" Silence. No humor offered his mother. "I'm afraid," she said, "in order to do this, I have to stay here for a while."

"Like how long?"

"I don't know, sweetheart." It was strange to hear his

American accent after a couple of weeks immersed in Scots and English. The harsh 'a's and long, swallowed 'r's, never noticed before, surprised her. "I've already done a lot of work. Maybe a month, but I'm just guessing. We've always just sort of drifted along, haven't we? What if I died next week? I'd have nothing to show for my life."

"I'm not nothing." He paused. "Mom, are you seeing someone?"

She hesitated. "No, silly."

In Chris's silence, the phone's echo mocked. "Silly."

"Listen, sweetheart, the doorbell just rang. You have my number in case of an emergency, all right?"

"Don't keep him waiting."

"Chris." But the line was dead. Not even a hint of her last words.

Helen was there, holding a plastic shopping bag weighed down by something heavy.

"Lovely morning, but clouding up a bit." She squinted skyward.

"Did you see the northern lights last night?" Rosalind asked.

"No, but I understand you did."

Chris's suspicions still rang in her ear. "We had a nice evening."

"I have a little pressie for you." Helen hoisted the bag as they ascended the stairs to the kitchen. "Gosh, what a good job you've done. Good for you. You know, once you begin, it moves along quite quickly."

"How about some tea?"

"Funny you should mention that. See what I've brought you." She put the bag on the chipped, yellowed counter and pulled out a cobalt blue teapot.

"Oh, that's a beauty."

"There's more." Next came matching cups and saucers, four of each in the Blue Willow pattern.

"Helen. You shouldn't have."

Then a big tin of Twinings loose tea. "Would you like me to show you how we do it?"

Rosalind remembered the full mugs of tea both Helen and Clive had quietly left on their last visit. "Guess you'd better."

"Don't they make tea in California?" Helen unwrapped the plastic from the tin with sharp, precise tugs.

"Sure. You put a teabag in a mug, fill it with water, and nuke it in the microwave."

Helen glanced twice at Rosalind over her spectacles.

"I know," said Rosalind. "My poor Scottish mother."

"Aikman and Terras is my favorite shop for tea. Right. First, fill the kettle with cold water. Oh dear, you'll have to get a new kettle, but I suppose this will do for now, if it doesn't electrocute us. Let the tap run for a moment to get it fresh and cold. And this being Scotland, we probably have lead pipes, so let the water run in any event. Now, while the kettle is heating, warm the teapot."

"But aren't you wasting a lot of water?"

"In Scotland? Let the kettle come to a rolling boil. Empty the hot water from the teapot, put in as many teaspoons of tea as there are cups, plus one for the pot. Bring the pot to the kettle, not the other way round."

"But what difference could that possibly make?"

"Then pour the boiling water over the tea leaves. Have you got a cozy?"

"I never seem to be able to get warm, but I'm pretty comfortable."

"A tea cozy. You really do need one. If you like, you can warm the cups as well. You want a thin lip on the cup so as to be able to taste the tea. There we are. Leave it to steep for five minutes."

"And Bob's your uncle. Thank you, Helen."

"Survival tactics," said Helen. "A good cup of tea cures anything."

"Have classes started yet?"

"Yes. I have a good bunch for my special subject class on the Vikings. We'll be going down to York next month. They're about half way done excavating the old Jorvik. You know," she said, "speaking of such like, I think Angus is on to something. Something really big."

"How do you mean?"

"He's found something in the cairn, I'm sure of it. And I don't think it's from the Neolithic era."

"Is that possible?"

"The milk should be poured first into the cup. There." She poured the tea. "Try that."

They perched carefully on the rickety seats at the table. "That's really good tea," Rosalind said. She watched Helen sip from the delicate teacup, noted her high forehead, a long nose with delicate nostrils above thin lips, defined slightly square jaw, giving her a handsome rather than merely pretty appearance, even if the heavy-lidded eyes gave the appearance of sorrow.

"A lot can happen over four millennia. For instance, there's a splendid Neolithic chambered cairn on Orkney, called Maeshowe. It was used by the Vikings as a favorite place for meeting, for courting and the like. The walls are covered with Viking runes and drawings. Usually these old tombs have a lot of legends associated with them, which is a good thing as it helps keep people from plundering them. But not everybody through the centuries has been frightened away."

"Is he acting differently?"

"He is. It's not like him to be secretive about his work. To the contrary. He's so excited, yet won't talk about it. He keeps putting me off, says he'll tell me as soon as he can. I've never seen him like this, almost boyish." Helen smiled. "But then, it could be something else."

"Oh, come on, we've gone out once. Okay, twice. Three times counting your dinner."

Helen lifted her thin shoulders. "I'm simply making an observation."

"We are fond of each other, but really, we just met."

"Do you ever regret," Helen took her glasses off and rubbed her eyes, "being too prudent in a younger day?"

Far more than she was willing to admit, and look where it got her. "What, do you think I should be less prudent now?"

"Can't advise you there, but no, I was thinking of a young man I knew in Cambridge. He was desperate for me to marry him. I was too young and uncertain. The reason I didn't get involved, I suppose, was fear of some unnamed retribution."

"Like pregnancy?"

"No. I couldn't have children anyway, as it turned out. I mean societal mores. Upbringing. He was too working class, I suppose, for my family to approve of. A self-made man. The blood will out, they insisted. So instead I married the appropriate Clive a few years later. Why did I knuckle under and impose these things on myself?"

"Because people who don't, ruin their lives?"

"Good heavens, Rosalind." Helen looked up. "Do you really believe that?"

The smug comment had slipped out unthinking. "Well, yes. Or I did. I always did what was expected of me, too. My parents epitomized the American work ethic, especially my immigrant mother. They made it work. Their lives were quiet and hard-working and, and ..."

"Deadly dull?" Helen laughed.

Rosalind was shocked into being defensive. "I don't mean that. I've never thought about it. I mean, that's best, isn't it? Look at all the problems people bring on themselves."

Helen looked surprised. "Bring on themselves? But what if not taking action causes the worst difficulties in the end? Don't you think that's more common?"

Rosalind felt threatened, and couldn't puzzle out why. "I don't know."

"Oh, pay no attention," said Helen. "I'm merely expressing my own disappointments. I want to see the garden."

Relieved at the strange conversation's ending, Rosalind stood and showed Helen to the back.

"Oh, a rowan tree," Helen exclaimed, clapping her hands. She stood under its ferny yellowing leaves, festive with overly ripe bunches of red berries. "We used to string the berries for necklaces as children." She reached up to pluck one, and rolled it between her delicate fingers. "It's traditional in Scotland to have a rowan tree at the door. They keep witches away."

"This one must be defective."

An apple tree had been trained along the south wall, under which rotted a few sad little fruits. "So much wasted potential," Helen wagged her head. "Shame, but if one is a bachelor sea captain, well, there you are. What did you think of the guests at dinner?"

A flood of happy memories returned. "Alastair was a character. I enjoyed his company, even though I can't quite figure him out, but I like him. Mary and Niall seemed..." Rosalind couldn't think how to avoid saying the wrong thing.

"Niall and his Celtic saints, honestly. He's trained as a clergyman, not an historian. It's a waste of time discussing things with such people, because of course they have an agenda, coupled with a very narrow viewpoint. But Alastair wanted to meet you."

"Me?"

"He's such a dear. Always on the lookout for interesting

people and art. He's a playwright and actor, you know, rather famous. He used to be known for getting too involved with his leading ladies. Or was it the men? Both probably. Well, must go. Have a tutorial in fifteen minutes." Helen hesitated at the door. "Oh, I meant to mention, just in case I mean, Angus has told you about Elspeth Weeks?"

"Who?"

"His girlfriend in Edinburgh? They've been together a couple of years. If you can call it that. More like that inertia business I was mentioning."

Was it foolish to feel a surge of despair for something there was little chance of having in the first place? Rosalind stroked the smooth wood of the door. "A handsome guy like that is bound to have a girlfriend."

"She's a bit of a wee Mary. Mousy, poor thing. Not particularly bright. It's a sort of on-again, off-again affair, and evidently just now it's off-again. The question is, ought one to grasp the nettle? Or whatever it is one ought to grasp. Ha ha."

"Helen!"

"But isn't that what we were just talking about? No, stay, I'll let myself out."

The gray sky had begun to mist with a light rain. Rosalind took a deep inhalation of the clean, cold sea air. Yes, why not? What harm would it do to have a fling with Angus who was obviously smitten with her? It was just that she'd never done anything like that before. Henry had been her only serious lover. As Rosalind tilted her head back to feel the coolness on her face, she noticed Morag Gilbride's black cat sitting on the wall, watching. "Kitty," she chirped. It stayed put, disdainful.

Helen's attitude surprised her. She thought of Brits as being uptight and proper, but there appeared to be an underlying, almost humorous ease with sexuality that Rosalind lacked.

A flurry of black wings erupted from the rowan tree. Something thudded to her shoulder and clung, a shocking silent presence. It seemed huge, terrifying, yet incomprehensibly weighed almost nothing. Rosalind very slowly turned her head to see a dully gleaming beak an inch from her eye.

"Oh, my God," Rosalind whispered. Her first impulse was to slap at it, make it go away, but if she hit it, what might it do? Attack her? And she didn't want to hurt the bird. The top of its beak had little nostril holes. Striations of subtle color followed the beak to its point. Rosalind's thudding heart rocked her body, and her eyes widened with fear, until she considered the bird might peck them, and then she squinted till she could hardly see and turned her head to the side. It had a subtle scent, not unpleasant, a cat fur smell. Its feet shifted and clung like little elfin fingers. Rosalind shuddered violently, but couldn't move.

"Good bird. Go away. Shoo."

It appeared to be content to perch on her shoulder. Rosalind steeled herself to slip a finger under its talons to lift it away from her face, still squinting. It ignored the finger and nibbled her ear ring.

"Ow!"

A whistle came from the other side of the garden wall. Morag's voice called. "Macha!"

With a spread of wings and a startling fan of air, the bird lifted and flew into the branches of the rowan tree. It gave one look back, as if weighing its options, them hopped down and out of sight, with the cat close behind.

*

They might have been mistaken for Titania and Oberon, as the High Priest and Priestess, escorted not by fairy trains, but by the overly excited coven of four younger initiates, Sarah and Janet, James, and Robin, the same young man Morag had happily seduced the night before. All but the High Priest and Priestess carried bags and magical implements. They stepped out from the forest path and into the natural amphitheater of cliffs and tall trees, bordered by a stream swirling around the low edge of the Druid's Den.

The High Priestess, Charlotte Gillespie, swooped through the leaves in flowing kaftan and shawl, feminine counterpoint to her tall cloaked husband, David Gillespie, Senior Partner of Gillespie and Forbes, St. Andrews Architects. Charlotte raised her slender hands, tilted her head back, eyes closed, and pronounced the vibrations to be perfect, ancient, and powerful.

"And see," cried Robin, gesturing at brook and stone cliff,

"all the elements are here!"

"James," said the High Priest to another of the men. "Make a tour round the area to be sure we are alone."

The scout scrambled up the slippery stone steps in the cleft of the Bell Craig, to the top of the rock ledge, and jogged a little ways up the path towards the kirkyard, to return soon after with a thumbs up.

David stood in one place, then another, head bowed, till it came clear. He caught Charlotte's eye, and she nodded agreement. "Here's where the circle will be. Come on you lot, let's start to gather."

"Altar table just there," indicated Charlotte. "Arrange it properly, you know how."

Sarah and Janet carefully unpacked and placed two bowls, knife, candles and chalice onto a black cloth over a small folding card table. Sarah unstoppered a bottle of sherry and poured it into the chalice, taking a quick surreptitious swig, as Janet took the other bowl to the stream and filled it. She sniffed it and made a face, then shrugged and brought it back to the altar.

"My sword please, James," said David.

"But," said young Sarah, "oughtn't you to measure the circle with the cord?"

"I think, Sarah," said Charlotte, "he's done it enough times to know the proper circumference. We'll need a bit of light, very shortly. Sarah and Janet, please light some candles and carefully place them round the circle, in front of the trees. We don't want to draw attention, and we most certainly don't want to start a fire. It's been a bit dry, you know, wouldn't do to make the newspapers."

"Isn't this the perfect place!" exclaimed Robin.

"Compass points, please," said David.

James was already bent over his Swiss compass. "North's that way."

"Gather, everyone," said Charlotte. "Feel the vibrational qualities." She stretched out her hands, fingers wide. "This is quite the special place, on a major ley line."

For a couple of minutes all stood with eyes closed, until Charlotte lowered her hands and smiled.

"Remember," David said as he began to define a circle on the leafy earth with the tip of his ceremonial sword, "we leave the north open at this point."

James and Sarah went to the altar and stood ready with the knife and a small bowl of salt.

David took the knife from his assistant and dipped it into the bowl of water held aloft by Sarah. "I exorcise thee, O creature of Water, that thou cast out from Thee all the impurities and uncleannesses of the Spirits of the World of Phantasm, so they may harm me not, in the names of Aradia and Cernunnos."

Robin watched with the keen eyes of a new initiate. When it came time for the blessing on the creature of salt, Robin reached for the bowl, but was shouldered out of the way by Janet, who glared at him. He retreated as more circumambulations were made around an ever-widening circle.

"You may light the altar candles," said Charlotte.

"But I always light the candles," said James, matches in hand by the altar.

David spun on them. "You will all be silent and do as you are instructed."

As James made way, he slammed his shoulder against Robin. "Sorry."

Robin, face burning, took the box of matches James had tossed to the altar, to find they'd been dipped in the bowl of water. He stood with the soggy matches in his hand, feeling the puzzled gaze of the High Priestess on him. Janet sniggered. He tried to scratch a match over the sandpaper side, and the box broke apart. He looked up helplessly, to see Sarah coming to his aid, hand shielding one of the lit candles from the circumference of the circle. She handed it to him and smiled encouragement.

"We don't play about with fire," David scolded. "It's a volatile element. Now, concentrate." David raised the sword to the Bell Craig, the rocky face of the cliff. "I summon, stir, and call thee up, thou Mighty Ones..."

"Sod," Robin whispered in James' ear.

"Nancy boy."

Charlotte, arms raised in invocation, shot a glance at the young men to silence them.

"I summon, I summon," began David again, voice raised in annoyance "... stir and call thee up!" He traced a pentagram in the air, and as the sword moved, a line of bright light appeared at the top of the cliff. Everyone stopped and stared.

The light was fire, which rose inexplicably higher until a sheet of unnaturally writhing flames spilled over and curtained down the cliff face, as if the Bell Craig were enflamed by dragons' breath.

Janet gasped and grabbed James's arm. Sarah cried out, and Robin stood with his mouth open, as the yellow fire danced across the stone. They all stumbled back a few steps.

"I...I...bid thee retreat!" David called, quickly making a banishing pentagram.

"Retreat!" called Charlotte in a shrill voice. "Disperse, thou creature of fire!"

At that, the flame extinguished entirely, plunging the grove into dark, shot through with searing after-images. Sarah gave a little scream, hands to mouth. The High Priest and High Priestess exchanged glances of astonishment.

"Bloody brilliant!" shouted James.

*

Morag tossed the empty can of liquid paraffin into the black Volvo's boot, and drove slowly past the forested glen of Dunino. The coven's few cars were still parked in the school drive. The trees along the path gave nothing away, no lights moved there, and it appeared the burning paraffin had not set the forest alight. She imagined they were still in their magical circle, trying to make sense of the literal manifestation of their invocation. She suspected the dumbfounded David and Charlotte would let the young coven-mates arrive at their own conclusions about the marvels and wonders of magic, and the power of their High Priest to invoke the very elements into being in such dramatic fashion.

"I, mighty Hierophant of the secret coven of Strathkinness, conjure and stir thee up!" she intoned in a sonorous voice. "Oopsie, now see what I've done!" Morag howled with laughter until she had to drag her sleeve across her streaming eyes as she drove down the country road through the dark fields. "We don't play about with Fire, young man! There's no telling what might happen!" Morag shrieked and gripped the steering wheel. She replayed the scene, still going on, no doubt, over and over again, laughing harder every time until her belly and jaws ached.

As she crested the hill, she slowed to see the moon-painted spires of St. Andrews below, and the luminous sea rolling in on the sands. Here was true magic. Here the mystical imbued the old stones and their history just as much as in the earth and its creatures. She stopped the car, still chuckling, to look out over the medieval town. Even in the moon's light, the stars twinkled merrily in the dark heavens, and a shooting star streaked across the horizon.

"Brilliant," she whispered. "Bloody brilliant."

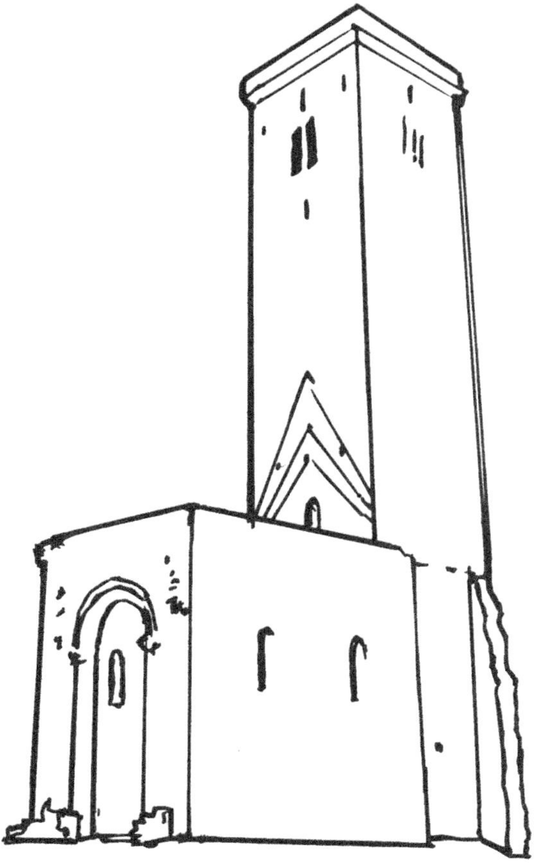

Chapter 9

The wan light from the impressive stained glass window behind the altar bathed the sanctuary in a bejeweled glow. Rosalind stood in the chancel, looking for the best angle. She was eager to try a drawing as if sketching a landscape, but from within an architectural space.

She quietly padded across the floor, her breath audible in the stillness. The pews shone in a light brown gloss, offering an inviting wash of warm color against the cold stone. The church was built on the old cross-shape, with transepts extending stubby arms in either direction off the nave, and curious plaques and alcoves inviting exploration. A gallery for extra seating fringed the church. The pulpit glowed sea-green, backlit through thin panels of marble.

Rosalind began a preliminary sketch of the pulpit and organ. As the pencil moved over the paper, her eye and hand stayed with the work, but her thoughts wandered back to their current obsession. The pencil paused, her head fell back, she recalled Angus's kisses, drawing in her breath at the intense pleasure of the memory.

And always prowling the perimeter of her mind was Morag, as bizarrely intriguing as Angus was conventionally desirable. The butt of the pencil tapped on the paper. She leaned against the stone wall, enveloped in the dim light, in the peaceful silence. She was very tired, not only from the cleaning of the cottage. The emotions must be taking a toll, too, the problems with her dying Uncle mixed with the budding romance, ripe with possibilities and at the same time highly improbable, given her circumstances. She yearned for a way to enter this new world, leaving the old one behind.

A strange sound came from across the transept. Wood creaked against wood. A sigh speared into the dark recesses, soughed around pillars built to uphold the church's vast ceiling six centuries ago. All those years the stones brushed by feathery sighs and whispers from countless throats. And this one heartfelt sigh containing within it all the rest, riveted Rosalind to the wall behind the organ.

She had not thought anyone would be in so late, at dusk, just before Niall had said the church would be closed. She pushed away from the wall, sketchpad in hand, and began to walk down the aisle, when the voice spoke.

"My Lord, I believe. Help my unbelief."

Rosalind stopped. It was Niall's voice.

Another sigh. In the medley of faint echoes, her eyes located him before her ears could, across the wide chancel in what she assumed must be a side chapel. The soft light above glanced off his bowed, balding head. He sat in the first pew by the side altar, face in hands. Rosalind cleared her throat, and was about to speak, when he began.

"Dear God," he said in a voice accustomed to solitary prayer, the voice of a supplicant who did not know the church was not empty. "Holy Father. Thirty years ago today I was ordained. Thirty years! In that time I've had my ups and downs, you know better than myself, and I realize..." his voice cracked.

Rosalind backed away, into the shadows. She glanced around for an unobtrusive exit.

"I've spoken to you and at you and on your behalf, and listened to silence. I've spoken your name every day for thirty years and more... I've prayed for a clean heart, for strength and guidance, for discernment, but I feel it's all been for nothing."

He must have come in through an unseen door out of her line of vision. Maybe the south door, the one she'd entered, through a small porch. It was less than a hundred yards down the wall from the transept where the minister sat. Rosalind started for it, then hesitated. If he turned his head even slightly, he would see her.

"I look for your kingdom, but never with more than a token nod to the incarnate mystery present here and now, maybe because it's the last place, and if you are not here, then everything, my life's work, will be meaningless."

Rosalind swayed in indecision, clutching the sketchpad. She crept behind one of the large pillars. It was more than likely he'd locked the doors before beginning his private devotion. If only she'd seen him come in. If only he'd seen her behind the organ. She looked for another door on her side of the church but nothing revealed itself in the frustrating pattern of fading light and black shadow.

"What does a man's life matter? I'm nothing, an insignificant speck of dust in the vastness of this universe. I am no man but a worm."

She could see Archbishop Sharp's large marble memorial, the once Presbyterian minister turned Episcopal Archbishop and eventually murdered for it in late sixteen hundreds, but not before he'd consigned a certain Isobel Lindsey to don the branks for taking issue with his preaching, as Angus had gleefully informed her.

"Everything else has been vanity. Oh, I've not been a bad husband or minister. To the contrary. Constant. Temperate. And some days I feel you in the prayers. But not others, not most of the time now. What did your saints have that I lack? What kindled the fire in their bosoms?"

Silence. Rosalind felt a leap of hope that he might be done, but then a new voice burst from the same throat, deeper, strained. "Thirty years I've lived through your death and rebirth every day. Yours, not mine, never mine."

Rosalind squatted down behind the pillar. If she couldn't bring herself to interrupt him, she'd wait him out. But would she end up locked in? A night in the cold church did not appeal in the least. Perhaps when he was done, she could pretend she'd fallen asleep in a pew and just woken up. "God," she whispered. Each desperate idea was more absurd than the last.

"I have died all the little deaths of self-denial. To what end?"

"Oh, help," she mumbled. His voice stopped. Rosalind held her breath. But he had only paused.

"Oh, Colum Cille, oh, Father Aidan, oh, Michael militant, oh, saints and angels speak to me!"

High above, the last daylight from the windows bathed the sides of the columns, but it was getting too dark to read the inscriptions on the shadow-painted wall directly in front of her. The smell of wax and stone filled the huge cavern that darkness had extended upward into a void.

All right. She would wait him out. Surely it would be possible to exit the church when he had gone. Because she'd stupidly hesitated when this absurd predicament began, she'd lost the chance to leave gracefully. After a while, as he continued his strange prayer, to pass the time, and to take her mind from the cold and discomfort, Rosalind began scribbling in her sketchpad, experimenting with the play of light under the Gothic windows. The scribbles became more serious. Not bad, not a bad sketch. She could take it home and finish it there. She did a quick drawing of the transept before it was plunged into total darkness, an attempt to salvage her original mission, though not an angle or light she would have chosen. Then, across the pew tops, out of boredom, a sketch of a minister at woeful prayer.

"Here tonight on my anniversary, don't leave me to struggle through my last years like a foolish old pretender. Bring me into a new revival, show me the way. Impart in me the passion of your saints."

Wood creaked. Rosalind cautiously peeked around the pillar. Niall hoisted his body up, then stumbled three steps towards the side altar. His face, bathed in the gentle glow of the subdued lighting, stretched in a silent wail, as if he were in unending pain, breath stilled, all creation stilled. Rosalind put down her pencils, then took them up again and sketched him standing there, too, considering that perhaps all clergy prayed like that when alone.

Through the dark vastness of the opened universe he had invoked, the chimes of the clock tower above marked the hour. People would be having their dinner, plates of hot food, fires burning in hearths, the lights of the houses glowing cheerfully behind drawn curtains. Rosalind's fingers became too numb to draw with, and her backside on the cold floor seemed to be absorbing all the dank chill in the church. She silently placed the sketchpad down and tried to warm her hands by jamming them under her armpits.

Niall gasped, and she turned to look again. His features began to change. The lids of his eyes grew heavy. He began to make a rumbling deep in his throat, a sound that, by some acoustical trick, seemed to come from all corners of the church at once, seeking Rosalind out, as if an audio floodlight had been turned full on her, huddled behind the pillar, appalled.

He fell to his knees, arms still outstretched. "Yes," he whispered.

This was her chance. Rosalind tucked the hem of her skirt into her belt, and crawled across the space between the chancel and the first row of pews. She paused. No sign he'd heard. She continued, catlike, down row after row of the huge church, an endless procession of wooden pews. Her cold knees quickly became bruised and scraped, and a cramp seized the arch of one foot. Her hands grew accustomed to the floor and began to detect every little ripple or rough spot, and once her palm fell upon a hard candy, still sticky, perhaps secretly expelled by a child. She peered over the pew tops. No sign of Niall. She cautiously stood, then dropped back down. He was still there, sitting on his heels.

"Is it you?" Niall suddenly asked.

Rosalind held her breath, eyes wide.

"It is you."

Rosalind peeked again over the pew. He was speaking to someone in the chancel, though she could not see anybody in the dim light. Good, that meant there was an unlocked door somewhere. She looked for the exit, then maneuvered her way directly through a pew row, heading straight for the door.

"Yes," he said, in a completely new voice, one of wonder. "Yes. I understand."

She stopped, still on hands and knees, listening. If he was still sitting on the floor, she could make a dash for it, but surely the door, if it opened at all, would make an awful racket.

"Of course," Niall continued. "It's so obvious. It's been staring me in the face for years, and in my stupidity I overlooked it. How simple, yet ingenious."

She steeled herself to walk boldly across, as if everything was normal, and she'd just come in, and not seen anything. If need be, she would say to him, "Oh. Sorry to disturb you. I'll come back another time." But what if the door was locked?

"But I am unworthy. How can I possibly...? Ah, the solution is plain. Like Columba I will fast and pray and sing praises. I will live on God alone, God and onions and nettles." Niall stood. "Like Saint Aidan, with renewed integrity, I will preach and baptize. No more foolish indulgences." He hesitated. "What about Mary? And her incessant lasciviousness?" He made a sound of dismissal. "No. No more. She has my brotherly love and that is more than sufficient. I will be pure as Saint Kevin, and she will support me in this holy rebirth. Never again will we rut like the beasts in the field."

Meeting him now was absolutely out of the question. Rosalind sank back down onto the cold floor.

"God grant me strength to once and for all shake loose from the world and spread the faith as they did," his voice boomed into the darkness. "I shall be a living example of ascetic discipline. Oh, my dear dear brethren, all the sacrifices and God's work you did fifteen hundred years ago for the conversion of this country, all in danger of being swept away by this insidious secularism and absurd New Age rubbish. And we know where the evil resides, indeed we do."

Rosalind measured the distance to the door and resolved to make a run for it. But suddenly a shoe scuffed the floor. She crouched back down. A shadow moved along the wall. It drew closer, a mix of irregular footfalls and eager mumblings. Rosalind stretched out flat, as quickly and as closely under the pew as she could move. If he saw her now, their mutual embarrassment would be unbearable.

Her breath stirred a little puff of dust. She glanced down in alarm. It dawned on her she was probably lying on a grave. She clearly pictured a body underneath, inches below, paralleling hers, grinning its moldy smile under her chin, a gruesome lover delighted that she'd lain with him.

"Therefore the wicked shall not stand in the judgment, nor sinners in the congregation of the righteous!" Niall passed by, down the center aisle, headed for the back door, his steps purposeful, and thankfully receding. Rosalind felt certain he hadn't seen her, lying flat under the pew, finger pressed hard against her upper lip to stifle a sneeze the dust was invoking.

"For the Lord knoweth the way of the righteous: but the way of the wicked shall perish." He opened a door at the back of the nave and exited without closing it. Rosalind struggled to her feet and almost fell back, gasping at the pain and stiffness. Hunched over, eyes set on nothing but escape, she scuttled across the aisle, past the smaller side row of pews, skidded to a halt at the side door, frantic with hope. It opened effortlessly. She ran through the little porch, out the gate, down the steps, and onto the pavement along South Street, taking deep breaths of the cold night air. She clutched the pikes of the metal railing. The solid street lights gave sanctuary, the knowledge that now he would never know.

"Oh, my God," she gasped, "oh, my God." She weakly laughed, then stopped, hand clapped to her mouth. Her sketchpad. The drawings. The renditions of Niall at prayer, lifting his arms to a silent God; the sketchpad lying forgotten behind the pillar.

Rosalind turned, uncertain, doubting she could make

herself go back in, when Niall came briefly into sight from within the church, and pushed the outer doors shut with a decisive bang. A lock clunked into place.

She stumbled down the pavement, head bowed under the searing images of the perplexing episode, emotions whirling. She turned the corner on the empty street.

Someone was standing at the east wall of the church, peering up at the dark windows. As if knowing what had just happened. Absurd. Rosalind gathered her courage to walk past, when the figure turned bright eyes to her and murmured something.

"What?" Rosalind said.

"Are you going to heaven?" asked Mrs. Pearse.

Chapter 10

It wasn't like Clive to panic. But wakened from a deep sleep by the British ring-ring of the phone, Rosalind heard an inflection in his voice she could not fathom.

"Sorry to phone so early," he said. "There's a team from our Aberdeen office coming in this morning to discuss a joint project. Could you possibly man the library just while they're here? It may take up much of the day. I'd be ever so grateful, I can't tell you."

Rosalind paused. Angus was due to take her out for lunch, which she'd been anticipating so eagerly it was almost embarrassing. The thought of canceling the lunch filled her with an equal amount of distress. Angus would be downcast as well. But it was the right thing to do.

"All right, let me make a phone call and I'll be there."

"Oh, thank you!" he cried. Then, "Oh, is it Angus?"

"Yes. Is he still at your house?"

"Oh, God, he said something about lunch or some such. I'm so sorry, my dear, but he certainly will understand. I'll take his ire, he can blame me."

She phoned Clive's house. Angus was still sleepy and his voice was deeper, softer. It brightened so much when he knew it was her she could hardly bring herself to disappoint him.

"Angus," she said, "Clive just phoned. He needs me today."

A pause. "I'll kill him."

"I'm so sorry, I was really looking forward…"

"Me, too. A rain check, eh? How about a nice walk tomorrow?"

"You know I'd love to."

"Four o'clock?"

"Yes, four o'clock."

"Until then!"

She replaced the receiver, hand still resting on it, amused at how the language of affection simplified the deeper in one went. And absurdly relieved, with something to look forward to the next day to replace the stolen time with Angus.

*

The throttle of the architects' little world opened wide. The secretary trotted the halls clutching papers. Elsie's phone rang frequently, eliciting little cries of despair as the fingernail file had to be put aside again and again. The normal geniality of the two young architects was replaced by a sharp focus on their duties as they exited and entered the conference room with creased foreheads and set mouths. Rosalind managed to stay the course, locating and delivering building standards and trade literature as it was requested. Whisky the cat fled to the far corner of the library and holed up behind Rosalind's desk.

The few glimpses she caught of Clive, pacing hollow-eyed up and back the seated phalanx of visiting architects, showed him to be chewing his nails or tugging on his ear, visibly struggling to collect his thoughts when he spoke in clipped syllables, or forcing laughs at appropriate times.

When the meeting finally ended, and the guest architects departed, the other senior partner, the dapper, blue-suited, bow-tied David Gillespie, came to lean his tall body against the door frame of the library, and sighed deeply. "Baptism by fire, eh?" Whisky rushed to brush his sides against David's legs, erupting into purrs.

Rosalind shook her head and smiled, secretly proud.

"Any chance you'd be relocating to Scotland?"

"I can't see how it would work out right now."

"We could certainly use you. Keep me informed, would you? If you are going to stay, even for a bit, I'd like to talk to you."

"Why, yes, thank you, I will."

He smiled kindly at her, and left to find his coat. Rosalind drummed her fingers on the cluttered desk. Whisky jumped on her lap. She absentmindedly stroked the cat's head. "How about that, Whisky? Did something momentous just happen?"

The conference lasted until well into mid-afternoon. Rosalind went home, tired and hungry. The sketchpad abandoned on the floor of the church would have to wait. The buffer of a night's sleep and the day spent with other, pressing concerns, pushed back the immediacy, the feeling of crisis from the embarrassing incident of the previous night at the church. At this point she'd be glad to just forget it ever happened.

Rosalind swung by the book shop on the corner and bought another, larger sketch pad, thinking she may never see the incriminating one again. She also found an artist's slender bag, orange-red on the outside, black on the inside, large enough to hold the new sketchpad, with delightful pockets for all her supplies, including sections for palette and paint. Her eye passed over small easels that could be set up in the field, just too expensive, still a conceit at this stage, but the beautiful plump silver tubes of acrylics and perfect soft brushes proved too much to resist. Well, she reasoned, was she going to be serious about it, or not?

She walked the short distance to Morning Star, and had no sooner trudged upstairs when the old doorbell rattled. She sighed, turned for the door, heart lifting at the thought that it might be Angus. Instead, there stood Helen. Rosalind squelched a slight disappointment.

"Please come in!"

"Good afternoon," Helen almost jumped over the threshold as Mrs. Pearse emerged from her Meeting Hall a few doors away. "Heard about the Aberdeen team. Just came to see how you were getting on."

"Far as I know everything went well. Want some tea? Watch me do it and see if I get it right."

"I hope Clive wasn't too demanding this morning. He's a bit of a perfectionist."

"No, I was glad to help. It's a lot more enjoyable than my job back home."

"Well, it's not my place to say, but he'd probably keep you on as long as you're here."

"David Gillespie insinuated the same thing. I hardly know what to think."

"David? Did he now?"

The kettle came to a boil and clicked off. Rosalind poured the water with a hollow splash and gurgle into the teapot. Helen watched, thoughts elsewhere.

"Wretched Angus still will not tell me what he's discovered in the cairn. God. Archaeologists can be so bloody zealous."

Rosalind caught herself studying the lines and planes of Helen's face and realized she was looking at things differently now, through an artist's eye. It pleased her inordinately, that this forgotten joy was resurrected. It wasn't simply an enhanced awareness of objects, but how something within them could be rendered and exposed through her attempts at painting. Helen's dark straight hair framed an aquiline nose, her face made all the more elegant by troubled but gentle dark eyes, the face of an accomplished woman beset with sorrow.

"Would you mind," Rosalind asked, "if I sketched you?"

"Me? Good heavens. Why would you want to sketch me?"

"Well, two reasons. One, because I need the practice, and two, because you have a truly beautiful, interesting face."

Helen laughed, embarrassed and dismissive. "Nobody's ever said that before."

"May I?"

"If you feel you must. But may I drink my tea?"

"No problem." Rosalind reached across the table for the new artist's bag, drew out the new sketchpad, opened it, placed it on her up-drawn knee, and studied Helen's features.

Helen squirmed. "Gosh, the artist's gaze is very direct."

"I suppose our mothers must have talked to each other over tea, like this."

"Perhaps in this very room. They both left about the same time, yours to the States, mine to Cheltenham, to have me."

"And now here we are, our mother's daughters returned to the same place. What do you think they talked about? Have an oatcake."

"May I move? I suppose they spoke about the price of things. Rations. There was a POW camp not far from here."

"I wonder if my mother told yours about the American soldier she was seeing." The pencil traveled freely across the paper. "Dad used to say the kids would run up to them and say, 'any gum, chum?'" Rosalind held her pencil at arm's length and closed an eye to take Helen's measure.

"Is your father still alive?" asked Helen.

"No, he died a long time ago. War-related injuries was what I always heard."

"Sorry." Helen laid her glasses on the table and rubbed her eyes.

At first Rosalind thought Helen was commiserating about her father, but it was something else. She put down the sketchpad and reached for the teapot. Below the heels of Helen's thin hands, her mouth turned down as if in sorrow.

She sighed and moved her fingers under her dark bangs to the skin of her temples. "Tell me. What was it like when your husband died?"

The cozy hung over the teapot for a heartbeat. "Helen?"

"I want to know." Her expression was vulnerable but resolute. "Were you left with feelings of guilt over issues never resolved?"

Select memories, highlights suspended like old photographs, were easily recalled. "Yes. At the time they seemed so important, and now I can't even remember what the issues were. It was sudden. About as sudden as you can get. One of the strangest flukes, a lightning strike."

"You're joking."

"I thought it was crazy, then discovered it's not that uncommon. The guys he was playing golf with said they should seek shelter with the storm coming in, but he waved it off and insisted they keep playing. These were business colleagues, in Florida. They got into a fight about it, and were arguing when it happened. He was standing a little apart from them, waving a club around. Sometimes he'd have these temper tantrums. I wonder all the time if I'd been with him whether I might have been able to do something, call an ambulance in time. I'll never know."

"Or you might be dead."

"Henry and I had had an argument earlier. I can't remember what that was about either. Isn't it ridiculous how you lose sight of the big picture?" Rosalind stood, a dim trepidation knocking in her chest, and poured a bronze stream of tea.

"Perfect color," said Helen.

"He was painted by the lightning. They call it Lichtenberg figures. It's like the lightning etches itself on the skin like a tattoo. It was actually very beautiful."

"I've never heard the like."

"But his death – it was a shock. Numbing. Beyond comprehension, that in the course of an ordinary day, everything changed in an instant. I never did get over that. And how fragile life really is. You get used to things and take it all for granted. After eighteen years we'd settled into a kind of routine companionship. Not particularly happy, I have to admit. The worst thing was the feeling of being cut loose, you know, from an anchor that was imaginary in the first place.

But it wasn't only his unexpected death. I mean, Henry died and Chris went to college and there I was, somehow ending up stuck in a job I hated with a life I'd never intended."

"I suppose every case is different."

"This must sound pretty silly to you, a university lecturer."

"Well, but I wanted children and couldn't have them." Helen traced the lip on her teacup. "Probably for the best. But the loss itself. How did you cope?"

"Hour by hour. Days slowed or zipped past like watching a movie. The sun rising or setting always surprised me. Days kept happening somehow. I fell into a routine. God, it was so tiring. I was angry at Henry. He pretty much neglected me – and his son – for his work when he was alive, then left us suddenly, through no fault of his own, but the anger would boil up anyway." Rosalind took up the sketchpad again, but her thoughts pulled her away. "Eventually I welcomed daily tasks, so I wouldn't lie there and sink back into depression, playing the same stupid thoughts over and over in my head."

Dusk shadowed the dreary kitchen. They stared at the bleak sky through the window.

"I haven't even admitted this to myself until now. I don't know if I was mourning the loss of Henry or of myself. Isn't it strange that the choices we make based on love can be the most damaging?"

Helen, brow creased, gazed dully into her tea. "Sad, but true."

"Anyway," Rosalind said, "no use indulging in regrets. Aside from financial worries, I'm actually feeling better all the time. Looking back honestly, I think it was more the shock of being bumped out of a routine in which Henry's and Chris's needs filled my life. You get used to things. It's not like we were young lovers."

Helen gave a rueful smile. "You're a plucky soul, Rosalind. What about your son?"

"He tried to be the strong guy, taking care of everything: me, the funeral, the details of clearing out Henry's things. There was so much shuffling and reorganizing. He never let himself grieve, and recently went into a tough depression, which I think he's still battling."

"I suppose the threat of loss put things into perspective."

Rosalind's tea was gone. She didn't remember drinking it. "You'd think so, wouldn't you? We never had a chance."

*

Morag's Quair of Light and Shadows

This is really difficult to write. I mean because it's impossible to describe. But never mind, here goes.

To begin with, there was the most extraordinary mix of passions. Fury at Clive. Oh, aye. Blood red rage stoked by the fear that he would escape retribution, and worse, gloat every time I saw him. Grief for Catriona. Deep sorrow for my sister and Aunt. Lusty desire for the American, tempered with caution. Destiny follows in her wake, even as she is all unaware. And I might as well be, too, for the lack of foresight.

At least I'm a good enough credit to my foremothers that I know such a cauldron of powerful emotions can be harnessed and directed into magic if...if!...controlled. Since the little revelation I'd gleaned after my Dunino fun, of the invisible world that flows under and through the visible one, its ethereal music sounding in rising waves; and that the thoughts, ideas, and dreams we have are also part of the music, I'd been thinking about Scotland's ancient places. Here, the Goddess stands at the in-between. Between the worlds, between day and night, at the turning of the seasons, between life and death. So much of our magic is accessed in the thresholds, also at the seasons' change according to the old calendar. Often enough, in the old Celtic way, standing in a threshold, I'd see what auguries presented themselves. There's far more than that, though. The 'special' places in Scotland are thresholds, as well. What occurs there, among the stones, or fairy mounds, or sacred wells and mountains, is spontaneous and not necessarily brought about by me. Many are the times and places I and my ilk have been visited unexpectedly by mysterious beings.

Regardless of which situation – mystical doorways in the ancient earth, or making magic in my living room or best of all, my bed, I'd pass between the worlds, out of this one and into that, then back again, to put what I'd gleaned into practice, in an ever evolving path.

But, I considered, if the ancient Goddesses were themselves liminal beings, what if, rather than merely pausing for auguries, or passing through, the threshold itself was the key to enter into the deepest realms of existence? If my theory was indeed true, I should be able to experience it. I resolved, therefore, to try, and see.

So, here's what happened, until words fail.

I took off all my clothes and tossed them into the corner. I sat Japanese style on my feet, hands at rest on my thighs, and let the lively force of my power ignite, like a sun inside my belly; and my second sight rouse and open. I stood to take up my ritual sword and encompassed a space, three times round, with the caim of the goddess Bride. All the magical energy awoke and bent to my craft, as the power uncoiled, lifted, writhed through my body and expanded to meet the life-force all around. I bent my magical will to the construction of a mystical doorway, there directly before me, large and strong, within the circle. The power flowed from my hands in blue-blazing light, to define the threshold. It had no door as yet, and I had no idea what it would open to. Once the frame was constructed, called into a shining, humming existence, I paused to admire it. Don't think I hadn't done this before, many times. Magical doorways to other worlds are common enough, and used for all sorts of magic. This one was different. Its purpose was different, and therefore the elements going into its creation matched its raison d'être. This was far more powerful and weighty than anything I'd called up before. Through the door frame, the far wall of the room swam in and out of sight as the curtain of effervescent energy within the threshold shimmered and shone.

I stepped into the threshold. The sheet of energy danced through my body like an electrical shock. I put hands to the frame, eyes half closed to better feel the movement of light. This was fine in and of itself, nothing unfamiliar as yet. I waited, with no expectation, lest I be guilty of creating a fantasy of my own desire, which would defeat the purpose. All nerve endings tingled in a familiar, delicious warmth, the hair on my body lifted, and my visions shifted to more clearly see the dance of colors, of dark and light in the magical forces. My mind cleared. The ever-cycling energy rose and fell and rose again on my breath. So far, business as usual as I slipped ever deeper into trance.

It took me almost unawares, when something began to happen. The boundaries of my body dissolved. A shift occurred and I ceased being a creature standing in a magical threshold, and became the threshold itself. A sudden expansion, and the cosmos opened and I was plunged into an empty but lively void. I let the flaring energy transport me until I existed no longer. Here was a Great Presence I knew better than myself, closer than the eye, farther than the sun. Inseparable, indistinguishable. And thus! we entered the pathways of the deepest magic from beyond time.

*

Rosalind shuddered and pulled back her sweater sleeve to see the fine hairs on her arm all standing up. "Brr!"

"Someone's walked over your grave," suggested Helen absentmindedly. "Is it too dark now to draw? Have I ruined your picture, talking too much?"

"Not at all, we'll just pick up where we left off next time."

"Did you know," Helen said, "Angus is going to move in with Patrick Buchan? The Medieval chairman. I think we've driven him off. Honestly, Clive is such a bear these days."

Helen looked tired. Her chin and nose seemed more pronounced, and a ridge of vein throbbed down the center of her pale forehead. She smoothed her hand over the table. "Would you get married again?"

Rosalind poured more tea to hide her ongoing discomfort. "There's another hard question."

"Or is it better to marry a friend and leave out all the ridiculous sexual complications? The disappointment that's bound to follow." Helen got up and went to the window. "White curtains, don't you think? Or yellow? I like blue and yellow in a kitchen. Oh!" she suddenly cried, and quickly stepped back.

"What is it?"

Morag Gilbride's big jackdaw hopped along the outside stone sill.

Rosalind laughed. "This bird keeps trying to make friends, and finally I gave in. I've been putting crumbs out for it. Here." She broke off a piece of her oatcake and slid the window open about six inches. Instead of waiting for food, the jackdaw ducked its head and shot through, flying to the back of the chair where Helen had been sitting.

"Oh!" Helen gave a little scream. "Get it out. Nasty thing."

"It's never done that before." Rosalind offered the oatcake morsel again. The bird inspected it, head tilted, then politely took it in its beak. Its foot came up and grasped the piece, turned it, and popped it into its mouth.

"What should we do?" said Helen, backing away.

The jackdaw ruffled its feathers and shat.

"Oh," cried Helen, "look what it's done."

Rosalind eyed the white splatter. "I'll try to grab it and you open the window, okay?"

Helen made a wide berth to the window, watched intently by the jackdaw. With its attention diverted, Rosalind picked it up by grasping its folded wings to its body. Each soft feather was perfectly in place, the ridges down the center of the pinions supple as a birch whip. Alarmingly rapid heartbeats drummed in its hot body. It gave an almost human sound of disappointment, legs peddling in the air. Helen pushed the window wide open, and Rosalind reluctantly tossed the bird out. It flew in steady wingbeats away, sad cries diminishing in the dusk. Her heart yearned after it, as if she'd thrown something out that should have been given welcome.

Rosalind looked at the wet splotch on the floor and started to laugh.

"Well, gosh," said Helen. "Fancy that."

"Come sit back down. Watch your step!" She laughed again.

"No, must be going." Helen folded her reading glasses and stuffed them into her handbag.

The floor creaked. Rosalind leaned over to see into the landing. "It's the ghosts," she explained to Helen's puzzled look. "I've been wondering what my family looked like. I think those old photographs set my imagination off, like what they'd be doing in each room. When the house creaks and groans, it's as if I can match the sounds and little things that happen with the families that have lived here."

"Things?" Helen sounded skeptical.

"Doors that won't stay shut. Sounds like footsteps, as if people are walking around. Small objects getting moved. Of course, it could be that I'm getting absentminded in my old age." Rosalind did not mention the sighs and whispers that came with more frequency from behind the old walls. "I'll have to ask a priest to do an exorcism if this keeps up. Speaking of which, what kind of reputation does Niall Sinclair have?"

"We don't really know him, bad parishioner that Clive is. I'm actually Anglican. Far as I know Niall never rocks the boat, if that's what you mean. A model of ecclesiastical decorum. Toes the party line. Basically what you'd expect of someone in that unenviable position, except. . . " she paused.

"Yes?"

"Well, funny you should mention him. I crossed his path coming over here." Helen stood and pushed the chair close to the table. "I can't understand the man at all."

"What do you mean?"

She shook her head and frowned. "He was spouting off some rubbish about a revival of the old Celtic church. All the usual nonsense. I suppose his research, such as it is, has gone to his head. Of course most of these men are brainwashed in seminary and live a fantasy after that, safe in their secure enclaves of the Righteous. He's modeling himself on Saint Aidan or Columbanus, can't recall which. Mortify the flesh and preach the Gospel sort of thing. And he was encouraging me to do the same." She laughed. "Honestly. I think the man's gone mad."

Rosalind knew all too well what Helen was referring to. She decided against sharing her embarrassing story of being stuck in the church during Niall's revelations. There had been a frightening undertone to what would have otherwise been an amusing incident.

*

"Morag. Wake up. Wake up!"

For the life of her, she could not open her eyes. With a massive effort a whisper passed her cold lips.

"She's conscious," said a man's voice.

"Morag. Can you hear me?"

Then she was back, body like a frozen stone, heavy and immobile. It hurt to breathe. Hands and feet began to ache, but Morag drifted above it in a state of pure delight.

"Morag!"

Kirsteen's creased brow came into view. As her hand came close, Morag watched, amazed to see it gloved in dancing light. The penumbra touched her before the flesh did, and she gasped at the near painful shock. Kirsteen frowned but kept her deliciously warm palm on Morag's brow. By looking at her, Morag saw into her. With a small flex of will there was Kirsteen in various places, past and future. Kirsteen with a clarsach on her knee, finding solace in the music, Kirsteen cradling a new baby, Kirsteen screaming, glistening in blood and firelight. Morag could even see the fear in her, a quaking brown color, as she bent over the bed, mixed with tentative love. Kirsteen was connected to the ligaments of snaking energy that twined through everything, and Morag suddenly wished with all her heart she could convey to the troubled lass that the final destiny of all creatures was a good one.

Another density in the filaments of light proved to be Calum, hanging back a bit. He murmured to Kirsteen and she moved away, and in her place, smiling, were Morag's deceased grandmother and mother. Their pale hands touched her shoulders in an electrifying saining.

"Welcome," they said, "to the Clann an Fritheir. To the Children of the Shining Ones."

Her heart burst open. It was a new place, in a new threshold between the worlds. She waited for the remarkable state to dissipate as the ancestors departed, but it held steady. A veil had lifted, exposing the subtle swirls of energy, a layer under and through the mundane.

It quickly proved to be a challenge, however, as they battled for attention. Kirsteen mistook her tears.

"What the hell were you doing?"

"Where am I?" Morag asked, truly not quite certain.

Kirsteen gestured at the obvious with her hands. "In your bedroom."

"Oh," she said. "So I am. What a lovely bedroom!"

"I found you stark naked on the floor in the sitting room, unconscious, with a sword. Do you know what I thought?"

"Kirsteen," Calum gently chided.

"I could not find a heartbeat. The fire was out. Your body was like ice."

"Oh, aye," she remembered. "It was incredible."

"Morag." She was about to cry.

"Yes, dear one?"

"It was your magic, wasn't it?"

"Could I trouble you for some tea?" Morag asked hopefully.

"I'll get it," said Calum, no doubt glad for an excuse to be useful.

Morag had always known the myriad creatures that existed, as if in a parallel realm, a mystical world of sprites and spirits, of the Sidhe and unknown presences, who were more interactive at certain times of the year; or the glaistig or urisks willing to let themselves be known during magical spells. But now this commonwealth was visible all around, moving here or there like a school of fish in the ocean, or a lazily grazing herd of deer. They fell into an opaque veil when something powerful asserted itself, such as the spirits of her mother and grandmother, as if according to some mystical rules in that world.

Kirsteen was ablaze in youthful passion. "You look beautiful," Morag said in wonder.

"Is that all you have to say? You looked dead. I thought you were."

"Don't scold me, lass. You know I'm given to that sort of thing. How did I get upstairs?"

"Calum. He carried you."

It entered her head that she must have been naked. "Oh!" she laughed weakly. "How embarrassing."

Kirsteen softened a bit, then resumed her scolding. "The cat had no water. What if I'd not come by this evening?"

"Evening?"

Her eyes rounded in exasperation. "Aye."

"What day is it?"

She gave Morag a long, fearful look. "Sunday."

Morag puzzled it out with a great deal of difficulty. She'd been gone from the conscious world for more than twenty-four hours. "Just a night," she lied. One of the magical creatures, in the form of a delicate, human-like sprite, made itself comfortable on her left shoulder. When she looked at it, it comprehended that her perception had altered, and it fell off, onto the sheets, in surprise. Morag realized that she knew this creature, as well as a few others who crowded about her with a newfound interest. They were a mix of animal-like creatures with ethereal humanoids.

Calum entered, clearing his throat, bearing a tray with teapot, mugs and a steaming bowl of porridge. Morag almost sobbed at the sight. Kirsteen, the efficient nurse, put a pillow behind her head and Calum carefully poured tea and offered a cup.

"Well, seeing as how you're not dead and the cat might

survive, I'm off to work."

"You're coming by for supper after?" asked Calum.

She stopped by the door. "Oh."

"Kirsteen." His shoulders slumped.

"I'm sorry, Calum." It came out in a petulant whine.

"You broke off..." he glanced Morag's way, tightened his lips against further speech.

"I've told you..."

Kirsteen displayed an almost comical combination of feeling badly for hurting the lad, with her wild temper. Ah, the warring of love. Morag held her tongue, still lost in wonder at the new world soughing like the winds of bliss all around.

When Kirsteen's wildness won, she left, and Calum brought Morag the bowl of porridge.

"She says I suffocate her."

If he could see even into a glimpse of the vision Morag had had, he'd be as speechless as she. How does one convey the curious sense of impending tragedy in the context of divine eternity?

"Patience," she said at last, after a bite of porridge. "She must undergo a struggle of some kind." Calum hovered over her like a mother hen, but despite the incredibly delicious porridge, the spoon dropped from her fingers. Her body was turning into light again, and her dear fore-mothers, pressing back into awareness, were being joined by others that wanted to make themselves known.

*

"Up!" Angus trotted to the top of the hillock, hands in his jacket pockets. "Down!" His head disappeared. Then he galloped around the side. "Clippity clop! Clippity clop!"

"Wait up," Rosalind called, laughing.

He descended again over the next hillock. "Wup!"

She ran to find him, and almost slid into a sand trap concealed in the side of the slope. He climbed out of it, slapping his trousers, puffing with laughter. The sand stuck to his waxed jacket. She brushed it off his shoulders, hesitant to touch him when such a small gesture held such significance.

"Are you sure this is legal?" She surveyed the links. "I don't see anybody else."

"That's because it's getting dark. It's a public right to walk the Old Course on Sundays."

"Really?"

"Every good Scot knows they'll roast in hell if they play golf on the Sabbath. Do you see," he knelt and caressed the edge of a green, "each little blade is a separate plant. Beautiful, smooth stuff."

The sea to their right, out of sight beyond the dunes, thundered and hissed in a steady rhythm. From time to time jets roared out of RAF Leuchars, only their lights visible, like a succession of stars rising and descending. Rosalind turned to see the sun sinking behind the town. Its rays illuminated the rippled clouds and infused the faint mist, creating a swirl of opaque reds and gold over a wash of silver.

"How beautiful the sky is," she said.

"In fact, an odd micro climate exists here, similar to another where the Findhorn meets the Moray Firth. Both have less rainfall than other parts of Scotland. Maybe it's the way the land lies, where it meets the sea."

She was keenly aware of his warm presence, so close. "I forget that nature can be so beautiful. Almost heartbreaking."

"Auld nature swears, the lovely dears," Angus sang as they strolled along. "Her noblest work she classes, o: her prentice han', she tried on man, an then she made the lasses, o."

They stopped near a small golfers' shelter backed by a steep hill. Bracken and gorse covered the slope, softening its silhouette.

"Perhaps we should cross over to the sands," Angus said. "It's getting dark faster than I thought. We can get back and have a pint before dinner."

They stood still and gazed at each other. "All right," she said. "Though I am reluctant to go back, this is so lovely."

"I ought to appreciate my surroundings more, but when you live with it, you get used to it and don't notice much." Angus skipped ahead like a schoolboy, hands jammed into his jacket pockets. "I've something very important to tell you. Come on, where nobody can hear us. It's a secret."

"There's not another living soul out here," Rosalind said.

But as they approached the shelter, a man's voice murmured something unintelligible from the far side, in the dark at the foot of the steep hill.

"Wait." Angus took her arm and backed a little away. They looked over their shoulders at the shelter, only its outline distinctive against the hill. Another sound, a whisper and soft sigh.

"Don't move," he whispered.

"What is it?"

"Shh!"

After a space of silence filled with an acute awareness of Angus's bearded proximity, a slender figure stepped away from the shelter, a woman, her long, thick hair falling below her shoulders. She stopped and turned back to look at the shelter. A second figure quickly moved toward her with an arm outstretched. He embraced her and they kissed passionately.

Rosalind started to move, but Angus still held her.

"Wait."

The woman broke away, and with a laugh, ran up the hill, sliding in the sand. A branch snapped under her foot. A moment later her companion, more clearly discernible in an overcoat and fedora, walked in the opposite direction around the side of the shelter. With a chuckle and a brisk step, he turned up the fairway towards the town, and was quickly lost to sight in the depressions of the links, but for a familiar tune whistled from the dusk. As soon as Rosalind realized where she'd recently heard the tune, an avalanche of dread crashed in on her.

"Is there anywhere we can sit for a moment? Only not there," she said, indicating the shelter.

They climbed the hill and walked a little down the course, till they reached a second shelter, and sat on its bench. A crescent moon and bright stars appeared behind the still luminous clouds, where they parted to inky space.

He took her hand and held it in his callused fingers.

"Angus," Rosalind began hesitantly. "How shall I say this? You are handsome." He gave a dismissive grunt. "And well-educated, and fun to be with."

"If you find me so, it's because I'm with you. You ignite the best in me." He lifted her hand to his warm lips and kissed it reverently. "I'm actually very boring."

Rosalind searched for a diplomatic way to find out if Helen's news of a girlfriend was true. "There must be someone else?"

He leaned back against the wooden wall. "Ah." He cleared his throat. "I have a friend in Edinburgh. But she's just that, a friend." He smoothed the back of her hand with his palm. "Sometimes you sort of get stuck in situations that are not what you might hope for, do you see?"

A large V of geese flew overhead, visible below the low clouds, then lost to sight against the black sky. Their honking breathy cries continued eerily long after they disappeared into the crack of light on the horizon.

"It's silly my even mentioning it," she said.

"Is it?"

What she would not have given to just turn and kiss him and let anything happen. But the incident they had just witnessed held her back. She traced some lovers' initials cut in the wooden frame by her shoulder. "That was Clive, wasn't it?"

Angus pushed at the pea gravel under the bench with his shoe. "I think it was, yes."

"Do you think...surely this doesn't just happen to be the first time. Do you think Helen knows?"

"She's never spoken to me about it, but that doesn't mean anything. Can you be married and not suspect? Or does one just carry on?"

"My God."

"It's no use trying to second guess in these matters. I think it's been going on for years."

"How?"

"Rumors. Hints that have slipped out between them in conversation. I'm sorry this happened. It sort of spoils my little surprise, but there you are."

He stood and offered his hand to pull her up. "Come on. Have you tried hundred-and-eighty-shilling ale at the Russell?" When she hesitated he bent down to take her hand in both of his and rubbed it solicitously. "They have good cider, as well."

She smiled for him and stood up, and they stepped over the rough, to the road between the golf course and the beach. Enough moonlight filtered through the clouds to sparkle on the low moving backs of the waves. They entered the dunes, stumbling through the thick grasses, then walked sedately on the smooth sand.

"Now," Angus said. "Put all thoughts of unpleasantness

aside. I shall divulge my secret."

"Fire away."

"Well!" Even though nobody was visible, he bent close and spoke in a confessional tone. "I have found something extraordinary in the Neolithic cairn."

"Uh-huh?"

His eyes sparkled. "It will change my life, certainly. It's an archaeologist's dream come true. I can't tell you how important it is."

"You'll be catapulted to fame and fortune?"

"Fame anyway. In rather limited circles, I grant you. As soon as it's public, there'll be all sorts of activity. That's another reason I'd rather have moved in with the chairman when the news breaks. He doesn't mind a little publicity. To the contrary, but the Forbes would absolutely loathe it."

"Well?" She pulled his arm. "What is it?"

"A treasure hoard. Hidden in the tomb."

"No kidding? A real treasure?"

He threw back his head and laughed. "Aye. Whoever hid it probably was desperate, didn't have much time. And had good reason to hide it, as they never made it back to retrieve it. What I mean to say is, it's priceless. The few pieces that are exposed, a brooch and silver bowl, are in themselves, simply, utterly splendid." Angus shook his head in wonder. "Unbelievable good fortune. Do you remember I told you how the cairn was shaped? A walled-off cist close to the damaged part collapsed. That's where I believe the rest of the treasure is. A bit of work's needed to uncover it."

"I see why you didn't want it made public."

"Rosalind," he stopped and placed her palms over his broad chest. "I want you to come and be with me when I excavate. You can help, take notes and the like."

Somewhere on the dark waves a seabird peeped. A cold breeze blew off the water. It lifted the scruffy curls on Angus's forehead.

"But isn't it kind of unorthodox to let a lay person like me stomp around an important site?"

"Listen, it's unorthodox for a professional to enter an enclosed site prior to excavation and take some rather serious chances, as I've done. But I saw a bit of the gold spilled out. I can justify any fuss raised. The treasure is so valuable I must remove it before the excavation proper begins, in just a few days. Short of posting an armed guard day and night it's the only way I can be assured of its safety. If it were stolen or damaged, the loss would be catastrophic. In fact, I've pressed the farmer into service, to keep a watch over the field, just in case. I'm not worried. If you didn't know it was there, you'd never find it. But still, not worth a risk."

He was avoiding the question. "Why me?" she asked.

"Do you Americans always ask such direct questions?"

She smiled. "My mother warned me about guys who want to take me into tombs. No, I mean, why not another archaeologist? Why not Helen? She's dying to know what you've found."

"I've been a good boy all my life playing by the rules, and where has it got me? Years of unemployment. Stuck in archival work in museums that any school kid could do."

"I know the feeling."

"I even had to sell insurance at one point. I was climbing the career ladder, slowly but surely, and a brief mini-television series was great, as far as I got before I lost my job here. Cutbacks everywhere, and rumors that the entire department will be closed soon. There's no money for archaeology. Important sites falling into the sea all over Britain, damaged by weather, all this historic wealth disintegrating and nothing to be done about it. When this story breaks, and it will as soon as the artifacts are secured, there's no way I could even get you close to the site." He stopped again, face to face. "It's a sort of unique gift I want to give you, and only I can offer it."

He was very close, his mouth inches from hers, on the verge of overwhelming her senses. "Are there, you know, bodies?"

Angus blinked. "I haven't seen beyond the first collapsed section."

"Is it dangerous?"

"No, I don't think so. The structure of the cairn itself seems quite stable. If anyone should happen by, which is highly unlikely, I'll say you're my assistant, which is true."

She hesitated. "I've got to tell you the idea of going into a tomb does not fill me with joy."

His face registered a dawning fear that she might say no.

"But I've spent enough years in abject boredom, too. You're on."

"Hurrah! Good!" He skipped away on the sand, and bounced a few times. "Splendid! How about Tuesday afternoon? I'll have the entrance cleared by then, make quite sure it's safe. I can't tell you, Rosalind, how alive I feel, as if my life is just starting, as if it's all been leading up to this. It's because of you. You bring me good luck."

Angus gently pulled Rosalind to him, and they savored their kisses in that perfect time of having just begun a romance, with all the excitement and passion yet to unfold.

The waves pulled off the sand with a dying hiss like a carbonated drink being poured, and the mysterious seabird called. An orange glow hovered over the town, but this time it was only the lights reflected off the clouds.

Chapter 11

Morag straightened the painting's frame, then stepped back to see.

"That's a really lovely gift, Morag," said Kirsteen. "A real work of art." She lifted the harp from her knee and placed it on its stand in the corner. "It's the first really nice thing in my home, ever."

"You're very welcome, my lass. It will be worth something before long, mark my words." The mystical world had never departed, but it was possible to function in both simultaneously, even if people did look oddly at Morag from time to time, or to be precise, more frequently and with graver concern. Another in a long list of curiosities, was the way music affected the non-material realm, as if it were a bridge between them. As if harmonic resonances were a common language. Morag could shift more fully into one or the other of the realms, usually in order to focus attention on a matter pertaining to that world. Music kept its integrity, flowing between both worlds, eternally interacting.

"Do you think?"

"Aye, I do." The acrylic was of the far corner of the cathedral ruins, where the gravestones clustered under a magnificent old tree with corkscrewed branches that looked like a wild tangle of hair, and the aqua sky behind, hazy with brooding clouds. Morag had watched Rosalind painting it from afar, watched how the will to paint possessed the American. All to the good. There was a rare passion under the woman's veneer, which Morag had been starting to worry about, to be honest. She'd need courage to go where Morag hoped to escort her.

Kirsteen tossed a blanket over the harp. The rehearsal had gone very well, most of their performance pieces from the Border ballads. She poured tea into two mugs, then a splash of milk, and handed one to Morag. She had something on her mind, and finally spoke it. "You won't mind if I don't come to Samhuinn at the stones?"

"Of course I won't mind. Why would I mind?"

"I'm not easy with it."

Why would Kirsteen enquire after something she had hitherto avoided like the plague, as if she'd had a change of heart? She wasn't lying, but was definitely trying to connect in order to conceal. "You're meaning the whole thing."

"Aye."

"You've never made a secret of that. It's not for everybody, Kirsteen. It's not for most folk. I never assumed you'd take that path."

"I feel as if I'm letting you down."

This was even stranger. "Ach, no. How'd you get that idea into your head? I wouldn't wish it on anyone if she were not called to it."

"I think my Mum was secretly hoping you'd apprentice me or whatever it is you do."

Morag laughed. "I can see the weavings of destiny and I can read the auguries and I can shape-shift with the creatures, but sometimes I can't see what's under my own nose."

"Too many times we're a laughing stock. I don't know if folk are scared or find it contemptible."

"And are you perhaps a wee bit scared of it yourself?"

"I don't know." She bit her fingernail. "Yes, I am."

Morag waited quietly. The glowing energy around Kirsteen was pulled close in. She was hiding something. It couldn't be Clive. Surely not, after Catriona's funeral. Surely not?

"You gave me such a fright the other night."

"You needn't ever worry about me, my lass. And as for the Auld Ways, only a very select few have that honor offered them, and that's as it should be. I know fine you're not keen on it. My grandmother was the last one I knew of who could exist between the worlds as easily. She was unusual."

"It frightens me, and it frightens me what it will cost you."

"Cost me? The Goddess claimed me, and that's that. I'd not have it any other way."

"Then, what happened the other night was...?"

How to convey the unimaginable joy and returning home to a true and eternal love? But all she said was, "my heart's desire, Kirsteen."

"So you've no expectations, I mean, you're not disappointed?"

"Ach, no. You're more interested in laddies and lipstick than the mysteries of the universe, correct me if I'm wrong."

To change the subject, Morag reached for a red rose in a small bunch on the kitchen table awaiting placement in a vase. "Aren't these lovely. Calum's a dear lad."

A flicker of fear passed over Kirsteen's face as Morag lifted the stem.

Immediately, like a flash vision in her mind's eye, there was Clive, his leering face and the flowers in his hands being offered to the flustered Kirsteen.

There was more than that. Morag dropped the rose. Kirsteen got up and stepped back.

"Why do you persist in seeing him?" Morag demanded. "Are Catriona's dealings with him not enough?"

"I'm not seeing him! It's not like that."

"Enough duplicity!"

"It's nothing. We've done nothing. It's just a friendship."

"You were with him in his car yesterday..." Morag looked deeper into the vision, "...Anstruther harbor."

"How can you know that? How can you possibly know that? This is not fair!"

"Why would a man like that be interested in a young lassie?"

She lifted her chin. "For intellectual stimulation."

Morag snorted.

"It's true, he says he finds my ideas interesting, that I offer a new perspective on things. An informed, feminist perspective. He says he finds me fascinating."

"I'm sure he does."

"Morag!"

"Never mind the rest, he's married."

"Clive says she doesn't mind."

"Oh, have they discussed you, then?"

"He says.... I don't know. But what of it, if there's no harm done? It's no business of hers then, is it?"

Morag stood up, heart thudding dully in a quiet fury. But there was equal parts fear to it.

Kirsteen shrank back. "Why are you so angry?"

"Because I know nothing good will come of this. Why do young women blind themselves so?"

"I'm perfectly capable of fending for myself."

"Like Catriona?"

"You can't compare us." She paced up and back in agitation. "So what if he's had lovers before? His wife is a cold fish from what I hear. You have lovers all the time! Why is it all right for you and not me? You've slept with married people, I know you have. You're a hypocrite!"

"Catriona was sixteen," Morag said quietly.

"He wasn't her first, you know. And I'm sorry, but you can't link him with her death."

"I most certainly can."

"He probably tried to help her, pay for things, ken?"

"What's the use of that if she was unable to even consider it?"

"This is 1979!"

"Perhaps some day the world will see things your way."

"When I moved here, Mum said you'd help keep a watch on me, but it's turned into a prison of suspicion. I'm telling you there's nothing going on I can't handle."

Morag was too angry, risking saying the wrong thing. And something very strange was happening. A brilliant deep red vortex had formed and began swirling about her, drawing in the light and tendrils of energy as if feeding on them. Kirsteen's aura was being pulled apart where the red brushed past her, creating a jagged edge like a frayed carpet, or broken storm clouds. Morag's emotions were apparently tied to her newfound ability. She would have to exercise massive self-control to avoid hurting someone like Kirsteen.

And indeed, Kirsteen suddenly went pale and put a hand to the table.

Morag took a deep breath and called up her love for the young lassie. It took a moment, but when it clicked into place, the change was dramatic. The vortex disintegrated as Kirsteen began to cry. Morag made an effort to speak calmly. "Kirsteen, if it were anyone else I'd turn a blind eye. Calum is perfect for you."

Kirsteen threw up her hands in exasperation.

"I think you are naïve in the face of what a man like Clive intends," Morag said. "I know you won't listen to me, but I think that with your father leaving when you were a child, you've been looking for another father since."

"That is such a load of bollocks."

Kirsteen had a gleam in her eye and a set to her mouth there was no moving past. Morag knew she'd drive the lass deeper into Clive's arms if she didn't back off. "All I'm saying is, be canny, lass. And for the love of the Goddess, tell me if he hurts you."

"He's not going to hurt me."

There was nothing more to be gained just then. Morag sighed, took up her jacket, and walked out. When the door closed behind her, she leaned back against it, eyes shut. A dreadful premonition had come with the holding of the rose. How did one reason with a headstrong young lassie when she was enticed by a charismatic seducer like Clive? Well, Morag reasoned, if she couldn't get through to Kirsteen, she bloody well would with him.

*

Rosalind went to the Cottage Hospital first thing in the morning, hoping Uncle Rab would be awake and alert. Instead, he was sunk deep into a kind of torpor, back on the heavy drugs. She had an hour before she was meant to be at Clive's architects' office, and decided to sit with Uncle Rab in the hope that he might awaken. She quietly drew out her increasingly worn sketchpad from her bag, half the pages filled with drawings and ideas, some holding promise, but most pretty dreadful, if truth be told. Still, she knew the discipline required to give her attention to it every chance was the only way forward.

She decided to start with his eyes instead of sketching out the shape of his head. As the pencil's satiny darkness began to define his old eye sockets and the prominent bridge of his nose, she considered how difficult it would be to suffer the visits of well-wishers at their leisure, not at his desire. How vulnerable he was lying there, in a hazy valley between this world and the next.

The drawing was by no means near completion when she had to leave for the architects' firm, but for some reason the loose and free sketching from the center of Uncle Rab's face, the proportion of this area to that, resulted in the most promising yet of her drawings, one that could be the basis for a painting. The unfortunate thing, were she to show it to him, was how absolutely awful he looked. And yet she'd captured an excellent likeness that held a softer edge to his irascible nature. She knew it was a 'keeper' as she used to call those pieces that came together well, in the early days of her arrested artist's career.

*

Trade magazines went in a rack by the library door. The architects checked them out by signing a notepad Rosalind placed conspicuously next to them, but she often had to call reminders as they unthinkingly carried things off, a lingering influence of the previous lack of order.

From the mail addressed to "Librarian, Gillespie & Forbes," a stack which increased dramatically every day, Rosalind pulled out the glossy November edition of *Architectural Digest*. No sooner had she replaced the old edition than the blue-suited David Gillespie bustled in.

"Morning, Rosalind." He shot her a friendly glance over bifocals, then lifted the magazine with a "jolly good," and exited.

Rosalind jotted down his liberty. The senior partners, benevolent patriarchs, were above the law. David Gillespie was always cheerful and helpful. She considered how pleasant it would be to stay and work for him, and equally rueful that it was not at all likely. She sighed and returned to the job of removing obsolete pages from a trade catalog and began to insert the latest literature the company had sent when the telephone on the small desk buzzed.

"Hello?" she said. "I mean, 'library.'"

"Rosalind," Clive's voice said.

She had only seen him in passing that morning. He looked the same, a little less strained, neatly dressed as always, and had called a greeting through the door in his usual upbeat way.

"Hi, Clive." A deluge of thoughts pressed in on her. He with a paramour in the golf shelter. Helen's role in all of it. How she should deal with her shifting emotions and sense of trouble brewing. It was not her business, but would he detect a change in her voice or demeanor? "What can I do for you?"

"Could you please nip down to the storeroom – there's a few black ledgers on the shelf, straight in front as you enter, with accounts from the previous five years."

"Certainly."

She had not yet been down to the basement, with its older archival material and building samples. As she entered the dark hallway at the foot of the stairs, hand feeling along the wall for a light switch, she heard a man's low voice coming from a door just slightly ajar. A dim light spilled out into the hallway from the room. Assuming this was the storeroom, she raised her hand to push the door open, when something made her stop. It was David Gillespie's voice, quietly reciting in a sing-song rhythm.

"String to wind and magic to bind, so your will shall now be mine."

She peeked through the crack in the door, to see the back of a man's dark suit. In his left hand he held a short stick, an irregular shape, as if carved into a crude human form, and was winding a cord tightly around it. The light came from a candle stub burning in a saucer on a table. She started to enter, thinking he was being playful, or entertaining a child, till his voice became intense, hissing from behind bared teeth.

"Bound fast, bound tight with all my might, so Clive be bound and theft indict!"

Rosalind silently turned on her heel and hurried back up the stairs to the library, where she sat, motionless, bewildered. Whisky looked up at her and mewed.

"I wish you could talk, Whisky," she said. "The things you've probably seen."

Not three minutes later, David Gillespie's cheerful face peered into the library. "Hullo, Rosalind. Bearing up all right?" All signs of his secret wizard's persona had vanished.

"Yes, doing fine, thanks."

"Don't suppose you've made a decision about staying on?"

"There's nothing I'd like better, David, but I still can't give you an answer."

He tapped the side of his nose and pointed his index finger to her as he exited.

When she returned to the dark basement to collect the ledgers, back to the same room, which was indeed the storage room, only the faintest scent of an extinguished candle was any indication of what she had witnessed. Why would a grown man, and a distinguished British one at that, be doing what looked like a spell? And of all places, why there?

She gathered the ledgers and ascended the stairs, and was passing by her library door when the intercom buzzed.

"Me, again," said Clive. "Glad I caught you. One more thing if you don't mind. We had a collection of plans for a contest for a community building on Iona. Do you think you could dig them up and bring them to the conference room? I'm with a client. Oh, and the Standards book that just came in."

"Right away." Rosalind scrawled 'eye oh nuh', and 'com bld' on a notepad. She sat back in her creaky office chair. If Helen and Clive had a serious falling out, where would that leave her in her relation to either of them? She shrugged. Never mind. If things proceeded as planned, like it or not, Rosalind would be gone back to the States soon enough. And Angus? Oh, Angus the bringer of dreams. She shook her head clear and returned to the job at hand.

Work had quickly become a combination of orderly filing, which she enjoyed, taming structural elements into usable, cooperative units, and the utter chaos of not knowing where things were, having to present them immediately, or dig them out of obscure, haphazard manuals. Although nobody, and Clive least of all, expected her to do more than "tidy up the library," the requests that a real librarian would have received began streaming in after the Aberdeen conference.

Rosalind picked up the phone and punched the internal line to Andrew Burns, the overly helpful young red-haired architect.

"Hallo, down in that oasis of calm," he said.

"You must be joking."

"No indeed. You've done an admirable job taming the beastie. The last librarian left it, shall we say, a wee bit untidy. No doubt you Yanks have all your information on computers. They haven't been discovered here, yet."

"Can you tell me where the old plans are? Did you work on an Iona project? And what is an Iona?"

"An island off the west of Mull. Which is an island off the west coast. Birthplace of Christianity in Scotland. St. Columba, you know, back in the sixth century."

"Columba?"

"Well, of course that was before he discovered America."

She held the receiver away from her ear until his laughter died away.

"That reminds me," he said, "of the American tourist in Edinburgh who was heard to say it was a pity the castle had been built so close to the train station."

"Andrew, where are the Iona plans?"

"Oh, aye. My entry should have won, but what can one expect from a huddle of handwringing, deadly earnest

Presbyterians? One crow-step gable too much for them. Look in a big chest with pullout map drawers in the entrance to the secretary's office."

"Thank you, Andrew. I'll call again when I'm in the hot seat."

"Wait! Say the last three letters of the alphabet."

"Andrew, I'm in a hurry."

"Ach, come on, just say them. Please."

"X Y Z."

There was shouting in the background. "Zee! She said zee! I'm rich, I'm rich. How do you pronounce 'deity'?"

"Deity. Goodbye, Andrew." The receiver clicked off the sounds of hooting and argument.

The telephone buzzed again as she was getting up.

"Transatlantic call, line two," said Elsie, "from a Chris Ehrhart. Is that your son? Is he handsome? I suppose he must be."

Rosalind sank back down into the chair. "Oh, heavens. Put him through."

"Hi, Mom. How's it going?"

"Chris. Is everything all right?" Rosalind glanced at the clock over the door.

"I just wanted to be in touch, you know?"

"I'm sorry, honey, it has been a few days, hasn't it? Listen, I'm going to have to call you back later. I'm supposed to have some material in the boss's hands right now."

"So how serious is this new job getting to be?"

"Well, this isn't a real job. Not yet anyway. I'm doing a friend a favor. Chris, I really do have to go. I promise I'll call as soon as I can, all right?"

Silence. The thunderclouds of depression gathering.

"You know I'm trying to do the right thing, Chris. You need to have faith in me. Heaven knows I have little enough. I need your support right now while I figure out how to deal with things."

"I guess."

"I miss you, honey, you know I do. I promise I'll call soon. Give Gran my love. I'll call. Bye, sweetheart."

"Bye Mom."

Chris had phoned simply to be reassured, to be in touch, and now she felt awful that she had to cut him off. She scurried down the hall to the secretaries' office, thoughts convoluted and sad as she uncovered the Iona plans in the bottom drawer, mixed with fifty others, all out of order.

"The whole world's in a spin," said Rosalind.

She extracted them, rushed back to the library, grabbed the Standards book and ledgers, then hurried to the conference room, and laid the material on the huge table next to Clive. He winked at her. She blanched and quickly returned to the library.

Scandinavian furniture trade literature, which had arrived with the post, awaited placement. Rosalind popped open the binder's rings. Out with the old, in with the new.

Just outside the window, bonneted head swiveling like clockwork, Mrs. Pearse stood on the sidewalk, holding out pamphlets to passersby. There were only a handful of stores in that end of South Street, but cars filled the road with constant movement, and the broad pavement was busy with locals and university students. Town and gown. Rosalind could now discern various individuals and groups, and watched the familiar clusters of brown uniformed girls from St. Leonards school, freed for lunch, giggling and nudging one another as they approached Mrs. Pearse.

In contrast to their well-laundered looks, a young girl, maybe seven, kept passing the window. She wore a dirty cotton dress and heavy sweater, much too large, and her feet were bare. She trotted alongside adults as they hurried by, lifted face and small hands beseeching. A short man in a tweed jacket and bowtie bent to hear her, then rummaged in his pockets. Rosalind had seen him walk past the window almost every morning, shuffling loose papers, carrying stacks of books. She suspected he worked in the Medieval department with Helen, only a few buildings down. He pulled out a wallet, extracted paper money, and gave it to the girl, then continued on his way.

Beggars. Beggars in Britain. That was a surprise.

The girl ran across the busy road to a woman waiting on the far side. They bent their heads over the money. The woman had a dark tartan shawl over her shoulders. Her face was young but smudged with dirt, her hair uncombed.

A policeman strolled up to them. The two adults exchanged words. Soon after, when Rosalind glanced up from her work, the child and woman were gone.

Clive came in. Hands in pockets, he leaned against the

door frame. Rosalind shook her head in exasperation over a card catalog all out of order.

"David and I have discussed it. This job's yours if you want it," he said. "A permanent part time position."

There he stood, dapper, trim, and she couldn't look at him.

"I'm grateful," she said. "You've no idea. But I just can't say right now."

"How about this, then? Carry on as you are, and when you do make a decision, let me know." He turned to go.

"Clive?"

"Yes?"

Rosalind flipped the catalog open to the Swedish cabinets. "Would it be possible to get something like this? I've brought the dimensions."

He came close. She studied his attractive face, his well-groomed moustache and goatee, and inhaled his scent of fresh pipe tobacco and cologne. He took the folder in his hands, and as he held it up to read, she imagined those same hands moving over the young woman's body in the semi-darkness of the golf shelter.

A sudden leap of sexual feeling stunned Rosalind. It was because of Clive's proximity, because of his hands. It was a physical sensation she had never before experienced, an echo of orgasm in her lower belly, which flowed through her and met her pounding heart and baffled mind.

"Easily." He snapped it shut and handed it back. "Leave it with me. I'll get a price and shipping date."

"Thanks." Clive appeared to be oblivious to her burning face and the bizarre passions pounding through her body.

"Mr. Forbes," Elsie called from her desk. "Caller on line one. Do you want to take it in there?"

"Yes." Clive walked around the bookcases to the desk, and spoke quietly. "Yes? Well? Look, I've told you not to phone me... I don't care. Tell the bloody world, then. You... Christ! Well, let me tell you something, you're in no position to..."

Rosalind quickly left the library, past Elsie whose plucked eyebrows danced up and down suggestively, and headed for the bathroom up the stairs. She leaned her hands on the old porcelain sink and looked long and hard at the face in the mirror. It had changed. Definitely. Despite the long hours of work, both at the cottage and with the architects, the unpleasant lines around the eyes and lips which had deepened in severity at Henry's death, had disappeared. Her tanned skin was softened with the Scottish climate, and most noticeable of all, her eyes were bright, the whites so clear as to have a bluish sheen.

"I don't get it," she said. "What's happening to you?"

Chapter 12

The horse and carriage turned the corner and rumbled away down the street. Bride and groom, blushing with massive self-consciousness, sat in the back, she in a voluminous white gown, he in kilt and formal jacket. Children chased the coach, grabbing at streamers waving off the back. Cars began pulling away, faces behind windows bright with laughter.

"Oh, no," Rosalind groaned. "A wedding."

The high wall of the chancel blocked any view of the front of the church, as Rosalind approached the corner, hoping nobody would notice that she had, three times in the past two days, made this same fruitless expedition, encountering a service, an organ recital, and a meeting. This trip was Rosalind's final attempt to salvage her sketchpad.

At the same time, Morag mingled with the happy wedding party by the door. It was a festive delight, made doubly pleasurable by the fact that Morag had initiated both of them into the sacred pleasures of sex. They'd enjoy a far more robust first night of wedded bliss than most. And on that note, her mind turned to the more savage pleasure of baiting the minister who'd just wed them.

The wedding party quickly thinned out, but a few lingered in small groups, breaking ranks for conversation or a fag. Niall Paterson stood outside the church door, wringing his soft hands, as the ladies gazed upon him with a reverence which he duly accepted with humble piety, vested in his usual somber, threadbare clericals, old shoes with the heels well worn, frayed sleeves and collar, duly donned with all proper devoutness.

Niall glanced up to see the witch approach, his lips pursed in a slight smile, until he realized it was her, diabolically camouflaged among the wedding guests in frock and shawl and even a broad-brimmed hat with satin band. Trapped, all Niall could do was sigh and say, "Well, Morag. I suppose you know the happy couple."

"Oh, you may be sure, Niall, in every way."

His eyes bulged and the muscle along his lean jaw tensed as he gritted his teeth, but he could say nothing with the wedding party milling about.

"But I have another matter to discuss," Morag said sweetly.

"The reception is beginning. I must go." He made a show of pulling his sleeve off his wrist watch.

"Not for another half hour," she retorted.

Just then Rosalind walked cautiously around the shoulder of the church, headed for the door, and almost bumped into them. She stopped short with a look of dismay, but to Morag's surprise it was directed at the minister. As with Niall, there was no flicker of recognition from Rosalind as her gaze passed over Morag.

And it was yet another surprise to see his expression lift, and an almost sardonic smile touch his thin lips. The unexpected bond between them offered a magical glimpse of a dark space filled with incomprehensible emotions and passions. This was a mystery worth investigating.

"Rosalind Ogilvy." Morag drew her in, lightly touching her shoulder, as Rosalind turned a puzzled look to Morag, which changed to dawning recognition. "A talented artist, wasting her skills in some office job."

"That's not a very accurate introduction."

"Yes, I know Rosalind," said Niall with forced patience. "We met at a dinner."

A young man in a morning coat and pinstripe trousers jogged past. "The flowers," he said. "They're gone! I can't find them!"

"It's taken care of, Douglas," Niall called to him.

"Is the church going to be closed?" Rosalind asked. "Can I go in for a second?"

"The church stays open." He made a show again of pulling the black sleeve off his watch. "But I must go."

"We were just discussing something, Rosalind," Morag said. "You see, Niall refuses to help start a counseling center for chemical dependents…"

"For heaven's sake," he sputtered, "is that what you wanted to talk about?"

She plowed on regardless, "… initially financed by a small group who heard about Catriona's overdose in Leuchars, and wanted to help, to see if this tide of drug abuse in Scotland can't be turned. We already have the backing of a local doctor and volunteers offering professional counseling."

"That's great," Rosalind pulled her arm from Morag's fond

grip. "But my opinion doesn't matter."

"This is neither the time nor the place..." Niall turned to go.

"The point is, there are some who are less than enthusiastic, because we want to locate the center here, perhaps even in this lovely old tower, eh? Some redress for it being a... what was it they called it, Niall?"

"I don't know what you're talking about."

"House of correction for errant women. That's it. The fanatics of the Reformation used to imprison people in that tower who disagreed with them, and funnily enough most were female."

But Niall was walking away.

"One word from you, Niall, and we'd be able to site the center here. It's very important. Won't you please consider it?"

"It's out of the question."

"Clive Forbes is backing the project. Did you know that?"

He glanced back, surprised, then pointedly ignored her. As he approached the church door, he passed by a lone figure unnoticed against the church wall. She spoke quietly yet her voice carried easily. "Have you accepted Jesus Christ as your personal savior?"

Niall spun around to see it was Mrs. Pearse. "Of course I have. What are you thinking, woman?"

'But you don't *know* him," she replied, unruffled.

"Mrs. Pearse," Morag cried. "How lovely to see you."

The evangelist's eyes grew round as she realized who it was. She clutched her worn Bible and immediately scuttled away.

"You're good for one thing, at least," Niall muttered under his breath.

The door to the church opened, and an elderly woman emerged, carrying a bundle of linens. She almost ran into Rosalind, who quickly stepped back. "I'm just going to launder these, Reverend Paterson," she said. "Everything's put away."

"Thank you, Mrs. McCubbin."

"Someone's left a notebook," she said, and Rosalind snapped to attention. "I've put in on the table by the door just there." She carried her ecclesiastical laundry away, heels clicking on the cobbles.

Rosalind sidled to the church entrance. "I'll just look in for a moment. There was an architectural detail...." she trailed off with a nervous laugh as she pulled and pushed at the huge door's handle but couldn't budge it.

"It will succeed," Morag called as she walked away, hips swinging enticingly in the tight dress, "despite your censorship."

"Lord give me patience," Niall sputtered. The veins on his neck were magnificent in their throbbing.

Rosalind jumped back to let Niall yank open the door with unnecessary vigor.

"Did you say you wanted to come in?"

"Yes," she said reluctantly. She glanced back, but Morag had disappeared around the corner of the church. She stepped through, and the big door boomed shut between them. Niall strode purposefully away down the aisle, as Rosalind stood for a moment to let her eyes adjust from the bright sunlight. The slightly dank, moldy smell brought back vivid memories of the bizarre ordeal of being trapped in the church, though today flower arrangements transformed it into a pleasant scene. Rosalind found the table near the door. A small brown notebook was on it. Not hers.

"Damn!" she whispered.

Rosalind hurried through the empty church, up the far aisle, till she reached the pillar where she'd left the sketchpad. Nothing. She looked around the pillar, along the wall, and in the seats. She got down on hands and knees, still sore, to look under the long pews. A great dark space stretched away, one or two fallen wedding service bulletins, and a sticky candy, but nothing else. She hoped someone in the wedding party had not discovered it in the middle of the service.

A pair of men's worn black shoes appeared under Rosalind's nose. She could smell the polished leather. She slowly lifted her head.

Niall held, over his knees, at the level of her face, a familiar artist's sketchpad, open to the drawing of himself standing with arms spread before the side altar. It was an excellent likeness of his profile, the mask of agony successfully portrayed. Another "keeper," she couldn't help but think.

The minister towered over her.

"Are you, perhaps, looking for this?" he said.

"Oh," said Rosalind.

"What did your friend Morag just call you, a 'talented artist'?"

"Morag?"

"Was that her way of insinuating she knows about this?"

Rosalind slowly got to her feet.

"How did you get in?" demanded Niall.

"The door was open."

"Nonsense, I'd locked it. I remember quite distinctly."

Rosalind lifted her spread hands.

Niall made a strangled sound of exasperation, and flipped through the sketches. "I don't know what you think you have to gain from this..."

"Gain?"

"...but I can assure you your scheme will fail."

"Niall! You're completely wrong about this."

"Reverend, if you please."

For a moment she didn't know to whom he was referring..

"Are all Americans as obtuse as you obviously are?"

"I'd like my sketchpad back."

"So that you can show these... these pictures to your friend Morag? Certainly not. You have a lot of explaining to do. I suggest you come to the manse, where we can discuss what's to be done, unless you prefer I report this unforgivable invasion of privacy to the authorities today."

"I really don't think that's necessary. This is all a terrible misunderstanding."

"Rest assured I will be in touch shortly about this. You've a lot of explaining to do." He clasped the notepad to his chest and stomped away, leaving Rosalind to stare dumbfounded after him. She felt like a child who has gotten caught doing something very bad, mixed with indignation at the misunderstanding. Her stomach went queasy. She sat in a pew and gazed at the historic cutty stool on display, the stool of repentance once used to discipline errant parishioners.

Chapter 13

October

The last section of wallpaper in the upstairs bathroom required steaming, scoring, and two hours scraping with a putty knife before it surrendered its hold.

"Bloody hell," said Angus. "My shoulders are aching."

"This is hard work," Rosalind agreed. "Let's take a break." She led him into the kitchen and put on the kettle for the usual cup of tea, then changed her mind. "A glass of wine?"

"Oh, aye, that would be grand."

Rosalind gave Angus the wine bottle and corkscrew, and unsuccessfully searched the cabinets for wine glasses. She gave up and pulled out two drinking cups. The cork popped and they both laughed. In the atmosphere of their easy affection, little things took on a silly pleasure.

"Italian style wine-tumblers," Angus said as he poured. "That will do nicely."

"It's really kind of you to help when you've got so much going on at your site."

"Oh, but the benefits are many." He sat at the table and sighed happily.

She stood behind him to embrace him, and kissed the top of his head.

"It's a bit slow at the site just now," he said, "as I measure and take notes and prepare for my illustrious visitor tomorrow. All going as according to plan."

Rosalind gently began to massage his shoulders. He half-turned his head to say something, then sat quietly as her thumbs kneaded his neck.

"Oh, my God," he said, head bowed.

"You're so tense. Relax."

"That feels incredible. I've never felt anything like that."

"I'm not that good." She continued as he gasped and groaned. "Don't tell me you've never had a shoulder massage before."

"Never. This is Scotland, remember. We abhor hedonism."

"A shoulder massage is hedonistic?"

"God, yes." He pulled her gently by the arm to sit on his lap. She put her arms around his shoulders and he pulled her to an eagerly awaited kiss. "You are amazing," he said.

From in front, she continued the simple massage. His eyes closed and his lips parted. She kissed him again, breath coming more deeply to match his.

From one block away, the loud chimes of the Town Kirk clanged the noon hour. A deep sigh, almost a sob, came from Angus. "I have to go," he said. "Damn and blast."

"Thank you so much for your help," she said. "I couldn't have done it without you."

"You can return the favor tomorrow at my place of employment." He led the way down the stairs and took his jacket from behind the front door. "Rosalind, if I'm right, this might be one of the most important finds to surface in a long time." He kissed her once more, with lingering affection. She watched him walk down the lane, aching sweetly to see him go, then returned to sweep up the mess in the bathroom.

A doleful shipping forecast droned from the kitchen radio. The announcer sounded apologetic that the barometer was falling. Rosalind often listened to the forecast, the names a foreign litany from around the coast; Faroes, Fair Isle, Tyne, Dogger, German Bite, strange words strung along like a magic spell.

At last, too weary to rejoice, she stuffed the defeated wallpaper, most of it hard-won chips, into the trash bag and lugged it to the back gate. The bin was stuffed full, and six more lumpy plastic bags squatted around it, full of wallpaper and dirt and junk from the house. This was nothing to the amount she'd thrown out when she'd started, yet these bags were a victory, a sign of the worst job completed. Not much more to do.

In the garden, a flower border's outline was barely visible along the wall. She scraped leaf mold aside and pushed her fingers into the dirt, bringing up rich loam. Centuries of earth worked by her own ancestors sifted through her fingers. She imagined her great-grandmother bent over the garden to her left, pulling weeds from a bed of gooseberries and rhubarb, of leeks and cabbages. Her great-grandfather chopped seaweed he'd brought from the sands for fertilizer, and distributed it across the soil. Perhaps they took a little time from daily chores to indulge in a few roses and herbs. The cottage was working its magic on her, weaving a spell of excitement and belonging, and against her better judgment, drawing her in.

Her fingers encountered gnarled roots in the soil. Rosalind tugged at one thick root and it snapped off from what she suspected to be the remains of a long dead rose bush. She pushed earth away from the clump of roots, then tugged and pried at the base of the old bush, her fingers sore from the wallpaper removal, till the whole root ball lifted from the loosened soil, looking like a grotesque bundle of intertwined tentacles. She tossed it to the side and dug her hand back into the cool soil. Her questing fingers slid on smooth stone, a piece of slate, roofing slate perhaps. Beneath it was empty space.

A flurry of wing-beats brought Macha the jackdaw, ever curious, to alight on the wall, head tilted to watch Rosalind's hands remove the dirt from the top of the slate, until she could slip her fingers beneath, and slowly pry it up.

Instantly the jackdaw was there, peering down into the hole. A little dirt fell in, but Rosalind could see it was lined with more slate, creating a shoe-box sized receptacle, the lid of which she had removed. Macha shifted from foot to foot as if impatient. Fine silt had filtered in. Something lay at the bottom, half-exposed. She cautiously reached in to feel the edges of it, a container of some sort, rectangular, wrapped in decaying cloth. She and Macha looked at the box, then at each other, then back to the box.

A wave of unease came over Rosalind. "I'm guessing," she said to Macha, "this is a pet's grave. I doubt either of us would want to see what's in this box."

As if in reply, the jackdaw jumped in and pecked at the cloth, tearing and tugging it off faster than Rosalind could react.

"Hey, get away!" Rosalind pushed the jackdaw back. A wooden box lay exposed, with dull brass decorations at the edges. She lifted it out and picked off the last bits of rotting cloth, to reveal a hand-carved box, about six inches by two, and over an inch thick. The shape was unusual, tapered to one end, like a miniature coffin, complete with an inscribed lid tacked down with small brass nails. "See, I was right, Macha." Rosalind rubbed her thumb over the tiny brass plaque. "M G?"

Again, in a flash, the jackdaw jumped in and grabbed it, pulling it away in a flurry of wing beats.

"Hey, hey!" Rosalind retrieved the box just in time and got to her feet, as Macha flew scolding into the rowan tree. She took it to the back door of the cottage, and stood at the threshold, studying the fine craftsmanship that had obviously gone into the wood, while at the same time reluctant to bring a possibly decomposed animal into the house. Macha let out an ear-piercing caw that decided Rosalind. She found a shoebox among the boxes she'd collected to store things in as she tidied the cottage, placed the wooden coffin in it, and hid the box in the room with the vaulted ceiling. She closed the door behind her when she returned to the garden, lest the cheeky jackdaw enter and steal it.

*

It had not been difficult to filch a bit of Mr. Clive Forbes. Simply wait till the bastard left the hairdresser and chat up the barber before he'd had a chance to sweep the floor. When he was distracted by a client, pick up a pinch of the hair, and it would suffice quite nicely. Those tendrils of energy that connect all creatures? The strongest bond is in something parted from its host, a more direct link than your common-or-garden remote spell, particularly if the results wanted were on the incarnate plane.

This Morag had known. What was newly arising was an understanding of certain rules that were in place in the natural and supernatural world, governed by some essence flowing through it all. Close kin to nature, Morag appreciated the confluence of human and natural in the prehistoric places, where mystical doorways had come into existence over the millennia, and which she, by practice of her magical heritage, kept from extinction. Now her feet were traipsing along a new silver pathway running through the old familiar roads. No, not new, ancient, far older than what the mind could grasp.

Morag pressed the stolen hair into the wax effigy she had formed in her kitchen, as Auntie Meg chuckled and clucked and drooled with excitement.

"Come on then," Morag said to her. "Put in a bit of your own cantrips."

Auntie Meg seized the poppet and caressed it most lasciviously, mumbling her old curses into its ear. After a few minutes Morag wrested it away from her. "Good enough. Time for a little fun, Auntie."

She carried it outside, curious to see the actual magical link to Clive imbuing the poppet, with his admittedly enticing charisma. Before the revelations of the Threshold magic, she could tell when an object was charged, often by whom, and about whom, since the energy of individuals is as distinctive as a face. Now she could perceive it, as if a new sense had been born, beyond the sixth. The poppet exuded a combination of Clive's essence, with Auntie Meg's dark mischief, both contained within her own, where it became an extension of her intention. With the passing of her hand, or the flexing of her will, the veil of energy in the poppet could be moved this way or that, with equal effect, and the individual's energy reduced or brought forward.

The Entourage, as she had begun calling the little company of strange companions that moved with her between the worlds, seemed to like being in her home and garden. They and the cat and jackdaw had their own alliances, which Morag realized had already existed. She had been too mystically obtuse to notice before. She also found that when she did magical work, causing the energetic vibrations to rouse and dance, the interest of these creatures was piqued. A certain type of movement and color, caught by the corner of her eye, like the distinctive glimpse of a fox flashing through a field, signified the arrival of the Entourage. When they were absent, it usually indicated that she had shifted into the mundane world of matter. And their appearance now meant she was swinging back the other way.

True enough, as they did the poppet magic, Auntie Meg blinked her one eye and nodded her head to indicate Morag's shoulder. "Here! You've a wee kilmoullach."

"What?" The elven creature sat on her left shoulder. "Is that what it is?" She perceived the Entourage, not like Victorian drawings of Faeries, but as small densities of light and color. Her inner eye could sometimes ascertain a shape within the color, resembling human or beast.

"Ah havnae seen that since your ain grandmither's time." Auntie Meg tickled at the creature with her bent claw. "Killie killie killie." Then she snatched her hand away, clutching it with the other. "Och ye wee bawbag! Bite at me, will ye?" Auntie Meg followed Morag into the garden, sucking on her injured hand and glaring at the creature.

"Auntie," Morag said, as if to distract fighting children, "go back inside and bring out the bow, would you?"

Morag walked down the lang rig and lashed the poppet to the old straw target. She returned, there to string the longbow Auntie Meg handed her, stepping on the stringer to bend the bow and carefully fit the bowstring to the notch.

Morag sensed a change close by. She stopped to see her aunt standing quietly, staring at her. "What is it, Auntie?" Morag asked as she slipped on the glove and arm-guard.

"You. They came for you," she observed.

Morag knew fine what Auntie Meg was referring to. "Aye. They did."

Auntie Meg nodded in a mix of pride and excitement for Morag, with profound sorrow at never having reached that magical place herself.

Morag put a hand to her aunt's frail shoulder. "I was looking for it, but it came unbidden all the same. I can say this; the hands of the Fates are unravelling the threads of our lives, to spin them into something new."

She slipped on the glove and arm-guard. She tossed the quiver over her shoulder to the clatter of arrows, reached up and over, and slowly slid the first cedar arrow out, savoring the sound it made. Morag took the archer's stance, nocked the arrow to the string, and slowly drew the bow. Away, down the length of the shaft, down the garden, there to the virgin poppet awaiting penetration. Her fingers loosened, the bow thrummed, and the arrow smacked into the target with a sharp retort. The target, not the effigy. She scowled.

Granted, she was out of practice, but as arrow after arrow thwacked into a neat circle around the poppet, frustration began to get the better of Morag. It didn't help that Auntie Meg chortled and mumbled behind her, louder and louder with every shot. Not only her aunt, but the magical creatures were finding it all highly amusing, too. She felt her hair being lightly tugged, as if by the wind, and heard laughter that sounded like tinny echoes in a distant cave.

"Go inside," Morag said. "I can't concentrate with you dancing about."

"You need specs," Auntie Meg teased. "Getting older are

we, dearie?" She pinched the top of Morag's ear.

Morag snarled and drew the magnificent bow again. "Must I put up with the derision of both worlds now?" She released. The arrow missed the target entirely, hit the stone wall and shattered into flying pieces. "Ishtar's paps!" she cursed, as Auntie Meg shrieked with joy. "Has that blasted coven in Strathkinness put a protection spell on the villain?"

"Wow!" cried a voice from under the rowan tree. "It exploded!

Morag jumped like a spooked horse. She and Auntie Meg stared in disbelief at the intruder watching them over the side stone wall. "Rosalind."

Rosalind was so amused by the bizarre antics of her odd neighbors, and that she'd caught them by surprise for a change, that she laughed aloud. "What's that on the target?"

Auntie Meg and Morag glanced at each other. Nothing to be done now they'd been caught red-handed in their witchy mischief. "You might as well come and see," Morag said.

Rosalind straddled the wall and, clutching the branch of the rowan, slid down into Morag's prolific foxgloves.

"Do you practice?" Morag asked, pointing the tip of the bow to the target.

"Archery? No, but I'd love to try."

Auntie Meg chuckled knowingly, to Rosalind's quizzical look. "I'll just put the kettle on." She shuffled into the cottage.

"Isn't Kirsteen expecting you for tea?" Morag politely inquired after her.

"Eh?" Auntie Meg thought on it for a minute. "Is she? Oh aye. Bye the noo, dearies..."

In fact, Kirsteen was not expecting her, but let Auntie Meg totter over for a cuppa, and no harm done. Having Rosalind wander innocently into the witch's lair was too good an opportunity to have Auntie Meg hanging about like a scraggly old crow. "I can't hit the damned thing," Morag said. "My psychic sight is improving at the expense of my physical eyes."

"Is this some form of voodoo?"

"It's called sympathetic magic. The traditional methods bore me silly, you know pushing needles into poppets, that sort of thing. This is far more fun, and there's an element of fate. Who guides the archer's arrow?"

"Have you found this method to be effective?"

"When I do it?" She looked at the target. "Oh, yes."

"Can I try?"

"You won't be able to draw the bow." As soon as the words were out of Morag's mouth she regretted it.

"How do you know?"

"Sorry. Very rude of me," she mumbled. "Here, give it a go." She slid an arrow from the quiver and twirled the fletching. "Archery was the dominant sport in St. Andrews in medieval times, before golf usurped it. Mary Queen of Scots was an archer. They practiced on the bowling green behind the university quadrangle. That's why the lane is called 'Butts Wynd.'"

"Butt's Wynd?" Rosalind laughed.

"The archery target is called a butt. This is a longbow, yew, what they would have been using."

Rosalind nocked an arrow to the string and lifted the bow. "Like this?"

"Hold on." Morag stood behind, raised Rosalind's left wrist, and straightened her bow arm. She did not bother to tie on the arm guard, since she knew what was about to happen. The scent of Rosalind's hair was a great distraction, and the smooth skin of her enticing neck was inches from Morag's lips. "Now, draw the bow with these three fingers."

Rosalind pulled back. The bowstring came three or four inches, then wouldn't budge. She relaxed, then tugged a second time. "It hurts my fingers. Wait, let me try again." No matter how hard she tried to pull the bowstring back, it would not bend.

Morag waited patiently. Rosalind gave up and handed the bow back. "Here, you show me."

"Stand behind me and watch how the arrow flies." Morag turned to the target, lifted smoothly, drew, paused, and released the arrow. The arrow didn't even arc as it shot down the lang rig and thunked into the effigy's leg.

"Ha ha! Bloody well about time."

"How can you do that?"

"There's a double whammy of magic here, if you can read the arrow's flight. It's called belomancy."

"I mean how do you pull that bow? Is there some trick to it?"

"Brute strength. Years of practice. And this bow is only half the draw weight of the medieval war bows."

"So, does the doll represent somebody?"

Morag hesitated. "Clive Forbes."

Rosalind stepped back. "That's not funny."

"No. It's not."

A flush warmed Rosalind's face. "Why?"

"I have my reasons."

"You're making a fool of me." Rosalind looked for the back gate to the alley walk behind the gardens for a quick escape.

"No. I'm not. No. Won't you please come in? I've seen all the rubbish you've been carting out. You must be exhausted."

The effigy dangled pathetically from the target. Rosalind crossed her forearms and glanced at Morag.

"Ach, Rosalind, it's a little gallows' humor." Morag stepped between the string and bow, bent it over her backside, and slipped the loop off the top. "Please come in. Let me explain." Rosalind frowned, still unsure. "I have a lovely cottage. Really. Surely you'd like to see it?"

Curiosity, and Uncle Rab's high esteem of this strange woman won out. "All right. For just a little bit."

Morag led her through the back door and leaned the longbow and quiver in the corner of the kitchen by the stairs. Despite Auntie Meg's fussy little spellwork projects, the cottage was neat and clean. She was not one to slovenly leave occult paraphernalia lying about in pools of wax and ash and bones, feathers and elf-shot. Aside from a hint of stale incense, Morag's cottage was tasteful, even elegant in its simplicity. Subtle floral and gold wallpaper covered the hallway walls. The lintels and doors were natural wood, and as they ascended to the landing, Rosalind felt the sturdy softness of a Persian carpet beneath their feet.

Best of all was the living room, which was also Morag's primary ritual room, but unless one had a keen eye, or a sense of the slowly revolving energy in the air, one would never suspect. Ivy-patterned stencils climbed to dark wooden beams in the ceiling, as if the garden magically swept through the room. On every wall hung her collection of paintings, all good originals in a variety of styles. Macha the jackdaw perched close to the window, newspaper spread below, eyes lidded, but all ears as they entered, an almost imperceptible tilt to its shadowy head.

"How about a claret with a bit of bread?" Morag asked. "Would you mind putting a match to the fire?"

"No, please, don't go to any trouble," Rosalind said. "I need to go see my uncle soon."

But Morag was out the door as if she'd not heard. And by the time she returned, the fire was just licking the coals, and to the loud tock of the grandfather clock, Rosalind had settled uneasily into the wingback by the fire. As Morag entered, tray laden with wine and bread and cheese, Rosalind caught sight of her own sketch she'd done of the castle ruins, sold by Elizabeth Stratton's shop, hung by the door.

"Oh, hey. I didn't mean for this to turn into a party."

Morag merely smiled, poured the wine, sliced bread and brie and offered it on a small plate. "Fresh from the oven."

Despite herself, Rosalind took to the room, even to Morag, who was doing her best to be hospitable. "These old homes are so well built. For the most part I'm enjoying fixing up Uncle Rab's house. He's helped me realize I have parts missing from not knowing my past, good or bad as the case may be. Of course you don't have that problem. Your history is literally all around you."

"Aye, well, in the case of my family, that's not necessarily a happy thing, believe me."

"Can I ask a question? Your home is really lovely."

"Not what you expected, is it?"

"That's not what I meant. Look at this art collection. I hope you didn't go and buy that overpriced sketch from Elizabeth Stratton's shop?"

"I bought it. I won't be able to afford your work much longer."

"That's kind of you to say so." Rosalind inhaled the yeasty scent of the warm bread and took a bite and savored it. "This is the best bread I have ever tasted."

"I also bought your watercolor of the cathedral tree, for a friend's new flat."

"Thank you, I mean really, thank you for supporting my work."

"Stratton's commission is unfair. She gets away with it because there are so many artists struggling to make ends meet. You need an agent."

"First I need to become a real artist, let's not rush things. So, I'm curious. What do you do for a living?"

The jackdaw flapped to the mantel, where it preened. "I have a small gift of being able to nudge nature's course in some situations. Or of enhancing its resolve."

"Run that by me again." As she relaxed, Rosalind became aware of a new sensation, or perhaps something lost and regained. She stilled herself to better experience it, a lovely glow radiating from her lower belly.

"My ancestors, from way back, were sort of the village wise-women. Well, to be honest, I don't know how true that is, but we like to think it. The second sight has popped up fairly regularly in my family. Christianity forced us underground, but we've always kept the old faith."

"The old faith?"

"Pre-Christian."

"I'm not following you."

"Other than a couple of family grimoires, there is nothing more than oral tradition passed down. I'm afraid the secrecy was not good for us."

"Family what?"

"Like a magical journal. We stagnated, got stuck in trivial mumbo-jumbo for the sake of preservation. Families became isolated when we moved underground. Back in the day, we dealt with major issues. Rain to the crops. Fish to the net. A loved one to the lover's arms, a child to the womb. To protect from misfortune. To bestow victory in battle. In the interim we were herbalists, midwives, respected elders, until church and kirk eradicated any authority women had. Today we are in danger of ending up fussing with little things, superstitions and country charms, all that was left to us."

"Like shooting at dolls?"

Morag's eyes narrowed. "Rosalind, it might look petty to an outsider, but please believe me when I say there is far more to this than meets the eye."

"You're right, I don't understand. It looks to me like a sort of passive-aggressive way to take out your feelings."

Morag was so shocked at the American's blunt comment, that she sat back and actually considered the idea. "If the sympathetic magic were simply the physical actions, yes, I suppose you could see it that way. Like an ancient Roman pouring out all his fury into a lead cursing tablet. But you'll have to believe me when I say, what seems apparent on the surface in this instance is a thinly veiled image of what is really happening behind it. And that would take me hours to explain."

"Okay," Rosalind said. "So, back to your professional services."

"I find more freedom than my mother ever did, and we have been making inroads into reclaiming what was lost."

"I'm sorry, you just lost me again." Rosalind laughed as she relaxed more deeply and savored the warmth spreading through her body.

"No, I apologize. I am guilty of having gone too deep and too far into this life to make sense to others."

"This is just ordinary wine, isn't it?"

"It's rather good wine, actually."

"Maybe I'm not used to rather good wine. So, give me an example of what you do."

Morag chirped to the jackdaw. The bird spread its wings and lifted from the mantel and flew to Morag's shoulder, where it took a piece of bread from her fingers. "I sell the wind to sailors. A charm of a knotted cord, three knots. The sailor undoes the knots at sea as required. One for a light breeze, two for a strong wind, three for a gale."

"Why would a sailor want a gale?"

"His wife might wish for one," she laughed. "What else? Mostly divination. Herbal teas and remedies. Old country charms like woven wheat. A carved piece of wood to which the spirit of the tree has lent power. Like the wee charm I gave you. Did you know your Uncle used to make lovely wee carvings for my spells?"

"Uncle Rab did that?"

"The most frequent requests I get, as you'd expect, are to influence sex, love, money, and revenge."

"I don't mean to offend you, but how could an intelligent person not see this as mumbo-jumbo?"

"I'm afraid it mostly is. Apparently that's what people want. However, far as the real thing goes, if you are speaking of the powers in creation, yes, I open doors to the other world, to the mystical, and I do it through nature – the special places, the seasons, the celestial movements. We are immersed in the magical."

"The opposite argument could be made," Rosalind said. "That you are creating your own fantasy reality."

Morag watched one of the Entourage alight next to the sleeping cat, dancing light about the cat's twitching ear. Piseag Dhubh rolled to her belly and shook her head vigorously, and swiped at the sprite with unsheathed claws.

"She might have ear mites," suggested Rosalind.

"I'm not in the least interested in creating fantasies. Scotland has an immense legacy waiting to be uncovered. I have to admit, the trivial requests I get from the villagers are becoming increasingly distasteful to me."

"Oh no, job dissatisfaction."

"You are laughing at me."

Rosalind got up and went to the fireplace to study an antique print of fox hunters on horseback leaping a stone wall, the riders in the old position for taking a jump, leaning back instead of forward. "Well, I don't know, Morag. I think you put on a little act."

"Drama is part of making magic. More wine? Let me give an example. Now, suppose you were wracked by indecision as to whether or not to accept your doting paramour?"

Rosalind turned to stare. "How is it the whole town seems to know about Angus? I'm not considering anything. But okay, hypothetically, supposing I was?"

"To whom would you turn? Friends? Family? Ah, what about that woman who is known for being able to make things happen, because what you really want is to make him captive to your desires, and who among the others can do that?"

"People call you a witch."

Morag spread her hands. "Does that make you uncomfortable?"

"So I sneak in to the local witch."

A flash of annoyance crossed her face. "Granted, a few do find it necessary to sneak in, including God's Righteous. And who am I to refuse their coin? We discuss your choices. I am not bound by the old patriarchal games. Love comes in many guises. Shall I demonstrate?" Her hand hovered over a small wooden box on the side table.

Rosalind sighed and reached for her wine glass.

"I use the knowledge I have gained from speaking to you. You said Angus's name, not me." She flipped open the lid and lifted a card off the pack, the Queen of Cups, at which Rosalind rolled her eyes. "Let's see, a woman kept in reserve by a lover, a woman oblivious to his interest in another, because she can't see past the end of her little nose. Why, this card could easily represent Angus's girlfriend. You do know he has a girlfriend?"

"I hear she's out of the picture now."

"How odd," Morag said, "that the MacLeod family is pressing hard for marriage with this lass."

"They are?"

"It appears Angus didn't tell you. In fact, did he tell you about Elspeth at all, or just hoped you'd never find out?"

"You're saying I should tie the knot with Angus before she gets him?"

"Oh, good heavens, no."

Rosalind returned to the wingback chair. "No?"

"Right, well, you just showed your hand, didn't you? I consider you, who you are, who you could be, and I consider Angus, and marriage is the likeliest, if least fortunate choice."

"What's wrong with marriage? He has a lot going for him."

"He's a decent enough man," Morag admitted. "I know his family fairly well. But he is a Calvinist. And you are most definitely not." She stood to refill Rosalind's glass.

"No more. I can't stagger in drunk to the hospital, though Uncle Rab would probably be delighted."

"He's been brought up and formed by the church, in a clergy family. Once the novelty has worn off, sex will be an occasional vaguely sinful embarrassment. If you were not a sensual person yourself, that might be all right, but you're practically humming with a surfacing passion."

"Humming!" Claret made laughter come easily.

"Surely you can feel it."

"Something's changing," Rosalind admitted. "Maybe it's being here, away from the routine pressures back home."

Morag indicated her painting with a tilt of her head. "The artistic impulse is tied directly to the erotic. The place of creativity, of making."

"So you're saying this erotic energy is wasted on Angus?"

"Where he grew up, they used to padlock the swings in the parks on Sundays so the children couldn't play."

"Oh, come on."

"It's true! If whistling is not allowed on the Sabbath, can you image what else is forbidden and guilt-ridden the other six days?"

"And what if I just want an affair?"

"He'd feel as if he were making you into a whore. He'd be unable to resist taking you, then would despise himself for doing it, and turn his self-loathing on you."

Rosalind was growing increasingly uncomfortable as her

own sweet fantasy was ripped apart by the witch. "That's harsh. He's been very romantic. He's promised to take me to meet his brother."

"Oh, aye, Hamish. Now Hamish is one of my regular customers, which puts Angus into a rage."

Such gossip about her suitor was too compelling to ignore. "How do you know Angus?"

"When he lived here, years ago, we had a fight."

"You seem to clash with a lot of people."

"His brother Hamish, that you mentioned, a fisherman at Pittenweem, just down the coast, came to me for a bit of luck, shall we call it, for the fishing year. This is my specialty, if you like, the links between the sea and stars and human fate. Their father, a minister in Portree, got wind of it, through Hamish's wife, the silly woman. As if by helping Hamish I wasn't helping her, but she's a devout Catholic, and scared of me. The father ordered Angus to intervene. Angus intercepted Hamish at my very door, and all the neighbors came out to see what the fuss was about. It was dreadful at the time, but now it's rather funny. Angus puffed up with righteous indignation, while his brother was furious at being found out and worried that it would all spell disaster for the fishing. Anyway, the upshot was, we managed to get rid of Angus, who stalked off in a mighty huff, and Hamish and I undid the damage."

"What do you do for him?"

"I gave him a charm to keep on the trawler, a connection to the magic I weave here and at the seaside for him."

"What charm?"

"A crystal, I think. It works in tandem with me, and holds my power well. And of course the knotted cord. That's an old Scottish tradition. But it's not the charm itself exactly. It's what I do behind the scenes that makes the difference."

"And what is that, exactly?"

Morag paused. "Cynicism is glazing your lovely eyes, Rosalind. All that needs said just now is that Hamish gives me a portion of his earnings, which is not insubstantial. Combine that with about forty others, farmers, merchants, businesses, and you'll see, it's not a bad way to live. If they make a profit, they give me a cut. If they don't, I get nothing. There is a lot of bartering in trade."

"Your tax forms must be pretty interesting."

"Oh, aye, self-employed witches have it the worst."

Rosalind had to laugh. "Do you mind if I ask you a question about Clive?"

"I'd have been surprised if you hadn't."

"Why the antipathy?"

"The poppet?" Morag let her head fall back against the chair and closed her eyes, and the jackdaw plucked at a strand of hair on her forehead.

Rosalind studied Morag's features. Alastair was right. Beneath the facade of idiosyncrasies, she was indisputably beautiful.

"He may have vented his fury about me in your presence, but I doubt he elaborated. He couldn't without revealing too much." She swirled the wine in her glass, and watched it spin. "Do you remember when I spoke to you after a funeral? It was for my niece, Catriona. She wasn't but sixteen. Clive has an eye for young girls." Morag held up her hand against Rosalind's shocked protest. "Not my business, except when his unpleasant dealings enter my sphere. I tried to help Catriona steer through this mess, but she was enamored with a teenager's single minded obsession and wouldn't listen. She was easy prey. When Clive brought the whole thing to a predictably abrupt end once the fruit had been plucked, Catriona went a bit crazy."

"This is not the Clive I know."

"Be thankful! His lust turned to revulsion quickly enough when she asked more than he was willing to give. She was a fragile girl emotionally. She came to me in desperation, wanting advice – not that she liked what I told her. She wanted me to intercede, to speak to him, and to Helen. Och, what a mess!"

"These are serious accusations."

"He drove her to her death, the heartless swine. Look at him now, happily whistling as he walks down the street as if he's no cause for blame."

"I admit I don't know Clive that well, but…"

The jackdaw hopped up from Morag's shoulder and with one movement of its wings alighted on the window sill. Morag, breathing hard, leapt up and went to the window to let it out, and stared into the street. "I let Catriona down. I should have done as she asked and interjected."

"What about Helen?"

"If the poor woman knows anything, it's not from my lips. And now," Morag snarled, "he's after Kirsteen."

"Who's she?"

"The daughter of a friend, as close as a daughter to me."

Rosalind hesitated. "If what you say is true, I can see why you dislike Clive, but why does he feel so strongly?"

"Oh." Morag came back to her chair by the fire. She put on a sheepish air. "I blackmailed him."

"What?"

"Not for anything as vulgar as money. Aside from paying for Catriona's funeral. And for any outstanding expenses and medication the Health Service was not quick enough to provide. Plus a wee bit for Catriona's poor mother, you know, to ease the burden of her loss. He's been quite generous to charities I support, like the clinic we're trying to get started in spite of Reverend Niall's objections. Now, answer me this, if Clive is innocent, why is he acquiescing to all my demands?"

"But Clive helped me with the cottage, and got me some work at his firm."

"I find it hard to believe there wasn't a massive dollop of self-interest involved. He probably intended on buying the house from you at a low bid after you'd done the hard work of restoring it."

Rosalind did not want to believe it of Clive, but she couldn't deny that her own suspicions had already been aroused.

"So there you are," said Morag. "You know, you should let your hair loose. It's thick and lovely. Don't keep it pinned up all the time."

"I'll take it under advisement." She stood. "I've got to get to the hospital."

"Give the Captain my regards. I might look in later." Morag stood as well. "He asked me to bring him some whisky. Grouse is his favorite, but I might splash out on a good malt."

"He did? He asked me, too. And sandwiches."

For a moment Morag looked stricken. She started to say something, then stopped. She leaned against the door frame as if suddenly weary. "He doesn't have much longer. Why deny him his little pleasures?"

"I wonder why he asked both of us."

Morag shrugged. She escorted Rosalind down the stairs to the front door. She paused, one hand on the door knob, eyes level with Rosalind's.

Rosalind couldn't move without touching her. Morag watched Rosalind's mouth as she spoke, and licked her lips.

As if on cue, the steady world plummeted in a sexual gyre, Rosalind's amazement at the bold desire almost as strong as the feeling itself. She ducked her head and fumbled for the latch, accidentally placing her hand over Morag's, where it rested on the handle. She jerked away as if she'd been burned.

"You're blushing," Morag said, all innocence.

Rosalind was stammering an answer, when the doorbell rang. Morag's eyes widened.

"Oh sod it! It's Mrs. Matheson, the old hen. She'll have a fit if anyone sees her here. Quick, out the back," Morag hissed in a stage whisper as she hurried Rosalind into her kitchen and out to the garden. "How did I forget about her? Ha! Stupid question. Gate at the foot of the garden..."

The back door boomed shut, leaving Rosalind alone in Morag's world of absurdly prolific fruit trees and roses. She stood against the door frame for a moment, breathing the cold sea air, trying to figure out how on earth she could feel such strong desire for something so incomprehensible to her experience.

The archery target still had the wax doll bound to its bullseye. Morag had left in the arrow piercing its thigh. Rosalind withdrew it and molded the wax back over the wound. Let her figure that one out. She would unbend a little of Morag's arrogant magic.

Chapter 14

Uncle Rab sat tall in the bed, regaling a small group of three visiting patients in the room, willing or not, with an explanation of how the waters had been over-fished, and of the competition between fishing nations, of how foreign countries could infringe freely, even to fish in Scotland's rightful waters, but that was nothing new, was it? Scotland had always been a victim of relentless foreign interests, particularly those to the south, was that not so, and where the hell did they think all that North Sea Oil was going? Look at the poverty Scotland was heir to.

Rosalind stood at the door and watched his gnarled fingers eloquently imitate waves or the fishes swimming side to side, and lift in the gush of oil from the sea derricks.

He turned a ruddy face and spied her. "This is my niece, a famous movie star frae Hollywood." Blank stares greeted Rosalind's introduction. "Och weel, they're no feeling shipshape. Come away in, lass. And away, the lot of youse, so's we can talk!"

Rosalind waited until they were gone. Uncle Rab craned his neck to see behind her. "Coast is clear."

She reached into her purse and pulled out cigarettes and a bottle of whisky. She stuffed them under his pillow. "I can't believe I'm doing this." The bottle clinked against something. "Uncle Rab. You old sot. You've already got a bottle."

"Bless you. Bless you." He grasped her hand in his dry palms.

"Pooh. You've had a drink, too. If you mix alcohol with morphine, you know what happens?"

"Ach, I'm not going to go that way, you may be sure. What the hell difference does a drink make? A man's final wish, now you've taken care of all the rest. God will bless you, Rosalind. And sandwiches?"

"At least this is above board." She nudged a plastic bag full of sandwiches and fruit. "Is the food really that bad?"

"It's terrible! Terrible! Och, Rosalind, you've been very good to me."

"Your cough isn't so bad today."

"No, but my bowels are bunged up."

"Oh. Surely they can give you something?"

"Aye, and I'm having none of it! So, how's it going with yon laddie, Angus MacLeod?"

The old chair shrieked as she leaned back. "How did you hear about Angus? Let me guess. Morag Gilbride."

"Is he a good lad?"

"I haven't actually seen that much of him, we're both so busy. But he's asked me to visit his archaeology site, in Tentsmuir forest, later today."

"I ken his brother Hamish, in Pittenweem. A fisherman. Angus would make a fine husband. Good family, Highland MacLeods. A Skye man's a fly man, they say. Canny."

"Marriage, huh? But your friend Morag says it's a bad idea."

"Does she? Best not, then. She kens what's what."

"Well, you certainly trust her opinion. Anyway, what's all this talk of marriage? You never got married."

He grimaced in distaste. "Who'd want an ugly old bugger like me? I have my mistress. The sea. She's aye jealous of the time I spend with others. That's my real home. I dream of the sea every night. It's easy to catch a glimpse of Tir-nan-Og when the horizon is gone, and behind it the sun is sleeping."

"Cheer what?"

"Tir-nan-Og. The Land of the Ever-Young. It lies to the west, where the sun sets."

She considered it for a moment. "Most folks call it America."

"Eh! Aye! America."

"Speaking of the sea, here's something I did for you." She rummaged through her artist's bag and pulled out a folder that opened to a sketch of *The Reiver,* one she was particularly proud of.

Uncle Rab glanced at the paper with a look of alarm. "Put it away, there's a good lass. Aye, back in your bag."

"I thought you'd like it."

"Och, it's lovely. Just keep it in the cottage just now. Don't mention the boat till I've decided what to do with her, will you promise me that?"

"Whatever you want." Rosalind was puzzled and hurt, but bit it back.

He noticed. "It's just a superstitious sailor's quirk. It's a lovely picture. Morag's right, you're very talented. Tell me, how's the wee hoose?"

Rosalind made an effort to quell her bewilderment. She'd wanted so much to please him with the sketch. "It's really beautiful, if I say so myself. I've painted the walls off-white. See the paint on my hands? It's in my hair, too, but I've been enjoying it. The wood of the lintels and baseboard is sanded. My friend Helen Forbes loaned me an electric sander. It would have been way too hard without it. Next I'll have a shower put in the upstairs bathroom, but keep that nice old tub. So there's a metal track suspended from the ceiling which the shower curtain goes on. And a big water heater."

Uncle Rab watched with bleary-eyed fondness. "That's grand," he said from time to time. "Aye, aye, good."

"I should take some pictures to show you. Maybe Helen has a Polaroid camera."

"Aye, do that."

"Soon I'll start on the cellar, if my funds hold out. And then it will all be done. I hope you can get back soon to see it." As soon as she said it, she mentally kicked herself. But he took it in stride and actually comforted her.

"My time is done, my lass. Morning Star is yours now, to make into the sort of place you need."

Rosalind took the rope with the three knots, and fiddled with it to hide the tears that were welling up.

"Here," he said. "Don't untie those knots."

"Will I start up a storm?"

"A storm wi' me, anyway. Aye, away ye go, then. You've been an angel in my last days." He lifted his arms to her. "I'll just say goodbye."

He pulled her head down to his stubbly cheek and embraced her tightly. "Here, give my love to your mother. Don't forget."

"But I'll see you tomorrow." She stopped at the door and looked back. Her uncle's eyes bored into her with a serious intensity. He lifted a hand in farewell.

PART 2

Chapter 15

The road made a sharp bend around the little Romanesque church in Leuchars. Rosalind wanted a closer look but was already late, having been stopped by acquaintances for little chats all the way from the hospital to the garage complex where Helen kept her car. It was, in fact, Helen's offer to loan the car that had enabled Rosalind to escape the confines of the town for a day, but Helen would have torn her thin hair in frustration if she had known her own car would be arriving at the mysterious excavation before her. The duplicity sat uneasily on Rosalind.

As she rounded the old church, the high, thin windows in the half-circle of the chancel came into sight. Helen had informed her they were used by lepers in medieval times to peer in at the proceedings, their only means of getting as close as possible to a vision of the Incarnation.

By the time she'd driven slowly through the small town, it began to dawn on her that Angus's directions to the Neolithic cairn were inadequate. Once out of Leuchars on the Tentsmuir Forest road she was to watch for a line of cottages on the left then carry on past fields, toward the sea. The site entrance was in a cultivated field within the forest.

No sign appeared for Tentsmuir. Rosalind traveled what she hoped was the right road, past a little row of council houses, then through fields defined by low stone walls. The dark edge of the woods came into view. Forestry lanes went off in all directions. She stayed on the paved road curving around isolated farmhouses. The trees abruptly closed in, and broom and dry bracken brushed the car as it passed. In one clearing two ponies grazed. No sign of Angus. A car came up behind and tailgated for a bit, then roared past, a young man scowling his displeasure at Rosalind's slow pace. She was having to concentrate every moment on keeping to the left, having the body of the car on her left side. Thank goodness she had learned how to drive a standard, but the gear shift was on the left side and often her right hand would unthinkingly bang against the door when she needed to shift gears.

After half an hour of dead ends and circles, she gave up, mind racing ahead to explanations. Rather than waste the trip, she considered exploring the beach, or driving down to the fishing villages south of St. Andrews, but she was too upset.

The road ended in a small picnic area. Overhead, the tall pines, with the gray sky beyond, created a dark, shadowless atmosphere. Rooks cawed from deep in the forest. She turned the car and headed back, starting to weep with disappointment. When she pulled over to blow her nose, something caught the edge of her vision, a flash of dark metal through the trees. She bumped down the grassy track, absurdly relieved to draw up beside Angus's old Land Rover. If it hadn't been there, she would never have found the site. As it was, she could see nothing beyond a deserted field carved out of the forest. She opened the door to the soft whisper of wind through the upper branches.

The earth in the open field had been tilled into ridges of stark furrows. At its edge, perhaps two hundred yards away, the plowed pattern made an oval detour around something, like raked gravel in a Japanese rock garden.

Rosalind skirted the field through the trees, stepping high over lumpy grass and bracken. The soft needles of feathery larches, yellow-gold with autumn color, caressed her. She came as close as possible to the plowed aberration without leaving the shelter of the forest. A large flat stone the same color as the soil lay beside a dark rent in the earth, fringed with wispy blond grass.

Had Angus not said the site consisted of a large cairn? Rosalind looked in all directions. The tall pines all around were actually a forestry plantation. It was disappointing to finally be in a Scottish forest, only to find it was artificial. Small mounds and hollows buckled the pine-needled earth, but did not break the trees' sentinel lines. Sets of a man's footprints made a trail from where she stood to the little chasm. She'd expected a roped-off, layered archaeological site, or at least some visible edifice.

She stepped in the troughs of the tilled soil to the carpet of grass surrounding the dark crevice. A gash of silver streaked the length of the upturned stone where the plow had caught it.

By going down on hands and knees to peer into the hole, she could see, about five feet below, a couple of rough stone steps. These led to a shallow chamber, but it was too dark to ascertain its size. As she peered into the hole, a glow formed in the blackness. Something moved.

"Rosalind! Hurrah!" boomed a deep voice.

She cried out and sat down hard.

Angus's handsome, bearded face appeared below. He held out his muddy hand and she took it. His eyes, glistening, were a little red.

"Are you all right?" she asked.

"Tears of joy, my lass. Tears of joy. Come, let me show you." His head descended into the earth.

"Wait. Stop. Where does it go? I can't go down there."

He shuffled his way back and materialized under her again. "Of course you can. I've spent hours clearing the entrance and putting in steps here, so you could get in. See the curve of the mound, right behind us? That's it. Come on. What do you Yanks say? Piece of cake." He disappeared.

"That's what?" Her desperate sight took in any number of mounds among the trees. "Angus? Wait."

His voice floated out, distant. "Not as bad as it looks."

"Oh, Lord." The forest wore a facade. Its depths were dark and sinister as the underground tomb. Only the tilled field seemed safe, subdued by the plow, under a steely sky. It was unnatural that the bright earth was deserted, while there were scrapings and movements in this black cavern. At the field's edge the car offered a last chance to return to the familiar.

She put her feet into the hole.

"Sorry, it's an awkward angle," he called, voice muffled. "Face the other way and it'll be easier."

Rosalind rolled to her stomach and lowered herself down, toes searching for the step. The grass shuddered under her chin. Her thighs felt vulnerable, exposed to the darkness. The wounded earth seemed to close over her head. When her feet touched after an eternity of groping, she sank to her heels and pivoted, looking wide-eyed over her shoulder. Stone touched her forehead. A sound escaped her throat. She would have to go down the slippery steps, set at an awkward angle, to be able to enter the cairn.

Rosalind's tennis shoes skidded across damp rock, and she careened into darkness.

After the violence, peace. A hard pillow – the bottom step – cradled Rosalind's head. Her thigh hurt where it had glanced off the stones, but she lay comfortably, looking between up-drawn knees into a dark cell. Her palms expected slimy, wet rock, but it was dry, almost a softness in the ancient floor.

The sudden cessation of wind left a deep silence but for faint echoes coming from within. The odor of damp earth was strong but not unpleasant. It brought to mind the good earth in Morning Star's garden.

Above, suspended over her body, a lintel stone stretched into the dark; immense, massive, a single clean rock of unimaginable weight suspended over her body. At the other end of the small section, a pale glow illuminated the opening to a larger chamber.

"Hey, Angus? I can't do this." Her head tilted back to see the circle of gray clouds. Better to get out before the panic overwhelmed her.

His deep voice murmured something. He re-entered the space, bent double. She quickly sat up.

"It's very secure," he said, slapping the wall. "It's been here four thousand years. It's not going to move now." He gestured behind him. "This is just a small adjacent section to the main chamber."

"Wait. Tell me again exactly what this is." Rosalind's voice thundered off the wall into her startled ears.

"A chambered cairn."

"Can you be more specific?"

"It's a tomb. Didn't I say? Probably built originally for a Neolithic community or family."

"Didn't you say there were no skeletons?"

He considered. "No. I meant what I found had nothing to do with the tomb."

"So, are there?"

"Aye, a few bones here and there. Nothing to get excited about."

Rosalind touched the lintel stone. The black hole through which she'd have to crawl yawned open like the gullet of a monstrous animal. "I've got a touch of claustrophobia, I think."

"You're so close. It's not so bad once you get into the central chamber."

She fought down extreme reluctance. "I'll try."

"Good lass. I'll be right here. I'm just adjusting the camera." He slipped out of sight.

When her back scraped the rock ceiling, she clenched her teeth but crawled into the earth, feeling the smooth walls. Her fingers encountered odd ridges and hollows, incised rings, with little round concavities set among them. Their oddity calmed her a bit.

"What's this?" she called. "This carved stone?"

His head ducked into the passage. "That's a rather typical cup-and-ring marked stone. Usually incorporated into Bronze Age monuments, but sometimes found on exposed surfaces of boulders or standing stones."

"But what is its purpose?"

"It's a haggis trap."

"Angus."

"Aye, they're very curious wee beasties, and they come to study the maze and get dizzy and fall over, and then they're much easier to catch. That's how these ancient people survived the harsh winters. They brewed beer and trapped haggis."

She started laughing then couldn't stop, belly tight, on hands and knees in the ancient cairn, all her nervousness spilling out.

"Come on," he called.

She moved forward, the field above now a fantasy. Her hands touched the rock framing the entrance to the chamber. Angus crouched against the far wall. It was a small room, perhaps six feet across. A lantern hung from one of the jutting stones that lined the sides. The corbelled walls curved in and up and were capped by another flat blue stone. Fallen stones and rubble littered the floor. Among it all Angus's modern paraphernalia looked jarringly foreign.

Rosalind crawled into the chamber and saw the skeletons, their disjointed bones as brown as the tilled earth. The skulls were flattened, part of the bones disintegrated. Broken pottery pieces and flint utensils lay beside them.

"It's all right," Angus said gently. "Come in." He beckoned. As if the tomb were his living room, he bustled about, bent over but still banging his head on the ceiling, removing papers, picking up his scattered things and clearing a flat stone. "Here. Sit on this and I'll pour some tea."

"I'm such a wimp." The mug of tea he offered from the flask was hot and sweet. "Thank you." She nodded at the bones. "I suppose you get used to that after a while."

"To what?"

"Human remains."

"Oh, well, but after millennia, what's a piece of bone? Assuming it survives in the first place." He knelt beside her and filled a plastic mug for himself. The cairn was so small they moved carefully between the bones, the hanging lantern, and each other's knees. "I'm not very sentimental when it comes to these things, Rosalind. I lack imagination. My work has more of the scientific about it than any capacity for recreating visions of history. It's a mistake to impose our way of thinking on ancient peoples. Inevitably it becomes romanticized and inaccurate." He stood again, as best he could, tea untasted. "Shall we proceed? You've no idea how difficult it's been for me to wait. This is a great moment."

Large flat stones covered a series of compartments along the base of the walls. Rosalind feared they were more burials and was relieved Angus had not begun excavating these. The overall feeling, sitting in the middle of the cairn, was like being in a child's imaginative stone house, a hollow sculpture, and if she could forget the idea of bodies interred in those little cubicles, almost pleasant.

Angus pointed. "Just to the left of the passageway where we entered. Do you see it?"

A collapsed group of flat stones, two medium sized still standing against the wall, spilled a little way onto the floor. The stones that were still incorporated looked loose, sloppy.

"It's not as well built as the others," Rosalind said.

"Exactly. It's a more recent facsimile." He went to the section and squatted by it. "We must be very careful. Would you bring the tripod here, with the light, and the camera?" He began lifting the fallen stones from the pile and placing them on the floor. Bending over to help, she saw a glint of metal.

"As I suspected," he said. "They're in a reliquary."

He moved a few more stones and rubble from the wall. Delicate splinters of wood and cloth fragments gave way to dull metal. Angus paused and looked at Rosalind. His eyes sparkled, his breath came faster. "Rosalind," he touched her arm, "I am so glad you are here to witness this. Ready?" Angus removed a piece and held it to the light. "Good. Coins. But surely not. It is. No. Yes, it is, I'm sure of it. Anglo-Saxon. And Celtic. Look at this one. There was a time the Celts copied Roman coins. This is of a chariot, though it's so abstract you have to look for the wheel, see?"

"It's beautiful," she said. "Is this the only one?"

"Just a moment. This must be done properly. But I can hardly wait!" Angus picked up a notebook and scrawled something in it. "How are you at taking photos? It's ready. Just focus and shoot."

The flash coated the metal for a moment, revealing pieces buried in the rubble, then orange spots danced against the stone. Angus was intent on his work. With exaggerated caution he removed little pieces of disintegrated casket, and placed them in plastic bags.

He half-stood, and reaching over to his pile of equipment pulled two flat wooden boxes from a leather case, which when opened revealed beds of a soft fabric on which he began placing the coins. "It's better than I imagined. Look."

He blew away a coating of dust and picked out bits of stone. Circles of gold appeared. He carefully lifted one. "Rosalind, my heart is pounding!"

She insinuated her hand between the buttons of his shirt and pressed her palm to his chest. "Don't have a heart attack, and leave me alone in a scary tomb, Angus," she laughed. "What is that piece?"

His voice was husky. "A penannular brooch, seventh century. Dear God. The flanges."

"Can I touch it?" Beasts intertwined into complicated patterns around its flattened circle of gold. Its pin was three times as long as the brooch it hooked to. "How does it work?"

"They put the pin through the cloth, then pressed it through the opening here, between the terminals, then twisted the circular bit to lock it in place."

"How clever. What's the other?"

"A torc. To go around the neck. Look at the detail on the knobs. These are solid gold, not plated bronze like you sometimes find. See the little brooches? They used them like buttons. A lovely chalice. A silver bowl."

"There's a spoon," Rosalind laughed.

"And a belt buckle. Look here." His voice failed him. He

licked his dry lips and spoke again. "A gold cross. It might be a pectoral cross. For a bishop, like the one we found at the Holy Trinity dig. But this one, I think it's..." he hesitated, then whispered, "gold. And a ruby in the center." He took a shuddering breath and carefully laid it in the box, then picked up a coin and studied it, turning it this way and that. "Ninth-century coinage."

"But you said thousands of years, then seventh century, then ninth? I'm confused."

"That's the really interesting part. I think the cairn was used by a local man, a monk? No, I don't think it's ecclesiastical, aside from the cross, but we're not done yet. A trader, a local wealthy family, or even a reiver, hiding his treasure for whatever reason. Invasion. Family quarrels. Tribal battle. We may never know. He – or they – must have thought it would be safe here. Even then the cairn might have been covered as it is now, probably sand blown up from the beach in storms. A hoard of gold and silver, just, just..."

His voice cracked. He pulled a crumpled handkerchief from his pocket, but instead of wiping his nose, moved the dust away from an engraved silver bowl. "Think of it. Lost. Until now."

"Suppose I stole this cross and sold it. What do you think I'd get?" Rosalind hefted the solid weight of it, the gold cross the length and breadth of her hand.

"What a devious little mind you have, Rosalind." He opened another lidded box and reverently placed the bowl in its lined interior. "Let's take a break. It's all too much."

They sat down and he jotted notes again. Then he closed the notebook and beamed at her. "I'm giddy," he said. "It's better than I could possibly have imagined."

"It's so old. So beautiful. It's incredible to touch something like this after hundreds of years."

"You know, it occurs to me, these artifacts need to be drawn by hand. Could you do that sort of thing? It would have to be very precise, exact measurements."

Rosalind hesitated. The truth was that she was starting to consider herself a painter on the rise, maybe even eventually taking her rightful place among the worthy and notable, making a smooth come-back from the years she felt cheated at having lost. Not an illustrator for a textbook.

"A good drawing brings out more than film does," he

explained. "There are professional illustrators, of course, for archaeological publications, but given what's about to happen with this hoard, I'm sure I could insist on my own illustrator. Just think of all the students pouring over your work. Would you be interested?"

She did not much care for the idea, and was slightly annoyed that he didn't appreciate her talents and aspirations. But she was in love, too. "Well, let me think about it. Maybe you can show me some examples."

Angus couldn't resist gazing at the treasure again. He lifted the box with the golden cross and studied it.

"All right, I'll admit it." Angus's voice changed. "I disappointed my father. He wanted me to follow him into the Kirk, to be a minister like himself. That's the only thing that matters to him. The thought of my being an academic, oh he was not pleased. What's worse, I've turned my back on God, and every time I see a bloody cross, I'm reminded that I'm a failure in my father's eyes, and as far as he's concerned, I'm doomed."

"Surely he doesn't believe that of his own son."

"All the better an example, his own son. He revels in misfortune." Angus shrugged. "Maybe he's right. Too much good luck is a bad thing, you know."

"Angus," she laughed, "have you lost your God but kept your superstitions?"

He scowled, then relaxed and shook his head. "What a mix of contradictions I am, eh?" He wiped a little dust from the face of the cross. "But you're right to inquire," he said. "About thievery. It certainly happens. There are professional treasure hunters out there happy to plunder tombs. As for archaeologists, rest assured temptation like this doesn't often manifest itself." His eyes half-closed as he stroked the gold cross. "If I sold it all for a fortune, would you come and live with me in Argentina?"

She laughed at the somber tone to his question. "But seriously, what do you do with a find like this? Where does it end up?"

"It ends up in a museum. On the way it's studied, analyzed, recorded, et cetera."

"Do you get anything for finding it?"

"Not money, not directly, if that's what you mean. Of course there is eventual publication, documentaries perhaps, talks and the like, and a better chance at a good position."

"So, if I were to sell it undercover to a museum, it would end up in the same place as if you did it by the book. But I'd be rich. In other words, dishonesty pays?"

"The choice is fame or cash. Can't have both." He was still for a moment, then shook his head. "I'm not smart enough to be a successful crook. I plod through life, with little to show for it. Until now. You've brought me good luck. The best." He squeezed her hand, eyes brimming over with emotion.

"Oh, no, not too much, I hope," she teased, then gently pulled her fingers away and sipped her tea. "Who do you think these two skeletons were?"

"I think it's a male and a female. Important persons, judging from the grave goods. But these Neolithic tombs were used over and again. Sometimes the original burial was moved aside, or even removed to make room for others. And you can see the additions along the original walls. Here, look." He picked up a smooth stone from the rubble. "This is a magnificent axe head. And I found a few pieces of simple jewelry, which I've already removed to the department to be classified."

"I'm beginning to understand how important this is," she said.

"Not frightened anymore?"

"No. To the contrary. This is really neat. I feel at ease, almost cozy."

"Rosalind."

He was gazing at her with what was becoming a familiar adoring look. Angus was so handsome yet so shy, completely self-possessed in his little empire of excavation, and so desirous of her.

After the first touch of lips, the kiss lingered. Their breathing came faster, his eyes closed and he kissed with more passion and hunger than ever before.

The axe-head slipped from his grasp. It hit the bones with a dull thud.

"Christ!" He ducked to frantically inspect the damage. "Oh! Bloody hell!"

Rosalind covered her mouth with a hand, waiting to know if a catastrophe had just occurred.

Angus looked up. His eyes squeezed shut and he put his forehead on her knee. His shoulders shook. Then his entire back. She placed a tentative palm on the thick curls of his head.

"Is it…damaged?"

He took a huge gulp of air and raised his head. At last the sounds rumbled out of him, a belly laugh that brought tears streaming into his beard. "Your face! Ah!"

Rosalind slumped with relief. "I thought you were crying!"

He battled for control, the laughs winding down into chuckles and sighs. "No harm done. You see the effect you have on me?"

They kissed again, Rosalind eager to feel the intoxicating softness of his lips, the warmth of his breath. A dizzying welter of emotions spiraled around the circular chamber. She drew a little away. "How old did you say the bones were?"

"Judging from their decay, the nature of the tomb, and the grave goods, I'd say late Neolithic, maybe 2500 B.C. These two on the floor I suspect are younger. I'd like to excavate the entire site, not that the farmer will cooperate."

The entrance through which they'd come, when she looked for it, had disappeared in the annoying glare of the lamp.

"Why is it shaped like this?" Rosalind asked.

"Back to the womb of the earth perhaps, to a god of death and rebirth? Your guess is as good as mine. You could take the compass in that bag and try to find an alignment of the entrance way. I think the way we came in is actually the original entry. Hard to tell just yet." Angus's head was bent once again over his treasure. "If it is, it will probably align to the southwest."

The lamp's light spent all its energy illuminating the treasure. She squatted in the dark entry. A turnabout had occurred. Rather than being eager to scramble out, she now preferred to stay in the chamber, with its treasure and Angus's preoccupied presence. The entrance, even with a pool of cold daylight, presented a gauntlet of danger. The slabs of rock were too close on all sides. She'd have to brush along that mysterious incised stone.

Her fingers slid down the wall, the flat Swiss compass in one hand clacking along the side. Then her knuckles dipped into a small hollow, and she stopped. She placed both hands against the incised stone, and traced the whorls and loops. Something familiar was there, hidden in the pattern. She leaned her cheek against it. From that angle the spirals and indentations filled her vision, the shadows deep in the light from the chamber. She'd go to the car and retrieve her sketchpad, and try to pull out some expression of this ineffable stone.

Four thousand years old. What hands made this? Smaller than hers? White, dark, female? Laughing? In a hurry, or squatting under the sun with a stone and chisel, gossiping. It was a trigger, a map of the stars. It was occult knowledge contained in what the fingers could feel, what the fist could fit into and roll along, the neuropathways of the universe, waiting.

"Was I right?" he called.

She touched her cheek to the soft stone, mouth open, nuzzling. How could such a remarkable edifice be hidden for so long? People had been living here all this time, but here was proof that even tangible things surviving millennia were forgotten.

"Is it southwest?"

"Just a minute," she murmured. "I dropped the compass."

The afternoon sun jarred her senses. It split the clouds and descended over the forest in a bright haze. She stood on the middle step, head above ground level. The glare on the compass rendered it indecipherable.

As she blinked and shielded her eyes, a muscular bare arm reached from within the passage for her thigh. Rosalind froze. Angus playing a joke? No. The arm was adorned with tattoos, from fingers to shoulder, of spirals and lines. Indecipherable Celtic patterns. Bright eyes in a savage face appeared in the darkness below.

She stumbled back against the wall of earth. The compass clattered down the steps.

There was nothing there. Nothing. It was the cup and ring incised stone, still lingering in her vision, imprinted on her retina against the brightness of the sky. Any artist worth her salt understood an after-image.

Yet it took all the courage she possessed to stoop down and pick up the compass.

"Any luck?" called Angus.

"Wait. What is wrong with this thing?" The needle would not lie still. Whenever she turned the compass to put north under the red line, it bobbed off into another direction.

"You do know how to work it?"

"Yes. It just won't cooperate."

Rosalind clambered out of the hole, not caring anymore how muddy her clothes had become, and stood straddling the passageway under the earth. "Now I've got it," she shouted into the black pit. "You're right, southwest."

Angus didn't hear. He was singing, his voice barely audible from the tomb, a distant, otherworldly hymn from his own past. A mighty fortress is our God, a bulwark never failing.

*

Kirsteen paused in the doorway to the restaurant.

"Don't you like the look of it?" Clive asked. When she didn't answer, he gently but firmly took her elbow and guided her in. "Come along, my dear."

They were seated by the window, where they looked out over the inn's sloping lawn in the early evening light, across the plowed field and to the distant spires of the town, the horizon bisected to the right by the dark line of the sea.

When their bottle of wine arrived and was duly swirled and tasted and approved by Clive, Kirsteen leaned forward over the table. "It's very posh." Her cleavage enticed in the low neck of her cardigan. She was oblivious to the perfection of her bosom, or its effect on him. Sweet innocence. "It must be very expensive."

"Not so bad," said Clive, raising his wine glass to a toast. "And anyway, why not? Don't we deserve it?" Her breasts were just large enough that his fingers would not be able to envelope them. Kirsteen was slightly plump with a girlish roundness to her soft cheek. Her lips were full and sensual, wanting tasting. The hips beneath her cardigan were rounded with the supple softness of a young woman's body that has not yet made the decision to develop into firmer muscle or soften into fat.

"I've lived here all my life," said Kirsteen, eyes shining from two drinks had previously in the adjacent pub.

Clive's mouth twitched at the thought of how long that could possibly be, but he merely smiled to encourage her. Warm bread was brought to the table by a discreet waiter. "Here," Clive shook out her napkin. "This goes in your lap."

"I was brought up in Anstruther, just down the road, but it would never enter our heads to come here."

"High time, then." Not that it was likely, but if anyone from Clive's social circles should show up at the quiet restaurant, he didn't care. He had plenty of transparent excuses. Courtesy would prohibit awkward questions, and he rather enjoyed the unspoken envy other men would be bound to harbor.

Candlelight glimmered in the panes of glass. The dining room was dark and romantic, a perfect setting.

"Oh," Kirsteen suddenly sat up straight. "I've to...." She was flustered, not sure how to express herself with him. "Will you excuse me?"

"Of course." He inclined his head. "Shall I order for us?"

"Be grand." She got up a tad unsteadily and walked back to the entrance hall, her forgotten napkin falling to the floor from her lap.

A perfect heart shape to her buttocks. Still toned and tight but with a welcoming softness, every part of her. He imagined her belly, the soft smoothness of it, imagined his hand trailing down to brush through the soft curls.

Clive took a deep breath and closed his eyes. This was far and away the best part. The pursuit, the game, the mastery. The inevitable conclusion.

She ate her dinner of steak with the gusto of youth, speaking excitedly of her life through mouthfuls. "Jane said, my pal Jane, said it was a better job in St. Andrews than in Kirkcaldy anyway, so that was fine. So I was able to stay here, with family close by, though I'm glad to have my own flat."

"Oh, yes," said Clive. "A young woman needs her own place, must cut the apron strings and become the unique young woman you are meant to be."

"Oh, aye, my pal Jane says exactly the same thing, mind you, she..."

"Would you like another glass of wine?"

"Oh, yes, I would. I never knew wine tasted so good. Oh, but I suppose I shouldn't. I've to be at work the morn wi' a clear head, ken?"

"One more won't hurt." He poured. Her East Neuk accent was growing stronger the more she imbibed, and her girlish chatter was becoming slightly annoying. Time to press on. "So. Kirsteen. Tell me. A pretty thing like you is bound to

208

have an army of admirers."

She giggled and looked down at the ravaged remnants of her dinner. "Nobody important," she mumbled.

"I find that hard to believe, a lovely girl such as yourself."

"Well," she confessed. "There is one."

"Only one? I thought there'd be twenty at least."

She laughed and slapped his forearm. "No! You're a caution! Only the one, Calum."

"And what does Calum do to deserve such a prize as the beautiful Kirsteen?"

"He's a baker, he works in the town."

"A baker. My." Clive took a sip of his wine and watched the disappointing realization dawn on her. "Will you have some dessert? Perhaps a dessert wine to taste with it."

She perked up. "That would be lovely."

Clive signaled for the waiter. "And is he very romantic, your Calum the baker?"

"Oh no, he's a big puppy, a daft laddie. A big galoot." She laughed, a gob of bread in her mouth.

Clive leaned toward the attentive waiter and gave his order for trifle and chocolate éclairs, with coffee and a sauterne of the chef's choosing. When he had gone, Clive sat back and studied Kirsteen. "And would you be content with that?"

"I'm not sure what you mean."

Oh, but she did. "You know there's more. Much more."

She became very still and studied him with round eyes. "Yes," she breathed.

He had her. He knew it then. He could play her like a trout in the undulating Tweed.

They pulled up in front of her refurbished council house that had been sectioned into flats. He turned the engine off and sat quietly. Kirsteen stared straight ahead through the windshield into the dark night, hands folded in her lap.

"Thank you," she began, unsure of the protocol.

He leaned to her, she turned her head toward him. The kiss from those sensual young lips was as delicious as he'd anticipated. The usual train of reactions happened in the kisses that followed, laughably predictable. First she was astonished and swept away that such a sophisticated man was actually kissing her. Until the touch of his lips, it was still an adolescent's fantasy which could go in any direction, but the kiss changed all the rules. Then she drew back a little in fear, as he transformed, his desire revealed. He tugged his tie loose. Encouragement murmured, whispers of endearment. Then after another tentative couple of kisses in which he held back, giving her time, it became delightfully obvious when she felt her own desire rise. She reached for him in wonder, shifting in her seat, gently pulled his head down, hungrily taking his mouth with hers. A neat transition from girl to woman.

And when he knew she was completely his, he disengaged and sat back, a hand on the steering wheel.

"Goodnight, Kirsteen," he said.

*

The High Priestess of the coven in Strathkinness abhorred publicity of any sort. It had not been but a little over two decades since the Witchcraft laws of persecution had been repealed in England, and the old precautions still affected this curious strain making its way north in various ways, secrecy being the norm. Not that anyone used the word 'witch,' if it could at all be avoided. Morag was well aware of all this, secrets gained from the young lover in the coven, and cared not a pin.

A lifetime of habit made her pause in front of the lovely old stone cottage on a side street in the small village, bow her head, feel the atmosphere and gather the magical threads in and about her to spin the caim of protection. When one entered a potentially adversarial situation, in particular one operating on the psychic level, some safeguard was never amiss. A slight shift in her perception however, in the ever-fluid conjoining of the worlds of matter and of non-matter, revealed that it was unnecessary. This was something new, another revelation following the plunge into the Deep Magic. Morag had become aligned to a multi-leveled expression of magic, and could no more be affected by psychic ill will than a lion would need fear from a mouse. She felt like a lion, completely in her element. Some of the Entourage of magical creatures had come along for the ride, literally on her shoulders, including the faithful wee kilmoullach. They had become such a part of her, she usually forgot they were there.

A plaque beside the unassuming door of the cottage boasted the Saltire Award for architectural renovation. Not to be wondered at, given that one of Gillespie and Forbes Architectural Firm's senior partners lived there, in the very house he'd renovated.

When Morag boldly knocked at the cottage door, Charlotte was not pleased.

"How dare you come here," she hissed. "Anyone could see you."

"Invite me in, then," said Morag.

"Well, get inside!" She shut the door decisively behind Morag. "Have you lost your mind coming here in broad daylight? What on earth do you want?"

"Is this any way to welcome a guest?"

A dainty snort came from Charlotte as she shouldered past and led the way into the living room, where two young women waited, listening, eyes cautious. "This is Janet and Sarah. Janet and Sarah, Morag Gilbride."

They recoiled slightly and glanced at Charlotte.

"If you must know," Charlotte said to Morag, "two of my priestesses."

"What a curious concept," said Morag absently, glancing around the room. "This house is absolutely beautiful!"

The interior had been completely gutted and redesigned, some walls and half the ceiling removed to create a light-filled, sparse but comfortable post-modern open concept. All the woodwork, but for the hardwood floor, had been painted a creamy white. The large stone–faced fireplace dominated the living room, illuminated by skylights above, and a carpet defined the sitting area of off-white, modern furniture.

"What are you, then?" demanded Sarah.

Morag looked Sarah up and down, and considered that she looked a very tempting morsel. Both young women were dressed in the English style of the day, the 'Yahs' as the University students called them, with oversized pullovers half-way down their thighs, over knit tights. "I would be hard pressed to say."

Charlotte eased into a throne-like upholstered chair and gestured to Morag to sit in a lesser version. No tea was offered, no social niceties. "Well?"

Straight and to the point. "Niall Paterson. He's been

intruding too much into my personal affairs. I intend to see to it that he leaves St. Andrews for good."

"And why, Morag, would we wish to be involved in this business?" Charlotte asked, sitting primly upright.

"Paterson has an agenda against our kind."

"Our kind?" Charlotte raised her eyebrows.

"His station gives him free reign. It's high time he was dealt with."

"You mean he has an agenda against you," offered Janet. The two young women sat on the elevated stone hearth of the fireplace.

"Let him cause me grief with no opposition, and you can guess where he'll turn his attentions next."

"Mind the threefold law you should, three times bad and three times good," offered Sarah, silenced by Charlotte's raised hand. She knew Morag would eat the youngster alive.

"I don't agree, Morag," said Charlotte. "I have no love for Paterson, but he has nothing to do with us, nor we with him. He doesn't even know we exist. And," she gave Morag a sharp look, "that's how it's going to remain."

"What are you insinuating?"

Janet and Sarah looked with wide eyes from Morag to their mistress and back again.

"Mischief follows you, Morag."

"True enough," she laughed, thinking of the prank she'd pulled on the coven only a few nights past at Dunino Den. The three women appeared nonplussed by Morag's mirth. "Give me the key to the town kirk's tower. That's all I want."

Charlotte looked surprised, then chortled. But her lassies didn't relax their vigilance. "You never cease to amaze me. And just how did you know I have it?"

"You were giving historic tours last month, for your husband's architects' fair, which included a look round the tower."

"And what will you do with the key?"

"Best you don't know."

"It will be traced back to us," said Sarah.

"No," Morag said. "Don't worry. You have my word."

Charlotte sat back and considered. "Equal exchange, Morag, tit for tat, or it's no deal. What will you give me?"

"Proof of Clive Forbes's embezzlement from your husband."

"What!" Charlotte rose to her feet.

"Well, from the architect's firm, to be precise."

"How do you know about that?"

Morag merely smiled. "Yes, or no, Charlotte?"

"You two," Charlotte gestured to the kitchen. "Go make us some tea."

They obediently left the room, their soft voices rising in the kitchen.

"This is a serious matter, Morag, very serious indeed."

"Indeed yes."

"The future of the firm, possibly of my husband's career, is at stake."

"I have my own reasons to see the firm survive. And for redressing the balance where Clive is concerned in my private affairs."

Charlotte sat back down, breathing hard. "What proof?"

"A copy of the financial records before they were altered three months ago."

Charlotte put her fingertips to her lips, head bowed in thought. When she looked up at Morag, her eyes were blazing. "The key is the least I can do."

"Then we are agreed."

The young women returned with a tray laden with teapot, cups and saucers, a sugar bowl and milk. Sarah placed it on the coffee table between the chairs, and leaned over to pour. She glanced up to see Morag's appraising eyes on her. The tea splashed over the rim of the cup.

"Do pay attention," murmured Charlotte.

"So," Morag took the proffered cup and settled back in the chair. "Tell me about your group, here, young priestesses and all. I'm very curious."

Charlotte smiled and raised a hand to settle the reactions from the young women. "It's all right," she said.

"But you know," Janet said, "we've had secrecy drummed into us from day one."

"And that's as it should be," said Charlotte. "Regardless, there are changes afoot. The mysteries must be respected and cherished, and yes, kept secret, yet now we have the chance to disseminate a little – just enough – information to put paid to some of the dreadful accusations we are heir to."

"Such as?" inquired Morag.

"Devil worshipping sex maniacs, that sort of thing."

"Ours," pronounced Sarah, "is a civilized and forward-looking path."

"At the present time," said Charlotte, "I am only aware of perhaps nine other covens in Scotland, of our particular lineage. Though one in Perth is hiving off others at an uncomfortably fast clip. There's been a bit of the inevitable bickering among the higher-ups, but regardless, David and I have been content to be practicing here for a good little while. I'm quite proud of my coven, and our new initiates. Interest is growing. I feel a new day dawning for the Craft of the Wise, and these young women, and more like them, will usher in a new age."

"How do you go about making magic?" asked Morag.

The young priestesses protested, but again, Charlotte held up an elegant hand. "There's no harm done in explaining our theories," she said. "Morag may be a Scottish country witch, but I believe our roots come from the same ancient source. We may even find we have much in common."

Morag politely said nothing.

"We focus an intention by raising psychic power, through movement or sound. Or simply by sitting in a circle and 'beaming' the vibrations to a transmitter. One of us, myself or David, act as a receiver, then as a transmitter, you see. The intention flies to its purpose through our will. It's really very scientific, if you think about it."

"Done within the context of ritual, of course," said Sarah. "In a circle conjured for purification within and protection without."

"From what?" asked Morag.

"Cast the circle thrice about to keep the evil spirits out."

"Evil spirits?" asked Morag.

"When one enters the psychic realm," explained Sarah, "there are many unknown influences which must be guarded against." She eyed Morag with a mix of accusation for her rumored black arts, and pity for her ignorance. "Though I must say, our High Priestess and High Priest are so powerful..."

Charlotte raised her hand to quiet the young woman, but her eyes gave away a false modesty. Not to be wondered at, if one believes one can create a conflagration from the ether.

"It is rumored that you sometimes are naked in your rites. How beautiful a sight that must be," Morag sighed.

The younger women drained their cups of tea, as Charlotte smiled.

"What about you?" asked Sarah.

"Go naked? If the occasion calls for it."

Morag had noticed that the Entourage loved food and drink. True to form, one of them hovered just above the table, at the sugar bowl. A small fistful of the crystals almost imperceptibly lifted up and disappeared. "Em, a circle conjured? Sometimes, though I prefer to go to the house of the gods in places that have existed from the most ancient times." Morag frowned at the greedy sprite to leave the sugar. As it stuffed its mouth again, she subtly flicked her hand to warn it away.

The three women displayed frozen smiles, and no-one spoke.

"We do share a common celebration coming up," said Charlotte eventually. "Halloween!"

"Oh, aye, we call it Samhuinn."

"There are Celtic aspects to the Wica," said Charlotte. "Our ways go right back to the Stone Age, before there were these tribal differences. I believe we have a common ancestry in the Old Religion."

"Who are your gods?" Morag asked, as the sugar spoon fell to the table.

"The Lord and the Lady. The Great Mother Goddess and her consort."

"Don't you," asked Janet, "worship the Lord and Lady?"

The creature had taken a fancy to Sarah's teacup, and was pushing and pulling on it. Morag had long since ceased to wonder at the motivation of the wee ones.

Slightly distracted, she considered her world of deities. "Scotland has her own gods," she said, "who live in their ancient homes. They travel on the wind, too, and in the storms and in the places where things are begotten and grow. Sometimes in animals."

She looked up from the subtle quaking of the teacup to see knit brows. "It's a large topic," she offered.

"More tea?" Janet reached for the teacup and just as her fingers came close, it upended and flipped over, trapping the sprite underneath. Janet jerked her hand away as if she'd been burned. She and Sarah shrieked and stumbled back, clutching each other.

"Oh do be careful," Charlotte snapped.

"Here, I'll just, em..." said Morag as she righted the tea cup and the wet sprite burst out, scolding.

"Telekinesis," Janet hissed in Sarah's ear.

"Do you have a towel?" Morag asked.

"Leave it, please!" said Charlotte.

"We both saw it," whispered Sarah.

"They're not very biddable," Morag said to the young women by way of apology, who stared wide-eyed back at her, brows creased, and breathing hard.

"You know, Morag" said Charlotte, "I quite like the idea of perhaps learning from one another."

Morag doubted there would be much in the way of real magic to be gleaned from this foreign group, who seemed very staid and rigid, but her purpose that morning, other than the tower key, had been to form an alliance. Despite herself, she appeared to have succeeded. "How shall we begin?"

Charlotte tapped her slender fingers on the armrest. "I should like very much to attend your Halloween gathering. With David."

After a stunned pause, Morag said, "Oh."

"Knowing what little I do of your rites, I suspect it will prove quite interesting."

The priestesses sat with mouths open. "It's far too risky," said Sarah. "On many counts."

Morag stilled herself. An unexpected door had just opened in the place where the worlds bisected, and a strong impulse to pave the way surprised her as much as the boldness of Charlotte's request.

"And likely to go against our Rede," said Janet.

"Probably," smiled Charlotte.

"Reed?" asked Morag, shaking the magical reverie out of her head.

"Eight words the Wican Rede fulfill; an ye harm none, do what ye will."

"I see I have lots to learn," said Morag.

"This is ludicrous," cried Janet. "They're dangerous. Who knows what they'd have you doing?"

"Or even that you'd be safe," chimed in Sarah. "It's all very well talking about things. Theirs is an old, superstitious, dark folklore." She spoke low and ominously.

"Will we be safe, Morag?"

"But they are right, Charlotte," said Morag. "We are followers of the Dark One, the Cailleach. The magic we enter into is not of our making, and one which no man can control."

Morag stood, and Charlotte followed suit.

"I will consider your request," Morag said. "There are conditions."

"Yes?"

"I would have to have a guarantee of your trust." Morag looked at Janet, who clutched Sarah's arm. "Perhaps a hostage."

"She's just joking, sillies. Or I hope so, anyway. David and I can assure you of our complete discretion and respect for your ways."

"Whatever we do, you must join in, wholeheartedly and without reservation."

"I understand."

"I normally would not even entertain the idea of outsiders joining us, but it so happens something unusual is afoot with this Samhuinn. However, I must bring this to the Elders for a final decision," said Morag.

"I thought you were the leader," said Charlotte.

"We are all on equal footing. The gathering takes place because it is the time of Cailleach. She calls us together. This gathering is so ancient, it goes far beyond the memory of our ancestors."

All were quiet for a moment. Charlotte spoke. "I apologize if I gave a bad impression. I want to say that I should feel very much privileged and grateful were David and I allowed to attend. Please convey this to your Elders."

"I will," said Morag. "And insofar as I am able, I promise no harm will befall you at my hands. More than that I cannot say."

Charlotte nodded. "That's fair."

The two young priestesses looked from Charlotte to Morag and back, puzzled. They would learn soon enough, as their mistress knew, that there was no worse enemy, but no better ally than Morag Gilbride. And even High Priestesses are too often starved for the ancient magic.

Chapter 16

"Oh," Heather exclaimed softly when Rosalind sat down. "That's Hamish's chair. I'm very sorry. Will you sit here?" She indicated the sofa along the wall.

"Oops." Rosalind hoisted herself from the deep armchair and demurely sat where she'd been instructed.

"There now," said Heather, much relieved. "All right?"

Angus had been standing silently at the window with Hamish during the gaffe.

"I'll just bring you some tea, Rosalind."

"We'll have a dram," said Hamish. The men moved to sit in the two plush chairs on either side of the coal fire. Hamish, a younger version of his brother, with the same untidy hair and beard, the same element-etched creases on every facial surface, lifted a pipe from the small mantel. Although their features were remarkably similar, where they had come together handsomely on Angus, they sat askew on his brother, the ear lobes too large, the lips too thin, the teeth crooked and stained.

"How's the fishing?" Angus asked.

"Not bad. Not bad. It's, eh..." Hamish pulled a crinkly envelope of tobacco from his pocket and opened it. "Overall, not the best year, but for me, not bad at all." He sucked on the pipe and squinted down the stem as if it were a pistol. "These days it boils down to luck, and some people know how to court it and others don't."

Angus crossed his legs and cleared his throat.

Plump Heather hurried back in with two tumblers on a tray, half-filled with golden liquid. "There you are. The water o' life." She offered one to Angus, who said his thanks, and the other to Hamish, who pointed the stem of his pipe at his brother.

"Have you heard from Father?"

As Heather passed Rosalind she whispered, "The kettle's just boiled."

"No," said Angus. "I sent him clippings from the paper, but I've had no word back."

Hamish thought. "Oh aye, that business with the cairn."

"Well, it is rather important."

"I'm sure. Cheers," said Hamish. They lifted their glasses to one another. Angus glanced at Rosalind, apologetic. He opened his briefcase and took out the Scotsman newspaper. On the bottom of the front page was a photo of himself at the site of the cairn in Tentsmuir, with a short article on the treasure trove. He handed it to Hamish, who glanced at it. "You're needing a haircut."

The sofa had the advantage of a good view of Pittenweem harbor. Across the street the masts of the boats, their heavy cables taut between poles adorned with nautical instruments, swayed in a gentle rising and falling of the invisible water below the quay.

The MacLeod house was situated at the end of a row of similar homes fronting the harbor. They were centuries old, harled stone buildings, historic plaques displayed on a wall here and there. A motorboat chugged through a passageway between two piers, into the calm inner harbor. The outer, curving seawall, the far boundary of a second harbor, threw a protective shield between the active sea and the calm waters the boats bobbed on. Lobster traps and nets, crates and barrels piled high on the stone pier, suggested an active fishing village, much busier than St. Andrews' small harbor. Beyond it all the sea rose to the thin horizon, into a sky as gray as the water.

Heather alighted next to Rosalind with a cup of tea.

"Thank you."

"So how are you liking Scotland?"

"It's different from what I expected, but I definitely like Scotland."

"I heard you're Captain Ogilvy's niece."

"That's right."

Hamish began to stuff tobacco into his pipe with a yellowed thumb. "Does he not..." Hamish put a lit match to the pipe's bowl and sucked. A puff of smoke escaped his lips, then another, then another before he tossed the match into the fire and finished the sentence, the group of three a captive audience politely waiting. "...have a boat at St. Andrews?"

Rosalind rested the cup and saucer on her knees. "Yes, he does."

"Sailing boat? *The Reiver*."

"Yes. We just saw it the other night."

Angus sat quietly, with an affable, slightly puzzled air.

For the first time Hamish really looked at Rosalind. The shipping forecast cackled and droned from the kitchen radio. Hamish raised his pipe in the air for silence when his area was mentioned, and everyone acquiesced. There was no doubt Hamish was king of his castle.

Hamish took up his glass. "Here's to Captain Robert Ogilvy. And *The Reiver*. He's a good skipper, he understands the ways of the sea."

"Captain Ogilvy," smiled Angus, oblivious.

"More whisky, Heather."

"They'll be dancing a jig here in a wee bit," Heather winked at Rosalind as she left for the kitchen. Hamish's singsong Highland accent was not difficult to understand, but Heather's east coast tongue took more concentration.

"Put off the wireless," Hamish called. He waved his pipe at the window. "Did you hear about Ian Robertson, lost at sea twelve weeks past?"

"Aye, I remember," said Angus. "Why?"

"But do you remember the details?"

"No."

Heather put her head around the door, heard what her husband was talking about, and nodded sadly.

"Is this a local family?" Rosalind asked.

Hamish stared at Rosalind as if he'd forgotten she was there. "Ainster."

"Just up the road," Angus explained.

"Hamish will never be considered anything but an outsider," Heather called from the kitchen, "even though he's been here twenty years and married me."

"But that's not the point of what I'm saying." Hamish leaned his elbows on his knees to come closer to Angus. "Young Ian took the watch at two a.m., while his brother – you remember him – Tom – and Tom's engineer slept below."

"Aye, aye," said Angus.

"Do you no mind the story?"

"No. Three months past? I was working in Glasgow."

"Well," said Hamish. "This is what happened. Tom doesn't usually sleep well on the boat, he keeps an ear open for the propeller, you know. Or sometimes they'd go up for a fag on deck, as Tom doesn't allow smoking in the bunks. But that night they both slept soundly. Ian should have called the next watch at four a.m., but he never did, and also – this is the strange bit – they slept in till after eight. All night till eight."

"It's tiring work, certainly," Angus suggested.

"There's more to it than that. When Tom awoke, the deck and wheelhouse were deserted. The boat was fishing on autopilot. Ian had vanished."

"Vanished?" said Angus.

"Aye but listen. All they can think is a trawl wire snagged across the stern as the boat changed course. Maybe it caught Ian, but he's done it hundreds of times."

"Done what?" Rosalind asked.

Hamish blinked at her. "Em, waited for the roll of the boat to slacken the wire, then lifted it clear. The gloves he'd have worn to do it were missing. Tom let go the gear to save time and shouted up the other boats in the area and called the coast guard. No sign of the boy."

"A terrible shame," said Angus.

"Tom's been having bad luck."

"It doesn't get worse than that."

"But that's not the end of it."

"How?"

"There's nobody pays you for lying in harbor, whatever's happened."

"No."

"Tom told me he'd a feeling about it when they went out later for the nets, isn't that right, Heather? Didn't I say?"

"Aye, you did," she called.

"When they went out, twelve weeks to the very day -" Hamish punctuated his words with jabs of his pipe – "to the very same morning watch, that's when it happened."

"What?"

"Ian came up in the nets." Hamish sat back, grim-faced.

"Good God," Rosalind said.

"That's right," said Heather from the kitchen.

"Think of the lad rolling around down there," said Hamish. "All that time. The sea is not kind to human flesh."

"It's shocking," said Angus. "It's a terrible tragedy." He knocked back the last of his whisky. "And that's all it is."

"Then you just explain the coincidences to me. And how they slept like that, a thing that's never, never happened before in all Tom's life."

"And when the minister," Heather put a defiant fist on hip and stood half through the doorway, "blesses the fleet at the gala, does that count for nothing?"

"Away to your kitchen, woman!"

Two teenage boys came through the front door with fishing rods and a bucket. A ruckus carried on in the hallway, with a shaking off of wellies and hanging up of jackets, and soft dialogue in their gentle lilting voices. They came through the door, shyness abruptly silencing them, cheeks glowing from cold sea air, their mops of curly brown hair lending a younger appearance than Rosalind expected they were.

Heather came back from the kitchen. "Oh, you're a' glaur," she cried, and introduced them as Jamie and Duncan. "Awa' and gie yer faces a dicht!" Heather shooed them out and invited Rosalind, who fortunately understood the request, if little else, to come and speak to her as she worked in the kitchen.

"She's bonny," one of the boys said from the back of the house.

"You have beautiful children," Rosalind said. "You must be proud of them."

"Oh, aye," Heather beamed. "They're good lads. They help their father with the fishing during the holidays. I don't know how we'd manage without them. But oh God, if one of them was taken like poor Ian."

"Do they like fishing?"

"Well, I've never asked. It's no an easy life. Himself," she cocked her head in the direction of the living room, "goes away out to sea for the prawns and whitefish. He could catch lobster and crabs close to shore, but he got a sixty-five-foot trawler from his grandfather – his father's a minister, you see, away on Skye – and the trawler's better, though he's away longer. We've had some close calls with the weather, but somebody up there keeps an eye on him. I hope you like fish, that's what we're having for our tea."

"Sounds great. Can I help?"

"No, no. Everything's ready."

The men's voices rose in argument. Hamish appeared to be making a case for the proper propitiation, something lacking in the Robertson's sad tale.

"Did Hamish ever consider becoming a minister like his father?" Rosalind asked.

"Oh, no." She laughed. "Imagine him! He's a born fisherman. He understands the sea." She looked out the kitchen window into the murky light. Then she raised her hands and laughed again. "Och, I'm just as glad. Imagine me a minister's wee wifie, and the Church of Scotland? We were raised Catholics, my family."

"Does Hamish go to your church?"

"No." Heather looked sad. "But he's allowed me to raise the boys in the faith."

"Ah."

"I've got some smokies for you to take back." She lifted two leathery fish by a piece of string tied around their tails. Their eye sockets were empty; the flesh peeking out from their slit bellies was bright yellow. "Arbroath smokies. They're the best."

"Thank you. How do you cook them?"

"I like to poach them in milk. Then they're no sae salty."

"Heather!" Hamish called from the living room.

"They'll be wanting another whisky." She wrapped the fish in paper and hurried out to the men. Then back again, to lift the top off a pot on the stove and check whatever bubbled beneath its steam.

"So," she glanced up from her stirring, "is our Angus going to be famous, then?"

"Yes, his lucky break. Have you had a chance to see the treasure?"

"Och, no. I'm pleased for Angus, it's important for him of course, but we're not really keen on all that old history."

Hamish called. "We're just going down to see the boat."

The men paused at the door. Angus smiled for Rosalind.

"Can I come?" she asked. "I'd love to see your boat. Do you mind?" she asked Heather.

"Away ye go," cried Heather, granting permission. "Just don't set foot on the deck."

"Bad luck," Angus explained.

"Because I'm a foreigner?"

He smiled. "Because you're a woman."

"Here!" Heather called. "Your tea will be ready in twenty minutes." To Rosalind she said, "They say you need a lang spoon tae sup wi' a Fifer."

"We'll not be long," said Hamish.

"What did she mean?" Rosalind asked Angus.

"Ah, Heather's full of couthy wee sayings. It means that Fife natives are... how to say... parsimonious."

They had only to step outside and cross the street to be on the quay, looking down at the squat fishing boats jostling each other gently in the rising tide. An oily fuel leak ringed one of the vessels.

"Some of the boats were damaged in the last storm," Hamish said.

"But not yours," Angus finished the unspoken thought.

A dark creature broke the surface in the middle of the harbor, black and glossy, rolling a sleek hump over the surface.

"There's a seal," Rosalind pointed.

"No, no. There's no seals in the harbor," said Hamish. The round head appeared again, and the huge body glided through the water, then went under. "Christ. 'Tis. Think of that. Must be after the fish."

Hamish, followed by Angus, climbed down iron rungs set in the harbor wall, and jumped onto the wide deck of a substantial fishing boat. Tall support beams of heavy pipe canopied over the wheelhouse, and another beam with winches and pulleys pointed away over the stern. Bright orange nets were rolled up among cans and balloon-shaped buoys. Coils of rope covered much of the prow. The boat was painted a medium blue, as many of the Pittenweem boats were, the bridge and deck white. The colors, the stone and the water imparted the flavor of a Greek island's harbor.

Angus looked up at her. "Far as you go. Sorry. Have a look at the Gyles, the houses I told you about."

Rosalind looked over the pier at the buildings, white-harled three and four story cottages of obvious antiquity, where the outer pier joined the shore. Enticing subjects for a painting, with distinctive Scottish crow-step gables and red tiled roofs above the sheet of water and harbor wall and boats.

Below on the deck, Hamish opened the door for Angus to step through into the wheelhouse. Rosalind strolled along the quay, which was permeated by the smell of slightly decayed fish. The two men were visible through the windows and easily overheard as Hamish explained a radar device to Angus. Thick sweaters and rain gear lay neatly stowed in an open locker. And at the window over the bow hung a fairly large wire-wrapped crystal.

Angus saw it too. "It isn't what you believe or don't believe," he said. "It's that you give her so much of your earnings, like a tithe. I mean, all that hard work, and..."

Hamish jabbed a stiff finger at Angus. "Don't you be

lecturing me about hard work and what I do with my earnings. If it weren't for her, I'd have no earnings at all, aye, after that coarse year we went under. And I'm telling you," he poked his brother's chest, "there's nothing so foolish as crossing her."

"Oh, Christ, I can't believe you said that. Take that ridiculous charm and throw it into the sea. What would our father say? A grown man believing in fairy tales, and paying for it! He maybe thinks little enough of me, but this absurd superstition? You could have saved hundreds of pounds by now."

Angus reached for the crystal. Hamish hit his arm down and shoved him away.

Rosalind crossed the street to leave the brothers to their fight, and re-entered the house, to find Heather smoking a cigarette beside the fire.

"Are they quarreling again? Ach, leave them. They're like wee boys. Always fighting over that Morag in St. Andrews."

"How do you feel about her?"

"Will you take a lager or a sherry? Well, as I say, Hamish does better than almost everybody. I've spoken to my priest about it, but Hamish would never go and see him. Still, he doesn't tell me how to cook his tea, and I don't tell him how to fish. He's a good husband, a good provider."

"I wonder why Angus gets so upset about it?"

"Oh, now Angus, that's another matter. I think he fancies her but won't admit it to himself."

"Morag Gilbride?"

"Him and every other man in Fife. Oh, dinnae fash yersel'. You're every bit as bonny and much pleasanter company, I can tell you. She frightens me. I don't agree with Hamish going to see her, but some of these men, they know things out there on the sea we forget. As I say, it's not my business. No, I shouldn't have spoken. Angus just feels what most men feel around her, but it's nothing to do with reality, ye ken. She doesn't care a pin for him! Don't you be worrying. It's you my brother-in-law is in love with. Sure as death."

*

Angus seemed preoccupied on the short drive back to St.

Andrews, but accepted her invitation to come in. She doubted it would be difficult to bring his attention back to their romantic progress, which was certainly filling her every moment. Now, alone after the somewhat awkward socializing and brothers' quarrel, she thought it an excellent time to take things up a notch.

They took their coats off in the hallway. She pulled him by the hand up the stairs. He hesitated, but she attributed it to shyness, and brought him into the small living room. It was nowhere near as classy as Morag's, but at least it was now clean and neat. Helen's advice – ought one to grasp the nettle – mingled in her mind with Heather's words, "It's you he's in love with." That, combined with the gentle wooing Angus had been lavishing on her, all came together in a perfect romantic symphony of sweet expectations.

She guided him to the sofa, sat him down, and playfully straddled his lap.

"Rosalind, hold on," he began, "I'm not..."

She bent her head to kiss him, and he received the kisses yet displayed none of the enthusiasm he'd shown before.

She pulled away. "Are you all right?"

"I'm fine." His hands remained on the sofa.

She went back to kissing, to stroking his hair and chin to better guide his mouth to hers. She was eager for some serious sensuality, her lips and tongue relaxed, eyes dreamy. It was the first time the excitement of their romantic interaction was moving into a compelling arousal, and the timing was perfect to take things a step further. She pressed against his thigh, delighted, after such a dearth of physical sexual expression, to feel how aroused she already was. She began to undo the top buttons of his shirt, sliding her fingers down the warm skin.

His hand clamped down on hers. She looked up in surprise to see the glitter of anger, and – was it possible? – an expression of stern disapproval.

Rosalind was so taken aback, she couldn't speak as he firmly removed her from his lap, stood and went to the door in a chilling calm.

"What just happened?" she asked.

"We are both tired, I think." He left the room. In a few seconds she heard the front door close decisively behind him.

Chapter 17

Rosalind lay on her back in bed, staring at the exposed beams of the rafters and the creamy plaster between the wood, with tired, aching eyes. Her thoughts circled back to every interaction she'd ever had with Angus, down to the Neolithic tomb, mulling over what forces had been set in motion over the past few weeks. His sudden change in demeanor baffled her. He'd acted as if she'd deeply offended him. But how? What was different? It felt as if she'd crossed a line she didn't know existed.

So low did her spirits plummet, swinging from fear to anger to anxiety as her mind picked over every nuance in their speech and action that she realized in hindsight what a high she'd been building up to.

Her old sensibilities crashed back in. She'd been concerned about making a fool of herself, and now she had, though it was still not clear exactly how. She'd been chasing a silly romantic fantasy which he obviously did not share. Yet he'd been the one making all the advances, the dates, the treats and even the kisses, so she must be wrong. She could swear his reaction was to the sexual aspect, but couldn't figure out why. Maybe he was upset by the fight with his brother. Yes, that must be it. She was so self-centered, just plowing ahead with what she wanted, she never noticed how upset he must have been, then pushed him beyond where he wanted to go. And yet. Morag's warning entered her thoughts, about his Calvinist attitude, but she had no context for understanding what that meant.

And then she thought of all the heartfelt romantic moments they had shared. She must be mistaken. Angus had become a continuous, happy presence in her musings. She constantly thought of the wonderful things they'd done, the incomparable romantic settings, while casting her hopes ahead for the next exciting meeting.

She'd forgotten the power of love and infatuation. She'd also forgotten the depths to which one could plummet over the smallest things. She groaned and rolled over, hands clamped between her thighs. Never had the erotic taken possession of her like this before. It was almost unbearable. She threw the sheet aside and padded to the window, then spun on her heel and paced the small room, till the cold drove her back under the covers.

All right, she resolved, tired of this ridiculous bewilderment. It was a strange country where strange opportunities were flying at her from every direction. She would talk to Angus tomorrow, figure out what happened, and make a decision as to how to proceed. Should she let him phone, or give him until the evening? How best to convey her disappointment without appearing clingy or letting her anger out?

"God," she said. "I'm acting like a teenager."

Her time in Scotland was slipping past like lightning. She resolved to try to gratefully accept whatever was offered her in the short time remaining, doing her best to deal with her Uncle's death, and savoring what was indisputably one of the biggest adventures of her life.

And right now, the sensual feel of sheets and warmth over her entire body was exquisite, begging to be noticed. For the first time in her life, Rosalind had taken to sleeping nude. Why had she not done this before? Having a young son in the house required modesty, but she even did it in the privacy of her own bed, since Henry was not comfortable with nudity in general. She slowly moved her hands over her breasts, down her belly and thighs, eliciting another sigh of pleasure. She'd been living in this body for more than forty years and previously seen it only as something to fight against or criticize. Why not savor pleasure for a change? Perhaps Morag was right, perhaps creativity was freed and enhanced by sensuality. Maybe this was the way to get out of her censoring, critical head and into the flow of creation, for the sake of her art.

*

A low laugh came from outside. It sounded as if it were at the bedroom window, which was absurd, since it was three stories above the garden. Rosalind slid out of the bed again and padded to the window, pulling aside the curtains. Dark clouds scudded across the waxing moon's face and a silver blanket of light covered the town. She blinked and searched the gardens below, and was not surprised to see Morag in her garden, a cloak of some sort tossed dramatically over her shoulders.

Morag turned to look directly up at Rosalind. She made a motion of lifting, signaling Rosalind to open the window. The old wood stuck, then the window came up and cool night air flowed over Rosalind's arms and breasts, reminding her she was naked. She squatted down, forearms on the sill, and put her head out the window.

"Come down," Morag said softly, but in a low voice that easily carried.

"It's past my bedtime," Rosalind said.

"Ach, come on. Come join me in a real ritual."

"And why would I want to do that?"

"Because you may never have the chance again?"

She dropped her forehead to the window sill. This was far too bizarre for her to seriously consider. So much for her lofty aspirations to experience whatever came her way. She looked down at Morag, who was waiting patiently, and wondered what bad thing could possibly happen. The answer was, she had no idea whatsoever. Go down, or go back to her bed, back to her overwhelming sexual frustration and mentally bewildered and disturbed mindset. "I'll get dressed."

"You are dressed perfectly," said Morag. "Come through the gate in the garden."

"What gate?"

Rosalind put on her white bath robe from the brass hook on the bedroom door, and belted it tight as she descended the stairs to the back door.

Morag's broadsword cleaved through the gooseberry bush and rosemary. The old ironwork on the solid wooden gate needed a great deal of coaxing to loosen its grip, which it had held for half a century. Timid rustlings came from the far side.

"Can you work the bolt free?" Morag called.

"My God, there's a gate here!"

"Twist it up and back, hopefully we won't need oil."

"It's so overgrown back here I would never have known."

Iron creaked and screeched as it slid. The gate was caught fast between the earth below and settled lintel stone above.

"Push," Morag said.

It came an inch. Morag insinuated fingers around the old wood, braced a foot against the wall and heaved it open. A fan of loam appeared under the sweep of its base and it came about two feet, enough to see the wondering Rosalind in her white dressing gown.

"Come through." Morag held a hand into the threshold.

Rosalind took the hand in a tentative grip and stepped gingerly through, from chaos into order. "Was the gate never used?"

"Not in my lifetime. I'm afraid some of your ancestors were a wee bit leery of what went on, on this side."

"Did they have a good reason?"

"I'll let you be the judge of that." Morag went to the small lawn in the garden, where the trees did not obscure the moon, and rested both hands on the basket hilt of the broadsword, its tip to the earth. The grass was soft and cold. Her cloak was tartan, draped under one arm and fastened at the shoulder with a silver brooch, the same ring and pin type Rosalind had seen in the Neolithic cairn's treasure.

"What's going to happen?"

"One never knows. The best one can hope for is revelation; the least, nothing but pretty words."

Rosalind felt edgy but let Morag take her hand again. They stood side by side facing the moon's glow behind the clouds. The shadows in the garden were pools of darkness that deepened or lightened as the clouds sailed across the night sky.

"This is an old poem from the Gaelic I like to use." Morag tilted her head back, her long dark hair swaying across her shoulders. "Daughter of heaven, fair art thou. Thou comest forth in loveliness, the stars attend thy blue course in the east. The clouds rejoice in thy presence O moon! They brighten their dark-brown sides."

Her voice was low but she enunciated every syllable with pleasure. Still holding Rosalind's hand with her left, she lifted the sword in her other hand as if saluting the moon.

"Burst the cloud, O wind, that the daughter of night may look forth! That the shaggy mountains may brighten and the ocean roll its white waves in light." She tilted the blade of the basket hilt this way and that, sighting down the steel. The clouds broke and the moon's radiance flashed on the blade as if collected in it.

Rosalind blinked, her vision riven by streaks of light. Morag's eyes closed and her grip on Rosalind's hand tightened. She started to breathe with deep, measured inhalations. Her hand suddenly became hot, pulsing, and from the hand Rosalind felt the tingling rise through her arm to fill her body. She savored the curious sensation, at the same time wondering how it was happening. Her body felt buoyant, alive.

Morag let the sword's tip fall back to the earth. Her profile, eyes closed, was stunningly beautiful in the moon's glow. She lolled her head over her left shoulder and opened her eyes to stare straight at Rosalind. Her face had changed to something Rosalind had not seen before, the face of a creature that is entirely self-possessed, calm yet perfectly attentive.

Without a word Morag led Rosalind to the back door and into the house. She placed the sword, its blade now almost invisibly dark, in a corner of the kitchen, and ascended the stairs to the living room. The chairs had been pushed back from the fireplace, and candles lit on every surface. The venerable old room with its exposed wooden beams and low ceiling, lit by candle and fire, was truly enchanting, as was its resident witch, who moved through it with animal grace.

Morag put her hands out as if testing the air. She slowly pivoted in a complete circle, eyes half-closed, face relaxed but concentrating. There was a hush, a stillness as of something waiting in the chamber.

"Rosalind," Morag said.

"Yes?"

"How do you feel?"

"I feel great. And scared."

Morag's speech had changed with her demeanor, to an even-toned murmur. Out the window, its curtains drawn back, the moon appeared like a gray sliced disk as the heavy clouds blew across its face, then flashed into brilliance in their fleeting spaces.

Inexplicably, the hair on the nape of Rosalind's neck and arms lifted. Morag made another strange movement, as if enticing something to rise up her thighs and torso. When her hands reached her heart, she opened and spread them to the side. Rosalind felt a draft of warm air move around her bare calves, a prickly warmth spreading over her entire body underneath the robe. She closed her eyes and felt it flow through her. Then she found its source. It was undeniably the very crucible of the pervasive sexual feelings. Her eyes flashed open.

"Good lass," Morag murmured. "Let it happen."

The portcullis of caution readied itself to descend. This was so intense a feeling as to be all-consuming, overwhelming her ever-vigilant control.

"What are we..." Rosalind began.

Morag held up a hand. "We'll do only as we are moved to do." She stood quietly. "And I will do nothing without your permission."

"All right," Rosalind said slowly.

"The way is found through desire. Do you understand?"

"No. I'm sorry, I don't."

Morag searched for an analogy. "Like Tantric sacred sexual techniques, yes, like that."

"You are giving me way too much credit, Morag."

"You're joking."

Rosalind spread her hands haplessly.

"May I touch you?" Morag asked. "Show you? It's not a time to discuss things, but to experience them."

"Maybe I should go home."

"I can shift the magic into another current if you wish. Not an erotic one. It's a shame, as this one is beckoning very strongly. But it makes no difference ultimately."

Rosalind wavered. "I'm afraid."

"This may surprise you, but I am as well."

"Why?"

"I'm not controlling this magic. Nor your destiny, nor choices, nor mine. I've no idea where it will go."

"I'll mess it all up."

"Please stop or we'll not accomplish anything."

"Is sex part of this ritual?"

"I hope so."

"But I don't know what to do. Or if I should."

"All you have to do is want and be present."

A mighty internal struggle physically rocked her body with pounding heartbeats. Rosalind closed her eyes and took a deep breath. A mental crossroads appeared again. Stop and go home, or stay and yield to the moment. She reigned in her thoughts as they tried to take off on the typical route of sensibly weighing all the pros and cons before inevitably choosing the conservative path. Instead, she made a conscious effort to turn her awareness inward to find the answer. There was no doubt there. All the sexual heat that had been building up so inexplicably over the past weeks erupted into a fire that filled every part of her. Yet there was one more thing that had to be clarified even in this sexual maelstrom. "I want to know that whatever happens, it stays in this room."

"That is a given. You have my word."

At last Rosalind could surrender to herself. "Yes," she whispered. "All right."

Morag came close and brushed her lips down Rosalind's neck, to find the pulse of her heart, which leapt wildly. Rosalind started to step back, then held her ground. Morag's proximity was overpowering, her gentle touch electrifying, turning the erotic counter higher degree by degree. Her breath was sweet, her skin fragrant, and her beautiful face was so close.

"What are you moved to do?" Morag asked. "What is in your heart?"

In a second, Rosalind forgot herself, her past, everything, and let the plunge into the ocean of sensuality happen. There was nothing she would rather do than kiss the witch, than feel those hands on her flesh. In a near-swoon, she drew Morag's head closer and kissed her soft lips. She pulled back and tried to catch her breath, then kissed her again, surprised to feel the woman trembling. Morag's mouth was hot, velvety. Rosalind trailed her fingers, hyper-sensitive, up Morag's arms, feeling the soft skin over the hard muscle, the fine hairs along the forearm.

Morag unloosened the belt of Rosalind's robe and slipped her hands inside, slowly touching along her ribs to her breasts, and closed her eyes with a sharp intake of breath. Rosalind groaned in a mix of sensuality and surprise to feel the sexual warmth radiating from the touch, another new realization. It was as if she'd been sectioned before, partitioned, not the integrated body she had apparently become.

Morag slipped the robe off Rosalind's shoulders and let it fall to the carpet. For a moment Rosalind felt the old shame and vulnerability. Morag untwisted the penannular brooch at her own shoulder and shrugged off her cloak. She was naked underneath. They paused to savor the sight of each other, Rosalind entranced by the curve of waist, the dark hair against white muscled hips, the weight of breast over ribs. She gave over to the beauty in Morag and stopped thinking of her own fears. When their bodies touched in an embrace, breast, belly, and thigh, it was foreign, shocking, enticing. Morag's soft breath came in sighs as Rosalind began to caress and explore the athletic body in her arms.

The room pulsed with sexual energy, candle flames ringed by a dancing penumbral glow. The same luminosity surrounded their bodies, the tingling space around expanded and filled the room in a delicious haze of lazy, swirling energy. Rosalind drifted through a sensual sea. Morag's hands and mouth conjured waves of sensations that flooded her, and she completely surrendered. When Rosalind touched Morag's body with abandon and wonder, it was as if she were touching a mirror image of herself, and what echoed in her own body equaled the pleasure Morag was obviously receiving. Every touch and kiss was exquisite in itself, and neither wished to push on past the wonder of the present.

Morag whispered something, but Rosalind was so far gone, marveling at the new sensations, she was not immediately aware that Morag had spoken. She'd forgotten that the reason they were together, ostensibly, was for some mysterious ritual. The witch coaxed Rosalind down to the carpeted floor. She sat with her back against one of the chairs, and held out her arms for Rosalind to sit in the curve of her body, with her back to Morag's belly and breasts. Her head lolled on Morag's shoulder, so that both sat facing the fire, Rosalind cradled in Morag's arms, her thighs open and resting between Morag's legs.

The heat of the fire entered Rosalind's body. Morag's fingers brushed over her skin and through the flaring energy of each part. Rosalind turned her head to kiss Morag, struggling to keep her mouth pressed there, until breath became sound and sound became movement, and she turned away in abandon.

Morag's husky voice spoke in her ear. "Open to Her." Her hands lightly traveled down Rosalind's inner thighs and slowly gathered and enticed all sensation to focus there. Ecstatic awareness expanded to fill Rosalind's senses in an explosion of pure sexuality.

She gradually became aware of another presence in the room. Rosalind blinked to clear her hazy vision, suspended in an ecstasy that would not cease. An elusive dark figure stood before them, slightly blocking the fire.

The figure seemed appropriate, as if their passion had knit together its own identity, projected in some way to stand apart from them.

"Ah." Morag gave a sound of recognition.

For an indefinite, unfocused time Rosalind accepted the new presence. She could shut her eyes in the ecstasy and consider it a manifestation of the rapturous dream-like state, and she certainly had no wish to break the trance. But slowly her rational mind grasped the impossibility of what was occurring. She opened her eyes to see the figure, more apparent than before, resplendent before the fire. Acceptance turned abruptly to cold fear. She willed the incomprehensible to disappear, insisted on it, and still the figure stood. It was like being caught in a childhood nightmare, when the scary monster in the bedroom wouldn't go away in the paralysis of sleep.

Frozen in alarm, Rosalind could not make a sound. Morag's measured breath on her shoulder stopped when she felt Rosalind go tense.

"What is that?" Rosalind hissed.

"What?"

"Can't you see it?"

"There are many things to see."

"By the Fire. Her."

"Excellent," Morag breathed. "You're doing beautifully."

"No. This can't be happening." Rosalind sat abruptly forward, broke from Morag's embrace, and scrambled on all fours away from the figure and the fire.

Morag's speech was slurred as if she'd just woken from a deep sleep. "No, no, no," she murmured. "Don't be afraid."

Rosalind grabbed her bathrobe, climbed to wobbly knees.

"Rosalind, don't go."

And still the figure remained, imperious, as solid in the candle and firelight as Morag's body leaning against the chair. It was a woman, resplendent in amorphous cloak, long hair of silver, and the demeanor of a queen. Rosalind was so terrified she could not speak, not even utter the apology she absurdly felt she ought to give. She stumbled down the dark stairs, drawing on her robe as she made her way through the rooms to the front door, banging against a chair. Something in her demanded she stop, go back, back into the warm love and pleasure upstairs, to connect with the enigma, but she could not. As she fumbled with the door and its lock, her terrified imagination conjuring strange figures at every turn, she heard Morag chuckle ruefully, then weep in exasperation, a bizarre sound going back and forth between the two.

She fled the witch's house. The door banged closed behind her as she stumbled the few feet to her own front door, and pulled on it, only to realize it was locked. She looked desperately this way and that, then hitched up her dressing gown, ran up the cobbled street to the little lane that ran along the back of the gardens, and to her own back door.

Morag rolled to hands and knees and pulled the curtains aside, to see whether Rosalind could actually open her front door or would have to come back into the witch's lair, chuckling weakly at the absurdity of the situation. She watched Rosalind run and disappear into the wynd, then half-snapped out of the magical reverie when she saw the dark car creeping along the cobbles. It slowed to a stop as the driver witnessed Rosalind's hasty retreat from Morag's cottage, and she knew fine whose car it was, though why the pious Reverend Paterson should be keeping watch on her doings at that late hour was a mystery.

*

Helen carefully but firmly pushed down the plunger in the French press coffee pot. She watched the grounds being herded, flattened under the filter. She poured a cup, resenting having made the usual full pot, placing Clive's favorite mug beside it, so that he could have some as well. Little daily acts of kindness in the face of unspoken cruelty.

Clive entered, adjusting his tie. Their gazes did not meet. He poured coffee into his mug and bent over to open the fridge for milk.

"I didn't hear you come in last night," she said.

"I was late. Didn't want to disturb you. So I slept on the sofa."

"That can't have been very comfortable."

"No, it wasn't particularly." He sat at the table with his coffee.

She picked up her briefcase and umbrella and finally looked at him, and he at her with a dull stare. She wanted to ask if Angus had seen him sleeping on the sofa when he left early that morning to catch a flight for London, if indeed Clive had come home at all, but knew it would only lead to a row. She took a different tack.

"Is this going to become a habit, because honestly, we might as well get another bed. It's too much bother laundering the cushions."

"No," he said impassively. "No need." He reached for the newspaper and snapped it open.

She stood looking at the spread newspaper for a moment. From behind it, silence.

"Right," she said, and left.

*

As to who should phone first, Angus or herself, the incident with Morag decided Rosalind. Inexplicable, terrifying occurrences were one way to put things in perspective. The strange figure that had appeared by the fire was, if anything, more powerful than even Morag's enticing presence. Rosalind could not get it out of her mind. Even with distance and unrelenting examination from every angle during a sleepless night, it contained such an immense and foreign, yet strangely familiar attraction that she did not know what to make of it. The interrupted love-making had taken her light years beyond anything previously known, but then the inexplicable thing manifesting was far too disturbing to brush aside. She had to admit she yearned to be back with Morag, yet she could not accept what had happened.

As her thoughts spiraled around, she idly let her drawing pencil move over the artist's paper, just a small doodle in the margin, a line of long hair, a sleeve, a fold of velvet gown. A tongue of fire behind. No concept of a face, but authority distinct in the silhouette.

She tried to locate Angus. She only wanted to hear his voice, hoping against hope for his infatuated and clumsy endearments, to put the familiar world back to rights. She would apologize for being too forward, he'd forgive her, cultural differences and all that, and they would take up the happy romance again. She stood in the kitchen and dialed Helen's house. While she waited, something passed by the kitchen door, just a hint in the corner of her vision of a long skirt sweeping the floor. Her heart skipped. When she turned to look there was nothing there, as usual.

She turned her attention back to the phone. There was no answer. She phoned the Medieval department and finally managed to connect with Helen. Angus had taken the shuttle plane to London, called away unexpectedly to take care of some business at one of the big museums.

"Oh, I didn't know," said Rosalind, surprised.

"Good heavens, he asked me to tell you, and I completely forgot," cried Helen. "I'm so sorry. It's just for a few days. I expect it's something to do with the cairn and treasure hoard. Yes, yes, the news broke. As you can imagine, the archaeologists are rushing in. Clive is helping him set up a temporary display here in the department. I don't know the details yet, but it really is a major find. Did Angus warn you the press will be at the ceilidh?"

"The what?"

"Oh, you know, the massive party, or is it a media opportunity, ha ha, the Chairman is hosting for Angus."

"I don't know anything about that, Helen."

There was a pause. "Are you saying he's not told you?"

"No."

Another pause. "Oh, dear."

"I guess," Rosalind felt like crying, "I guess he doesn't want me to know."

"I expect he's not had a chance yet to speak to you about it, he's so preoccupied. Not to worry. Oh gosh, sorry, I've a lecture to beetle off to, I'll be in touch by and by, cheerio."

The world crashed down on her again. He'd left without a word. And not told her about some big upcoming party.

No sooner had she replaced the receiver and prepared herself for a good cry, when the phone rang loudly. Rosalind jumped. She picked up the receiver, heart thudding, hoping it might be Angus and terrified it was Morag. "Hello?"

"Rosalind Ogilvy? Can you hear me?"

"This is Rosalind Ehrhart."

"My dear, Alastair Comyn. Remember me? Forbes's dinner. There seems to be some static on the line. Hullo? Ah. Do you recall I asked Angus MacLeod to mind my castle for the week I was away?"

"No." She thought back, and met a blank "I'm sorry, I don't remember."

"Thing is, the dear boy can't, says things are far too frantic at his dig or whatever it is. But Morag suggested I might ask you. She thinks you'd enjoy having a castle to yourself for a bit. From say October twenty-fifth , for a week. Does it appeal at all?"

"You want me to castle-sit?" Rosalind slid into the polished wooden seat of the kitchen chair and switched on the lamp, sending the Ogilvy clan of curious ghosts decisively down to the dank cellar. "That would be great. I'd love to. What would I be expected to do?"

"Two shipments are due. Wine and a painting, much too valuable to be left at the back door, you see. If you could be here to meet them, that's the main thing. Trouble is, I'm not exactly certain which day. We do things up here on Highland time. "

"That's fine," Rosalind smiled.

"The only other thing is the service in the chapel on the thirty-first, an annual Evensong. If you could open the front door for them, say four p.m., and lock up after the party. It's the Reverend Paterson's turn this year."

"Niall Paterson?"

"Hello? Beastly contraptions, telephones."

The offer suddenly didn't sound so attractive. Rosalind was so dreading the upcoming confrontation with Niall over her sketchpad that she'd put the whole ordeal out of her head. Now it all flooded back. "A lot will depend on my uncle's health."

"Oh, but Helen Forbes would spell you, surely, and you could be back within an hour and a half, if need be. Heavens, darling, you needn't attend the Evensong if that's an issue. An old heathen like me understands these things."

If she could avoid Niall, the opportunity was too good to pass up. Not only that, she could buy time to deal with the strange situations she was quickly finding herself in. "I'll have to make a few arrangements, but I can't see any difficulties. I'm so pleased for the invitation, but if you don't mind my asking, why me?"

"Because you couldn't possibly ever find a better subject than my castle for your developing style of painting."

"My painting?"

"A week from Thursday, then? I'll be by at some point with the keys. Thank you so much. *Au revoir.*"

She replaced the receiver and frowned at the new mustard colored curtains, and the heavy sky beyond. She could not recall ever having spoken to Alastair about her artwork.

*

Troubles come in threes, she recalled her mother saying, as she dragged her feet along the broad sidewalk down Queens Gardens to the Manse. Enough time had passed that Rosalind hoped the whole matter had been forgotten, and was willing to let her sketchpad be sacrificed as payment. However, unfortunately, a heart-stopping if strangely cordial note had been put through the door on behalf of the Reverend Paterson, which included the address and time she was summoned to appear.

A line of tall stately homes lined one side of the road, and lush private gardens behind low stone walls with iron railings graced the other. The wind was rising, a darkening, cold harbinger of winter, bending the shrubs in a swaying dance, tossing leaves to spin like pinwheels down the pavement.

She worked it all out as she drew nearer the grim entrance, clutching her artist's bag. If she did manage to retrieve the sketches from him, it wouldn't do to have the wind blow them around the town. Niall Paterson would unload his embarrassment and anger at her unwilling eavesdropping, then she could retrieve her sketchpad and leave graciously, avoiding him as much as possible in the future. It was all very simple and diplomatic.

Rosalind's finger was on the doorbell, when Mary Paterson and an older man moved into sight behind the door's glass panel. He wore a dark suit, belly rounded above the worn belt of his trousers.

Mary gripped his forearm, speaking earnestly to his thoughtful frown. He patted her hand and murmured in response, which did not lift the worry on her face. They saw Rosalind at the door.

"Come in," Mary called. She paused and closed her eyes. "Em, Roxanne, isn't it? Yes, no, sorry, we're in a bit of a muddle just now. Meet John Rolfe, one of our esteemed Elders. He's just leaving, I'm afraid."

Rosalind put her hand into the moist little palm he offered. "Rosalind Ehrhart," she said. He stared intently at her face through thick round spectacles, stooping close. He looked like an owl, magnified eyes roofed by feathery eyebrows thrusting heavenward. His hands were little and delicate, a young girl's hands in an old man's skin.

"God bless you, Rosalind," he said with immense earnestness.

She was nonplussed. How did one reply? He continued to look very holy, gazing through her with his owl's eye for the kingdom to come.

Niall's excited face appeared around a door to the right of the hallway. He rubbed his hands together. "All worldly strength, yea even in things spiritual, decays, and yet shall never the work of God decay."

His hair was different. Because his crown was bald, it took a second to figure out the front of his scalp and sideburns had been shaved from ear to ear over the top of his head.

"No, indeed." John Rolfe struggled, with Mary's help, into his overcoat. Niall hovered impatiently as John patted his pockets, pulled out a ring of keys, dropped them, picked them up, took a hat from Mary, exchanged it for a different one Niall offered, and searched for the steps.

Rosalind sidled up to Mary. "Perhaps I should come back later?"

"Not at all. Just a moment. John, will you be all right?"

"Oh, yes, not to worry. Cheers now. God bless."

To Rosalind, Mary said, "Would you care for coffee? Or tea?"

"No, thanks. I can come another time. Really."

Mary hardly seemed to hear. "Please come in." She led Rosalind into the spacious living room. "Let me just...I want to be sure..." Mary appeared to be so distracted she couldn't hold a thought. She was dressed less formally than at the Forbes's dinner, yet still modestly severe in tweed skirt and blue pullover, as befitted the minister's dutiful spouse.

The front door boomed shut. From the windows they watched John Rolfe walk down the pavement towards his car, head wagging at each step, a swirl of leaves encircling his legs. He misjudged the step into the street and pitched forward, but caught himself by jogging a few paces. The wind lifted his hat and flung it down the road.

"Oh, have mercy," said Mary. "His eyesight's dreadful, poor thing."

Niall came in. He reached past them to sharply tug the curtains shut over the plight of his visitor. The fact that it was still light outside did not bode well.

"I don't understand it," he said. "Of all people."

"Now, dear," Mary said. "I warned you. Didn't I say?"

"I am not interested in your perspective, Mary. You're becoming far too vociferous as it is."

"Oh, really, dear. I can't allow you to become a laughing stock."

"That's enough," he said curtly. "It's the time-honored Celtic tonsure, and if it's not stylish by today's standards, all the better. You may leave us to our business."

Rosalind cleared her throat, and tried to think up a reason to leave as soon as she had rescued her sketchpad.

"Excuse me," Mary said politely to Rosalind. "I'll make certain John finds his car."

Niall gestured to a small wooden chair beside the big coffee table in the center of the room. He sat in a much grander, adjacent wingback. "I failed to impress John with my ideas. But never mind. Thus has it ever been." Niall was plainly speaking more to himself than to her.

"Was this like a special visit?" Rosalind ineptly offered.

Niall's gaze was as unwavering as his departing guest's, but where Rolfe's eyes were misty and distant, Niall's were hard as blue ice. "Now, why would you assume that?"

A mistake. She backtracked. "No reason."

"I didn't ask you to come here to speak of John Rolfe. I think we both know that."

The wind outside whistled. Twice Niall formed soundless words with his lips, then frowned. "This is rather difficult," he said. "Just a moment."

He went into the adjoining dining room. Rosalind sighed and looked yearningly at the door. Niall opened a cabinet, took something out, and returned. It was the sketchpad.

She braced herself. "I'd just like to say, I'm very sorry about what happened, I really didn't mean to be there, in fact, I'm mortified, and I did try to leave as soon as I heard you... praying."

Niall held up his hand for silence as he flipped through the architectural sketches, paused at the unfinished drawing of Holy Trinity's transept, then turned to the first sketch of himself kneeling on the step. "Ecce homo."

Her heart thumped.

He tapped his front teeth with his knuckles. "Let's just jump in with both feet, shall we? Two things are of importance. One, what happened. Two, that you witnessed it. You did witness it?"

"It wasn't intentional." She swallowed, eliciting a comic gulp.

"It's true, then. A very unusual situation. You see, I really don't know you at all, what sort of a person you are, your background, your religion, and here you've seen me turned inside out, as nobody, not even Mary ever has."

"I thought the church was empty. Well, it was when I went in."

"Impossible. The door was locked."

"No, it was open. Could I just ..."

"Hold on." He held up his hand. "Why were you thinking I asked you to come tonight?"

She hesitated. "I thought, from your reaction in the church....to reprimand."

He sat back and steepled his fingertips. "And why would I reprimand something God hath wrought?" He rolled the 'r' in *wrought* with relish.

"Sorry?"

"This was no accident. I want to know why you drew the pictures."

It was difficult to know how to reply to what she feared was a cover for another ambush.

"I was making some drawings in the church, and after you started praying... I couldn't bring myself to disturb you, and to be honest I got bored waiting, and I sketched. Things. I wasn't thinking."

"Bored? Surrounded by signs and wonders, and you were bored?"

"I didn't want to interrupt your worship."

"I would like you to tell me what you witnessed."

Rosalind sat dazed, her mind completely blank. "Well, not much. I mean the sketches say it all," she said as he breathed loudly through pinched nostrils. "Then you left, and immediately afterwards, I did, too."

"That's it?" Niall looked astonished at her apparent stupidity.

"Yes," she said cautiously. She could not bring herself to describe the embarrassing groans and shouts and prostrations, and surely they didn't need elaborated on. "May I have my sketchpad back, and I'll just go. Like it never happened."

"The heavens opened and the light filled the church and the voice spoke, and you were oblivious?"

She sat still, fearing she was in the company of a true fanatic. "I'm not religious."

"The scales fell from my eyes and I beheld the full glory of His revelation." Niall raised his hands in wonder. Then he cleared his throat and spoke in a confessional tone. "I'm sorry you had to hear the difficult bits leading up to it, but that was a vital ingredient. To understand our worth. We are nothing. Worse than nothing, sinful creatures, enslaved to our lusts and depravities. You understand of course, we needn't speak of any of that. But even Paul had a group of people with him. And now you can witness to the truth."

"But I don't understand any of this, Niall. I was only there to make architectural sketches."

He frowned and she remembered afresh he did not like the informality of being called by his first name. "You must demonstrate respect, as is writ by God's hand in Holy Scripture, thus: 'let a woman learn in silence with all submission.'" His eyes half closed as he dredged up his quotes. "'And I do not permit a woman to teach or to have authority over a man, but to be in silence.'" He looked at her as if waiting for it to sink in.

"Ah," said Rosalind. "I'm afraid I'm not a Christian."

"So many have turned away from the Lord's teaching. If they hear it from your heathen's lips, why, think what can be accomplished!"

"I'm confused," she said. "I think you have the wrong person." She stood up.

"Sit down. We've not finished yet."

Rosalind clutched her bag in front of her like a shield. "I really need to go now. May I have my sketchpad?"

"We are not done."

"Look, Niall, Reverend, this is all a confused mess. I'm

going to go now."

"I know where you were last night."

It took a moment to understand what he meant. Morag. Her knees buckled and she sat heavily. The corner of Niall's mouth pulled sideways in an undecipherable grimace.

Mary came through the door holding a tray with two mugs on it. "Here's your coffee. You did want coffee?" They both ignored her at first, staring at each other like feuding cats. "Oh, heavens, I'm in such a dither, I couldn't remember."

Rosalind felt sorry for Mary and almost took a mug, but didn't, lest it delay her escape. "You're very kind," she said lamely.

"So you see," Niall said, "the Lord does indeed work in mysterious ways."

Mary, still carrying the tray and mugs, left the room with a backward glance of annoyance. Rosalind suspected it had nothing to do with the coffee.

"That woman has been a thorn in my side since I arrived here." He spoke with soft venom.

"Mary?"

"You know perfectly well I mean Morag Gilbride."

"I don't see what this has to do with me," said Rosalind. "I'm just a visitor."

"Not only does she vex me at every turn, she plots to cause discord in the church, in the community. Mark my words, there's an agenda behind it."

"I have a job back in California, you see." She might as well have been talking to the curtains. "I'll be returning home soon. I just don't see how I can help you."

"And now it seems she's cast her spell over you. Would I be right?"

She couldn't help it. A blush heated her face. Her thoughts raced away. How could he know about last night? A vague memory of the dark car creeping down the lane returned to her, though why on earth he would be driving down a small lane in the middle of the night was a mystery. Did he know? Did Morag have a reputation for seducing the ladies, as well as the men, so that Niall could put two and two together with her emerging in her robe? Rosalind knew to keep her mouth shut. She seriously doubted lesbianism and witchcraft were positive topics in his church.

Niall studied her more closely. "You've nothing to fear if you turn from wickedness and embrace God's word. Stand with me and expose her for what she is." He waited, eyebrows raised, skin crinkled horizontally across his bald pate. "What is she, exactly, what things has she had you do? You can tell me."

"She's my neighbor, and she's only been kind to me." The blush deepened.

"She has seduced you into nefarious, unnatural activities."

Her stomach sank.

"Sorcery, divination? The raising of the spirits of the dead? Sacrifices of animals perhaps? Or is it worse than I suspect?"

It couldn't be contained. She was so relieved, she leaned forward and choked on a laugh, covering the unwise action with her hands.

He stood, drew himself up and spoke thunderously. "Scriptures plainly counsel give; suffer not a witch to live!"

She stood as well and with all the courage she could muster, asked again for the sketchbook.

"Do you have the faintest idea how valuable these drawings are?"

Rosalind realized he was holding the notepad high with both hands, as if with reverence.

"No," she said slowly.

"A witness, and drawings made at the very moment of this most sanctified event. The precious transmission itself, captured in images that will be revered throughout time. Do you realize no other man thus chosen by God has been given such a remarkable gift? There is proof to the prophesy!"

"Oh, please, take them. Here, let me...." she gingerly retrieved the sketchbook from his hands and to his gasp of disbelief, ripped the drawings of him out and handed them back.

"You might have damaged them!" He carefully inspected the paper, and heaved a dramatic sigh of relief to find them whole. "You would give these to me?"

"Gladly."

"This is a great thing you have done."

"I'm glad you like them. I'll be leaving now." She headed for the door.

"Child, the choice is yours. Do you not realize you have been the very instrument of God's hand? That it was He guiding your pencil? Side with the sorceress and court damnation. Or, join me in the new reformation of the chosen."

"I'm sorry, I feel that this doesn't involve me."

"Darkness covers the earth once again with the resurgence of this despicable paganism."

Rosalind left the room, Niall on her heels like a snapping terrier.

"Take heed! She will pull you down into the very jaws of hell," he cried out after her as she fled through the door and down the now familiar pavement of the old town.

*

She opened the door and almost stepped over the envelope that lay under the mail slot. It was addressed to her, but had no return address. She opened it as she ascended the stairs, her eyes going directly to the signature. Angus.

> Dear Rosalind,
>
> Would you be kind enough to consider accompanying me to a special event in my honor? It's a ceilidh, a Scottish party, hosted by the Chairman of the Department, an old friend of mine.
> I'll phone with more details upon my return.
>
> Fondly,
>
> Angus.

Rosalind leaned against the silky plaster of the old kitchen wall and almost cried with relief. He'd conceded fondness. She was not as excited as she thought she'd be with his invitation at first, too many emotions attached to it, but soon the familiar feelings of infatuation and obsession crept back in.

She sighed and looked out the kitchen window at the rooftop across the lane as darkness closed in. And in spite of everything, her heart lifted at the thought of going with him to a party.

Chapter 18

Two men in jeans and sports jackets disengaged themselves from the group milling around at the entrance to the Chairman's house. They stepped in front of Angus and Rosalind, halting their progress down the pavement. One poised a pen over a pad. The other shot a photograph, flash bright in the dusk.

"Dr. MacLeod! Is the treasure really priceless? What will become of it when the archaeologists are finished with it?"

Angus stood a little straighter. "Archaeologists will never be finished with it." He patted Rosalind's hand where it rested on his forearm.

"But which museum will get it? We understand there are squabbles breaking out already."

"Please," Angus said. "Come to the press conference tomorrow, and I'll answer all your questions."

"What's the lady's name? The lucky lady. What's your name, love?"

Angus smiled and brought Rosalind's hand to his lips and kissed it.

"Did you really miss me?" he asked. It was as if nothing untoward had happened. He had been late in coming to collect her. She could see why with the formal kilt. It would have taken a while to put the outfit together, the bow tie, the sporran, the elastic for the knee-high socks with little matching tartan flashes, the cufflinks, which he had been unable to fasten, and held his hands out for her to fix, after a shy kiss hello, and a "don't you look lovely." Not a word about anything else. He was excited, eager to go, his mind only on what awaited. She wondered if all her angst had been over nothing, projected fears of her own making.

She squeezed his arm in reply, self-conscious in front of the photographers.

He beamed and patted her hand again. "It was a grand wee trip. British Museum, interview, request for articles. Things went better than even I expected. And now this." He gazed at her, and she knew his unspoken thoughts which he'd frequently voiced; all because of her, his good luck charm.

As they neared Patrick Buchan's house, guests awaiting them outside the front door called out, "Well done! Congratulations!" A few thumped Angus's shoulder. The chairman stood among them, calling them in.

A familiar voice spoke quietly in Rosalind's ear. "Do you know the destiny God has chosen for you?"

Camouflaged in tweeds against the stone of the house, Mrs. Pearse held out pamphlets, head bent at a coy but insistent angle.

"Go away," Angus said. "You're not wanted here." As they passed her, Angus hunched his shoulders. "Brrr," he said. "Old woman. She makes me shudder."

"Angus. I'll be an old woman someday."

"You? Never. You'll always be young and beautiful." His arm slipped around her waist. When she reciprocated by pulling him closer, his delight was obvious. He almost leaned over to kiss her, but caught himself at the last moment when a flash went off.

Patrick Buchan, a short, stocky man with a cheerful round face, wore a double-breasted blue suit and bow-tie, his hair a soft gray tonsure. His eyes winked and twinkled when Angus introduced Rosalind. She recognized him as the man who had given the beggar child money outside the architects' office window.

"Delighted!" He lifted her hand to his lips. "I daresay some treasures are more valuable than others. Come in, come in."

Rosalind stepped down below street level into the large paneled living room of a medieval house. The furniture had been arranged for guests to view the far corner of the room, where a small stage-like area had been set up, curtains arranged behind two chairs. The house was quickly filling with guests. Most of the men wore kilts with formal jackets, and the women, in a fairly successful ploy at competing with the men's Scottish splendor, wore either ball gowns or cocktail dresses. Through the open front door, Rosalind spied a small group of black-suited men emerge from two Rolls Royces.

The guests were still rather quiet in the first awkward moments of a gathering, but most had drinks in hand, and were drifting into an adjoining dining room to sample sandwiches and fruit. A lovely young dark-haired woman in a simple indigo blue dress seated herself in the stage area. She inclined an ear and plucked at an unusual small harp she held on her knee. The noise level rose in reply, becoming a low roar they had to shout over.

"Rosalind, at last you're here." Helen, wearing a highly uncharacteristic floral party dress, plucked her sleeve, taking her away from Angus, who'd been immediately engaged in explaining the treasure to an attentive group. "I was afraid I'd be stuck with familiar academic faces all night. Mind you, there are some very distinguished visitors." She nodded at the black-suited group clustered round the drinks table, in a serious discussion while lifting glasses of wine to the lamplight. "From the Continent. Trust Patrick to seize an opportunity. I must say, you suit that dress far better than I."

"It's a beautiful dress, Helen. It'd make anyone look spiffy." Rosalind ran her hands across the fine black wool over her hips.

"I look like a stick in it. You fill it out nicely. Keep it, won't you?"

"Helen."

"No, do, please. Make me happy." She drew Rosalind to the wall, where they watched Angus being mobbed by academics. "Have you seen the treasure?"

Indeed she had, only that morning, where it was on display, neatly laid out and labeled in three glass cases, a security guard hovering close by. A vague memory had troubled Rosalind as she studied the treasure and an accompanying medieval manuscript. Something was different, but she could not think what it was.

"Yes," she said with enthusiasm.

"Isn't it marvelous? Still, he should have told me. I feel I'm the last to know anything." Helen searched the roomful of guests. "Angus is moving here, to this house, did he tell you? Oh, of course you know, silly me. He was gracious about it, saying he was cramping us, and just Patrick knocking about this enormous old place. And," she cocked a thin eyebrow, "I suppose he can have you to come visit without us breathing down his neck." Helen went up on her toes to see over the heads. "There's Clive by the fire with David Gillespie and his wife, Charlotte. They have a cottage in Strathkinness, done up really nicely, though a bit modern for my taste, as you'd expect for an architect. They are a lovely couple. I'll take you round to meet them." Helen was unusually talkative, almost manic. "Will you be at Carlin Castle this weekend? I heard a rumor."

"Yes. I'll leave Thursday."

"Dear Alastair. Take my car again."

Rosalind started to protest, but Helen cut her off. "You'll need a car up there. It's just sitting in the garage here. Angus will drive us out on Saturday for the Evensong party. It should be lots of fun, and the castle is simply magnificent, a real Highland castle. It's small, mind you, as castles go, two old towers and a wing between them, but lots of interesting history. Lovely gardens, too."

"Thank you, Helen."

"Oh, lovely, champagne." She took two glasses from a proffered tray held by a young man and passed one to Rosalind.

"Clive's not wearing a kilt," said Rosalind.

"If you saw his knees, you'd know why." Helen glanced across the room and stiffened. "Oh dear. What's that woman doing here?"

Morag, regal in a cream colored knit dress, with a tartan sash fastened at her shoulder by a penannular brooch, was adjusting a chair on the little stage. A series of emotions tore through Rosalind. How would Morag react to her being Angus's date? Or was that even a consideration? She didn't know the rules to this game. Rosalind had not expected to see Morag at an academic gathering, and it was the first time they'd been in the same place since the night they'd had the sex-magic ritual, or whatever it was. With the acute eye that near panic invoked, Rosalind realized anew how beautiful Morag was. She wore black leather shoes that resembled ballet slippers with laces, tied around her slim ankles. As she bent over, speaking to the young harpist on the makeshift stage, the white mounds of her bosom were barely captured by the tight bodice.

"Morag the witch," Rosalind said. She shut her eyes against a wave of erotic yearning, then was chagrined to have felt it. She quickly searched the room for Angus, and saw him with the chairman, craning his head this way and that to see her over the crowd. He gave a little wave.

"May I please have your attention, everybody," Patrick shouted. An obedient hush fell over the gathering. "Welcome to you all. We are here, as you know, to honor Angus MacLeod." Patrick put a hand on Angus's shoulder. "Most of you know him, and know that until recently he worked in the

Archeology Department here. A loss which I doubt we will ever recover from. But the University of St. Andrews has survived five centuries, coping with little things like the Black Death, Reformation..."

The good natured chuckle of a group bent on enjoying itself spread through the company.

"And now Angus and scholars like him are leading a revival, and he has been kind enough to utilize what resources we have available. It is particularly fortuitous that Angus was the one to be called in to excavate the Culdee foundation, which incidentally is still untouched, if any of you would like to volunteer, and subsequently, through a serendipitous event with a plow, I understand, to discover a treasure that spans the centuries. Although I am jealous, no, actually, very indebted to Angus, that my current research must be revised with the dating of certain of the artifacts found with the hoard, I think Angus is very well deserving of this opportunity fate has offered. Aside from myself, I can't think of a more deserving person."

A sprinkle of applause sounded. A couple of men shouted, "Hear hear!"

"Thank you, Patrick." Angus looked past his sporran at the toes of his brogues.

"Tomorrow morning Angus will be giving a lecture on his find, in the Younger Hall. Many of the artifacts are on display in Swallowgate. Eh, what? Yes, don't worry about security. And the press has been invited tomorrow afternoon. I know many of you are eager to view the cairn itself, and we will be taking a minibus out after lunch tomorrow. May I suggest wellies and jackets? For now we won't inflict speeches on anybody. We'll do that tomorrow. Tonight, as befits Angus's heritage, we shall celebrate into the wee hours with a proper ceilidh. Everyone please, enjoy the music, eat, drink, make merry. Are we ready?" Buchan looked to the stage area, eyebrows arched.

Morag raised her hand.

"Allow me to introduce a truly talented duo, Morag Gilbride and Kirsteen Tait, who will delight us with some grand old Scottish entertainment. Let the ceilidh begin!"

Patrick came to stand beside Rosalind and Helen. He poured himself an Irish whisky from the table behind them. "Helen," he whispered under Morag's introduction. "How are you?"

"Couldn't be better," she lied. "Lovely bunch of special subject students."

"Good, good. Helen," he said to Rosalind, "is one of our star lecturers. Groundbreaking work on the Vikings. Yet another book coming out this month."

"Please, Patrick, don't embarrass me," Helen said. "I'm going to get something to eat."

He watched her move away. Rosalind was startled to see an obvious fondness animate his round face, uncloaked when Helen was not aware. How strange. How remarkable. Patrick was in love with Helen.

He turned his attention back to Rosalind. "Angus tells me you're an American."

"Yes, Californian. My mother's family actually came from St. Andrews, which is why I'm here. A relative needed some assistance."

"The mystery lady, the lovely American, materializing at the suddenly famous archaeologist's side. I hope you don't let the gutter press upset you."

"Should I brace myself?"

"Quite possibly. The reputable newspapers will be concerned only with the find itself, but I'm afraid the others might focus on you. Angus is staying here, with me, for as long as he's needed in St. Andrews. He asked me to show you the back entrance through the garden."

As Morag praised her companion's musical talents, Rosalind suddenly realized she'd been so taken aback to see Morag there, she'd hadn't realized that the harpist was Morag's young friend, who she'd seen flirting with Clive.

"No," she said impulsively, half-listening to Morag speak. "But thank you." Now that she'd made the connection, it was obvious that Clive was watching Kirsteen's every move.

"Sorry?" Patrick leaned a little closer. "Did you say no?"

"Oh," she brought her attention back. "I'm not..." she searched for a word, "completely settled into a relationship with Angus. The truth is, we really haven't known each other that long. The idea of sneaking in the back..."

"I would never have thought anything or anybody could take precedence over Angus's work, never mind the find of the century, but my dear, I must tell you, you have."

"I'm flattered, I really am. Angus is a great guy, and I am very fond of him. But I don't even know how long I'll be here.

I feel like I'm being swept away in this tide of events."

"Of course you must. How thoughtless of me. Allow me to simply say that you are very welcome in my house, at any time."

A single lingering note plucked from the harp cut through the noise. Morag's low laugh came from the far end of the living room.

"They're really good," Patrick nodded at Morag and Kirsteen. "Won prizes round Scotland, plus a few in Canada, I understand. I'm a bit surprised they agreed to play for us tonight. Do you know them?"

"Morag is my neighbor. I had no idea she was a performer."

"I've also got a really good piper," he looked around the room. "Calum Hardie. Don't think he's arrived yet. I believe he's Kirsteen's new fiancé. Little town gossip for you."

Another surprise. "That's sweet."

Helen passed by with a full plate of sandwiches. "Do you want to come and sit?"

"You go on. I want to watch for a bit."

"May I join you, Helen?" asked Patrick.

"But of course," she said.

Rosalind hung back at the door to the dining room. Angus was in the center of the room, looking this way and that. She waved for him to sit down. He gestured at Morag and rolled his eyes, frowning comically.

"We Scots," Morag began, "can be justifiably proud of a long and rich tradition of ballads and stories." Her dark hair was loose, hanging down her back, but for two thin braids from each temple, fastened wreath-like around her head. "Did you know, for instance, that Scotland has its own goddesses, known for their prodigious sexual appetites?"

"They're the best kind, I always say," one of the guests shouted.

"I quite agree," she said. "One in particular, the mighty Cailleach, has left a legacy that extends all through Celtic myth, from beyond recorded time, to the West Highland tale, *The Daughter of King Under-Waves*, right down to the Arthurian legend of *Gawain and the Loathly Lady*, and Chaucer's *The Wife of Bath*'s tale, in all of which a hideous old crone demands sex from a man."

"Bloody hell," shouted another of the men. "Thought it was only me!"

"It's never a good idea to say no to the Cailleach. She'll take what she wants and snuff out a man's life like that!" Morag snapped her fingers.

Clive slipped through the laughing guests past Rosalind. "If she thinks I'm going to sit there and listen to this claptrap..." He stopped at the table and poured himself a large whisky, then pushed through the kitchen door. As he did so, Rosalind glimpsed a man in a kilt lift the splayed drones and limp pouch of bagpipes from a case. Patrick also noticed the piper. He leaned over to whisper an apology to Helen, and followed Clive into the kitchen.

"Normally, in our Scottish myths, mortals are enticed to the Otherworld through beauty and desire, but the story of the Cailleach is pulled from far deeper in our psyches, and is far more disturbing in its sexual anarchy."

Kirsteen touched the harp strings and a ripple of notes filled the room. Against the background of the music, Morag began the Hebridean story in a mellow, pleasant voice.

"Wild was the keening wind and sharp the icy blast, when the men of the Fhinn sheltered in the fire-lit hall below Ben Eudainn. But no sooner had they fallen asleep, when at midnight there came a great pounding on the door." The audience jumped as Kirsteen banged on the table. "A monstrous creature entered. This fearsome hag first demanded of the warrior Fionn that he welcome her into his bed."

Among the ribald laughter, which Morag played up beautifully, Rosalind relaxed into the music and story, berating herself for doubting Morag's intentions. Her own fears were surfacing. As lovers went, the beautiful witch-woman who held the company captive with her voice was a prize. Except that the whole thing was too bizarre, too foreign, and Rosalind was no nearer in making peace with the mix of magic or whatever psychological manifestations had occurred during that wild night. She'd have a friendly talk with Morag later, she decided, and make sure there were no expectations. The world could easily be put back to rights.

She felt eyes watching her and turned to see Patrick and another man at the dining table, speaking quietly, with inclined heads and appraising glances, obviously directed at her. It was the piper from the kitchen, his bagpipes sprawled like a bundle of sticks on the table. But not until he slightly inclined his head to Rosalind did she realize it was the burly young man she'd seen with Kirsteen at the funeral outside the town Kirk. His black jacket was different from Angus's, almost military, double-breasted with white lace cascading from his wrists, and under his neck, like a collie dog's ruff. Celtic silverwork of knotted spirals adorned the top crescent of his sporran, which was of a fine-sheened pelt. A sgian dhu's jeweled hilt protruded from the woolly sock clinging to a muscular calf.

Applause spread through the living room with the conclusion of Morag's story. Angus waved insistently for her to join him. As she threaded her way through the seated guests, he looked up, broke into a grin and patted the seat next to him.

"And so to the Border Ballads, and Thomas Rymer," Morag said, "a story about a man living in the thirteenth-century, abducted from the Eildon Hills by the beautiful, 'brisk and bold' queen of Elfland on her milk white steed, and returned to this world seven years later with the gift of second sight. Sort of our Scottish Nostradamus, who spoke his prophecies in rhyming couplets."

"Do fairy queens still roam the Eildons?" shouted someone.

"They certainly roam St. Andrews," she pointedly shot back, and even Angus laughed. "Whilst on the journey with the fairy queen, Thomas was shown three roads. Listen carefully to the ballad. Chances are you are walking one of these roads."

Calum walked around the guests to join them on the stage. Kirsteen struck the harp, Calum lifted a penny whistle to his lips, and they began.

"True Thomas lay o'er yond grassy bank,
And he beheld a lady gay,
A lady that was brisk and bold,
Come riding o'er the fernie brae."

"You'll be at Carlin Castle," Angus said softly. He held a glass of whisky from which he frequently sipped, almost absent-mindedly. "I've attended the party in the past; I usually go up with Clive and Helen. It's a very romantic setting," he smiled, his gaze lingering on her face.

She squeezed his hand, to his obvious delight. Something in the music moved Rosalind, which even Angus's impatiently tapping feet could not distract. She relaxed into the enchantment Morag's voice wove, into the story of magic and transformation, the lovers embarking on a fantastical journey. She felt integrated, wanted, desirable, all of which rekindled a happy self-regard that had apparently gone into hibernation many years ago.

Angus, only half listening, beamed at Rosalind, face merry with pleasure, and patted her hand. "Did you bring dancing shoes?"

She slid her skirt up to reveal simple black pumps. His gaze lingered on her calf in an exaggerated glance of appreciation.

"O see not ye yon narrow road,
So thick beset wi' thorns and briers?
That is the path of righteousness,
Though after it but few enquires."

Someone leaned over from behind them, to whisper in her other ear, and she smelled cucumbers. "That's a clarsach, the Celtic harp." Rosalind turned to see Helen perched on the edge of her chair, still eating sandwiches. "Not easy to play, assuming one can play a harp in the first place."

"And see not ye that braid braid road,
That lies across yon lillie leven?
That is the path of wickedness,
Though some call it the road to heaven."

"The auld songs are all very well," Angus sighed, "but I wish we'd get to the dancing."

"No, I'm enjoying the songs, Angus. I've never had the chance to hear them before."

He nodded and touched his mouth as if to say, 'I'll shut up now for your sake.'

"And see not ye that bonny road,
Which winds about the fernie brae?
That is the road to fair Elfland,
Where you and I this night maun gae."

Rosalind found herself overwhelmed by a sense of homecoming, all the ingredients at that moment combined in a crucible of revelation: her Scottish legacy, the words of the song sung so simply and beautifully, her new friends and amour, the cottage of her kith and kin one street over. Until that moment she had no idea how alien her previous life had been to her soul's desire.

The three singers sang the chorus and finished the ballad

with an instrumental flourish.

After a time Rosalind realized people were clapping, and dabbed her eyes with a hankie. When the eager applause ended, Angus leaned close again. "Pat Buchan's a sly fox."

"How's that?" Rosalind whispered. She felt giddy with all the attention, as if in the eye of a hurricane.

"I've counted, in this room, nine top archaeologists, including five from the Continent, plus an editor or two. Patrick's pulled them in to be at the scene as it unfolds."

Glancing around the room, it was pretty obvious that many people were keeping a surreptitious watch on Angus. And on her.

"Thank you," said Morag. "We've lots more, but perhaps if we can prevail upon an accomplished piper in our midst to lead us in a dance?" She held out her hand to the young man beside her. "Our own Calum Hardie."

He rose and went to collect his bagpipes, calling, "If the men could clear the floor for a Gay Gordons." He hoisted the bag under his arm, arranged the drones, puffed into the blowpipe, and punched the bag. It hummed and quacked into life. He twisted one of the drones, then launched into a lively tune, fingers lifting and pressing on the chanter.

In the ensuing genteel confusion in which the men moved the chairs aside while the women hovered in a low buzz of conversation, Kirsteen left her harp on the little stage. She drifted to the drinks table where she took a glass of champagne, glancing from side to side. Within moments Clive came up behind her and whispered in her ear, at which she smiled. His eyes danced in a sparkling intensity. She nodded her head. Clive left her side as surreptitiously as he'd appeared. Rosalind quickly looked away when Kirsteen glanced around the room to see if anyone had taken note.

On the floor couples began forming. Angus turned to Rosalind, eyes brimming with ardor and intoxication. He gently pulled her to the dance.

"Do me the honor?"

"But I don't know these dances," she protested.

"This one's easy. I'll walk you through it."

After a couple of times, she learned the steps well enough to relax and watch the swirling kilts and dresses circling with them. Feet thudded on the wooden floor, taffeta and velvet hissed softly as they flowed around and around. Angus executed staid steps, back inflexible and arms stiff, and he stepped once on Rosalind's toes, but at least his kilt gave the illusion of fluidity.

When the dance ended, rosy-cheeked couples drifted to the table for a drink. Patrick opened a window to the street.

Rosalind waited while Angus fetched another champagne and poured himself more whisky. A sheen of sweat shone on his forehead. "Since I've been back from London, herds of archaeologists and students have been dropping by the department to inspect the treasure. A short documentary was filmed a few days ago, not just now with anything particular in mind, but for when the full story is pieced together. A couple of journals want articles, and the newspapers keep pestering me. I've even had a couple of job offers, one from a London museum and one from a college. Isn't it absurd? It was pure luck, but suddenly I'm famous." He took her hand. "It's because of you. Your coming into my life has brought me all good things. Do you want to sit? Or go into the garden for some fresh air?"

"The garden."

The chairman's home was not far from Morning Star Cottage, literally a stone's throw over the roofs of the houses in the back. Angus detoured to pour another drink, then joined Rosalind out the back door, where at least a dozen guests, most smoking cigarettes, lingered and talked and laughed.

A man in a plain black suit sidled up to Angus. "I must now ask you an important question," he said in a German accent. Angus excused himself, indicating to Rosalind that he would rejoin her in a moment.

His place was instantly filled by Morag. "I would join you in the next dance," she said, "but Angus is scared silly of me."

Rosalind stiffened self-consciously with Angus watching as he half-listened, distracted, to the German scholar. "Scared?"

"Sometimes the most cynical people have the deepest superstitions. In any event, he needn't be frightened of me. Not like some." She looked around the assembled guests. "Have you seen Kirsteen? I can't find her and we're due for another song."

"No, not for a while. I really liked your songs and stories. Especially that Thomas ballad."

"But not my magic, so much?"

"I'm fine," Rosalind answered honestly. "I'm having the best time of my life. I'm just sorry I spoiled everything. It was too much for me."

"You were brave to join me, and if I may say so, all told, it was a fantastic night. Please let me reassure you that you will always have my friendship, just as your Uncle has always been dear to me."

"Thank you," said Rosalind, equal parts relieved and grateful.

Morag touched her forearm. "Good. One never knows where magic will go once it's set in motion." She cocked her head at Angus. "It appears you've won the heart of the hero. Maybe you'll be a good influence on him." She looked around. "Now, where's that lassie Kirsteen got to?" She shut her eyes and seemed to grow taller on a deep inhalation. Rosalind was not surprised to feel her own skin tingling. Morag's head snapped up and she looked directly across the garden to a shadowed area behind rose bushes and a large bay tree. The outline of a couple was barely visible behind the bay.

By the time it had registered on Rosalind, Morag was already halfway there. Rosalind glanced around at the guests, but they were oblivious to anything beyond their own interests. Morag glided silently over the soft grass behind the roses. A muffled curse, angry words spoken in low tones, and Kirsteen ran out from behind the tree. As soon as she came into sight of the guests, she slowed to a walk, but went as quickly as she could into the house without calling attention to herself until she almost ran into Helen at the door. They did an awkward dance to get around each other, Kirsteen glaring, Helen puzzled.

"If it weren't for you..." Kirsteen began.

"Sorry?" said Helen.

Calum came up behind Helen, still cradling his bagpipes, face rosy and cheery.

"There you are, my lass!"

"Oh, Calum, just get out of my way." Kirsteen pushed past them and ran into the house. After a bewildered look around, he followed her in.

From the shadows, Morag stalked out angrily in Kirsteen's wake, but Clive came after her and took her arm, spinning her around to face him.

"You will not!" he hissed.

"Take your hands off me," she said. "I've warned you twice now."

"And I'm warning you, stay out of my business."

"Your business?" Morag's voice had risen in anger. A few of the guests stopped talking and turned to look. "After what you did to Catriona..."

"Be quiet!" He glanced up to see Helen watching.

"You will not see her again."

"Or what?" Clive said. "Or you'll curse me?"

"Oh, you fool."

"Oh no, oh dear, the wicked witch wants to curse me," he sneered. "You delusional bitch."

Helen's hand covered her mouth. Patrick came to stand next to her, bewildered by her expression. He looked to Rosalind for an explanation, brows knit.

"You complete and utter fool," Morag said. "You've gone too far now."

The contained fury in Morag's face was unlike anything Rosalind had seen before. It rooted her to the earth and flooded her senses like a nightmare.

"I'm sick to death of you and your childish games." Spittle flew from Clive's mouth. "You fucking cunt."

"So be it!" Morag stepped back and pointed the stiff fingers of her left hand at his solar plexus and slowly turned her hand as if spearing into his guts. "Clive Forbes," she said in an arresting voice that captured the attention of everyone in the garden, "I swear by the moon and the stars, and before these witnesses that before November is out, I will be dancing on your grave."

The guests fell silent but for one who guffawed, thinking it was still a performance. Rosalind looked to Angus, who appeared every bit as stunned as she felt.

Clive was past all the niceties of social constraints. He shouldered past Morag. "And may you be damned to hell, you meddling bitch."

Helen stood in the light spilling from the doorway, as still as stone. Clive hesitated when he neared her, then continued by. Patrick tried to speak as Clive passed, and was rudely rebuffed.

"Take me home," said Helen to no-one in particular. "Take me home."

"A car?" Angus said to Patrick's stricken face.

"In the lane." Patrick fished in his pockets and handed the keys to Angus, then hurried before them to open the gate. Rosalind took Helen's elbow and walked her across the lawn. Angus opened the car door for Helen. She had gone quiet, still, but her hand trembled violently where it lifted to touch her forehead.

"Can you drive?" Angus asked Rosalind.

"Me?" she said in surprise.

"Well, it would be best." He gestured at the house. "I ought not to leave just now. It would call attention if the guest of honor fled the party. I'll see if I can smooth this over."

She took the keys and got in the driver's seat.

"Oh, God." Patrick wrung his hands. "Helen."

"Get Calum to play another dance," said Angus. "Most people didn't see what happened. Come along, the night needn't be spoiled."

Rosalind started the car. Angus bent over and she rolled the window down.

"All right?" he asked.

Helen would not look up.

"We'll be fine." Despite her small panic at having to drive Helen home, Rosalind smiled for him, for his anxious face, patted his hand, and slowly drove down the dark narrow lane. In the rear view mirror she saw Angus hurry back to the party, while Patrick stood alone in the middle of the street, watching them go.

Morag stormed across the living room and plucked up her heavy woolen cloak where it lay in a corner of the little stage. She flung it over her shoulders and burst out the front door, striding past guests who were so inebriated and jolly that they hardly gave a glance, and no-one noticed the subtle ripple of movement in Morag's wake, as clothing and tablecloth and chairs and artwork shifted ever so slightly, as if pulled along with a wind. Clive and Kirsteen had scattered, only Calum the dutiful remained at the party, pulling together another dance. Morag could sense the direction they'd taken, which at least was not the same. She had to get far away, immediately, unable to contain her fury. Somewhere where her brilliantly flashing anger could cause no damage, somewhere immersed in the elements.

Down the Scores, under the canopy of the old trees along the narrow street, out across the lawn by the Martyr's Monument, down to the path to the sea and West Sands. She left the tarmac and stumbled through the soft dunes till she came to the smooth beach that stretched away into the darkness. The gibbous moon put a silvered sheen on the tops of the waves as they plunked and hissed along the sand. At last she could let go, and teeth bared, roared into the night breezes.

After a time, she slowed her pace, and stopped when a broken wave washed over her feet. The shock of cold brought her back. Her lovely soft dancing brogues were ruined.

Morag had become inscrutable even to herself. The night held its own intelligence, into which hers extended and found a harmony beyond her making. The moon's radiance filled her body, and the North Sea, with its sliding and bucking waves, demanded she be still, to remember that other forces were at work.

The first concerned Clive and the destiny she had just unlocked with her curse. Had she done nothing, but left him to his own devices, perhaps his ill treatment of others would have resulted in some vague retribution from the offended ones, and he'd have sloughed it off with disdain. Now things were entirely different. The hand of fate was coming down hard on all concerned. She could not see what form it would take; still, even now, she could not see. But she could trust in the forces gathering, and was content.

The second had nothing to do with Clive. She pushed the night's events from her mind, and cast her awareness out into the distant elements. Like the quiet at the pause of the tide before it peacefully reverses and begins gathering speed on the flood, to plummet into the great whirlpool of Corryvreckan, the rocky tidal channel where the Cailleach washes her plaid to herald the storms of winter, so Morag felt the deceptive stillness in the air and sea. Good. All things were in place. Tomorrow the plan, so long in the making, would be implemented.

Morag turned and walked calmly back the mile of beach, under the jewel-blazing stars. A flicker of lightning at the edge of night, where the sea met the dark sky, illuminated the gathering of a company of dark clouds, building up one on the other.

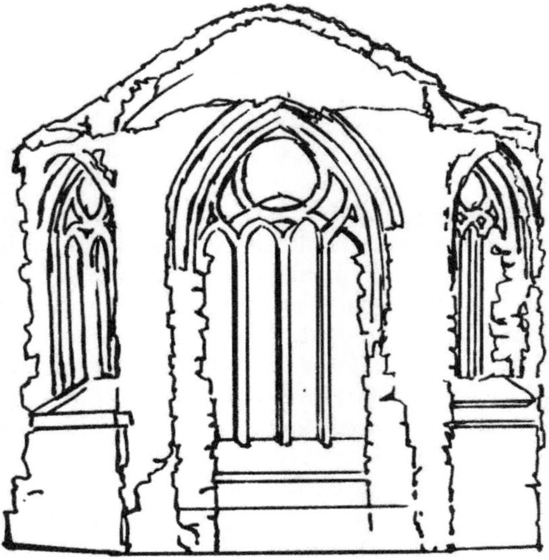

Chapter 19

The cold, wet weather made the walk to the hospital unpleasant, and it was doubly disappointing when she entered Uncle Rab's room, to find him drifting in and out of a morphine-induced haze from which she could not awaken him. Sometimes his eyes would open and he'd speak unintelligibly, then fall heavily into unconsciousness.

Rosalind sat by his side for a while, studying the sunken features, the white bristles, the labored breaths that sometimes stopped until she grew concerned, then with a snort, resumed again. Touching his hand or speaking to him elicited no response.

She went to the window and looked out at the heavy drizzle and gray skies. Uncle Rab's occasional ramblings coalesced into a fragment of song.

"The ship of my dreaming…will of fate is speeding her way swift as…as a bird…love song draw me, O Tir-nan-Og."

His heaven, his Tir-nan-Og. She wondered what images were moving through the old sailor's mind. Finally, when he'd fallen silent for a long time, she kissed his forehead and left the room, wondering if his time had come, if she should return that night for a death watch.

But first, life went on with an errand for the stricken Helen.

*

The harsh glare of overhead lighting inside Boots the Chemist bathed the milling shoppers in stage-like illumination, rendering the gray sky out the front glass doors all the gloomier. Rosalind carried her few items to the girl perched on a stool at the cash register. With practiced efficiency, the girl tapped out the numbers, put the shampoo and soap, and the bottle of paracetamol into a plastic bag and immediately turned her attention to the next customer. No pleasantries, no familiar faces to detain Rosalind.

The desultory drizzle thickened to rain, stealing what small wish she had to step outside. A young mother pushing a baby pram came to the door and Rosalind held it open for her. She nodded her thanks, red cheeked and puffing. "Dreich day," she said.

It was truly a dreich day. Umbrellas didn't do much good in that sort of coastal rain, which went in any direction the wind swirled. Rosalind had adopted the popular style with a hooded jacket, and fared slightly better, coming in less soggy at the end of expeditions. Painting or sketching outdoors was impossible, and she'd given up for the time being.

Back in Palo Alto, her mother was probably sitting outside on the small patio, reading in the warm Californian sun. And Chris would be playing his beloved football, running over the fresh green grass of the practice field.

But the weather in Scotland was living up to its stereotype. She pulled up her jacket hood and plunged into the bleakness, down South Street, past Blackfriars, an isolated ruin with only a vaulted roof still extant over the small rounded chapel, wet gray stones encompassing a murky interior.

Rosalind detoured around townspeople queuing for a bus on the wide sidewalk between Blackfriars and the street. They appeared to be shoppers come in from the neighborhoods surrounding the town center, mostly women, mostly short and stocky. Plastic scarves or hoods drawn over their heads hid their faces, and all wore boots or thick soled shoes. As if by design, all the overcoats were black or dark brown or blue. Everyone bowed against the weather like a ghostly procession of hefty medieval monks called unhappily to midday prayer at the chapel.

Rosalind found her thoughts circling back to Morag's curse. Whether it was the vehemence with which it was spoken, or the setting of events in motion that could actually lead to a crisis, it stuck in her mind, as pervasive as the dark clouds.

Two young men in motorcycle leather crossed Rosalind's path; one, unhealthily skinny, a shaved head sprouting tufts of wheaty stubble, altered his course to pass close by.

"Do you want a sweetie?" His face was vacant, moist with rain. "Or do you just want tae fuck?"

His companion merely pulled him on down the street.

"I'd rather have the sweetie," she whispered, distressed. Nothing like that had ever happened before. In a town where a woman could walk alone through the dark night streets without fear, where babies were often left in their prams outside the shops while the parent went in, where children roamed unattended, taking the bus or walking alone, Rosalind had almost forgotten the dangers she normally took for granted. The rude, drugged youth was an omen, like the miserable weather and the dank ruin, a bad sign of what awaited at the Forbes's home.

Helen came at Rosalind's knock, lips set in a straight line. Dark skin circled bleary eyes. Her usual neat clothing was replaced by an old knit sweater and baggy pants.

"Perhaps I shouldn't have phoned," she said. "I'm not very presentable."

"I'll come back later, if you'd rather. Here's the paracetamol."

Helen leaned her thin skinned temple against the door. "Might as well."

She turned and walked into the house, leaving the door open. Rosalind stepped in, uncertain, hoping it was the right choice. She shut the door and followed Helen downstairs to the kitchen.

"Are you doing all right?" A tentative query. Other than a request for the analgesic, Rosalind had not heard from Helen since she drove her home the night before. Helen had insisted on being dropped off, no conversation at all.

"Well, no, of course not, but if you mean am I going to jump off St. Rule's tower, don't worry. I wouldn't give him the satisfaction." She slid into a dining chair. "I've got my own life to look after. Students are depending on me. One simply must carry on."

Gloom enshrouded the cold kitchen, the only illumination whatever sparse daylight could filter through the conservatory doors.

"I guess there's not much I can do, but if you want me to pick up groceries or anything," Rosalind offered.

"I just need to pull myself together. I have classes Monday, and I intend to take them."

The kitchen clock ticked the seconds. Just as Rosalind decided it might be best to leave, Helen stirred.

"This is nothing new, you understand. It's been going on for years. It was my choice to turn a blind eye, to just get on with things. I mean, honestly, do you break apart a marriage because of his idiotic proclivities, when everything else is all right? Was all right. At least I thought it was all right."

The enormity of Helen's confession, that she'd known all along about Clive and his illicit lovers, took Rosalind aback. She could not think of anything to say that wasn't an insulting platitude.

"It's the public humiliation that takes it to a new level," said Helen. "And that girl, she can't be but eighteen. Honestly."

"Could you get away, take a break?"

She snorted. "No doubt my students wish I would, especially the first years. They'll be terrified after one look at me. But I shall not disrupt my life. I shall not."

Music came from upstairs, a single violin playing a mournful tune she'd heard before, from Prokofiev.

"How much of my life do I change because of his actions, for God's sake? I hate him, but I love him. All the years can't just be erased." She jerked at her thin gold necklace distractedly, leaving a red scrape across the skin. "Angus is gone, of course. He moved in with Patrick this morning. You knew that. Thank God. Can you imagine having to cope with those wretched reporters at a time like this?"

"I know he feels bad about moving out, like he's letting you down."

"It's a relief, honestly. It was getting rather cramped here, for all concerned." Helen pressed her fingertips to her eyes. "Why am I so absolutely exhausted?"

"Would you like me to make some tea?"

"...be lovely."

No sooner had Rosalind turned the faucet off than Clive shuffled in. His dressing gown hung in loose wrinkled folds. Helen flinched as he passed behind her.

"Hullo, Rosalind. Survive the night?"

Sitting with Helen was a friendly, if difficult gesture, but the addition of Clive made her very uncomfortable. She had a separate relationship with each and did not want to get caught in their potential crossfire.

Clive limped to the far side of the table and sat slumped, staring at nothing.

"What have you done to your leg?" Rosalind asked.

"Such an idiot. Gashed it against a piece of metal when I was walking last night."

Helen glanced over, eyes surprised, but kept her features

expressionless.

"It was dark. A bit of the railing along the path above the castle must have been damaged by a car or something, and I blundered right into it." He touched the top of his thigh where bandages made a lump under the pajamas. "My shoe was soaked with blood by the time I reached the hospital. Had stitches. Hurt like blazes. Is that paracetamol?" He reached for the bottle.

"That's mine," Helen snapped. He dropped it back to the table.

Rosalind filled the teapot and put the cozy over it. Since her first lesson with Helen, the process had become second nature.

"Did Angus stay at Patrick's last night?" Clive asked.

"He was here briefly," Helen said. "Packed up and left this morning."

This was bad news if it meant Clive and Helen had not spoken to one another since the ordeal of the previous night. Rosalind poured their tea and tried to think up an excuse to flee.

"Are you not having any?" Helen asked.

"Well, maybe I ought to get back. The cellar is almost done and that's the final piece."

"Stay for a moment, Rosalind," Clive said. "There's something I need to tell you."

She tried not to look apprehensive as she poured half a cup and joined them at the table.

"The office. I'm afraid we were premature in offering you work. You see, we are in the process of negotiating, possibly having to close the St. Andrews branch, just keep the one in Aberdeen going. Until I know more…you understand."

"What?" said Helen.

"Yes, what's that word, 'downsizing.'"

"When did this happen?" Helen demanded.

"I've been trying to negotiate an alternative."

"I very much appreciate your help, Clive," said Rosalind, "both in letting me work for you and with…"

"So," Helen cut her off. "Are you moving to Aberdeen?"

"Helen, we can discuss this later."

"Tell me."

"I'm not moving to Aberdeen."

"A reputable firm that is a leader in awards and clients is

suddenly going out of business? A senior partner is suddenly out of a job? How odd."

Clive turned his attention to Rosalind. "I'll get your final cheque to you tomorrow."

"Thank you." She stood to go.

"Oh, and I promised I'd mention one other thing. How shall I put it?" He tapped the lip of his mug. "Angus."

"Clive," Rosalind protested.

"He asked me to say something. I suppose he's not able, being a shy Scot. He's in love. Fifteen years and I've never known him to be like this. Don't let it pass you by," Clive said. "Life is much too short."

"I like that, coming from you." The sparks ignited in Helen's eyes.

Clive placed his hands flat on the table and leaned over them. "Don't twist my words about."

"I should go." Rosalind stood and collected her coat from the back of the chair.

"Love," Helen sneered. "And what's happened to our love? You didn't care to nurture it much, did you?"

"Don't honestly tell me you think the blame can be laid on me."

"I know all this must dredge up painful memories for you, Rosalind," said Helen, eyes still on her husband. "But I gather things were all right with your marriage. No furtive *amours*," she hissed at Clive.

Rosalind made an effort to say nothing, angry and embarrassed for them. Helen swiped up the paracetamol and left the kitchen.

Clive stared glumly into his empty glass. Rain pinged on the conservatory roof. Rosalind moved towards the door. "I'll see you later."

"You're lucky. You can leave. God, so many people would give all they have for that opportunity. Sell the cottage and get out as fast as you can. Take Angus home with you, to your sunshine and American optimism. Forget this depressed, decayed, dying place."

*

The dreich weather meant nothing to Mary Paterson, dutiful

and long-suffering wife to the pious minister. Accustomed as she was to the perpetual dark humors encircling her holy husband's balding pate, what did the cold rain matter? As he often quoted Proverbs at her: "A continual dripping on a very rainy day and a quarrelsome wife are alike." Ergo, it was her responsibility to lighten the skies.

This, however, was proving to be a special day indeed. Since she had found the letter in her coat pocket that morning, and read it standing under her dripping umbrella on Queen's Gardens as cars passed with the distinctive sticky sound of tires on wet pavement, it was by far the brightest, best, most wonderful day she had had since she could remember.

Mary clutched the awkwardly typewritten letter to her over-brimming heart as she ascended the stairs up the kirk tower. The last thing she would have expected was for her pious husband to write such a romantic note, one which, while apologies for his behavior were conspicuously absent, at least conceded his lack of husbandly duty to his faithful and loving wife. For do not scriptures enjoin the husband to love his wife even as Christ also loved the church, and gave himself for it, that he might sanctify and cleanse it with the washing of water by the word? There were too many distractions and memories in the manse, particularly in the barren bedroom, where decorum dictated they lie, never touching, side by side in the cold bed. So would she do him the honor of agreeing to meet him for a private tête-a-tête in the only place he could think which might be suitable, the kirk tower, where, away from prying eyes and inevitable demands from parishioners, he promised to at least try to begin making amends?

And so at the appointed hour, Mary stood, moist-eyed in the upper chamber, having discovered, with a little squeak – oh, oh! – the bottle of champagne and large box of chocolates awaiting her. Mary had hoped the horrid medieval torture device, the Bishop's Branks, or Scold's Bridle, would not intrude too much in their loving reunion with its terrifying implications. But it was not there in its accustomed display. How thoughtful her dear husband was being! She gave a little jump when the bells clanged the hour, and covered her ears for the duration, not hearing the door close and the key turn in its lock, to leave her quite alone and imprisoned in the gathering gloom of the long cold night.

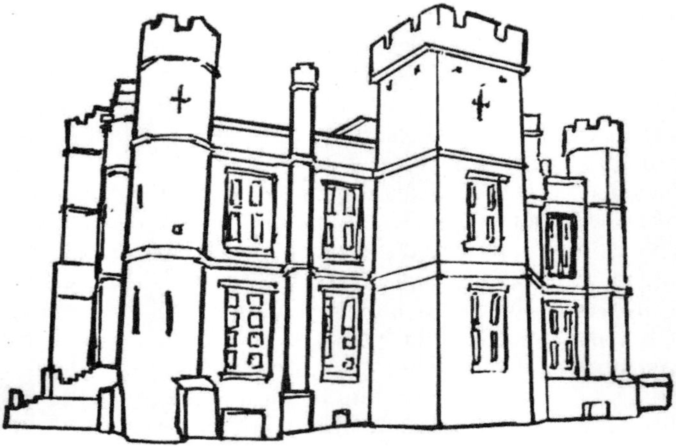

Chapter 20

Clive was right. It was time to go. Time to stop the strange progression of events, and go. That sentimental burst of emotion at the ceilidh was just that and nothing more. There were too many uncertainties. She would stay to take care of Uncle Rab in his final hours, then put the cottage on the market, return to California and beg for her job back.

But she didn't want to.

Rosalind walked aimlessly away from the town center, towards Kinburn Park. A month ago she'd have been marveling at every new sight, the old stone homes, the small gardens, the British cars and bicycles parked along the road where it was easy to see where iron railings had been removed from the low stone walls in front of the houses for the war effort. A direct legacy from her father's time at St Andrews. Now concerns pressed in, turning promise to despondency.

The idea of the tedious work in the college archives, and her cringing gratitude for it, the uncomfortable brown chair with the loose seat that assured her of an aching back at night, the ugly metal desk, the serious people she worked for, with their serious problems, the commute, the perpetual worries – about what? And that was it. That was the rest of her life. She did not want to return, but was her longing to stay an excuse, as her pragmatic mother used to insist whenever hard choices came up, to not face reality?

Was Angus reality, or wishful thinking? In spite of everything, she'd been entertaining a fantasy of the two of them sitting in quiet domestic bliss by some future hearthside, right down to a cute kitten playing with a string. Henry was allergic to cats, or so he said, so they'd never had one. Angus would go off daily and do whatever it was famous archaeologists did. TV shows maybe. Could she be the artist she was meant to be, while relying on his income and tending to his needs, his home, his social circles, his unspoken expectations? The income part was overly attractive, since the option would be a return to where she was currently, having to work to stay afloat with no time for painting.

The fantasy began to be eroded by a fear that eventually they'd lapse into a routine of domestic tedium, with infrequent intimacy, a pattern all too familiar from her years with Henry. No wonder she had been feeling so sexually crazed. There were years of pent up sorrow and frustration behind her. But never mind all that. The main question, she suddenly realized, was, did she want to live with another person at all, no matter who it was? She hoped she was mature enough, despite the joy of being in love, to see Angus's faults clearly, or at least the places she would be compromised by his wishes. Why not have friends and lovers, but be able to come home to blissful solitude? And why had she never seriously considered this option before?

Lovers. She couldn't help but compare the amorphous fear of domestic sexual ennui with the memory of the actual night of bizarre love-making with Morag.

And what on earth did that signify? Nothing bad had happened subsequently. Morag displayed no motive beyond the obvious. In fact, as the days passed, Rosalind felt a kind of victory. Perhaps her self-image as a sensible, boring, play-it-safe woman submitting to lessening expectations of middle age was not the whole story. Something had been unleashed that night. Not so much a defining of her sexuality, as an empowerment. If Morag did not surprise her with any unwanted expectations, she admitted she would be glad to have had the experience.

None of which, of course, helped make the decision easier. If, as Clive said, the architects' firm was closing, she had no employment, no prospects. No, he was right. Time to stop the fantasy, finish up, and go back home.

Not far beyond the Forbes's house, silent outdoor tennis courts and bowling greens glistened with the dampness that had settled over everything. In the center of the park stood a castle-like building, surrounded by rose beds and pathways. University students hurried down a path behind the building, a shortcut to a hall of residence not far beyond. A few older townsfolk meandered by, turning wistful gazes to the last roses. Multicolored petals festooned the garden beds, fallen under the weight of incessant moisture.

Rosalind draped her raincoat over one of the benches and

sat on it. The drizzle had slowed to a soft mist, cold but bearable. Seagulls wheeled above. The back of the bench supported her head and after a time her eyes, stinging with weariness, closed. Then she realized that to go would be the end of her artistic dreams and the tears flowed in earnest.

At the ceilidh, before the uproar, Morag had told a story from the Orkney Islands, about a seal-woman. This creature, a selkie, would come with her seal-people to cast their pelts and dance on the shore at certain magical times of the year. An islander, returning from a midsummer night's ceilidh, passed the beach near his home and saw the seal-folk dancing, melting in and out of the waves and rocks. He broke their spell with his clumsiness, and they all fled, but for one woman, whose seal pelt lay at his feet. Though she begged all night, he would not return it, but claimed her for his wife. He hid her pelt so that she couldn't go back, and took her into his home.

Years passed. They had six sons, and the husband loved his family, especially his seal-wife. She cooked and cleaned and cared for the children, appearing to be like other wives, except for the strange moods that came over her sometimes, sending her to the shoreline, to wander up and down, looking out into the waves. And the weird songs she sang, that echoed the temper of the sea.

All her sons were like the comely, blond husband, a Viking descendant, except the youngest. He had his mother's silver hair and sea-dark eyes. Playing one day, while the father and older sons were fishing, he discovered the pelt hidden in a rock cairn, and brought it to his mother. She said goodbye to her young son, and went to the sands, where the husband watched in despair from his boat, crying for her to stop as she put on the sealskin, and slipped back into the sea.

Into the sea. Images disengaged from her conscious mind and carried her back. Beneath the waves it was calm, restful. A familiar face appeared, Morag? No, not Morag, yet somehow associated with her, and familiar. The face entered her half-sleep to sing the selkie back to her true home, the sea home she'd left long ago. What heartache is there? Surely the Viking husband loved his seal-wife, yet this same love prevented him from revealing the place he'd hidden the pelt, a pelt that remained smooth and glossy over the years when everything else grew tarnished by time.

The selkie sheds tears into an ocean of sorrow for the years parted from the sea, and tears of longing for the promise of reunion. But on the shore, another man, another hunter-lover watches from the bay, waiting, and... what did Morag call it... Samhuinn is approaching.

"Rosalind," called a voice. "Rosalind Ehrhart?"

The images fled, closing out of sight like sea anemones, one by one. They seemed important. There was a link, a comprehension of something obvious that was suddenly vague again. The woman was calling her.

"Don't go," Rosalind murmured.

"Rosalind?"

She sat up and blinked her eyes awake, to see one of the nurses from the hospital who frequently had put up with Uncle Rab's black humor. "I must have dozed off."

"Thank goodness! We'd given up finding you, and I was just passing on my way for lunch. Is your uncle at home by any chance?"

"My uncle?" Her thoughts were still foggy.

"Robert Ogilvy. Has he returned home?" The nurse bent close, anxiety creasing her brow.

She sat up. "Oh, my God. What's happened?"

"I'm afraid he's gone missing."

It was the last thing she expected the nurse to say. "Missing?"

"Would you mind just seeing if he's gone home? We've knocked on the door but there's no answer." A sudden gust of wind whipped around them. The nurse clutched her coat tighter against her breast. "Good heavens, the weather forecast this morning said nothing about a gale!"

Rosalind got to her feet, took up her damp coat and put it on. "I'll go and check."

"It's very strange," the nurse said. "He was weak, I mean, it would never have dawned on us that he could simply walk out of the hospital. And with this storm blowing in, it's far too dangerous."

"Do you think he's fallen somewhere?"

"We've looked everywhere. Would you please just phone the hospital as soon as you find out? I'll be back on duty in an hour."

Another gust of wind roared through the beech trees along the walk. They dipped their branches and groaned like a ship's timbers. Heavy clouds gathered in the east, a bank of darkness against the gray sky.

Rosalind hurried down the glistening streets to Morning Star. The front door gave no sign of having been opened. She unlocked it with the heavy key and entered the hallway. The wind tore into the cottage, flinging the door back. Chips of plaster showered down from the freshly painted wall. "Oh no!" Rosalind put her full weight against the door to push it shut.

She hurried to the back door and opened it to the thrashing rowan tree. Golden leaves swirled into the hall, some fluttering up the stairs like demonic fairies. There was nobody in the garden. She turned and swiftly ascended the stairs. "Uncle Rab? Uncle Rab!"

She turned on lights as she went, fearful that he had come home to die, afraid of finding him lying on the floor, surrounded by the cottage ghosts.

All the downstairs rooms were empty. She tried the top floor, even though it was absurd, as if he could climb the stairs when he could hardly get out of bed. She hurried down to the kitchen and tried to remember their last meeting.

The whisky.

Rosalind suddenly felt weak and sick with guilt. She sank into a chair. Her wet overcoat hung heavy as a lead yoke across her shoulders. Uncle Rab surely had drunk all the whisky and was lying in a stupor somewhere, dying of exposure. She was responsible for his death. Rosalind stared dully through the kitchen door at the beautiful sketch of Rab's sailing boat, *The Reiver*, which she'd had framed and hung in the little hallway, hoping he would return to see it one day. She looked out the window and saw a seagull give up attempting to fly into the wind, veer away and flash towards the harbor. A burst of wind roared over the roof tops. The gale had come out of nowhere and swept over the old gray town like a vengeful wraith. As if the sailors had untied the witch's knots.

And then she knew exactly what Uncle Rab had done.

*

The tide was high enough. Captain Ogilvy was able to bring

The Reiver alongside the pier. The wild swell lifted the boat and she scraped a bit against the stone.

"Bugger me, Morag," he said. "Lost my touch."

"Last chance." Morag waited till *The Reiver* rose, then swept her cloak aside and hopped off the boat to the rungs of an old iron ladder clinging to the pier wall.

"You know the answer, my lass," he shouted. The wind ruffled his white hair, and his eyes danced with excitement. Back in his element. Morag pushed the boat away with a foot, and he motored along the length of the pier, the rise and fall of the water difficult to maneuver, even along the old stone sea wall.

She walked the pier above the boat's course, keeping pace until they reached the end together, and Rab eased out into the deeper waters, with a last farewell lift of his hand. He cut the motor and *The Reiver* drifted slightly. His voice barely carried over the waves, singing, and she smiled to hear "Speed bonnie boat like a bird on the wing." A few seconds later, the mainsail unfurled. With the breasting of the sail, the boat ceased being a sleek tub chugging along, and came into her true identity, moving off her belly and into her keel.

Auntie Meg, Kirsteen, and Calum stood well behind on the pier, keen eyes on *The Reiver's* white sails as she straightened, found her stride and cleaved away through the rising swell. The young lovers had been fighting like cats and dogs after the ceilidh. He'd demanded honesty and fidelity, she'd countered with independence and respect. Neither wanted to lose the other, but the best they could arrive at was an uneasy, hurt, fearful truce. Larger issues demanded their loyalty, so they'd put differences aside to come and assist.

Auntie Meg watched her oldest living friend and neighbor crash away through the spume, and began to weep. "Och, Rabbie, you were aye guid tae me."

The fisher-folk watched from behind their curtains. Don't think they didn't know. A few ventured out to the quay, braving the storm but keeping well back, half hidden behind the lobster pots, centuries of history, of relations between the sea-farers and the magical people in their footsteps. Their strong emotions buoyed Morag, mixed in an irresistible intoxicant with the elements.

She raised her arms to the rising wind, fingers outspread, each one dissolved in their tips into pure white energy. Her cloak caught the wind and snapped, and the waves smashed against the pier, sending spray over the stone. Auntie Meg tottered to Morag, carrying with some difficulty an old ship's timber about three feet long. Calum had placed a large stone, a blue stane they called it, from one of the local prehistoric sites, long associated with magic, at the pier's end, and moved well back. Morag stood over it, waiting for the perfect time.

The wind swirled through her opened body and lifted her out of herself. She flew through the silent few gathered, and through the sparkling spray and through the cracks of time. She became the wind's path, tasting the sea salt bursting below, feeling the heavier essence of black thick clouds speeding low over the small group. She entered and left the lungs of the people there and felt the warmth of their spirits, and almost digressed to feel the playful element in the feathers of the sea-birds plying the winds above.

It was time and she was in perfect accord. She bent her will to *The Reiver,* and far, far out, she curled into the sails and sped the ship to its destiny. All at the same time, at the pier Morag flew from the wind's eyes to her body, to see the heaving swell and white caps all the way to the horizon.

It took an effort to lower her arms, which were still wind. "Call the tempest!" she cried, and pulled her skirt high to reveal an old-fashioned garter, the sort worn in generations past, a strip of cloth. She untied it and drew it off, holding it up. It streamed straight out to sea. Then with blazing hands of white energy, she tied three knots along its length. It needed to be wet for this magic, and the spray off the crashing waves obliged.

She placed it on the blue stone. The gale was spinning along nicely under its own volition. She half-turned to Auntie Meg and gestured. Meg put the ship's timber into her hand then fell back, out of harm's way, where Kirsteen, wide eyed, clutched Calum's arm. Morag raised her arms again, timber in one hand, and recited an old, old charm.

"I knot this ragg upon this stane,
To raise the wind in my Lady's name;
It sall not lye till she please again!"

The garter and the stone and the end of the pier blazed in a blinding sparkling silvered aura. Kirsteen hid her face against Calum's chest, and Auntie Meg clutched his arm lest she be blown over.

Morag grasped the timber in both hands and slammed it down on the garter and stone, where it shattered into a thousand flying splinters.

*

Rosalind raced down the lane, cut across down The Pends and along the cathedral wall, the quickest route to the harbor. The wind funneled down the high cathedral walls, pushing her along with nightmarish force as her feet thudded hard on the road, breath coming in erratic gasps. Mercifully, nobody was out in the storm. Then she was running up and back along the harbor, clutching her hair away from her eyes, reading aloud the name of every bucking vessel on the choppy waves.

The Reiver was not there.

She cried out and stumbled over the uneven stones of the deserted pier, the far end invisible in the heaving sea. Tall waves crashed against the stone with thuds and explosions. She raced into deeper darkness and arrived breathless at the pier's end. She grasped the cold wet iron rungs of the ladder that ascended the streaming wall of the pier, climbing with difficulty to the circular, iron-fenced terminal, the highest vantage point. Rosalind embraced the thick pole of the old dark beacon, pummeled by the wind. She looked out in desperation over the black sliding sea. Lights, some blinking, some steady, came from buoys, then disappeared behind the waves.

Rosalind clung to the light pole in an agony of indecision. With fair warning, the coast guard might find Uncle Rab, or Leuchars' Search and Rescue helicopters, maybe when the storm passed. The earliest he could have left was that morning. Or could he have slipped out in the dark of predawn? She had no idea how far a good sailing boat could travel in a day, but felt certain that he, armed with whisky and cigarettes and sandwiches, had no wish to be rescued. The old fox had been putting on a show of being weak.

Who to betray? Uncle Rab or the police and hospital staff?

"What should I do?" Rosalind demanded of the wet pole, smacking it with a palm. If it were her instead of him? Her eyes clamped shut at the thought of being in pain on the open, cold sea, dying there in utter solitude. But Uncle Rab wouldn't think that way.

The sea was his home, his lover, more familiar than dry land. She tried to imagine their bringing Uncle Rab back, and him dying in the frantic hands of rescuers, filled with turmoil and rage.

"Oh, God," she cried. "What should I do?"

The sea, in enormous humps of whale-sized swells, rushed at the pier, as if to force her back, waves and wind joined into one element that burst over the wall and splattered to the streaming stones, drenching Rosalind's hair and coat. Farther out, the darkness of sea and sky melted together. There was no sun, no stars, no moon, no light above. The swell rose and the sea lifted all around, or the pier descended, she couldn't tell, and an inch of water washed over her feet. At last it occurred to her that she could easily be swept off the pier and out to sea, of no more worth than a matchstick in the awakened elements.

She clutched for the iron rungs of the ladder and put her foot on the slick bar. Looking down, she saw that where the stone walkway had been, there was now only water churning dizzyingly over the stone.

She pivoted in the roaring blackness. From where she stood, on the end of the pier's upper wall, a thin concrete walk extended almost halfway back, to where stone steps led down to the lower, broader walk. The lights of the town beckoned, a warm orange glow from the street lights, and in the windows of the houses. And suddenly, they went out. The entire world was plunged into blackness but for a soft glow from the hidden moon on the moving waves.

The only way back now was along the thin high ledge, and as if to prove it, the wind slammed against her, lifting her off her feet to toss her down on her back to the concrete walk, arms flailing wildly. There was no railing. The boiling waters fell. Far below dark waves thrashed into whiteness across the rocks she knew were there, hitting and traveling down the side of the pier in a roaring fury. She sat up and twisted around to hands and knees, scrabbling wildly at the concrete ledge. The sea rose again, climbed the side of the pier, and caressed her hand where it clutched the side. One foot higher and she would have been swept away. She froze in panic, on hands and knees. A sharp gust of wind made her start and cry out, buffeting her into rigid, mind-numbing paralysis.

*

Morag's old knife clattered to the floor as the revelation burst into awareness. Raindrops struck the window and drummed on the roof in a fury. The fallen blade gleamed in the candle light. Electricity in the town was out with the giant trees brought down. Macha the jackdaw shifted on the perch and ruffled her feathers, and the cat crept closer to the fire. Morag put a hand to her befuddled head and shifted her awareness from the progress of *The Reiver* on the open ocean, to the cry for help, so close by.

"Terrified. The stinging spray, temper of Manannan Mac Lir." The elements from the magic on the pier were still in her, and it took no effort at all to draw the power through and project it out to the one in imminent danger. There was the same creature of salt waves, but these burst over solid stone, over a tiny drenched spark of human life about to be dragged down, under, and extinguished.

"Duin an uineag a tuath, duin gu grad an uineag a deas," she intoned loudly. "Look for me!"

*

The only thing to do before the sea rose again, was crawl, and crawl fast. Rosalind had seen others blithely skip along this narrow ledge, especially the University students on their traditional Sunday-after-church walks, wearing their scarlet academic gowns. This image, as Rosalind scuttled along, tearing the knees of her slacks and the hem of her drenched coat, was pushed aside by a more likely vision of her body broken in the wild waters below, as the waves rose again and washed over her hands with a terrifying intimacy. She grasped both sides of the ledge and held on until the water fell away.

Two thoughts hit her simultaneously. One, that she was about to die a violent death, a death she had stupidly blundered into; and even while the stark reality flooded her mind with despair and sorrow, the second thing overwhelmed it. There was somebody with her.

Courage filled her, a surge of energy roused and propelled her down the high pier's wall. She gasped and cried, intent on the landward end of the ledge, and with single-minded purpose, she carried on, still crawling, knees bruised and bleeding. She reached the end of the high, thin section, and the pier widened below; she was past immediate danger. In a half-crouch she shuffled down the steep steps to the lower tier, the same place Angus had taken her when they'd watched the northern lights, feeling the way in the blackness with hands and toes. Here, the spray was still vigorous, but the powerful, deep waves did not heave so over the shallow sea bed, and the breaker on the harbor side calmed the water. She collapsed to the stone, breath wheezing through her constricted throat.

Captain Ogilvy, skipper of *The Reiver*, would be facing into the gale, laughing at the crashing spume over his bow, drinking whisky and singing to the old gods of sailors, joyful as an osprey riding the air. The unsinkable old monkfish, torpedoing off on a doomed journey to Tir-nan-Og.

Drops of rain struck her face. Rosalind forced herself up as the stones shuddered and a curtain of spray canopied over the wall. She stumbled down the remaining length of pier, tripping when the wind shoved her sideways, and paused at the steep path leading to the top of the cliffs, barely visible. Uncle Rab would hate her, would curse her if she had him dragged back, like a fish in a net, but surely even he could not weather a storm like this.

*

Morag slipped in the inky blackness of the night, on the steep path to the pier. She cursed and grasped the railing along the walk. And there below her, barely able to trudge up the path, almost bent double, came a bedraggled figure.

Morag heaved herself up and grasped the woman by the arms, peering into her face. "Rosalind! Are you mad?"

Rosalind let her head fall to Morag's shoulder, too exhausted to care.

"Come on, lass." Morag put an arm round Rosalind's waist

and helped her up the slick pathway, clutching the railing, as the wind howled around them. They stopped at the crest of the hill, Rosalind breathing in sharp gasps. The wind hurtled over the cathedral wall and the invisible sea roared below the cliffs.

"Uncle Rab. He's gone," Rosalind said, hand lifted to shield her ear and cheek from the stinging rain.

Morag kept an arm around her shoulders. "Yes."

"You knew?" Rosalind shouted to be heard as Morag pulled her along under the cathedral wall. She turned to look back before the road curved around a bend. She thought she glimpsed a figure in white walking behind them by the haunted tower, and she tried to stop Morag, but when she looked again there was nothing. Where the pier should have been visible, there was only impenetrable darkness. It had all vanished like the horizon, like *The Reiver*, like Uncle Rab, into the open vastness of the night storm.

Morag did not answer, as they clutched each other and stumbled over the wet cobblestones on the lane adjoining Morning Star's street. At last, the row of houses broke the roaring of the wind.

"He must be in terrible pain, and he's so weak."

"It was his choice. He was going to do it whether I helped or not."

"He's gone to die on the open sea." A sob burst out.

"Unless he's blown into Norway first."

"He can't survive this."

"No."

"Oh, God," cried Rosalind. "How could you let him?"

"You mustn't tell anyone." Morag stopped and held her by the shoulders. "Do you understand?"

"No. I don't understand." Rosalind began to cry. "I don't."

"We'll talk later. Someone is here."

It was Angus, standing back from Morning Star's front door, shielding his eyes from the rain as he craned his neck to scrutinize the upstairs windows in the light of a flashlight. He caught sight of them and hurried up, shining the light in their faces, tentatively putting a hand out then withdrawing when he realized it was Morag supporting Rosalind.

"What on earth has happened? You're soaked through."

"I'm okay, Angus."

"Don't tell me you were out for a stroll in this weather?"

"No, no."

"We were to go to the pub, remember? Then this storm came up, and you weren't here."

"Oh, God, I'm sorry. The storm came..."

"Here, let's go inside," he said. "I was so worried."

"No, Angus, I can't right now." She fumbled in her pockets with numb fingers and found her key. "Maybe tomorrow, I'm sorry."

He searched her face more closely, her soaked, battered clothing, and hair in wet strands. "What on earth has happened?"

Rosalind's trembling hands dropped the key and Angus bent to pick it up in the flashlight's beam, but Morag snatched it up first. She turned to open the door, only to find it was not locked. Rosalind moved past her to enter. When Angus stepped closer, Morag blocked his way. "She'll be all right, Angus. I'll have her call you tomorrow."

He didn't move.

"Really, it's all right. She wants a woman's touch just now. She's had a fright."

Rosalind trudged up the stairs. The front door closed as she entered the kitchen and stood in shock. Morag came silently into the hallway.

"I'll make the fire in your bedroom, draw a hot bath, all right? Will there be hot water? You'll never warm up otherwise." Morag found some small candles in a kitchen drawer, lit one and dripped wax onto a saucer to affix it, then did the same with three more. With Rosalind still standing in a growing puddle on the kitchen floor, lips blue and starting to shake uncontrollably with the cold, Morag hurried to fill the bathtub. She gently led Rosalind in by candlelight and helped remove her wet clothes. In spite of the circumstances Morag couldn't help but admire the beauty of her body, slender yet nicely proportioned, nipples taut and erect with the cold, smooth curve of hip pimpled with gooseflesh. Rosalind stepped into the bath, gasping as her cold foot encountered the water's warmth. The steam, scented with bath salts, rose like feathers up her body. She eased in, exclaiming with pain as the hot water touched her scraped knees, and sat. Morag left and quickly reappeared with a shot of whisky and offered it. Rosalind drained it, gasping as it burned its way down, then leaned back to let her head rest on the porcelain. The tears came again. Morag lifted her limp arm where it lay on the tub's rim, and drew a hot washcloth along the length of it. Then the other arm, and her shoulders, her neck, bringing hot water to cascade over her skin.

Rosalind sighed deeply and sniffled.

"He's probably still out there," Morag said.

They were both silent for a moment, then laughed a little.

"Morag, how did you know where I was?"

"Just trust that I did."

"Uncle Rab." Her speech was slurred with fatigue.

Softly Morag sang the answer. "Behind the waves, the ship of my dreaming goes wind-warding as of yore: the will of fate is speeding her way silent and swift as a bird."

The hypnotic croon caressed Rosalind's senses, her eyes clouded over and she was drifting, drifting.

"White barge, O leave me not in distress by the shore of the mighty sea. Depths of pain and of love song draw me, O Tir-nan-Og."

Chapter 21

Rosalind slept late, almost till one p.m., shocked by the hour when she shuffled into the kitchen. The electricity had come back on. She made a cup of instant coffee, wishing for the real thing, and stood groggily at the window, noticing the remarkable amount of branches and leaves covering the lawn from the storm's fury.

She roused herself to call California. Her mother answered.
"Mom, it's me. I'm sorry to phone so early."
"My lass. What's happened?"
"It's Uncle Rab."
"What's he done now?"
Rosalind sighed and sat down. "It looks as if he snuck out of the hospital and took off on his sailing boat, nobody knows where."
"When?"
"Last night. In a storm."
There was a long pause.
"Are you saying he sailed away on the open ocean?"
"That's the unofficial version. The people who know what happened insist it be kept secret." Rosalind braced herself for her mother's reaction. "I expect the hospital version will be that he wandered off and is missing."
"So, Rabbie skived off on his boat," Sheila mused. She began to chuckle. "Aye, trust him to pull a stunt like that. Aye, well, good for him."
"I thought you'd be upset."
"He did what he wanted, no matter what. That's the Ogilvy blood. No doubt there will be some sort of enquiry, though knowing what an excellent sailor he was, I'll be surprised if anything comes of it."

Rosalind decided against telling her mother about the trauma on the pier. It was still too close, a mix of terror and chagrin at her stupidity.

"So," said Sheila. "Sounds as if Morning Star cottage is yours."
"What?"
"The cottage is yours, my lass."

"Oh."

"What are you wanting to do?"

Rosalind rested her forehead in her free hand. "I don't know. I don't know."

"Give it a wee while, in case the old rascal pops up again." She chuckled again and said her goodbyes as Rosalind realized there were surprising depths to her mother's savvy nature.

*

Andrew Nicolson and Peter Caird, respected and beloved Elders of the Town Kirk, had received an anonymous letter which disturbed them greatly, proving in quick time that their suspicions were correct. The Reverend Paterson had gone round the bend. His poor wife Mary was currently locked in the Kirk tower, so as to not interfere with Reverend Paterson's agenda of The New Reformation. He had taken the branks from its display, and set off to preach in the town. Given his current state, it seemed likely that the police would have to be called, and the scandal on the Kirk would take years to mend. The letter urged Andrew and Peter to make all haste in containing the rogue minister. Signed, "A concerned Member of God's Body."

They hastened to the Kirk, only to find the door to the tower locked. They called. "Mary? Mary? Are you there?" A feeble sob was heard. The next hour was spent in chasing down a key, which also served to alert more of the Faithful that something was amiss. When finally the door to the tower chamber swung open, a small crowd of parishioners gazed in to see Mary Paterson sitting on the floor, slumped against the cold stone wall, an empty magnum of champagne tossed aside, chocolate on her lips, chanting something to herself in a small wee voice.

"Mary?" said Andrew.

She looked up and smiled at the amazed faces peering in. "Hullo."

"Mary, where is your husband?" asked Peter.

"My tears have become my bread," she sniffed, "by night and by day."

"We are here to help you," said Peter, "but you must tell us where he is."

"'And forth from the chapel door he went into disgrace and banishment,' she explained, "clothed in a cloak of hodden gray,' which I made for him, you see." She held out her palms. "With these very..." she inspected her chocolatey fingers "...pious..." then licked them, "...hands."

"My dear Mary," Andrew knelt down beside her. "Where is Reverend Paterson?"

She turned earnest eyes to him. "Why, he is out gathering the lost sheep," she said, "of the house of Israel."

*

"The reek of Master Patrick Hamilton infected as many as it blew upon," Reverend Niall Paterson thundered to the passers-by. "Martyred on this very spot! Blessed reek! Holy reek!"

"Ah, there he is," Morag said, as the attention of those passing by was captured under the tower entrance of the university's St. Salvator's Chapel. Niall had taken up a somewhat predictable preaching circuit round the old town, from one martyr's place of execution to the next. Most townspeople hurried past on their way to office, lecture hall and business, but a small group of the curious began to gather as the emaciated, Celtic-tonsured, barefoot evangelist, dressed in a simple wool homespun gown, warmed to his task.

Morag walked unobtrusively behind him, and merged with the onlookers, putting down her large shopping bag.

"Yes, martyred on this very spot!" Niall's commanding finger pointed straight down to the brick initials 'PH' set in the old cobbles. "Tricked in the end by those he trusted, this fervent man of the Gospel, this willing lamb to the slaughter for the sake of God's holy writ!"

A couple of American tourists passing by Morag noticed. "Hey, it's a street show, like at the Edinburgh Fringe."

"Let's go see, George!"

Above Niall's gleaming half-pate, the stone of the tower displayed a grotesque grinning human face, an accident of nature, etched by centuries of harsh elements. The stern finger pointed up. "Here, the imprint of his agony, seared into the very rock, six hours burning on the stake, where I now stand!"

As he turned to point above, Morag slipped around to the street, the shopping bag left slightly open under Niall's soapbox.

Two student divines in black gowns, a young man and woman, drew near and listened. They spoke together in whispers, the woman shaking her head 'no' to the insistence of the man. He would not be contained. "And when ye pray," he said loudly, "ye shall not be as the hypocrites: for they love to stand and pray in the synagogues and in the corners of the streets, that they may be seen of men."

"Thus says the Lord," Niall retorted, "I have sent also unto you all my servants the prophets, rising up early and sending them, saying, return ye now every man from his evil ways."

"It's another fundraiser," said a townswoman, summing up the situation with a pursing of her lips.

"He's quite good," said another. "Here, I have twenty pence."

"Far too much. Give him five p."

"Beware of false prophets," thundered Niall at the students, "which come to you in sheep's clothing, but inwardly are ravening wolves."

Mrs. Pearse arrived, and, with eyes gazing upward to the saint on the soapbox, worn bible clutched fervently, displayed a look of pure adoration.

"For it is a rebellious people, lying children, children that will not hear the law of the Lord!"

A couple of men hurried up the street, concern evident in their expressions and haste. Right on cue, the Kirk Elders, Andrew and Peter, who had been tipped off by the anonymous note.

"Do men gather grapes of thorns, or figs of thistles? Even so every good tree bringeth forth good fruit; but the corrupt tree bringeth forth evil fruit."

Morag moved to the edge of the crowd, arms crossed, settling in to enjoy Niall's final humiliation and demise.

Andrew and Peter pushed their way through. "Reverend Paterson, please come down now."

Their presence only goaded Niall to shout louder above the gathering crowd. "But for the fearful, and unbelieving, and abominable, and murderers, and fornicators, and sorcerers," the mighty finger suddenly sought out Morag. "Sorceress!

Her part shall be in the lake that burneth with fire and brimstone!"

The crowd applauded and cheered, and Morag laughed.

Andrew clutched Peter's arm and indicated the shopping bag beside the minister. Peeking out the top was an iron band. He picked it up and let the cloth fall away to reveal that it was, indeed, the missing branks. "Reverend Paterson, you can't just take things. Please, come..."

Niall spun on him, to see Andrew holding the branks. He drew in a breath of wonder. "Oh see, see what you have brought, for to perform God's holy justice."

"No," said Peter.

Niall pointed again at Morag. "Witch! Witch!" he cried. "Seize her!"

The crowd took up the cry, and a couple of men took Morag's arms, laughing and shouting. "Burn the witch!"

"Here," said Morag, still laughing, trying to wrest herself free. "Get off me."

Mrs. Pearse had an uncharacteristically hungry look in her eyes.

"A man or a woman that hath a familiar spirit, or that is a wizard, shall surely be put to death. They shall stone them with stones. Bring her!" Niall snatched the branks from Andrew and held it aloft. A small gasp went around the onlookers.

"What is that?" said the tourist.

"A torture device!"

"Reverend Paterson," Peter said calmly. "I think that's enough now. You've made your point." He turned to the crowd. "What a wonderful recreation, ha," he said, "by a talented theatre group. Big round of applause!" Peter and Andrew clapped vigorously, then tried to pull Niall away.

He shouldered them off, holding the branks like a rugby ball. "Bring forth the witch!"

The gleeful crowd, now grown much larger, laughed and pushed Morag towards Niall.

"Let go of me, I say!" Morag cried, suddenly realizing things had gone topsy-turvy. "Let me go!"

They ringed Morag, a couple of hands on her shoulders to stand her in front of Niall, as he fumbled open the metal basket. "You idiots," she cried. "Can't you see he's serious?"

Mrs. Pearse clapped her hand against her bible and

bounced up and down in excitement.

"I will keep your righteous judgments!"

Andrew and Peter clutched Niall's arms. "Stop this instant! You are making a fool of yourself."

But there was no keeping Niall from his rightful vengeance as he held open the cage to receive Morag's twisting and turning head. "Turn ye not unto them that have familiar spirits, nor unto the wizards; seek them not out, to be defiled by them. I am the Lord your God!" She was so close, she could see his eyes flashing wildly and the foam that flecked the corners of his thin lips.

Morag watched with horror as the open cage approached her mouth.

"Reverend Paterson! Enough!" The Elders seized him in a bear hug, then Andrew wrested the branks from Niall's hands, as the crowd booed. "You are to come with us now." Though Niall struggled mightily, they pressed him between them and hurried him away, practically lifting him off his bare feet. "Let's just return to the manse where we can talk sensibly."

"Judas," Niall hissed at them. "Unhand me!"

"Your zeal is commendable. But that's enough. Come along."

"Yea, mine own familiar friend, in whom I trusted, which did eat of my bread, hath lifted up his heel against me," Niall hissed at Andrew.

The crowd applauded again as Niall was led away up North Street. His words drifted back. "Ye have not inclined your ear, nor hearkened unto me! Woe to you!"

Morag snarled at Mrs. Pearse, who smiled primly, turned her back and departed the scene in Niall's wake.

"That was great," agreed the tourists. "We just love Scotland." The man pressed a five pound note into Morag's hand. "Thanks!"

Morag backed away, fuming, and stalked off to the castle sands. She took up pebbles and hurled them with all her might into the waves, cursing with each fistful. A remarkable whirlpool of savage energy swirled around her, sparks breaking off to cling to the stones till they hit the water element and exploded like meteor showers. Slowly she calmed down, and climbed to a large sloping ledge of rock under the castle wall where she could sit in peace above the waves rolling in, and shake off the unexpected close call. Hopefully, this would prove to be the final victory over Niall. A little humiliation was worth it, she decided. She'd brought it on herself, too clever by far. As a bit of spray refreshed her face with a cool mist, Morag started to chuckle. Her own scheme had backfired, and served her right. She wondered if Mary had been rescued from the Kirk's tower yet.

From where she sat, Morag had a clear view of the cliffs under the cathedral wall, and the pier where it jutted out into the sea. She slowly and methodically scanned the rugged coast line beyond the pier and East Sands, dreading to catch sight of a ship's sail or broken timbers. Nothing revealed itself, and she knew that despite his frailty, Rab was far, far out on the open North Sea.

Now, at last, no magic to be done, no persons to rescue and comfort, or confound, nothing to distract her attention, she closed her eyes and leaned back against the wall of the castle, listening to the ever-moving small waves gurgle and swirl over the rock. She reached out to the *Reiver* with her second sight, reached out to Rab Ogilvy. He was alive, this she discerned, but distant, and receding into his final journey. So calm was Morag in her sorrow, the tears came quietly, flowing down her face to be lifted off her chin by the sea breeze, so still a child skipping down the long sloping path and stairs to the little beach only noticed a woman sleeping under the castle wall, and paid her no more attention.

*

All trace of the tempest was gone from the late afternoon sky. The sun shone brightly, and though the air was cold and fresh as cool water, the storm-tossed episodes of the previous night seemed like a dream. Rosalind stepped out the back door and squinted at the sky.

"There you are, at last." Morag sat on the garden wall under the few golden leaves left on the rowan, drumming her bare heels against the stone. "Could you use some herbs? I've had to harvest what the storm spared." She lifted her hand high to show leafy bunches hanging from strings looped around every finger.

Rosalind lifted a hand to shield her eye from the sun's

glare. "Thanks," she said half-heartedly.

"Is there any tea going?" Morag asked.

"Oh, sure."

Morag trailed after Rosalind as she shuffled into the hallway. Rosalind stopped, head lowered. "That's why Uncle Rab wanted the food, wasn't it?" Rosalind asked. "For his final voyage."

Morag thought of the food store they had cobbled together on the boat, of his favorite Gitanes cigarettes and bottle of Cameron Brig whisky, and potted hough and sandwiches. She was caught by surprise when the tears came again. From the time she was a wee bairn and he'd tell tales of his ocean-going misadventures, to the meals and pints and all the little interactions of their magical relationship, he with his sailor's lore, she with her family's craft, Rab Ogilvy had played a joyful part in her life, from her birth to his death.

"Oh, Morag, I never even thought. I'm sorry," Rosalind said.

"He'll be missed right enough, irascible Rab."

"Will he return?"

Morag dried her eyes on the sleeve of her pullover and looked up. "No."

"He had it all planned, didn't he?"

"He did. Since before you arrived."

"What will happen now?"

"Och, it depends on whether anyone mentions the ship to the authorities. I don't think anyone would, but one never knows. It would get the poor Harbor Master into trouble, and nobody in the village wants to bring attention to what's been done. Best to hope for is a missing person, an embarrassed hospital staff, some perfunctory questions and all quickly put behind them. Will the boat ever be found, or wreckage? I doubt it, he was an excellent sailor."

"Come have some tea. And there's something I want to show you."

As they moved down the narrow hallway, Morag paused. "Oh, I promised Alastair I'd take a wee look at your artwork. Do you mind?" She handed over the herbs.

Rosalind stopped, one foot on the first step. "They're mostly in there," she nodded. "I don't know what you're hoping to find." She put her back against the cellar door and pushed it open. "Can you get the light?"

Morag stepped in. "By my Lady!"

"You may well be amazed."

Morag took a turn around the cellar, now a working artist's studio. The Victorian fireplace awaited a match to set the coals alight. Sketches and the beginnings of paintings were stacked along one side. A drafting table and chair gifted from the sweet young architect who had a crush on Rosalind, Andrew Burns, filled most of the space of the wall fronting Market Street, under the window. Two small armchairs flanked the fireplace, with a tall reading lamp behind one.

"The natural light's pretty worthless, but this adjustable lighting does the job for now," Rosalind said. "I only wish Uncle Rab could have seen it."

Morag raised her hands. "May it remain as is."

Rosalind put the bundles of herbs on the sloping table. She squatted down to pull a shoebox out from under the table and set it beside the herbs.

"Tell me what you think this is."

With a quizzical glance, Morag reached for the lid, then stopped. She opened her hand palm down over the box and stilled herself. "How strange," she murmured.

"Do you feel something?"

"Aye, it's like a bundle of, em..." she searched for the word, "stale energy or emotion."

"Be my guest." Rosalind gestured at the box.

Morag lifted the lid of the shoebox to reveal the delicately carved wooden container Rosalind had unearthed from the garden. She went completely still, eyes wide.

"Morag?"

"Where did you find this?"

"Buried in the garden."

"You've not opened it?"

"No."

"Are you wanting me to open it?"

"Yes, or tell me if you know what it is."

Morag lifted out the wooden box and carefully studied it from every angle. "Do you have a knife?"

Rosalind pulled a palette knife from a jar of artist's brushes on the table and handed it to her. Morag began to pry off the lid, sliding the blade tip next to each of the six brass nail heads around the perimeter. It came up bit by bit. Morag held the bottom part in one hand, and grasped the top in the other to pull it apart, glancing at Rosalind, who was equally intent, and nodded for her to proceed.

When the lid came off, they both drew in a breath.

"By my Lady," said Morag.

The figure of a woman lay inside, beautifully carved from wood, darkened with time. White linen lined the box. The similarity to a coffin was unmistakable.

"Uncle Rab carved that, I can tell," said Rosalind. "What the hell is it?"

"Unless I am very much mistaken, this is the curse object we have been searching for, for almost forty years."

"Oh my God, look at the face," said Rosalind.

One of the brass nails had been driven into the effigy's left eye.

"Oh, Auntie Meg," whispered Morag. She put it down and stepped back, shaking herself like a hunting dog with its hackles raised.

"Wait, there's something else." Rosalind gingerly lifted out the figure, to reveal a piece of paper folded underneath. She put it on the table, gently opened it and read. "'Meg Gilbride for what you have done may you be cursed by God for the evil hussy you are and may you lose your evil power and never find love.'"

"There's the proof," said Morag as if to herself.

"There's more, like a verse:
'Your Eye has blighted
but Three have blessed.
Stronger are the Three that blessed
than the Eye that blighted.'"

"She's invoked the Trinity against the Evil Eye, an auld charm."

"She?"

"Your mother."

Rosalind laughed in disbelief. "My mother!" She thought for a moment. "Okay, so at a dinner party Alastair mentioned this Ogilvy curse, which even Helen knew about, but nobody could really shed any light on what it was other than a love triangle. And Mom and Uncle Rab both brushed it off like they didn't want to talk about it."

Morag sat in one of the chairs by the fireplace in deep thought, then looked up at Rosalind. "There's something very bizarre about that wee coffin, but first I'll tell you the story as

I've heard it from Meg and Rabbie. Your mother and Auntie Meg were rivals for your father. How lucky was he to have two lovely young lassies fighting over him? One being a witch, however, complicated things. Auntie Meg was never above using spells to get what she wanted, and regardless of your mother's beliefs, I doubt she was thrilled to be in a witch's bad graces."

"So she fought fire with fire."

"The other complication was your Uncle. He took Meg's side."

Rosalind brought the effigy to the other chair and sat, studying it more closely. "You'd think family would unite." The figure's facial features were vague, but its long hair and full skirt were carefully carved.

"Not at all. Your mother was probably the only woman who would put up with him enough to take care of him, and the last thing he'd want would be her running off to the States, to leave him and the cottage all alone."

"Then," Rosalind said, "she got pregnant. With me."

"Aye, but by then it was too late, everyone had set a course and was sticking to it."

They were interrupted by a thunderous rapping coming from the hallway.

"It might be Angus," Rosalind gave the effigy back to Morag and went to the door.

"No," said Morag, "it's Alastair."

Rosalind pulled open the front door to reveal the dapper Laird Comyn, eyes just visible under a wide-brimmed hat, silver-headed cane raised to batter the oak again.

He lifted his chin. "Ah, my dear Rosalind. I have brought the keys to the castle."

"Please come in. Morag is here." She helped him remove his coat and hat and hung them on the peg by the door.

Morag rose to kiss Alastair on the lips.

"Is it done, and is it done well?" he quietly asked Morag.

"Aye, it is. Much to tell. And more." Morag held up the effigy.

"Good heavens." Alastair took it in his hands with a sharp intake of breath to see the brass nail in the eye. "At last. At long last. Time shall unfold what plighted cunning hides."

"Morag was explaining this to me." Rosalind gave Alastair the miniature coffin, and he sat in the chair to study them more closely, placing the effigy into the coffin to see how it fit.

"Do carry on," he said.

"So, yes, your conception raised the stakes on all sides," Morag continued. "The evil eye is a common enough device among the auld Scots witches. 'Droch shùil' it was called."

Alastair chuckled at this. "Wouldn't put it past Meg."

"May I?" Morag took the casket and figure, and made the same movement as before, holding an outstretched palm over the coffin for a moment, eyes closed. "There is a residue of emotion, of fear mostly, jealousy and passion in this object. But no real magic, no real curse. It might as well be a child's toy. It's very strange."

"And yet," said Alastair.

Rosalind gave him the delicate paper with Sheila's curse written across it. "Power of suggestion?" she asked.

"And see how the legend grew over time," said Alastair, "gaining strength all the while."

"I'm not saying I believe any of this, and I can't wait to talk to Mom about it, but suspending disbelief for a moment, why is it strange, if you think this stuff actually works? Does my mother have unknown powers?" Rosalind waved her hands in the air as if to summon the Dark Arts. "You cursed Clive," said Rosalind to Morag. "I saw you. What's the difference?"

"Morag, my love, did you do that? Oh dear." Alastair rose to inspect the drawings on the table.

"You'll be disappointed," Rosalind warned.

He tilted his head in her direction and put on a sorrowful air. "I have no time and certainly no inclination to indulge your trepidation or modesty."

He pulled out the largest sketchpad stacked against the stone wall and laid it on the drafting table. He switched on the overhead light, then slowly studied each drawing.

"First of all," explained Morag, "what passes for curses, or spells or any of the rest of it for that matter, is almost always nothing. Cursing is a desire in a symbolic form by people feeling thwarted or threatened. Like this," she held up the wooden figure. "Sheila was threatened by a rival, and terrified of what could happen to her and the baby – you – if your father chose Auntie Meg instead. The stakes were very high, especially back then."

"I still can't believe my mother would ever do anything like this."

"You may be sure," Alastair lifted his head, "that what people profess to believe to others in the light of day, may take quite a different turn in the secrecy of their own passions."

"So-called cursing has parallels in all human endeavors," said Morag. "Only the form changes. Business rivalry, who fishes which waters, academic squabbles, politics. Religious groups who use prayer as a weapon. And here is your poor mother having to deal with an hereditary line of witches stretching back generations."

"So she used something that spoke the language of the witch," said Rosalind. "But with no more real power than mud-slinging politicians, is what I hear you say."

"And yet," said Alastair again.

"So how does real magic work?"

Alastair shot a gentle warning glance at Morag. "Good luck, dearie."

"Everything is made of a kind of force, of energy. Light is the best word I have," said Morag, "Everything is joined in the dance of that light. Identities arise within it, which remain distinct. A true witch discerns those energetic movements and reshapes them. When that happens, change occurs on the physical plan."

"What?" said Rosalind. "No. You can't change the wood of that chair."

"Your whole idea is incorrect, you assume we are individual entities. This is why it's difficult to explain. It's not the me you think you know, waving a magic wand and entering into some project of altering wood. To effect the true magic, I employ what I am as a magical instrument on this plan and work in tandem with that force."

Rosalind shook her head. "Just tell me about Clive."

"A human is a density of light with a unique identity. If I look into you, I 'see' particles in the light, like droplets that make the mist, always swirling and moving. Or, I refocus with my physical eyes and see you, lovely Rosalind, standing there with your arms folded in skepticism."

Rosalind sighed.

"There appear to be laws of an incorruptible symmetry even in this realm of magic. I reached into Clive and pulled apart the threads joined at the core of his temporal existence. At his solar plexus. He is literally 'undone.' Clive will find himself swept up into actions and forces beyond his ken, as will I and everyone who is part of this unfolding. I do not know yet what form it will take on the physical plane. Yet I, Morag, in tandem with that power, have set it in motion."

"Hush, and be mute," said Alastair, light-heartedly, "or else our spell is marr'd."

"I'm sorry, Morag, I don't get it, at all."

"Why should you?" asked Alastair. "Leave your esoteric lecture aside, Morag, and let Rosalind enter into the greater mysteries through her art, which is as good a path as any."

"That's true enough," said Morag. "Rosalind, whatever we may think about your mother's actions, Auntie Meg has been affected by them. I know this is asking a lot, but may I have this," she held up the small coffin, "to do with as needs be for her sake?"

Rosalind was torn, reluctant to release a mysterious piece of her family's lore, and one of Uncle Rab's best carvings. She wondered what Uncle Rab would say, and the answer was clear. "All right," she said, "you can have it, but only after I've made a drawing of it."

"Thank you." Morag stepped close to Rosalind and softly kissed her cheek.

"Now then," said Alastair, "back to the artwork. You've had some good training," he stated.

"Rhode Island School of Design. A long time ago. Would you like some tea?" Rosalind asked. "I think I could really use some."

"In a moment." Alastair fished in his shirt pocket and brought out a pair of wire-rim spectacles. He put them on and resumed his study of her paintings up close.

Rosalind turned an armchair to face him. Morag did the same, and they patiently watched Alastair's scrutiny of every sketch and painting in the room.

"Throw this away." He chucked a detailed sketch of the cathedral spire ruins to the floor. "And this. Start again." Rosalind made a little cry of despair. He exposed yellowed teeth in a grin, and resumed his culling of her work. "You need to loosen up, stop getting stuck on details before the composition is really under way. Perhaps," he wheeled on her, "the week at Carlin Castle will be just the thing, if you use it properly. It's not technique. Or ability. It's your frame of mind. Do you understand?"

Rosalind considered. "I think so. It's the jump from illustration to painting. I appreciate your advice," she said, "but I'm afraid at the moment I'm flat broke. I've put everything I've got into this house. Those sketches you just tossed aside sell pretty easily at the local gift shop. I don't even know why I'm bothering."

Alastair tossed another sketch over his shoulder. "What sort of prices are you getting for these, if you don't mind my asking?"

"The last one that sold in Elizabeth Stratton's shop, a sketch of St. Andrew's church, the porch, with a simple frame," she said, "was sixty pounds."

They stared in astonishment. She smiled proudly.

"Please, please, oh please," Alastair begged, "don't sell any more in these gift shops."

Rosalind's smile faded.

"Oh, my dear, I shall weep." Alastair crossed behind the chairs to view an unfinished oil painting propped against the far wall. The scent of his flowery cologne trailed after, mixing strangely with paint and turpentine. "Well, who am I to judge? Do what you must, then. Sell your pretty pictures in the gift shop. But after your stay in Carlin, I should like to discuss certain matters with you." He stood and patted his chest absentmindedly. "Morag, my love, where is my coat? The keys."

"I'll get them."

"I don't understand," Rosalind said.

"All in good time, my dear." Alastair angled the reading light to illuminate the painting. "Now, this one..." he said.

"That's what I'm having the most trouble with, my worst work."

In the hallway, Morag felt around in Alastair's coat pocket. The keys were easy to find, along with a Durex, the old rascal.

"To the contrary," he was saying. "It's the best. This is the direction you want to be heading. Rendering reality through the abstract. It's time to loosen your inhibitions, to let yourself flow out, not get picky and uptight and spend too much time focusing on unimportant detail. Eliminate it! It does nothing for the composition, for the focus on the building, the subject itself. Find what will enhance the message."

"I don't think in terms of message."

"I feel," said Alastair, with unquestioned authority, "that you are on the brink of something, but," he dramatically wheeled to gaze powerfully at her, "you may not have the talent."

"Oh."

"Or the time to develop the talent, if you can find it. Your voice, your courage, cut free. Here's the thing. What you are doing now demonstrates a mediocre gift for painting, and good crafting talent for drawing. If you stay in this sphere, you may well get a good reputation as an illustrator, no mean feat in itself. I can't really tell just now which way you will go."

Rosalind sat in a state of shock. Nobody had ever laid it out with such blunt honesty, and she knew he was right.

Alastair gasped lightly and pulled out a drawing of the cup-and-ring incised stone from the Neolithic cairn. "Ah, there it is. The technique I'm looking for. Well done." He pulled a worn wallet from his trousers' pocket and counted out three hundred pounds. "May I presume to buy a painting created from this? I'd like to commission it."

"You want to commission a painting?" Half-disbelieving she accepted the money from him.

"Ha!" said Alastair. "Artists can be so blind with their noses buried in their paints and pots."

"Why this one?"

"Here, compare." He held up the overly meticulous drawing of the cathedral spires next to the Neolithic stone sketch.

She considered them. "The stone is fluid and relaxed, and somehow has a presence. The ruins are flat and too busy with detail."

Morag held up three huge keys on an iron ring four inches in diameter and shook them to chime like tuning forks. "Madam," she curtsied. "The keys to the castle."

"You'll see the door in the old tower." Alastair ripped a sketch of Pittenweem harbor from its pad, taped its corners up on a corkboard above the drafting table, and stood back to view it. "The fifteenth-century tower, not the seventeenth. Of course, you can wander through the rest, the newer wing. You'll want to see my paintings. In particular the Lucian Freud."

"Is there a security alarm?" Rosalind took the keys from Morag, marveling at their size and weight.

"No, my angel. It is, after all, a castle. I shall leave a note in the kitchen, where to put the wine and all. If you need a fire, there's a bit of wood stacked out the back. Take a bottle from the cellar if you like, though not the old Burgundies, please. And don't let that rabble loose on it. I'll put aside a case of plonk for the party after Evensong."

"Oh," said Morag suddenly. "Oh, look." She lifted the portrait of Uncle Rab done in his sleep at the hospital. They all stared at it in silence. Morag gave it to Alastair and rubbed the tears away with her sleeve. "I'll just put the kettle on," she said, heading up the stair.

The doorbell rattled. Morag paused where the stair made a turn to watch as Rosalind went to open the door. Angus, slightly damp, pushed in out of the drizzle, turned Rosalind by the shoulders to face him, and kissed her. She blinked in surprise but returned his kiss. Morag gave a slightly sardonic glance over her shoulder as she ascended to the upper landing.

Alastair, in the hall behind them, cleared his throat.

Angus's head jerked up. "Alastair."

"Dear boy. Don't I get one as well?"

Angus, red-faced, clapped him on the shoulder. "Good to see you."

Alastair assessed the situation with a lifting of a white eyebrow. "I'll just see about that cup of tea." He trudged up the stone stairs, bumped into Morag, and pulled her into the kitchen.

"What's he doing here?" Angus hissed.

"Delivering the castle keys," said Rosalind. "That's this weekend, remember?"

"Oh, right. I'd forgotten in all the excitement. What was going on last night?"

"It was to do with Uncle Rab."

They heard the splash of running water filling the kettle, and a chair being moved.

"Uncle Rab?" Angus asked. "Why didn't you phone me? I tried phoning you this morning but there was no answer. I've been worried sick."

"I must have been completely sound asleep. My uncle, the last time I saw him in the hospital, he wasn't doing so well, and then yesterday..." He waited, head tilted. "I'll tell you later, okay? Or I'll start crying."

"But you are all right?"

"Yes."

The smell of waxed cotton came from his jacket, worn and muddy from fieldwork. He took it off and hung it next to Alastair's coat. "Can we try this again?" He pulled her against the woolly pullover on his warm chest, and they kissed with more relaxed concentration. Something clattered upstairs.

She drew away, smiling at his enthusiasm. "You've cut your beard differently."

"Yes. I thought, since I'm to be in the spotlight, on the telly and such, that it was high time I took a little more care with my appearance. Do you like it?"

"Very distinguished," Rosalind said.

Morag shouted down the stairs. "Where do you keep your biscuits, Rosalind?"

"That's not..." whispered Angus.

"It is," Rosalind said, then called up, "I don't have any. There's crackers in the cupboard."

"Damn," Angus said.

"Do you want to come back later, or have that drink I owe you tonight?"

"I can't," he grimaced. "I've got another press meeting scheduled for seven o'clock."

"Come on, then." Rosalind pulled him up the stair. They paused in the doorway to find Alastair seated at the table and Morag rummaging around for mugs.

"Hello, Angus," Morag said. "You're looking quite dashing."

He self-consciously made a hum and looked at the floor. The bunches of dried herbs lay on the kitchen table. Alastair sliced some cheese they'd pulled out of the small refrigerator and ate it with crackers.

"I was famished," he said through a mouthful. "There were no biscuits," he added reproachfully.

Rosalind pulled out what snacks she could find from the cupboard until a small pile of grapes and apples and oatcakes was collected on the table for Alastair to pick over, fingers plucking up morsels like a dainty egret.

When the tea had steeped, Morag offered Angus a mug. He jumped when her fingers touched his in the exchange, and spilled hot tea over his hand. "Damn!"

"Hold on." She took a cloth from the sink and dabbed the back of his hand. He set the mug down, blushing, and backed up until he was against the wall.

"So, as I was explaining to the bewitching Morag," Alastair's eyes were as shrewd as his voice was jovial, "our own dear Reverend Paterson has been hauled across the coals by his Elders."

"What do you mean?" asked Angus.

"Well, it was rather odd. His wife Mary somehow ended up locked in the church tower, discovered in a highly distressed state by the indefatigable church ladies and a couple of Elders. Drunk on champagne, eating chocolates, and singing 'Amazing Grace,' or some such. Gone quite mad. The as yet unanswered question is, how did it happen? And why would she think her saintly husband was to blame?"

"Surely," said Angus, "Niall wouldn't do a thing like that?"

"Mary's gone to live with her mother for a bit, yet another cross for poor Niall to bear in this vale of tears," Morag said.

"Has he been fired?" asked Rosalind.

"On probation," Alastair said. "His tenure here is ended a bit sooner than anticipated. He's causing too much embarrassment to the congregation. Just this morning he was on a soapbox at St. Salvators railing against the town's evildoers, which of course includes our delightful Morag Gilbride. Which is nothing unusual for St Andrews, except that he's clearly acquired a Christ complex. Which also," he laughed, "is nothing unusual for St Andrews. Power tends to corrupt, as they say."

"He'll end up very happy," said Morag, "somewhere off the West Coast with the Wee Frees."

"That and the Mary incident was the final straw," said Alastair. "Just think, a wee while ago, we'd have all been locked in the tower with Mary, awaiting execution. Witchcraft, heresy, sodomy..."

Morag laughed.

"And what about me?" Angus said to humor the group.

Everyone fell silent and considered. Then Morag spoke. "I took the liberty of reading your cards yesterday, Angus. They implied that somebody crossed you."

Angus went ashen and put his tea-cup down on the counter.

*

Clive looked at his watch as he entered his front door. Forty minutes till he was due back at the office. There was still time for a quick lunch and a phone call to Kirsteen, before she began her shift at work. She'd not been in touch since the ceilidh fiasco, and having worked so diligently to pave the way to their mutual desire, he would be damned before he'd admit defeat. These twists and turns of fate could be used to one's advantage. Enough time had passed, she was probably frightened that he was angry. Kirsteen would be waiting on tenterhooks for him to make the first move. If, however, she proved too immature, too bound by convention or fear to play the game, he could relinquish her without any great cost. After all, her innocent idealism and youthful tactlessness could be incredibly annoying.

Two suitcases had been stacked against the wall. Helen emerged from the bedroom, grim and determined. He hated her when she looked like that, when she peered at him with those wounded equine eyes.

"Going somewhere?" he asked.

She drew herself up. "I'm leaving you," she said.

"What rot."

"That last episode was the final straw."

"You're just going to pack your bags and walk out?"

"I see no alternative at this point."

"I suppose you'll be staying with friends. Not that you actually have any."

"I'm going to stay in a B&B until I know what to do. I won't impose myself in this state on my friends, and yes I do happen to have friends, real friends. Perhaps with a little distance we might be able to see more clearly, work things out."

"You can think again. You won't humiliate me like this, then expect to be able to return when you like."

Helen weighed his words. "Right." She picked up her suitcases.

He stepped quickly out of her way as she bore down on him, a barely controlled fury in her pinched face. She struggled with the door, a heavy suitcase in each hand. He made no move to help. She marched down the front steps and along the pavement, door ajar behind her, toward the town's largest selection of bed-and-breakfasts. That promised to be an expensive interlude. Well, damned if he was paying for it.

Clive turned and smacked his palm hard against the wall.

"Bitch!" He went to the front door and slammed it closed. Good riddance.

He turned to enter the elegant sitting room and poured himself a whisky. Collapsing into the armchair, he picked up the phone and dialed the number to Kirsteen's flat.

"Hullo?" answered a tentative but hopeful voice.

Immediately he knew she was still his for the taking. "Kirsteen," he purred.

"Oh, God," she said. "I thought you'd given up on me."

Wasn't it predictably wonderful how a woman's first reaction was to take the blame on herself? "Don't be silly, things have just been busy."

"Oh, God, I was so worried, but I didn't want to phone your house, because you'd said before..."

"There, there, not to worry. I'm just on my way back to the office, but I thought I'd drop by for a couple of minutes, what do you say?"

"Oh, yes, oh please."

He hung up the phone without any further conversation, absolutely loathing the precious word games young lovers play to end telephone conversations. He was smiling already with anticipation. She'd be desperate for a bit of reassurance, willing to let him take liberties she'd otherwise have coyly kept from him. Oh, yes, there would be no obstacles to that cherry mouth, the soft flesh. But the trick was to hold back. He'd leave her weak with desire, reel her back in, tease her, get her ready for the inevitable.

*

"Thank God they've left," said Angus. "I doubt there's any tea left."

"There is."

Angus sat where Alastair had been and poked apart the herbs. "As I suspected. Hemlock. Monkshood. Deadly nightshade."

"What?" As Rosalind leaned over, Angus laughed and tugged her arm to sit beside him.

"They both go beyond the bounds of what's tasteful sometimes," he said. "I hope you were not offended."

Rosalind was surprised. "No, not at all, they're just being

playful."

"Well," he said. "Now. Rosalind. I came here for a reason."

"Angus," she began, uncertain that she wanted him to continue.

He touched her lips with a finger. "Granted, we haven't known each other that long. Just weeks, really, but what weeks they've been, eh? The best of my life. Hasn't it been fantastic?"

"Yes," she admitted.

"I've never felt this way for anyone before. I knew the first time I saw you, at the church dig, with Helen, remember?" His face softened with the memory.

"It's been one of the most wonderful times of my life. I'll always treasure it."

"I've waited all my life for someone like you. You make me feel complete, whole. Rosalind." He gathered her hands in his. "I believe I have come to love you."

"Angus. I'm not sure what to say. You know I have strong feelings for you."

"Do you? Do you really? I'm so happy to hear you say it." He took out a little velvet-covered box from his vest pocket and pushed the herbs aside to place it in front of her on the table.

From the hallway, the floorboards creaked.

Rosalind stared at the box. "Angus, we're not rushing things, are we?"

"Actually, I thought it a perfect time. You see, things are on the brink of change. I don't know what's going to happen exactly. I'm going to be caught up in this wave of research and work, and I'm not sure what it will all mean, where I'll end up. But I do know this; that I will be able to offer you much more than I ever could have before."

The little box emanated a powerful disturbance. Rosalind's mind had gone remarkably blank but for one question that nagged. "Angus, I hate to bring this up, but do you remember that night here before you left for London? Right after the visit with your brother?"

He sat back. "Vaguely."

"What happened?"

He considered. "You must remember that I'm an old bachelor. I think I was overwhelmed by the potential changes you are bringing into my life, wonderful though they are. And

I admit I was in a foul mood with the family dynamics. Think nothing of it. It's not important."

She wasn't convinced, but he seemed eager to put it behind them.

"You see," he said, "at the moment, while things are relatively calm and while you and I are still in the position of being able to make decisions before I really get swept away, I wanted to ask you," he brought her limp hand to his lips, "if you might consider, I mean, the possibility... can you tell I've never done this before?" He sat up straight and spoke formally. "Would you consider an engagement?"

The cottage ghosts were stilled, waiting. Time stopped.

"Engagement?"

"To be married."

There, he'd spoken the words. "Angus," she began. "Hasn't it been fine the way it's been? I mean..." She rubbed her tired eyes. "I'm so tired I can't think."

"You don't have to say anything just now," he hastened to add. "Go on, open it."

She lifted the box's lid to see a modest diamond set in a silver band of minute Celtic knot-work. "How unusual. How beautiful."

In the hush she could hear his breath whistling through his nostrils. In out, in out.

"I know it must be a surprise," he said, "but I've been thinking of nothing else." He started to speak rapidly. "Of course I'd just as soon whisk you away to Gretna Green and wed you now before I lose you to some other admirer, or you leave, God forbid, for the States, but I'm trying to be a prudent wooer and do things properly. Please realize, even the treasure is nothing without you."

The treasure. His other passion. She seized on the subject, teasing to dissipate the tension. "You think fame will go to your head?"

"I wouldn't want this change in fortune affecting your decision, either."

She bit back a smile. "Probably wise. But it really does seem very sudden."

"I won't risk losing the only woman who's ever stolen my heart. I can offer you the means to stay. You would want for nothing."

Such a powerful part of her wanted to shout, yes! and

throw her arms around him. Everything would be so easy then, but something held her back.

"The thing is," she said slowly, "I'm in the middle of realizing how much I gave up for my husband."

"As I would do for you." She started to speak, but he kept on. "I understand your reservations, but it's also true that when a priceless opportunity presents itself, would it not be a shame to lose it by not seizing it, regardless of current circumstances?"

"We haven't even made love, Angus. How do you know we'd be compatible?"

"I wouldn't insult you," he said, "by having sex be a deciding factor in this decision. I'm not saying I don't madly desire you, but this is something that transcends the physical. For me, it's plain, you are the one. Everything else is secondary."

Such a burden of expectations confounded her. "Angus, you've honored me. I really am at a loss for words. I didn't expect... I mean...." He watched her anxiously. "I don't know what to say. I'm completely overwhelmed. Uncle Rab's just died, at least I think he has, and I'm flat out exhausted."

"He'd lived a good life, from what I understand, which is a rare thing."

"I guess so."

Angus looked at the ring and back at Rosalind.

"Please, can I have a few days?" Her mind raced to find a means of delaying. "I'll give you my answer at the castle. Would that be all right?"

"Of course. Of course!" He seemed almost relieved. "And now my love, I must dash. My public is waiting." He stood and drew her to him and kissed her with such passion that she had to sit when he had gone, and clutch the edge of the table, immersed in the pungent scents of the fresh-cut herbs.

A slow shuffle started up the stairs and stopped at the kitchen door. Rosalind knew it now for what it was, the lifelong trudging up and down, up and down her great-grandmother Mairi had done every day of her life.

The ghosts came to the table. Where before Rosalind had merely imagined their daily chores and interests, now they sat still and watched her with eyes like black marble. Was their message to join in the mundane destiny of human existence such as theirs had been, or to avoid what they gave their lives for? Their stony faces revealed nothing.

*

It had been absurdly easy to find the contact in Amsterdam. A couple of phone calls, a bribe, a visit from a former archaeologist gone bad from severe disappointment, betrayal by colleagues in his former university, taking revenge by using his knowledge for the black market.

They'd met at dusk, under the spires of the cathedral ruins. The gold and ruby cross, easily slipped into a jacket pocket, had never made it into the showcase at Swallowsgate, and thus went undetected in all the excitement. Had the wretched Chairman of the Medieval Department not raised questions, with his bloody manuscript list, it would have fallen away into obscurity. Angus would be the only one to know, and he'd be too scared to say anything, lest it be pinned on him.

The cross in its cloth wrapping was brought out under their bowed heads and quickly examined. A nod, an envelope extracted from the archaeologist, its contents of banknotes quickly riffled through by Clive. Mutual smiles, quick nods, and they parted ways.

Clive whistled happily as he strode out of the grassy cemetery. Time to celebrate with a good whisky, and finally purchase the plane ticket, one-way, to Costa Rica, where he would put the cash down-payment on the estate he'd decided on, in the colorful, tropical hills above the deep blue ocean, and where he could live like a king with his well-deserved ill-gotten gains. He would slip away, never to be found, living out the rest of his life in a very inexpensive paradise.

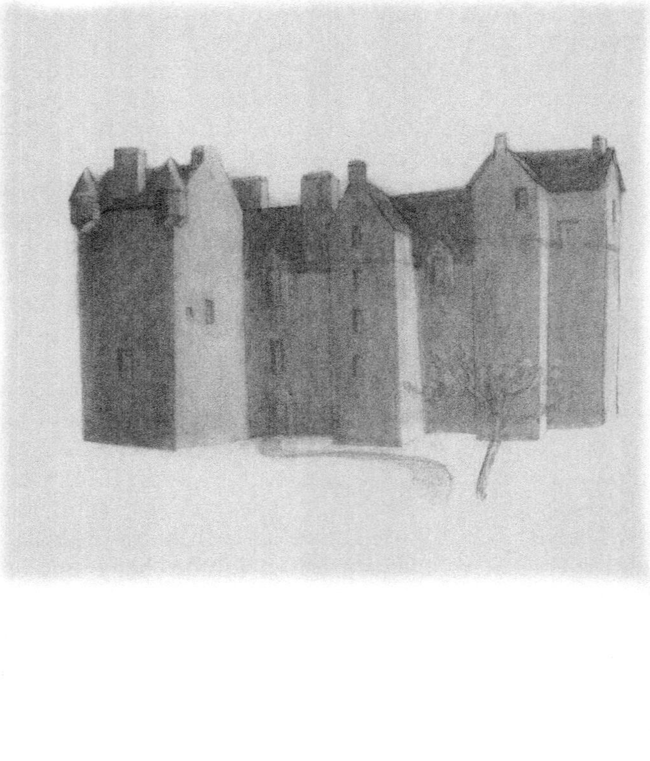

PART THREE

Chapter 22

Two days later a subdued Helen dropped by Morning Star with the car keys, a map and a National Trust for Scotland handbook on the wonders of Carlin Castle. It wasn't until she was leaving that she mentioned, almost as an aside, that she'd left Clive and moved to a B&B until she could think clearly what to do.

"Why didn't you tell me?" asked Rosalind. "Why on earth didn't you say something?"

"I couldn't ever trouble others with my private problems."

"For heaven's sake, Helen. Stay here, in Morning Star."

"Oh, no, I couldn't impose."

"I won't even be here for a week. Oh, come on, Helen. Wouldn't you do the same for me?"

Helen progressed through stages of looking adamantly resolute, puzzled, then grateful. "Well, if you put it that way."

"You'll have peace and quiet while I'm gone. But stay for as long as you need to. Please, I insist. You can have a whole floor to yourself."

Helen mulled it over some more before she said, "Well, yes, all right, if I won't be inconveniencing you. All right. But only for a very, very short time." She thanked Rosalind profusely, with an embarrassing amount of gratitude, as if she'd never received a simple kindness.

They drove the few streets over to collect the suitcases from the B&B, explained the situation to the friendly couple who ran the place, brought the suitcases back, and replaced them with Rosalind's bag.

As they were about to say goodbye, Rosalind hesitated.

"Helen," she said. "Angus asked me to marry him."

Helen lifted her thin eyebrows. "Well. Fancy that. What on earth did you say?"

"I asked for time. I don't know what to do. It's so sudden, and he's adamant. Why must it be marriage? Why can't we just be lovers?"

"Gosh, I don't know what to say. I'm not much for marriage just now given my circumstances. As far as Angus goes, though, his background is emerging, I daresay, the minister's son doing it right, without the sin of pre-marital sex. I think he actually believes he is honoring you. He's not like you, a sunny Californian with the hippie movement just past."

"It's so foreign to me, this all-or-nothing."

"Well, good to know now, rather than later, don't you think? 'Marry in haste, repent at leisure,' as they say. But really, it's good you're getting away. You'll get some perspective." She kissed Rosalind's cheek, the first time she'd ever done such a thing. "Cheery bye. Not to worry about me. If I decide to attend the Evensong, I'll have your hopeful fiancé drive me."

*

Rosalind headed north. Once over the Tay Bridge, the road led through Blairgowrie, climbed into the mountains over the pass called the Devil's Elbow, and into Braemar. A narrow lane wound west down a deep, forested glen. Autumn color was everywhere, on the heathery shoulders of the hills, among the trees, in the deep blue of the sky mirrored in a stream below.

It was a great relief, far more than she could have anticipated, to look out over the golden bracken and soft grasses in an unbroken line of vision to the horizon of mountain silhouettes. No people. No buildings. No decisions bearing down on her. Just sheep and expanses of wilderness.

An hour's drive up a winding single track road, she came to the high stone wall of the estate, and drew up to the large entrance gates of thick ironwork. A herd of red deer within lifted their heads to stare when Rosalind got out to push the heavy gate open. Huge rhododendrons lined the way, under twisted, red boughs of scotch pine. As she continued down the meandering drive, craning her neck for the first glimpse of the castle, tantalizing shapes and shadows flashed through the trees, until she rounded the final curve, and brooding Carlin Castle was there, sheer stone walls rising to turrets under a slate roof, small windows beneath, little panes stacked one above the other. At the sight of it she drummed her fists against the steering wheel and cheered with excitement. A real castle all to herself!

The drive gave way to crunching pea gravel. On Alastair's instructions, Rosalind drove to the farthest door, modest compared to the two others, but a giant door nonetheless, and parked the car close to the tower. She got out of the car and entered the silence of the mountains, but for the soft soughing of distant wind in the pine forest.

The simple fifteenth-century tower joined a multi-storied, many chimneyed wing. This in turn adjoined the seventeenth-century tower, more elaborate than the spare original, with peaked turrets on all corners, and a semicircular wall between the wing and newer tower which could only be housing a spiral stair. The back of the castle, arrived at after an eager walk through an autumn garden, lacked the simple facade of the front, with room extensions jutting from the old walls. Modern plumbing pipes, bolted to the outside walls, ran down from the upper stories.

Rosalind stood quietly, taking deep breaths of a spicy mountain perfume she could not identify. The hoarse calls of rooks came faintly from down the forested glen, and beyond the birds a whisper of wind. She walked around the castle, moving from gravel to flagstone paths, then to lawn. A walled garden took up all the level space between the back of the castle and the steep hill rising above it.

She returned to the car for her suitcase and ascended to the tower door. A discreet sign at eye level read 'private.' This tower was still Alastair's residence, the rest of the castle in the care of the National Trust for Scotland, with the entire property to be given over to the Trust upon his death.

The largest key fit readily into the lock, and with a well-oiled, heavy clunk, the bolt withdrew, and the door eased open on smooth hinges to reveal a large barrel-vaulted kitchen. Shining copper pots dangled from iron hooks over the table, bunches of dried herbs and flowers hung along the wall. Another door at the far end was crowded about with walking sticks, boots and raincoats.

A note lay on the table, its corner pinned down by a bottle of wine.

> "Welcome dear kindly Rosalind, to my
> home. You will find the fridge more or less

stocked, clean sheets, fires laid. Wood at the garden door. A lady from the village does for me, a Mrs. Farquharson, one of countless Farquharsons in the area. Number I can be reached by the telephone. Village grocer/ post office ought to have anything you need. Watch for the painting, a Sorolla Y Bastida to be delivered Friday afternoon, vino as well. Have the man put the painting in the bedroom, wine to the cellar. Your only other duty is to open the main door 3 pm Saturday, for Evensong, and lock up when they're all gone. Otherwise, mi castillo es su castillo. Enjoy enjoy, and thank you very much.

P.S. There's a nice walk to the hillfort, prehistoric. Lovely views. Binoculars at back door. Look for ospreys from the loch, golden eagle if you're lucky.

Oh, P.P.S. The deer rut will be in full gear. Do not, I repeat, do not, get close to the stags."

Signed with an indecipherable flourish.

*

Rosalind went up the spiral stairs neatly built into the corner of the tower. A heavy ship's rope run through iron rings set in the wall, oily with use, served as a banister. Her heels hung off stone steps sculpted into wavy depressions by countless other feet. Some were overlaid with boards where the hollows had become too deep. The walls were creamy plaster, with the occasional stone and wooden beam left exposed.

Another flight up and she stepped into the bedroom, dominated by a huge four-poster. Its dark wood matched a large cupboard and the lintels over the narrow windows. A long chest stood at the foot of the bed. On it a massive Bible, propped open on a stand, had the Comyn family tree, in hues of ink depending on the century, recorded by widely varied handwriting.

Rosalind's attention was pulled to the vision of a nude woman with a blank stare lounging on a bed, a stark, unflattering Lucian Freud hung between the four-poster and fireplace. She put down her suitcase and walked to the painting, entranced, and did a thing she always longed to do in museums: touched it to feel the deep ridges of paint, the texture of the different planes of the subjects, the sensuous curve of brushstroke, the incarnate disciplined abandon she had not yet mastered, and realized then, that she never would. Up close it felt more like a sculpture than a painting, the paint pushed into its forms of expression.

A raven cawed from above the castle. As if a cue, the rest of creation fell silent, no more lowing or baaing or bird-song or pheasant's call. Only the raven's harsh voice over the forested glen. Rosalind climbed the spiral stair to the topmost floor, to find a library-cum-spare bedroom, filled wall to wall with old leather-bound volumes, and a grand sleigh bed covered by a white duvet

Charmed by the intimate size of the castle rooms, she spiraled down to her bedroom, tossed her suitcase onto the high bed, then opened it to unpack her few things.

*

The white mare arched her brawny neck and snapped her hooves high. She'd present Morag a challenge if she dismounted, but so be it. All good people of Celtic ancestry know that animals move effortlessly between the worlds, and Morag's magical abilities had no more effect in the energetic realm than the incarnate one where a beast was concerned. She swung a leg over the mare's broad back and stepped down. The mare circled as Morag bent over to grab up a fistful of pea-gravel, the other hand keeping the reins. The mare shied dramatically as Morag threw the gravel at the castle bedroom window, pulling her to her knees. Morag cursed, stood and grasped the mare's ear to bring her head down, and muttered the ancient secret words, "Both in one." The mare calmed a bit. When nothing happened upstairs, Morag threw another volley, this one eliciting merely a toss of the big head. Still nothing. Morag gave up and attempted to mount again, the mare circling on a short left rein while Morag hopped like an idiot with one foot in the stirrup, and managed to spring into the saddle. This the mare took as permission to pirouette and attempt a gallop, which Morag in turn cancelled, as pea gravel flew from the hooves and bounced off the castle steps. This was folly, thinking she could entice Rosalind down for a leisurely ride, but damned if she would give up now.

The high window unlatched "What are you doing here?" Rosalind called down. "And where did you get a horse?"

"Come for a ride!"

The mare in her beauty demanded attention as she made a royal mess of the drive, inscribing strange runes into the earth as her hooves rearranged the gravel. Rosalind's head disappeared and before long the castle door opened to reveal her hastily pulling on her jacket. She grabbed Alastair's birding binoculars from their peg, hardly pausing in the momentum carrying her out into bright sunlight, and stood at the top of the steps to study Morag and the mare.

"Alastair set this up, didn't he?"

Morag patted the horse's broad rump. "Come on."

"How?"

The horse was overly eager, but very well trained. A boot sliding back against the ribs, a pressure of the reins against the neck, and she stepped nicely sideways to the steps. Morag put a hand out and Rosalind grasped it. "That's it." Morag leaned to the other side, as Rosalind swung a leg over the broad back. Before she'd found her seat, the mare spun and crunched over the drive, then thudded down the turf of the field, freed from Morag's hand which was desperately trying to prevent Rosalind from slipping off.

"Slow down!" Rosalind grabbed Morag's waist and began to pull her off balance.

"Hold the cantle," Morag cried, fingers of her other hand twined in the horse's mane.

"What?"

"The back of the saddle. Lean back a bit."

Rosalind found her seat just before they both slid off, and settled in on the cushiony haunches. The mare swished her tail and became a bit more biddable.

"What are you doing here?" Rosalind asked, breathless.

"Didn't I tell you?"

"No."

"How thoughtless of me."

The mare lifted her hooves over lichen-dappled stones along the trail. Tall grasses, golden in their autumn finery, and ferny clumps of bracken complimented the vivid yellow of birch and rowan.

"The thing about Scotland," Rosalind said, "is the light. The light and the colors."

"There's lots of things about Scotland. I'm going to show you another."

"Is this your horse?"

"No. A mile down the road, a farmer who trains them for hunting lets me exercise one when I come. Does them good to get out of familiar territory."

They trotted down the narrow path, under the feathery golden larches. Ghostly beech limbs formed a canopy high above. The deep shadows of the forest drew in. Everywhere lichen greened and silvered trunks and stones, and moss appeared in patches on rock faces or fallen trees.

A hen-sized bird, dark feathered, dashed across the path and down to the stream. The mare huffed and feinted sideways in play.

"Capercaillie," Morag said, holding the mare to a walk.

"But you still haven't said why you're here," Rosalind said.

"My annual festive gathering. Samhuinn we call it. Alastair loves to host the event, even if he rarely attends. We bring special magic to his land. Generations of our families have colluded in this gathering, even though it's been truly dangerous for all concerned in certain periods of history."

The wide path led up the glen, following the base of a hill on the left. The land fell sharply away on the other side, down to a sizable creek. The sun flashed, dazzling, on the peaty water where it spilled, roared down small waterfalls and flowed over rounded boulders, then smoothed quietly out, the color of strong tea. Beyond the burn, the other side of the glen rose again to steep, forested slopes.

"What will you do?"

"Make magic. Dance. Have a party."

"Magic for what?"

"Something for you, perhaps?"

"I think I've had enough of your magic, thanks anyway."

The stream below flattened and smoothed out, and they emerged into a meadow. Forest gave way to heather on the mountainsides, which in turn sloped away from the clearing, ringing a natural amphitheater.

Morag wheeled the mare sideways and stopped.

"Oh, my God," Rosalind said.

In the small valley, massive gray-blue stones stood upright, spread out like columns to a temple, forming a circle about forty feet across. The two tallest, fifteen feet high, were butted against a single huge stone lying between them. The rest looked to be placed at equal intervals, about four yards of turf between, graded in size so that the smallest were opposite the tallest flanking the horizontal stone.

Beyond the stone circle, the field opened up to a dramatic view of the glen and distant mountains. The stones were shocking and incongruous in the gentle meadow of the valley.

"They look alive," Rosalind said, "like they were dancing, then frozen in the act."

"I always feel remarkable," Morag said, "when I see them again. Hang on!"

The mare sank back, then surged forward across the grass. Rosalind grabbed Morag again, pinning her arms in a panic.

"The saddle!"

The mare skipped sideways as Rosalind's heels dug into her groin. Then they both straightened out as they headed straight for the horizontal stone. Rosalind shrieked.

At the circle's perimeter Morag reined the mare to the left and cantered clockwise around the stones, three times, shouting out a chant in Gaelic to the horse's rocking rhythm before reining the mare to a halt. Rosalind slid down, a hand on the mare's big haunch which came sideways and knocked her off balance. She fell backwards a couple of steps then collapsed to her rump in the long grass. Morag kicked her boots from the stirrups and swung down. She led the mare to a tree at the forest's edge, put a hand on her strong neck, and reisted her, the old way of having a horse stay where it's asked. She slipped the bit from the mare's mouth and drew it up under the chin so she could graze.

Halfway back Morag leapt high and punched the air as she entered the stone circle.

Rosalind followed her in, marveling at the personality of the stones. Morag stood in the center, both arms raised, slowly turning. Rooks rose from the forest and flew, cawing, over the tall stones and down the glen.

"Can you feel it!"

"They have such a presence." Rosalind touched one of the big stones, warm from the sun. "It's a little Stonehenge."

"Well, sort of. These are called recumbent stone circles. I prefer these Scottish rings myself, especially as very few tourists see them. Just the occasional archaeologist. This one's especially private, being out of the way on Alastair's estate; there's no farming, so it's survived remarkably intact."

"How old are they?"

"Four to five thousand years or so."

"What were they for?"

"Come tomorrow night and find out."

"But surely you don't really do the same things they did back then?"

"No, actually, we don't. Society has dramatically changed over four or five millennia, and of course the rituals have as well. Nobody honestly has a clue. Nothing was written or inscribed. Roman and Christian propaganda colors what we do know. I can tell you what I experience, I can explain the importance of the seasons to the communities from which the rituals probably developed, but there is no actual historical record to build on. I try to be diplomatic, keep the old ones happy in their family traditions, but move into new areas as things are revealed to me."

"Like what?"

Morag thought for a moment. "Like one of the most venerable Highland methods of augury, when the seer stands in a door's threshold on four certain Quarter days of the year, having fasted, and opens his eyes to see what signs present themselves. So, I thought, if a door's threshold can be used as a magical in-between place for divination, why wouldn't a threshold like that," she pointed to the large megaliths beside the recumbent, "be even better?"

"And, is it?"

"Most assuredly."

"I'll take your word for." Rosalind knelt beside the massive recumbent stone. "Oh, my gosh. This design is just like a stone in the cairn Angus showed me." She ran her hands lightly over the cup and ring markings clustered on a section of the stone's face. The small bowl-like depressions were surrounded by arcs, up to five lines circling them. "What do these mean? Angus said nobody really knows."

"They were constructed by aliens from another planet," Morag said, "to mark landing sites for their UFOs."

Rosalind, hands still on the stone, half-turned her head.

Morag clapped her hands at catching Rosalind out. "The recumbent stones are always in the southwest. This one is aligned nicely. The solstice sun sets directly between those megaliths." She turned and began to clear away a section in the center of the circle, pulling the grass back to reveal a flat stone with a blackened surface set flush to the ground.

"The moon also moves through them. Where the sun takes one year to complete its solstice to solstice arc, the moon does the same, but it journeys nineteen years to the place it stops and reverses course over the recumbent. It's just fantastic, a piece of magic still active from the mists of our own history. You should come at the solstice to see it."

Rosalind sat with her back against the stone. "The solstice. A lot's going to happen between here and there."

Morag stretched out on the grass beside her, dusting the earth from her hands. "Will you marry him?"

"I promised I'd tell him tomorrow."

Morag sighed, and plucked a piece of the long grass and chewed on the end. "What's happening tomorrow?"

"The University Renaissance group is doing Evensong in the castle. There'll be a party afterward. I thought you knew."

"I may have heard. My thoughts have been taken up with my own concerns."

A whistle came from above, a small goshawk circling the glen.

"Why do you do it?" Rosalind asked. "What's the point?"

"I don't know if I can explain it as well as I can show you. It's something I am compelled to do, and after all, I do have my own little legacy to uphold."

The goshawk suddenly plummeted down the hillside. A bird at least as large shot out of the bracken with a whirr of wing beats and a cry like wood scraping on wood. The goshawk closed in, slid talon first underneath, and brought it down in a storm of feathers.

Morag scrambled to her feet, startling the horse, and raced to where the birds had landed. A brief altercation ensued, hawk and woman standing off over the prey, until the hawk, disgusted, flapped away. Morag returned swinging the limp carcass triumphantly.

"Pheasant for dinner," Morag said in an English accent. "I say, haven't I trained my little goshawk rather well?"

"Nobody's going to believe me if I tell them what just happened." Rosalind inspected the pheasant, the bloody punctures where the hawk's talons had gripped, the lolling head. She slid the long barred tail feathers through her fingers. "Just when I've seen this other world, I'll have to go back to where I was and take up that old life again. All this Scottish experience wasted."

"Oh, aye, the Scottish Experience. I should sell tickets."

They sat quietly, watching the circling breeze set the grass heads and bracken to dancing. Rosalind glanced around and heaved a giant sigh.

"What I think I will do," she said, "is take off and explore the hills."

Just as Morag began to speak, a roar and shriek echoed down the glen. Both twisted to peer past the stones to the meadow beyond. The sound came again, and again, a child's scream, or a woman's, but then lowering to a gruff male shriek, making the hair on Rosalind's neck prickle.

"What the hell is that?"

The white mare had turned her head and was listening as well, ears pricked at attention.

"Sika deer, rutting. The little stags are claiming their right to mate."

"That is the weirdest sound I've ever heard."

"Oh, just wait till you hear the Red Deer. Mind you avoid the herds. They can be very aggressive."

"If I go up the hillside, will I be able to see them?"

"Aye, I think so."

The uncanny roar was joined by another, rising to an unworldly duet.

"Incredible," said Rosalind.

"Join us tomorrow, a bit before midnight. As you see, it's an easy walk from the castle, but a world away."

"It's going to be a full program at the castle. Why don't you come visit me tonight, have a glass of Alastair's wine? Tell me ghost stories of Carlin Castle?"

Morag sat up, surprised and pleased. "I'd love to." Then she remembered. "But I'm supposed to drive back to St.

Andrews tonight and pick up some things for the gathering."

"Too bad." Rosalind got to her feet. "I'm off to climb a mountain."

"Aye, you'll tak the high road."

"Angus said there were human sacrifices at some of these sites."

"There were prehistoric remains found here, a charred skeleton with the head decapitated and placed between the feet. And I think a few more skulls by themselves. Not untypical. Here in Scotland we love collecting heads and arranging bodies in bizarre configurations. One of those little things that make us so lovable."

"So who's going to be the sacrifice tomorrow night?" Rosalind called over her shoulder as she headed for the base of the mountain.

Just as it had when Morag held Auntie Meg's hands and her sight burst open, it came again, riding on the sika stag's otherworldly bellow: the fire, the blood, the screams, a great gleeful roaring all around the circle, closer now, gathering strength at its source. Morag scrambled to her feet, blood pounding in her ears, head cocked as she invited more information from the wild. But this magic had the ancient in it, and was not in the least biddable.

From a distance the heather looked soft and inviting. Up close it was anything but kind. Thick, gnarled branches, higher than her knees, made walking almost impossible. Red-brown tangles of boughs curved over Rosalind's legs and grasped at her feet. The wood was supple, impossible to break, the roots sunk deep in the peaty earth. She stopped, breathing hard, heart thumping, and turned to find the deer. A small herd was milling about just up the glen, an anxious stag combing through the does. His rival appeared to have been driven off.

From the glen the hillside had given the illusion of an easy climb. Rosalind wanted to reach the highest summit over the standing stones, but a mere fifty yards through the heather and she was ready to abandon the attempt. The top of her thighs burned from lifting her knees high, pulling her feet from the clutching heather, with every heart thudding steep step.

Nor had the summit appeared to be too far, but this too was a deception. As she slowly climbed, panting, dismayed at the effort it was going to take to reach the top, the pressure to make the final decision whether to accept Angus's proposal pressed down with stultifying force.

Kicking back against a particularly cunning arm of heather, she teetered. A glance down revealed a hillside so steep that if she started rolling, crashing through the fiendish shrubs, there would be no stopping till the glen floor. She lost her balance, and saw the mountain moving in a spin as she toppled. She twisted and fell to the side, hands going painfully through the heather to the springy peat below. She remained on hands and knees for a moment, angry that a bare looking hillside could defeat her.

Something soft and cold squashed between her fingers. Little dark brown pellets.

But when Rosalind wiped the stuff off against the heather stems, she realized a path was under her nose, a thin, well-worn track. The pellets lay along the trail, their source revealed by wisps of wool plucked by the heather's elfin fingers. The sharp little arrows of deer hooves were mixed in, pointing the way. On the hill opposite the glen a handful of sheep were in the bracken, undisturbed by the deer, grazing on the sweet green grass below. And beneath her she could see a couple of these trails she'd stepped over without being aware of them, bringing herself to tears of frustration when it would have been easy to follow them up, one connecting to the other, till she'd crisscrossed the face of the mountain.

"Idiot," Rosalind said. "Idiot! Do you have to land in shit before you can see anything?" She pulled a tuft of cream-colored wool from the heather and rubbed it between her fingers. The lanolin glistened slightly. She crushed and pulled the wool apart, and breathed in scents of comfort and warmth.

Far below, the circle of stones still contained Morag, walking its perimeter. From the hillside Morag looked tiny, insignificant, but even from that vantage point the essence of her personality shone. Despite Morag's enigmatic character, Rosalind puzzled over her strong attraction for the woman. It wasn't as simple as she would have thought, emotions mixed up with everything else that had been happening. Nor could it be denied that Morag seemed to live by different rules altogether. So much so that Rosalind realized any sort of normal relationship was never going to be.

Down the forested glen the towers of the castle pushed up through the trees. It was not far from castle to circle, less than a mile.

Rosalind quickly ascended, following the path sideways and up, not making the mistake of looking down again. Before long, almost to the rounded shoulder of the hill, the track led over a sizable earthen hump, fifteen feet wide. She stood on its crest and studied the summit. The mysterious ridge encircled the hilltop. It fell away in a depression, then rose in a second ridge, two huge rings capping the hill. She was above the heather now, and climbed straight up to a flattened top. What seemed a natural path led to the center, ending in a U-shaped ridge. The series of earthworks encircling the mountain had to have been built by humans.

As steep an incline as that she'd ascended fell away from the back and far side of the mountain top. The open section, facing the direction of the castle, followed a gentler ridge, dipping then rising again to link with the next bareheaded hill. It finally dawned. She'd ended up in the Iron-age hillfort Alastair had mentioned. She could go back that way, the high road, and find an easy route down to the castle.

Her heart still thudded from the climb. It beat in her ears, a jumping pulse from feet to fingers. It felt good, a rhythm of life, strong and steady, in tandem with the unfettered wind rising on the summit.

She crossed the flat top of the mountain, to the far side of the earthworks, and stopped short. A magnificent vista opened up before her, of mountains and glens and forests below, but unlike the slope she'd just ascended, the north face fell away in a sudden gradient leading to a sheer cliff. Her shoes crunched down in the loose rubble, and a few stones slid and rolled away. One bounced loose from the earth, picked up speed, and sailed out over the cliff's edge.

Anyone there in the mist or rain or snow would never know until it was too late how dangerous the mountain was. Morag had warned her of the surprising number of lives the Scottish mountains claimed every year, usually by unprepared hikers who were caught by sudden changes in the weather.

But even with the earth slipping beneath her, rather than feel frightened, she was emboldened. The adrenaline was coursing, all her senses were acute. She turned, and went to her hands as the loose scree gave way beneath her feet, more of it plummeting away, but she calmly kept scrabbling back up to the highest point of the mountain, to the sure stability of the turf in the Iron-age hill-fort.

Movement of a large object caught her eye. A huge bird of prey was riding the updraft below the mountain's summit. A golden eagle, which she could have sworn glanced her way as it glided by.

She pulled out Alastair's binoculars and made a slow complete circle with them. To the west, snow-capped mountains glowed a festive rosy color in the low autumn light, the Cairngorms her mother spoke of with such fondness. The place where a compass is no use, where ghosts chase hikers, where fairies lead them in circles. The place where there are many doors to another world. Belief is not required. The ancient earth itself is the doorway. Behind the doors is a mirror, fashioned out of millennia of ancestors who viewed it in turn, most at their deaths, but everybody at some point. And what hands fashioned and held the mirror? Better to find the door and open it while there was still time to live out its revelation. Just like Uncle Rab had been trying to tell her.

His presence was so strong he could have been standing beside her. Her heart went out to him, and she blessed him for the strength he'd insisted already existed in her, for his dynamic passion for life and his insistence she find it in her self. When she returned to St Andrews, she would reclaim the clan name of Ogilvy in his and her mother's honor.

A wave of longing came over Rosalind, to be with her mother and tell her she'd seen what her mother dreamed of every day. They shared it now. Her heart ached for her son. She had not realized how much she missed her family, always thinking she'd be returning soon. She even yearned for Henry, for the love in the good times they'd shared, willing now to let go of the bad. The land quickened something in Rosalind, something that had to be awakened to, a switch that could not be tripped until her arrival.

She sat on turf the sheep had not soiled, then lay back, arms outstretched, and felt the mountain's spine lifting her, cushioning her head, so that she did not end where the mountain began. A mountain on which humans had lived untold centuries, no trace left of any individual, not even a dream of them but their leveled walls and distant memory, all gone into the earth below.

The clouds descended over the mountains, flowed down the glen, passed over her body. Rosalind saw her life as from a great height, her previous marriage and child, her home and daily responsibilities in California, and it was as a dream passing away.

Grass shuddered between her fingers. It tickled her cheek. There was nothing but the grass and the clouds, the air moving through her lungs.

She lay cradled by the mountain for a long time, between sleep and consciousness, not thinking anymore, anguished thoughts finally stilled, aware that the almost full moon had risen over the mountains before she actually saw it, huge, through the clouds, peeking over the world's rim; aware too, that she had moved over a boundary that had been there all along. A gentle, natural progression like the moon lifting above the ancient land. Nobody called her name. Nothing held her back, there was nothing to be held back from. There was only the air and the earth, and she between them.

Chapter 23

By the time she'd unpacked and made a simple supper of potatoes and savoy cabbage, with a glass of Alastair's delicious French burgundy, darkness was closing in over the vast estate outside the small windows. It began to rain softly, the clouds heavy and low.

Rosalind found herself buoyed up on a wave of contentment that remained, despite the impending decision waiting to be conveyed. It was such an unusual feeling, she stopped what she was doing a couple of times to better savor it. Everything was stilled within her. The little tasks, making dinner, eating it, washing up to the accompaniment of the Highland voices of the wind in the trees, the scent of food, wine, the British "Fairy" dish-soap, all effortlessly held her attention in a peaceful bliss.

Upstairs in the bedroom she lit the fire and sat before it with a book, relishing the newfound peace in the silence of the mountains. But the fatigue of all the frenzied work done over the last month caught up with Rosalind, and the bed became irresistible.

A puzzle awaited her at the four poster. When she actually stood at the bedside with the intention of getting in, she found the top of the wooden frame came to her waist. It was insurmountable, impossible to climb over without bruising a leg on the wood, or engaging in some acrobatics. She circled the bed, looking for an answer, and had almost stepped up on the chest at the foot of the bed to leap in, when she noticed small hinges and a knob in the bed's frame. This, when pulled open, revealed a small door, as on a carriage, with steps crafted into the frame. She laughed at the discovery, tossed her robe to the foot of the bed and climbed naked under the covers.

The thick duvet, the crisp white sheets, not a wrinkle on them, and four pillows, made for an alluring nest. She slid in gratefully and turned her thoughts to the day, to Morag and the horse, to the stones, and the mountain; the wild deer and eagle, and in the echo of a distant wind soughing through the Scotch pines, flew light as a kestrel into her expanding dreams.

*

Morag's Quair of Light and Shadows
So! This destiny had unlocked and revealed itself at last. I entered the bedchamber and called her. Not by her name, but by her nameless spirit. No trappings, no veneers, just ourselves as we are before and after and during, but elusive to find in the mundane. She was pleased to see me, no doubt. Kindred spirits, we. Like young otters, playfully circling in the stream of our affection. Oh, the irony, that she could have anyone she wanted quite easily, but her quest now was the maturation of self-sufficiency. And I, far too self-sufficient, vassal to my Goddess, called to live a constant lament of loneliness. To welcome sorrow and joy as equally honored guests. All one.

But it's not so bad. That invisible world from which we all came, and to which we return in a great homecoming? The brief interlude this world, this body offers, is saddled with a yearning to reconnect, that will always be. Lady, let my yearning be a constant reminder of the short, precious time I am gifted with independence, and let me find in my solitude the eyes of wisdom.

Our playful spirits went to hover over Rosalind's body. I reached out a hand of pure light and touched her forehead.

Let us open our eyes to the great mysteries that surround us, Rosalind, my love, for in them is our only true solace in this fleeting world.

*

A harsh cawing became a human voice and the voice formed words.

"Rosalind."

Intense dreams jumbled with the confused awakening to a strange room. Morag, she'd been dreaming of Morag, a warm presence, such love bent her way, leaving her feeling buoyed up by the pleasure of that love. Except that it wasn't exactly Morag, in the way of dreams. That liberating world, this straitened world, which one would solidify? Not that she'd forgotten where she was, but something was different.

A low rumble of thunder sounded in the distance. The only

light came from the glow in the fireplace. Her travel clock read midnight. Rosalind held it to her ear and heard the faint ticking. She'd been sleeping for only two hours, yet hurled deep into dreams. Her head wouldn't clear. With blinking eyes she searched the chamber to figure out what had changed.

It was the door, the stairwell door studded with iron nail heads. Opened like the cottage bedroom door. A low roar started in Rosalind's head, the sound of her blood pulsing in absolute silence.

Before retiring, she had quite certainly closed the bedroom door. She remembered hearing the heavy iron latch clunk into place.

She climbed from the bed, clutched her bathrobe to her breast, crossed to the door and reached a pale hand to the wood, to give it a little push. It creaked out over the spiral stair into silence as velvety as the darkness, as thick as the castle walls. The worn steps fell away into deep obscurity. Her skin prickled, and the white downy hair on her arms stood straight up. She reached into the cold stairwell, grasped the iron handle, and pulled the door back till the latch fell with a clunk, then pulled and pushed on it. Immovable.

What woman might have reached a hand to that same iron ring, six centuries ago, or gone to stand by the embers, as she did? What thoughts might have occupied her mind? Daily tasks, running the household, most likely. Would the woman have felt just as she did? The same sense of the cold and the stone and the presence of the mountains all around?

Despite Rosalind's bewilderment at the shift in the atmosphere, the room was actually very pleasant, cozy in its simplicity. Ceiling beams had long ago been painted with images of foliage, fruit and birds, and the stone of the walls was plastered and painted creamy white. The ornately engraved headboard of the magnificent bed went all the way up to the wooden canopy above, and the mischievous faces of Green Men adorned every post.

Rosalind was the haunting spirit, displaced from time and place, thinking of all the people who had been before, and who would come after, moving within the castle walls. She imagined a woman in the wooden chair by the fire, spinning wool, wimpled against the cold, bundled in many skirts. Children gathered, playing with carvings of animals and dolls, like those that Uncle Rab had carved, opening that cupboard to fetch some carded wool for their mother. Memories of people lingered on the stair with the futile sword, coughing in the smoke of battle, dying here, giving birth in this bed, a rough wooing among primitives? Or was their love a spark of light in medieval darkness? Voices and whisperings seemed almost audible running along the walls. Was their humor like ours? Their sorrow? Rosalind hoped they were more thoughtful than she had been with the first half of her life.

The door must not have been completely shut when she went to bed. No, she knew it was, but her certainty was going hazy. And in the dream someone had been calling her.

The rising wind was audible now, gusting in roars through the large trees around the castle. Rosalind put on her robe and lit the candle on the bedside table. Floorboards creaked under her feet. She hesitated by the small window. On the gravel drive below, illuminated in that eternal glow from the clouds, Helen's car had become an indecipherable shape and color.

She held the candlestick high and entered the dark stairwell, her other hand sliding over the thick banister rope. In the kitchen, the copper pots glowed and seemed to move in the candle's flare. The light switch was by the door, and she almost touched it, when an unbidden idea arose.

She would explore the castle by candlelight.

Her heart sped up at the thought. She knew she was going to do it. All her senses heightened till she heard her breath, thunderously loud in her ears.

The kitchen doorway led into the sixteenth century wing. She gripped and turned the knob and stepped through.

The vast cavern of the great hall opened up and receded into darkness. Nothing could have prepared her for its splendor. In an instant, by the light of one candle, wooden beams and banners soared high above out of dark recesses. Huge tapestries lined the walls. The sound of the latch's clank and the hinges creaking still sounded in tinny echoes from the far corners.

Her heel slipped off the edge of an unseen step, and she catapulted in, mind filled in that instant with irrational fears of deep wells and dungeons. The candle snuffed out, but not before she'd seen faces watching her every move. The box of matches hit the floor with a rattle.

Rosalind crouched, seeing nothing but the visual echoes of the silent company in the great hall. She gingerly moved her fingers over the place the matchbox had landed. Nothing. She put the candlestick down, wondering if she'd ever find it again, and searched with both hands along the floor. The hall's entrance was flagstone, giving way to polished hardwood. Behind her, the doorway to the kitchen was gone, swallowed up like everything else in the darkness.

She took a step, still hunkered down, and felt a sickening crunch under her heel. She groaned, then snorted with a fearful laugh, and moved back, till the scattered and broken matches were under her hand.

Go on, or go back? Her fingers, tingling with sensation, picked out the sandpapered side of the matchbox. It was in shreds, useless. She squatted there, certain there was a solution if only she could think differently.

She scraped the head of a match across the stone. A spark leapt off and the head broke. She tried another in the gritty seam beside the flagstone. It burst effortlessly into life. There in the small pool of blinding match-light, stood the candle in its simple sconce.

She touched the match flame to the wick and lifted the candle high. The circle of light expanded and diffused. At the far end of the hall, a man floated halfway up the wall. Rosalind put a hand to her mouth to stifle a cry. They stared at one another for eternal heartbeats.

"You're a grown woman," she whispered. "There is a logical explanation for this."

She steeled herself to walk towards the man. Just a few steps into the Great Hall, and more faces peered at her from either side. Portraits. She exhaled, feeling equal parts foolish and profoundly relieved. Of course there were portraits in an old castle. A flash of lightning startled Rosalind, yet also provided a second of perfect illumination. There were old tapestries as well, done in elaborate needlework between the paintings. Alastair had turned the hall into a gallery, perhaps a mix of ancestors and other works in his collection. Banners hanging from the timber beams above rustled slightly in a phantom wind as a low rumble of thunder sounded. Long tables stretched down either side of the room. In the middle of the left-hand wall a huge fireplace gaped like a doorway to hell in a medieval morality play. Swords affixed to the stone bristled in a semi-circle above the mantel.

The portrait on the far wall was of Alastair himself, resplendent in Highland dress. The tartan, predominantly light blue, green, and red, was half hidden behind an absurdly large and furry sporran. A belt for a basket-hilt sword went over one shoulder, and a tartan sash fastened with a huge cairngorm brooch adorned the other. If the somewhat stylized painting was honest, he'd been very handsome in his prime.

She pushed open the door under his dainty, stockinged feet and entered a long narrow hallway, which also contained a good number of paintings. Couches and chairs along the wall were grouped into little sitting areas. Four doors were spaced in regular intervals down the right-hand wall, and one larger double door was located on the opposite side. That would be the main entrance to the castle. A little welcome desk was placed just inside it, heaped with pamphlets and books and a box for donations.

Lightning lit the air again and the imprint of a white human skull lingered in her mind's eye. She blinked as the thunder came closer and louder, more unnerved than bemused by her silly jitters. Even through the thick castle walls the sound of the rain came pelting down in a dull roar. A large tapestry hung on the wall to the right. Rosalind positioned the candle to see a lively medieval allegory, its central figure a skeleton. There was the skull she had seen, not her imagination. Legs and arms akimbo, it danced and played a fiddle. A line of people followed, a beggar and a king, merchants and children, all walks of life. Some joined the dance, others wept, hands covering their faces, shoulders hunched in misery. Too late, too late.

Rosalind followed the tapestry to the first door and pushed it open to a familiar smell of wax and wood and stale incense. It was the chapel. Beyond a low rail the altar was set against the far wall, on it two gleaming candlesticks on either side of a simple bronze cross.

A life-size figure knelt at the rail, hands pressed flat together in a prayerful posture, dressed in green satins, the liquid folds of her gown picked out by the candle light in a very realistic way. Rosalind wondered if it were commissioned, someone in the Ogilvy family, maybe even Alastair's mother or grandmother.

The National Trust handbook had illustrations of the painted wooden panels in the chapel, all from the New Testament. It was difficult to see them in the candlelight, as the colors had darkened with time. Rosalind wondered why the incongruous green lady wasn't included. Maybe Alastair had placed her in the chapel as a little joke, since she was in a prayerful posture.

The pews on either side of the carpeted center aisle might hold five people each. A small window above the altar appeared like a round hole in the stonework, but when she looked more closely, the glow of the moon's edge through storm clouds was just visible beyond the black panes of glass.

Rosalind moved down the aisle, to study the portrait more closely.

There was nothing there. Just a bare altar rail.

She stopped, certain she was looking in the right place. Yes, the vivid color of the lady's gown, the paleness of her profile had been noticeable among the dim colors of the painted panels all around the chapel.

Her heart started racing, but puzzled incomprehension seized her mind. With a mighty act of will, she turned her back to the altar and returned to the door, to stand as she had on first entering, and raised the candle high. Nothing.

What if somebody else was in the castle?

"Hello?" Her voice sounded absurdly weak. "Is anyone there?"

Rosalind thought of all the places a person could hide. But why would a woman put on a formal dress and pray in a pitch-dark chapel? And in the absolute silence, she'd have heard such a magnificent gown rustle.

She backed out and shut the door, fighting down panic. In the space of a minute, Rosalind turned over a dozen absurd thoughts. One thing was certain. The nocturnal tour was over. As if to hurry her along, an escalating groan, then shriek and crack sounded. Rosalind cried out, and felt more than heard something huge crash and thud to the earth.

With a hand shielding the small flame, she hurried back through the great hall, under the moving eyes of its occupants, forcing herself not to look back. The hot fear did not lift until she reached the kitchen, calmed under the rude electric light. A large bolt was on the inside of the door, and she pushed it to with a firm hand, hoping this door would remain shut.

The kitchen had an old electric kettle. She filled it and switched it on. She searched the cupboards with shaking hands, and found cocoa and a mug, and made hot chocolate, pouring in a splash of cream, concentrating on each small detail of the process. As she sat and cradled the warm mug, her thoughts expanded to the spaces of the castle, both down the hall and above, to the tower rooms, an acute awareness of their lively emptiness, and beyond that of the wild mountains surrounding the castle. A tree must have come down in the wind, she thought, in this wild storm that rattled at the kitchen door and howled down the ancient chimney.

She wasn't so much frightened anymore, but the high level of excitement refused to abate. What if it had been a real ghost? She continued to think up preferable, saner alternatives, primarily that an image from the portraits had been imprinted on her retina and in the chapel, against the frame of darkness, imposed the lady's face and form, like seeing a phantom flash from a camera.

But there was no portrait of a lady at prayer. And she had appeared as substantial as the pews or the altar. Finally, unconvinced, Rosalind decided that trying to make intellectual sense of it was useless and even self-deceptive. The time had come to trust herself to evaluate experiences through her own faculties. She didn't understand what had happened. She would go back in the daytime and figure it out, or allow it to reveal itself.

In the meantime, she had a more important decision to make.

Rosalind sipped her cocoa, and thought of what the people sitting there six hundred years ago dressed in when they got up at midnight, and what they drank to warm themselves. How would a woman of that time who lived in Carlin Castle make the decisions she was faced with? Angus would arrive the next day for the party, expecting her answer. She considered making a list of pros and cons, because no sooner did she arrive at a conclusion than she could think up reasons against it. She was aware that the new-found calmness held the unvoiced answer, even as her over-active thoughts flew this way and that, trying to convince her otherwise. Could she separate her desire to remain in Scotland and keep Morning Star, from Angus's romantic influence? The scales hung in perfect balance. Something would have to be done to tip them.

When her feet got too cold, she went up the spiral stair to the bedroom. She pulled open the heavy door, and stepped in to a blast of heat and candle light. There, by the stoked fire, stood Morag.

"Sorry," Morag said, "I don't mean to intrude, but you never answered the door, and I couldn't find you." Morag's dark hair was damp, and steam rose from the shawl she turned one side then the other to the fire. "And I couldn't imagine you'd wandered out in this storm, having had, I suspect, enough storms to last you a wee while."

"I thought you'd left."

"Change of plans," Morag said. "Orders from the Laird. What say we open one of his better wines, and I'll fill you in?" She lifted a dusty old bottle. "Or shall we wait till breakfast? It's terribly late. I'll sleep in the guest chamber above, if you don't mind."

"Should I be worried?"

"Not at all. Did you enjoy the view from the hill fort?"

"It's beyond description."

"And did things come clear?"

Rosalind shook her head ruefully. "Well, open the wine, why not? The thing is, I'll have to go back to California next week. I'll try to find some mindless job that doesn't steal all my artistic energy, even if I have to eat beans and toast every day. At least my time in Scotland has given me that insight."

"That won't be necessary." Morag poured two glasses of burgundy and settled into a chair by the low fire. The wind whipped down the chimney and pushed out a small gust of smoke. Morag calmly stepped on a small glowing ember that jumped to the hearth stone.

"I'm afraid it will be. Could you advise me on a realtor? I can probably get enough from selling the cottage to pay off our debts and keep me going for a while. That might work. But I can't stay here. My God, everything is so expensive."

"Alastair asked me to impart something to you."

Rosalind broke her reverie and looked up.

"But first answer me this: if you could, would you stay?"

Rosalind spread her hands. "But I've just said, it's not possible."

"Never mind all that. Put absolutely everything out of your head except for that one consideration. If you could, all things being equal, would you stay?"

There was no hesitation. "Yes."

"David Gillespie will be here in a couple of days."

"Clive's partner at the firm? For the Evensong? I'm sorry, I don't follow."

"No indeed," Morag chuckled. "For *my* gathering."

"You are kidding. David is a...a..." Suddenly she remembered the bizarre spell to bind the effigy in the architects' storeroom.

"A guest. He'll be asking you to return to the office at St. Andrews."

"But they're in the process of closing."

"Apparently not. There was a little problem, of a senior partner embezzling."

"Oh, no. Hasn't Helen had enough to deal with?"

"If someone has no scruples over taking advantage of one set of the population, why stop there? He's so clever, it was not easy. He's been getting away with it for years. David suspected, but could never prove anything. But Clive finally crossed the wrong person. I'm just as clever as that bastard, and I will not give up till I have my revenge. I had to enlist the help of very reluctant employees, but we got it sorted out, and as you can imagine, the Gillespies are very grateful indeed. You might say I saved the architects' firm."

Rosalind sat back. "This puts things in a new light."

"There's more, perhaps more important in the long run, what I'm really here to impart. Alastair would like to be your dealer, if you will have him."

"Alastair?"

"Aye."

"It's kind of him to offer, but I don't want to be obliged to someone who means well."

"What if I told you Alastair needs your help? Don't forget you'd be earning him a bit of cash as well. This is a symbiotic, not an altruistic offer. He's not well off, either. That's why the castle is going to the Trust."

"He'll negotiate with galleries, you mean?"

"Aye, galleries, shows, collectors. He already knows everybody. He has half the art world in his pocket."

"My God, that would be great. But no, wait, all that stuff takes time, never mind the paintings that have to be finished... never mind finished, that have to be begun. I can't see how it would work out. Assuming I was capable of this, it would still take years just to begin getting some work together. Don't you remember when he said I may not have the real talent for painting? I'm afraid he might be right."

Morag reached into the clothing over her bosom and pulled out a folded check and held it up in the firelight.

"What's that?" Rosalind asked, suspicious.

"A tidy sum for that painting, the Pittenweem harbor, that Alastair liked in your studio."

"That's nice. That's great actually. But you don't understand. The rest is too big a gamble. To set up the business side of painting is a job in itself, which can take years."

Morag gave her the check.

She looked at it and shook her head. "Six hundred pounds? I really don't think it's worth that."

"Well, things are more expensive here, eh? He's getting a jump on the competition, and it doesn't hurt to push up the prices a bit. It's a gamble, right enough. Don't you understand, he's giving you the chance to see if you have what it takes, and no harm done. Meanwhile he gets some nice paintings out of the deal, and whether or not your paintings are masterpieces, they will be good enough to sell in British galleries. He likes your work. If you discover it's not what you ought to be doing, then do...whatever that is."

"I thought I had it all finally resolved, and now it's all broken open again."

"Stay."

Rosalind sat with eyes closed as Morag quietly waited.

"I think I saw a ghost in the chapel," Rosalind said.

"The Green Lady?"

Rosalind's eyes snapped open. "How did you know? How the hell did you know that?"

"She's very popular."

After a spell of companionable silence, in which she knew at last, beyond all doubt, that everything had just changed, Rosalind said, "You're behind all this."

"Not really, not beyond my affection for you," Morag said. "It is difficult to find one's way to the Bonnie Road, and most will not walk it, but once your feet are on it, you will find the universe to be a kindly place."

*

The castle telephone was a comical contraption of the original rotary dial, with a receiver that could double as a cudgel. Rosalind had to go through a switchboard operator, who wanted to know more than the American phone number – was it her family, she wondered, she was wanting to speak to, and did Miss... Miss? Ogilvy like being at Carlin Castle? She also warned Rosalind that the phone call would be very expensive, but finally put her through.

"Wait, let me get this straight," said Chris. His voice sounded as if it had got caught and echoed round inside the massive receiver. "You said they'd closed the office."

"Yes, honey," she explained again patiently. "But the architects' firm – David Gillespie the senior partner – decided to remain in St. Andrews, and closed the Aberdeen office instead."

"Hold on, here's Gran."

"Ogilvy, eh? I think that's grand, but then I would, wouldn't I?"

"Uncle Rab would haunt me if I didn't take the name. Or the cottage. He probably will anyway."

"Such good news, though I must confess, a wee bit bittersweet to not have you so close."

"Do you want to live here, with me?"

"Ach, no, I've all my friends, my church, my life is here. And Chris...we've been having our wee chats while you've been away...He's fine just now."

Her mother had evidently encouraged Chris into a better frame of mind, and though it hurt to think it, Rosalind's absence had probably allowed him to move forward.

"Would you like to come for the memorial service, and maybe stay for a while? Chris can get to know the place, and that might help."

"Oh, aye, Chris can escort me across. We'll work out the travel and I'll phone. He can see where you began your life, and he'll be easier in his mind to know you're all right. And you needn't worry about us, Chris will be close by if I need anything here. You carry on. I don't pretend to understand about how the painting business works, but I'm very pleased you've got the job back at that office."

"I'm taking it one step at a time," said Rosalind. "But I

think it should work out okay."

"And, em, is there anything else you'd like to tell me?"

"Oh. That."

"Do I hear hesitation?"

Rosalind bowed her head and sighed.

"I'm glad it won't influence your decision, then, to stay, if I'm hearing you right."

"It's funny. Twenty years ago the decision would have been easy and clear as day."

"Fate," her mother mused. "It's aye a funny thing."

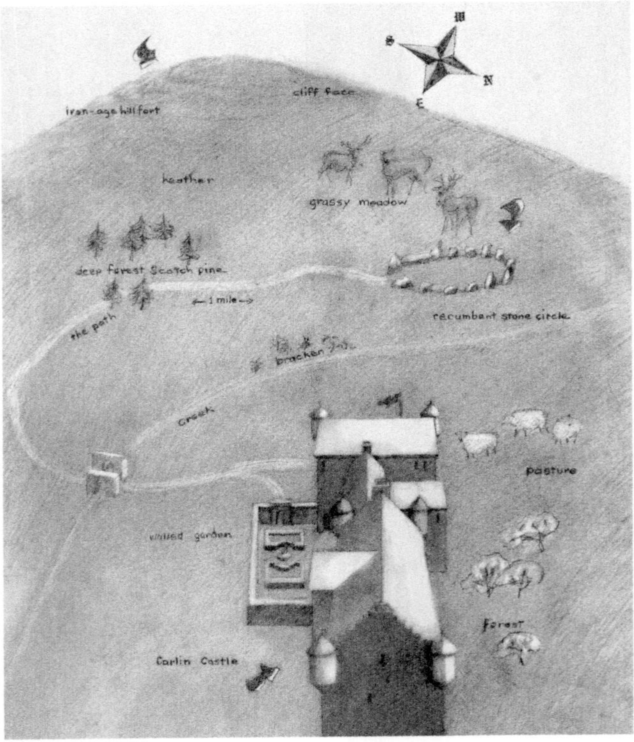
W
S
N
E
iron-age hill fort
cliff face
heather
grassy meadow
deep forest Scotch pine
1 mile
recumbent stone circle
the path
bracken
creek
pasture
walled garden
forest
Carlin Castle

Chapter 24

Angus's Land Rover roared up the drive and around the old oak tree that had split in half, and spilled a crown of golden foliage and gnarled boughs across a section of the parking lot. From the tower bedroom window, Rosalind watched him find a parking place amongst the other cars, leap out and go around to the passenger door. The storm had blown itself out, with only a few limbs down aside from the oak tree, but not enough to hinder the guests' parking. Angus was wearing his kilt again, informal this time, with a heavy white sweater and plain leather sporran. He looked fantastic, a man in his prime, so striking in his kilt and in his confidence that Rosalind imagined a laurel wreath gracing his brow. And the crowning glory would be her acceptance of his offer of marriage.

As Helen would say, "Oh, dear." Rosalind leaned her forehead against the cool stone beside the window, and sighed with foreboding.

And there was Helen, emerging from the passenger seat. Angus lifted solicitous arms to help her down. He escorted her to the castle's main entrance, head high, shoulders back, face cheery and expectant. Helen walked gingerly across the gravel, hanging on his forearm, almost being dragged off her feet by her oblivious escort, but game, and resolute. They paused as a car drove in and parked, a slender man in a clerical collar getting out with a wave to Helen. Rosalind remembered then that Niall Paterson had been reprimanded by his own church for his zealotry, and sent packing.

"Well, thank God for that at least," she said.

A small Ford crunched up the gravel on feeble tires, an older car with dings and dents in its dull green paint. A bare knee emerged, then a tousled head, and somehow the burly young man unfolded and heaved himself out. It was Calum, who had played the bagpipes at the ceilidh. He stepped around to the back of his car and gave the trunk a kick to pop it open. He lifted out a black rectangular case, slammed the trunk shut, which lifted up again, slammed it down a couple more times till it latched. Then he started across the drive, but stopped as another car veered around the fallen oak limbs. It was an almost equally antiquated Peugeot with a loose muffler. It steered into a space well apart from the other cars. A pair of shapely legs swung out of the driver's door, a short skirt above, high heels below, and a dark head came into view. She stood up and looked around, taking a deep breath of the soft Highland air. Clive climbed out of the passenger side, and they lingered for a moment, looking at each other over the top of the car. They exchanged words, laughed, and Clive came around the back of the car to offer the young women his elbow. It was Kirsteen, the one causing all the fuss. Calum lowered his head and quickly walked away to the castle door, as if he had not seen them. Rosalind groaned and rolled her head across the grainy stone when she thought of how Helen would feel upon meeting the defiant couple.

*

The small chapel had come alive, filled to capacity. Despite the presence of the congregation, it still smelled faintly of dampness and cold stone, of wood polish. The candles at the altar were lit, the sconces along the walls glimmered. Colorful embroidered kneelers hung from hooks on the pews before. The floor creaked under the reverent murmurs of the guests coming in, and pews groaned with their sudden burdens.

Helen and Angus insisted Rosalind join them in the service, which was, after all, the reason they were all there, and a real musical treat. The officiant was Helen's Scottish Episcopal priest from St. Andrews Church, who had kindly stepped in at the last minute after Rev. Paterson had been forced to leave so unexpectedly.

At precisely six o'clock, a cross-bearer entered. The congregation stood for the procession of choir and priest. The Renaissance Group wore their academic gowns, black for the divines, and scarlet for the arts faculty. They took their position in the old royal pew, a boxed in, canopied construction to the left of the altar. Their choir master, a jovial-faced, stooped older man in black gown, perched on the corner seat.

The priest, resplendent in embroidered vestments

belonging to the Comyn family, stepped up before the congregation, then turned and looked over the little, packed chapel.

"O God," he said, "Make speed to save us."

"O Lord," said the demure but eager congregation, some crossing themselves, "make haste to help us."

Angus, standing beside Rosalind, smelled good, of a warm wooliness, inviting and comforting. He was ill at ease with the service, and recited some prayers but not others. Helen, on her other side, followed easily along in the Prayer Book, slender finger pointing the way across the pages. Rosalind, unfamiliar with the old evensong, relaxed and enjoyed the Britishness of it.

*

The piercing notes from the bagpipes played by knowing fingers called up the dance from centuries of dances in the great hall. Murmuring voices filled the cavernous spaces above, twining among the heavy posts and beams and tapestries. Someone had kindled a fire. Everybody brought food and drink, and placed it haphazardly on huge tables on both ends of the great hall. The portraits on the walls expanded the gathering with their graceful, ghostly presence.

Calum plunged into a reel, a distracted intentness to his face. Rosalind and Angus and Helen took drinks and stood together to watch some students dance a hornpipe, then an Irish jig.

A couple of young men studied a display of swords on the wall, arranged in the shape of a circle, points to the center and basket hilts forming the penumbra. They glanced around, then gingerly removed four of the swords from their hangers, and ran to Calum, beaming with excitement. He bent his curly dark head to them, then smiled and nodded.

The young men crossed the blades into two sets on the stone floor, then stood erect behind them, put fists on hips, toes pointed to the side, and nodded at Calum. He pummeled the bag, adjusted the drones, huffed into the chanter, and began to play. The young men bowed from the hips, straight-backed, then raised an arm and began a dance, putting a toe between this blade and that, then stepping into the crossed swords, entering the dance with great skill. Everyone stopped to watch. Although the students did not wear kilts, the masculine, savage movements of the dance, their hissing breath and feet thudding between the bare blades, affected the party with a gaiety that had been lacking since the somber evening prayer. Angus whooped and raised his arms, and performed his own variation of their dance, to good-natured laughter and shouts of encouragement.

A couple of guests joined Calum with fiddle and bodhran, until the entire room was riveted by the spectacle, and the dancers finished, stepping back gracefully and executing the same bow. Applause sounded and guests yelled as the lads picked up the swords and retreated.

The musicians moved away for a break, and the hubbub of talk and laughter filled the castle hall. Clive and Kirsteen kept to themselves by the fire. Clive, with a satisfied smile, offered Kirsteen a glass of wine, and clinked his glass to hers. Calum turned away and took a long draught from a pint glass on the drinks table, then took a couple of deep breaths before turning around again and talking to the dancers. Rosalind watched a vein pop up and throb along Helen's forehead as she glanced at her husband.

"I can't believe his audacity, but you know, Rosalind, I'm not surprised. He's taking revenge on me for daring to leave him."

Angus went to the table and heaped a plate high with egg flan and sandwiches. Word of his treasure hoard discovery had spread by now beyond academic circles, and everybody wanted a word with him. He moved among the throng, dignified but excited, the center of all attention.

The students offered a madrigal, including a bawdy medieval song to make their director blush.

"I'm doing quite well, actually" Helen said with no prompting from Rosalind. "Your cottage is just the thing, thanks so much by the way, for a bit of sanctuary. Do you know, I'm actually relieved? Who'd have thought? I didn't realize how dreadfully unhappy I was, just being in the same house as him. And when I see him now, being the bastard that he is, a great weight is lifted."

"Helen." Rosalind slipped an arm around her stiff shoulders. "Stay as long as you need to."

"Thank you so much, more than I can say, but I intend to

find a flat quick as I can, and commence starting my life over. You've inspired me more than you know."

"I don't see how."

"You look different," Helen frowned. "Can't quite put my finger on it." Her eyes widened. "Of course! Angus. You've made a decision."

"Can you tell?"

"Yes. You've decided to marry him, haven't you?"

Rosalind shook her head no.

"Really? Oh, Rosalind, how could you resist Prince Charming? Does he know?" She searched through the guests and saw Angus speaking to a couple of students exuding the appropriate awe. "Obviously not. Oh, don't sigh like that. The only bad decision is a wrong one."

"I can't bear to hurt him. Making the decision ironically made me realize how much I love him. Why can't we just be lovers? His way of thinking is so foreign to me, and he just won't bend. How am I going to do this?"

"Rosalind." Helen pulled her to a private spot by a deep-set window, away from a student and a lecturer, who were having a heated debate over the Scottish or English origin of a tune. She put on a confessional voice. "I must ask you something. And you must answer me. It's very important."

"What's the matter?"

"Angus told me he'd shown you the treasure hoard as it was being excavated."

"Yes."

"Was there an ecclesiastical cross among it? Do you remember?"

A whirlwind of thoughts tore through Rosalind's mind. That's what had been missing in the displayed treasure, and she hadn't been able to name the cross specifically till Helen mentioned it. She recalled Angus's face in the Neolithic tomb when he'd found it, lit up with distaste oddly paired with a covetousness she'd never before witnessed, but one she'd shrugged off as a mysterious aberration, perhaps to do with his father and the church. Her bantering comments about selling archaeological treasures, his reply that the goods end up in the same museums, except that robbers got money, and honest archaeologists didn't. The mysterious and sudden trip to London, his assurances of financial solvency in his marriage offer.

"In fact," Helen said, "I'll describe it. Perhaps five inches long, gold, a single red stone in its center. Just say yes or no. I won't tell a soul, but I must know."

Rosalind figured that if Helen knew about it in the first place, there was no point in covering it up. "Yes."

"Oh dear. Oh dear, oh dear." The deep crease returned to her forehead.

"What's happened?"

"Professor Buchan uncovered a reference to the cross in a medieval manuscript, along with its companion pieces, all the rest of which have been accounted for. The cross had not been listed in the hoard's inventory, but it only just surfaced in Amsterdam where it had been sold on the black market. We can't jump to conclusions, but this is a truly dreadful development, whatever the facts."

"You don't think Angus is capable..." Rosalind began.

But before Helen could answer, Angus approached, kilt swinging merrily.

"A good way to get students interested, eh?" Angus passed a careful hand over his hair. "Have a little history in the making in their own university. Helen," he said tenderly, mistaking her pained look. "Can I get you anything?"

The wine on the table by the kitchen door was almost finished. "Excuse me," Rosalind said. "I need to put out a couple more bottles. Be right back."

Down the vaulted hallway to the kitchen, a small alcove contained two young people. She passed by quickly but not before seeing it was Calum and Kirsteen, all attention focused on an intense altercation. Her heart went out to them, especially to Calum, who was so obviously in love with the girl. And that turned her thoughts to Angus. Was he really capable of theft on that scale? Surely he was not that foolish. Were it true, though, how could she respect him any longer? She berated herself for spinning a romantic fantasy around a man she had to admit she really didn't know.

She entered the kitchen, picked up some bottles by the cellar stair, and was turning to place them on the table, when three deep thuds resounded on the private tower door.

Four children stood on the stone steps, illuminated by the light in the kitchen pouring out into the dark night.

"Well, hello. Who are you?"

All of them looked frightened, excited, and determined.

The two smaller ones wore costumes. A gypsy and a pirate. "Hello," eventually chirped the gypsy.

"Oh, my gosh," said Rosalind. "It's Halloween. Well, what can I do for you? Are you trick or treaters?"

They shuffled a bit and glanced at each other. Finally, the tallest child, a fair-haired girl not in costume, said, "Penny for the Guy." They all repeated the sentence obediently. "Penny for the Guy."

Rosalind squatted down to be eye level with the gypsy. "You got to help me out here, sweetheart. I'm from another country. Who's this guy?"

"Guy Fawkes," said the big girl.

The gravel on the dark drive crunched under heavy footfalls. Someone stopped just out of the light from the door. There was a rustle of cloth, and suddenly a glowing face appeared at waist level. The tallest girl grabbed the older boy. The smaller children shrieked.

"Hey, hey, someone's got a jack-o-lantern," Rosalind pointed. "We've got those where I come from in America. Is that your Dad?"

"A tumshie lantern, missus," said the pirate. "But I dinna ken who it is."

A deep feminine laugh boomed from the figure, and Morag, in a black, sweeping cloak, her hair loose, strode up to the castle door. The two older children fell back, but the little ones in costume held their ground.

"Guisers, eh?" she said. And to the older ones, "Where's your fancy dress?"

"We don't do that," said the tall girl. "We collect pennies for the Guy."

"That's an English custom," Morag spoke sternly. "This isn't Guy Fawkes. Samhuinn is Scottish, and we must make certain the old traditions are not replaced by foreign ones."

"We'll be off then if we're not welcome," the oldest girl said. "Come on you lot."

"I don't want to go," said the little gypsy, enunciating each word in her sweet child's voice.

"We've been practicing all day," the pirate explained to Rosalind.

The older children stepped away. "Let's try the other door," said the big girl, pulling her companion away. "Come on, I said."

Morag turned her attention back to the younger ones. "Let them go. Now, who's got a song or poem?"

"A bit of 'Tam o' Shanter'," said the pirate.

"Perfect," said Morag.

Rosalind watched amazed as the children recited in unison.

"Warlocks and witches in a dance:
Nae cotillon brent new frae France,
But hornpipes, jigs, strathspeys and reels,
Put life and mettle in their heels.
A winnock-bunker in the east.
There sat Auld Nick, in shape o' beast;
To gie them music was his chairge:
He screwed the pipes and gart them skirl
Till roof and rafters a' did dirl."

When they finished, they kicked at the steps and smiled shyly.

"That was great," Rosalind said. "Our kids just say 'trick or treat.'"

"Do you have something to give them?" Morag asked.

"There's lots of goodies from the party. Is that suitable?"

"Certainly. Especially for brave children who walked all the way on Samhuinn night down the dark drive to the most haunted castle in Scotland."

Rosalind went to forage and returned with Mars bars and cookies. "Here you go."

"Jings!" said the pirate.

An owl hooted down the dark glen, and a shriek from one of the dancers sounded particularly bloodcurdling. The main door to the castle had opened to the other children in a burst of light and music and voices. The younger children grew agitated, but it wasn't to join their friends.

"You are the Lady," said the little girl, pointing at Morag's face.

Morag only smiled. "Are those Sassenachs your friends?"

The boy shrugged. "They're no bad pals."

"Mind you keep Samhuinn. None of this Guy Fawkes business."

"But we like the bonfire," said the boy.

"We had our bonfires before they ever did. Ours is the true fire festival. There is a new spirit abroad in Scotland, and wee ones like yourselves have a natural feel for it. We must never forget who we are or where we came from. Take this." Morag handed the boy her turnip lantern. She opened her hand, fingers wide, above each child's head.

"Rising power of the Cailleach Bheur be yours, children, on this, her night of deepest magic."

They called their thanks as they went down the drive, heads bent together in animated talk.

"Will they be all right?" Rosalind asked.

"They go with the Lady's blessing." She raised her arms to the moon just cresting the eastern mountain. "I can barely be still!"

"Did you make the storm go away?"

Morag came closer to the door and put a hand on the stone frame. "It's much easier to call up a storm than to calm it down."

"By God, I can believe that."

"Hello, Morag," said a voice behind Rosalind. She jumped. Kirsteen stood with a glass of wine in her hand. "Thought it might be you." She was dressed to catch the masculine eye, in short skirt over tights and low-cut blouse.

Morag's face lit up. "Kirsteen, have you come to join us, then? That's fantastic. Everyone will be so pleased."

"No, no, as I said, I'm not interested in all that."

Brief puzzlement passed over Morag's face, then darkening realization. "You've come with him. For the party."

"Aye."

"Is his wife here?" Morag asked Rosalind. "Helen?"

She nodded.

"How could you, Kirsteen?"

"There you go again!" Kirsteen exploded. "I'm sick to death of it. His wife doesn't care, it's obvious. Go in and look if you don't believe me."

"How can you be so willfully blind?" Morag thundered.

"He's a philandering, misogynistic bastard," she sputtered, "who means you no good!"

"It's not like that." Kirsteen was on the verge of tears. "He's kind and he buys me lovely things." She fingered an exquisite silver necklace.

"He's only after one thing, my lass."

"I won't listen to this." Kirsteen went back into the kitchen and through the door to the hall. "...Jealous," her voice carried back.

Morag spread her hands open, eyebrows raised.

"Guess we've got to make our own mistakes," said Rosalind.

"I don't like this," said Morag. "I don't like it at all. There's something very strange in it, and I don't yet know what it is."

"Will you come in, join the party? Have a glass of wine?"

"No, I must be off. They're starting to gather. Keep an eye out for her, will you? She's headstrong but far more innocent than she lets on."

Rosalind waved it away. "There are lots of guests in there, they should be fine."

Morag calmed herself and studied Rosalind's face. "You've decided."

"God help me if I'm about to make the biggest stupid mistake of my life."

Morag stepped close. "It's good luck to kiss a witch on Samhuinn."

Rosalind had to smile. "I'm sure it is."

The kiss was strong, insistent. Morag sighed and touched Rosalind's face. "This is a very sexy night. In the myths, in the folklore, in my circles, in this very time when creation meets with destruction, this is the time when anything can happen, and nothing is as it seems."

"I'll take it under advisement."

Morag turned and strode to the glen path that led to the stone circle. "Join us, join us." Her voice faded away. Shadows moved against the trees and fell in step behind her.

Angus came into the kitchen. He popped a chunk of cake into his mouth. "Who are you talking to?"

But Morag was gone, not even the sound of her feet on the gravel.

Rosalind shut her eyes and took a deep breath. This was it. Her heart started beating like a kettle drum. "Some trick or treaters came to the door. Cute kids. They recited poetry and I gave them some treats."

"Oh, aye, guisers. My father frowned on the whole thing, calling it pagan, which I suppose it is."

"What is a..." she searched for the word, "Sassenach?"

He laughed. "Surely the guisers didn't call you that? It's generally used as a term for the English. From Saxon."

Rosalind closed the door. After the fresh night air the dank stone of the castle was overwhelming. Behind the light and tapestries, behind the seedy but elegant furniture, deep silences were brooding, just waiting for the lively party to dissipate. She thought of all the gatherings that had taken place in the great hall down the centuries. All these phantom collections of people, passing through the same rooms, holding their celebrations, full of life, then blinking out like a snuffed candle, replaced by the next generation, equally transient. And always light and music and dancing and love. And broken hearts.

Bagpipes wheezed and squawked, then set up a reedy, pure tune, a lively piece accompanied by the fiddle and drum. How did Calum have the strength to play for his willful girlfriend and her seducer joined together in the dance?

"Good, aren't they?" said Angus.

She felt the weight of tears gathering on lower eyelids. "Are people still dancing?"

"Aye, aye, that's why I came for you. They're playing Strip the Willow." He started to sing, "O you're the lassie o' my heart, my lassie ever dearer; O you're the queen o' womankind, and ne'er a ane to peer ye."

"Angus."

"It's easy. Just a lot of birling. I'll show you." He took her in his arms and whirled her around the kitchen. "'I maun hae a wife, whatsoe'er she be, an' she be a woman, that's enough for me!'"

"Angus."

He stopped but didn't let go.

"I can't be the wife you want," she said. "I can't do it."

He laughed. "Silly moo." He tapped her nose with a finger.

She gently disengaged herself from his arms. "I know what I would do. I'd always put you first. I'd always be thinking of what you needed, of what we as a couple would need, and in obtaining it I would have little thought for myself."

He gathered her hands in his, rubbing them absentmindedly. "That sounds admirable. Saintly."

"Eventually I'd start resenting the erosion of my own identity, and probably take out my frustrations on you. No," she interrupted his protest, "it has nothing to do with you and everything to do with me."

A slight change came over his face, a more focused

attention. "Every marriage is different," he said. "I would see to it you had everything you needed, especially now that I'm able."

She wondered how much of it was money he'd got from selling the medieval cross. "I know you would. You'd make a good husband. But I've done the marriage thing, and I don't want to do it again. Why can't we be lovers, enjoy each other's company, live in our own homes and see each other when we want to?"

He tilted his head. "Because I wouldn't cheapen you. And because I want to show the world, through wedding vows, how important you are to me, to the exclusion of all others, for the rest of our lives."

"That sounds so absolute, Angus." Rosalind pulled her hands away from his fervent grasp. "Given the choice between marriage or nothing, oh God, this is so hard...it will have to be nothing. I'd rather live alone." She closed her eyes against his earnest, searching look.

"Ach. Nobody really wants to be alone."

"I do." The answer was plain to her, despite being coated with sorrow. "You would be generous, I know. But the one thing I've never had is my own life. Can I make you understand that nothing is as important now as this one thing? There was a time I'd have been glad, honored, to marry you. But not now. I wish so much you could see it my way, I don't want to lose you. I am so sorry for the pain I'm bringing on you, on us, but I can't. I can't marry you."

"You need more time." He touched a tear running down her cheek. "It's all happened too quickly."

Rosalind steeled herself. "If the only choice is one or the other, then I have to say no. I can't thank you enough for the wonderful times we've shared. My fervent wish is that we continue as lovers, or if that's not possible, friends." She took the ring in its little velvet box from her pocket and handed it to him.

Angus's brows knit together. He held her a moment longer, but Rosalind's resolve did not weaken. He took the ring box and looked at it for a long time. "I can't believe what you just said."

She waited, resolute.

He frowned then shrugged. "I always suspected it was too good to be true, but thanks mate, we can be pals now? You're joking, right?" He rubbed his well-groomed beard. She forced herself to meet his hardening gaze.

"This is a bit of a blow. I assumed...I should never have assumed...We were...it was a perfect match. I thought."

Her hand lifted to touch his anguished face, hesitated, then dropped.

"Life goes on. Aye, life goes on." He walked slowly to the kitchen door, hesitated, head half turned, then exited.

Rosalind eased into the wooden chair. She folded her arms on the old pocked table and rested her head on them, and let the weeping flow out of her, listening to her own sobs contained in the little empty space of arms and table under her face.

After a while, the music stopped. Applause sounded, accompanied by a burst of talk and laughter. A gentle hand came to rest on her shoulder.

"You've told him." Helen pulled a chair close and sat beside Rosalind. "I just saw him stomping across the hall, with a face like thunder, headed straight for the whisky."

"Am I a complete idiot?" Rosalind kept her head down on her arms. "Did I just make a horrendous mistake?"

"Mine's disappeared with his piece of fluff, God knows where."

"I feel awful."

"I'm not one to cheer you up, I'm afraid." She snorted daintily. "Clive is doubtless in the process of seducing her this very moment, and wants me to know it. Though really, you'd think he'd shake my hand and say thanks, old thing, now I can go shag anything I like. But then, the illicit thrill will be gone. The faithful, stupid cow of a wife waiting at home to cook his dinner will be gone, he can't hurt her any longer, so what's the point?"

They sat quietly, staring into the old worn wood grain of the table.

"Aren't we the pair?" said Helen.

"Let's get out of here."

"At midnight? In the Highlands?"

Rosalind stood and gave Helen her hand to pull her up. "I happen to have been invited to a little gathering down the glen."

"You're not serious." Helen eyed her. "Oh, dear, you are."

Rosalind pulled her jacket off its hook by the door, found

one for Helen and held it up by way of invitation.

"No, quite seriously, Rosalind, these old Caledonian forests are eerie in the extreme, and dangerous, with craggy plunges into rapids and beasts and such like."

"It's not far. The path is clear."

"Well, gosh, I certainly don't want to be stuck here and see his smug face when he returns from his little..." she laughed, "nocturnal emission." Helen rubbed her hand over her pale cheek and considered. "Why not? Yes, why the bloody hell not? Jog on, jog on, Macduff!"

*

Kirsteen was a beacon to the young men. They asked for dances, they offered drinks, they chatted her up at every opportunity, or stood patiently waiting in small groups, speaking of other things but always keeping watch for an opportunity. She laughed, delighted at their hopeful advances, the sheen of sweat glowing on her soft brow. She twirled away from them to find Clive and take his arm, eyes a glancing mix of caution that he might be annoyed at her behavior, with a triumph at her new-found desirability. No matter. He had everything they had yet to discover, to master, these fumbling, self-conscious boys. She knew Calum's heart was breaking, and she caught occasional glimpses from him. She was sorry for him, but why would she give up the attentions of a wealthy doting sophisticate who could bring her anything she wanted, all in return for something he wanted as much from her? There was a power here she had not known before, and she began to comprehend the intoxication of using it, these feminine wiles that were already in place, awakened by Clive's desire for her.

Clive was indeed watching, and it was with a mix of annoyance and smugness. He was already frustrated enough that his beautiful Saab had ended up unexpectedly in the garage for new breaks following an inspection, and he'd had to suffer the ignoble humiliation of arriving in her piece of junk with the faulty muffler. He could only hope it would all be worth it. Kirsteen was drunk, giddy on all the attention. Let the young bullocks tease her, get her ready, do the work of pushing her into a new place and save him the trouble and blame if anything should go wrong, delicious as the process may be. Let Helen see what she'd given up, and serve her right.

"It's very warm," Kirsteen exclaimed, distracted and animated. Normally in his presence she tried to put on a more refined air, but in her excitement, her working class Scottishness emerged, a loud coarseness, talking and laughing through mouthfuls of food, lapsing into an almost indecipherable East Neuk village accent that sounded like baby talk, or the babbling of idiots. Watching her trying to rise above it, as when they'd had dinner at the Inn, was entertaining and even endearing. But seeing it come gushing out like this among the bemused guests was becoming distasteful. It was beginning to reflect on him. Time to put a stop to it.

"There's a garden out back," said Clive. "Shall we have a little walk, cool down a bit?"

"Oh, aye, that wid be awfee braw."

"I beg your pardon?"

"It would be jolly jolly hockey sticks nice, I say, wot."

Now who was making fun of whom? Anger tightened his gut, but as they left the castle and walked into the formal garden, the scent of her hair and youthful skin, and the curve of soft flesh exposed at the low neckline of her blouse, reminded him that her substantial charms were worth putting up with the rest. For now.

She grabbed his hands in hers and skipped around him, pulling him in a spinning circle down the garden path. "Slow down, Kirsteen," he said. The walled garden was nicely laid out, low hedges defining the sections with their respective flowers or borders, all centered round a sundial on a high plinth. In the soft darkness, with the orange moon cresting the mountain to the east, the layout of the garden was easily discerned. He guided her into the farthest section, behind the hedge where a stone bench stood against the wall. A clematis had been trained over a little bower above it, and though it had cast most of its leaves, the thick skeleton of its vines offered moon-lit privacy.

She was still gabbing on about something. He caught her in his arms and held her still. She gazed up at him, all attention now, eager to receive his mouth with hers. Her breath was sweet, her lips so soft and yielding that his teeth went past them and clacked against hers.

"Oh." She drew away and touched her upper lip.

"Sorry," he murmured, and pulled her back until she melted again in his mouth. A metallic tint touched his questing tongue. His hands undid the buttons of her blouse and slid inside the bra; ah how long had he waited for that simple caress? He impatiently pulled the straps off her shoulders with the top of the blouse, binding her upper arms and exposing her magnificent breasts. "Oh, God," he exclaimed, as she watched his face change, her scrutiny a pleasure in itself. He wrapped his arms around her and bent his head to kiss her neck, and she sighed with pleasure. He could tell she was self-conscious, a youthful mix of wanting and fearing, watching herself go through the motions. Mouth open, he dragged his teeth down her bosom, leaving a parallel red streak over her white flesh. He took her nipple in his mouth, in his teeth, testing its supple tightness.

"Clive," she attempted to raise her hands to his shoulders. "You're hurting me."

He returned to her mouth. "You are beautiful," he whispered, and she gratefully returned his kisses. He pressed his rigid penis, trapped upright in his trousers, against her belly.

Her eyes widened, but she said nothing, her mouth too occupied with his. When his hand slid up under her skirt, above the top of her stocking to find warm bare thigh, and higher to the damp warmth, she stiffened, but allowed his fingers to glide over the material of her underwear, over the intoxicating mound of Venus, to snake over and insinuate under the waistband and into her innocent curls. She tried to pull away.

"Clive," she said, "it's too quick."

"Yes." He stroked her, even as she tried to twist away from his hand. "You are ready, you're so ready."

"Yes, but," she grabbed his wrist. "That's enough just now, don't you think? I'm a wee bit nervous."

"I'm a wee bit aroused," he growled.

"Let's go back in, before they wonder where we are."

"Let's not." He kissed her again to stop her speaking. "Can't you feel how ready you are? Relax." He spun her around, and she gasped. "You know perfectly well you want to, you little bitch." He pushed her to the bench.

"Clive!" she cried.

When she put out her arms to stop the fall, the fabric across her shoulders tore. He lifted her skirt from behind and tore off the flimsy undergarments and when she tried to wriggle free, clasped the front of her thighs with his hands.

"Stop," she cried. "Stop."

"No, there's no stopping now, is there, 'my lass'?"

Chapter 25

A small group of Morag and Auntie Meg, three older women who were known respectfully as the 'Elders;' and two young men to escort and protect, arrived at the stone circle before the appointed hour, only to find that the entire group of around twenty-five participants stood in silence, waiting for them. In the dusky moonlight, standing stone and human appeared indistinguishable. Word had got out about the curse object having been found after almost four decades, and every one of the magical people knew immediately what would be done with it, when and where. Respect for the Gilbride family and affection for Meg gathered them all together in a silent witness.

Everything had been prepared earlier, and the two firestarters stroked bright sparks from flint and steel into the dry moss, the chaga and birch bark, which quickly set the little clumps of tinder alight. As they squatted on either side of the stack of wood, enticing the new little flames to leap to the dry kindling within, the Elders chanted.

"Choose the willow of the streams,
Choose the hazel of the rocks,
Choose the alder of the marshes,
Choose the birch of the waterfalls,
Choose the ash of the shade,
Choose the yew of resilience,
Choose the elm of the brae,
Choose the oak of the sun."

Morag stood as close as possible to the huge logs that made up the sacred fire. She raised her hands, palms open to the young blaze, welcomed and enticed up the creature of flame. It leapt through the wood and roared into life. As quickly as the fire element burst forth, so too did the inner blue fires of their magical rite. And yet a third black flame crept up the center of the stack, the flame of the dead.

Everyone stood back to watch the sparks and smoke rush into the night air. One of the white-haired Elders passed around the miniature coffin for all to inspect. As they marveled at the effigy and its blighted eye, Auntie Meg wept and wept, embraced by one woman then another, as they patted her bent back and shushed her like a baby.

It fell to Morag to awaken and call to the spirits of the land and the stones, to unite the sacred realms of earth, sea, and sky, and to greet the ancient Goddess of that glen and river and mountain.

"This beloved woman," she explained to the rising tide of magical creatures lifting their heads from the elements, "Meg Gilbride, rightful daughter of the Clann an Fritheir, has been held captive for far too long by a hidden curse. Now, at last, on this night of deepest magic, we destroy this object of sorrow." Morag raised the coffin high. "We release Meg Gilbride from all constraints. We release her from the binding of the hurtful past. We release her from anything that impedes her awakening to the gifts of her foremothers. We ask her mother Morag, and her sister, my mother, attend us now from the Land of Youth, and open the doors of magic to this beloved woman!"

Morag gave the miniature coffin to Auntie Meg, who held it over the fire, as close as she could stand by the dancing flames.

All the Elders extended hands to the coffin, banishing, ripping apart its essence. Meg looked to Morag with her one eye, and Morag nodded assent. With a high-pitched heart-rending cry, Meg threw it into the Samhuinn fire where it was consumed in an explosive conflagration.

*

The rising moon illuminated the well-kept path where it wound past the walled garden, into the forest. After a short time, the trickle and gurgle of the burn came from below.

The night altered Helen's form. She filled more space in its deceptive light. Her face shone, as did Rosalind's hands when she lifted them to see. Passing by trees that weren't quite where they first appeared, on the path that went down when it looked as if it were climbing, their senses strained.

"Where are you taking me?" giggled Helen.

"We're almost there." Rosalind felt reckless, untethered. If the decision to turn down Angus's offer of marriage had been one of the hardest things she'd ever done, she at the same time felt an immense relief.

The walk in the dark forest stretched on. Their fearful excitement enlivened every little detail, the branches of the beech trees like silvered dancers twined in muscular poses; the mossy edge of the path, dainty breaths and footsteps on the fallen leaves, the rise and fall of the land, and very shortly, the flicker of firelight through the trees.

The scene burst upon them as they stopped at the edge of the wood bordering the clearing. A large fire in the center of the stones illuminated a small group, perhaps thirty men and women, the women in cloaks, a few nude, the men bare-chested for the most part, kilted or in trousers, and in the middle of them Morag's naked athletic body, head thrown back, arms raised, a long straight sword in one hand, the blade flashing fire and moonlight. Bursts of laughter blended into the soft wind and the stream's restless gurgling.

Helen grabbed Rosalind's arm. "Wait," she said. "I only have so much courage. Let me see what I'm letting myself in for."

A large outcrop of rock jutting from the steep slope over the creek offered a good vantage point, so long as they did not forget where they were, and step back. Rosalind accidentally kicked a small stone, and it rolled down through the crackly ferns. They watched its bouncing moon-lit progress, horrified. It splashed when it hit the water, but the revelers gave no sign of having heard. The sound of the burn flowing over rocks below burbled insistently. Rosalind and Helen knelt and peeked over the top of the rock.

One young man, chest glistening with sweat, blew the pipes into life. "Gillatrypes!" someone called. He fingered a warm-up tune, as the men and women among the stones came together around the fire. A song rose, softly, strange words indecipherable to Rosalind and Helen. All joined hands and began stepping in a counter-clockwise circle, chanting a widdershins song. A fiddler drew her bow over the strings, and another young man bent an ear to a bodhran, drumming hand an invisible blur as the chant was joined. Some cast off their clothing, bronzed by the firelight. Those wearing cloaks became as empty spaces between them, into which things seemed to disappear, sections of the stones or fire or naked humans, when they passed by.

Morag leapt onto the recumbent stone. She gestured imperiously to someone.

Helen sucked in her breath. "That's...that's...that's..."

"Morag Gilbride. Didn't you know?"

"I'd heard rumors, but I didn't really think she did this sort of thing. I didn't think anybody did this sort of thing."

*

Morag's Quair of Light and Shadows
If there are punctuations in time, if there are times existing between times, between the worlds, if there are times that rend asunder the veils between us and the Goddess, between my Lady and creation, between the living and dead and those yet to be born, surely Samhuinn is the pinnacle, and surely our ring of stones is a most excellent vehicle?

Ask me now, and I would say I was born for this one night, born in the legacy of my ilk. The One whose ancient house this is, lifts her eternal gaze to our proud bodies, and sees in our nakedness living icons of herself. Here, her home, this perpetual wheel of conception and destruction. Here, our savage celebration, as has been done since the ancient hours when the worlds collided to ignite the great fire festival of our ancestors.

Habitation of our Goddess, joined to countless celebrations of divination and magic, the ghosts of history and our own beloved deceased drawn back to the oldest fire. Here, the Sidhe are passing by, bestowing bemused glances our way. Some I remember, and perhaps they remember me. Fully revealed to one another, we stand in truce and regard, as all the magical creatures of the wild are awoken on this night.

I shed my cloak and did not feel the cold. The spirits in the fire sprang up to dance, and the stones, those guardians of history, dissolved hard edges into their ancient essence, and the spirits of the living and the dead became indistinguishable. Sparks of the spirits, the wee folk and the forest creatures moved freely among us. All mystical flames twined and joined and risen to encircle the ring. This night was pure celebration of the deepest magic from beyond time.

*

A gray-haired woman, stout and strong with the vigor of a farmer's wife, reached up her hand. Morag took it and leapt off the recumbent stone, plunging the tip of the sword into the earth, where it swayed then stilled. Morag was handed off to a small group at the perimeter of the stones, where they dipped fingers in a pottery bowl and drew dark blue patterns on her body. Loops and swirls and circles and spirals. Creatures came to life in the patterns, the horse, the raven, the serpent, the bull and boar. The others commented on the artwork, teeth flashing in laughter, until Morag was covered head to toe in blue zoomorphic symbols. A young man stepped close to reverently place a silver torc about her neck. They stepped back to see their witch transformed into barbaric splendor.

Auntie Meg stood close to the fire, her long gray hair in tendrils over the black cloak on her bony shoulders. She clutched a staff with a stag's skull and antlers affixed to its top, her single eye glancing up, tongue dancing between her lips. "Here, my dearies," she said to no-one in particular, "whit's that, there?" She tipped her staff to the edge of the forest.

Two young men, in conversation with a few of the young women, glanced over, then at each other, puzzled.

"You laddies, awa' and see!" she scolded. "By the burn."

They stood and walked to the edge of the stones. One stooped to take up a broadsword from where it leaned against one of the megaliths. He pointed to the right, and his companion nodded in acknowledgment. They split apart, jogging in a wide half circle to meet behind the trees where Auntie Meg, her one eye apparently keener than theirs, had indicated.

"How splendid," Helen exclaimed. "Like Druid rites of old, or some such." She swept all around the clearing with binoculars. Something odd manifested in the binoculars, a squared pattern, out of focus, which swayed to and fro. She lowered the binoculars. "Oh," she said, to the kilt and bare knees in front of her face.

The two young men stood on the rock above Rosalind and Helen, broadsword resting on a shoulder, quizzical expressions on their handsome young faces.

Rosalind slowly stood. Helen raised herself as well, and to Rosalind's astonishment, said, "Oh, hullo. May we join you?"

Morag was suddenly standing between the two men. She laughed to see them, and extended a woad-marked arm to Rosalind, who stared speechless at the designs trying to think where she'd seen that image before.

"Come," Morag said. "It's all right."

Helen, proffering a delicate hand each to the young men, lost no time in turning to academic inquiry. "How long have you been doing this?" she asked. "How do you know what to do, I mean, you can't presume to know what the Celts actually did, never mind whoever built these stone rings, or surely it's a mix of various trends in history, don't you think? Of course, records are very scant, particularly in Scotland..."

As they drew near the circle, a challenge rang out. "Who dares?" demanded the stout woman who had helped Morag off the recumbant. Auntie Meg keeked sideways and squinted.

"Speak your names," said Morag.

"Helen," Helen piped up.

"Rosalind."

"Helen Forbes, that is. I say, please may we join you?"

All eyes looked to Morag. "Bid them welcome," she said. "Tonight there are forces at work beyond our ken."

"Then enter, if you dare," said an Elder with long white hair beautiful down her black cloak. She handed them each a handle-less pottery mug of dark wine. "Because once you have entered this place, nothing will ever be the same."

From a group standing slightly apart, a slender woman in a heavy cloak, satin-lined and with an embroidered hem, giving her a regal air, approached Helen. The firelight glanced off a silver circlet of a large crescent moon at her forehead. "Do I hear an English accent?"

"Hullo," said Helen. Then she looked closer. "Charlotte Gillespie? It can't be."

"Good heavens, Helen. What on earth are you doing here?"

"A lark!" She laughed. "I suppose I'm a guest."

"Let's stick together, shall we, in the midst of these rather wild Scots. And here is David." She indicated the equally regally cloaked man beside her.

"David! I had no idea you did this sort of thing."

"How lovely to see you, Helen," he said. "We are guests here. I trust we can keep this our little secret?"

"Of course. What fun!"

More figures gathered around. One of the youngsters uncapped flying ointment in a small glass jar and rubbed it in small circles on Rosalind's temples, and brushed it over her lips, then to Rosalind's surprise, kissed her. Another, naked, unstopped a small vial and held it under Rosalind's nostrils. "Come on, just a breath, aye, that's it."

A wave of euphoria rolled through Rosalind. A breath of pure light, and she was calmly flying, light as air.

*

The little vixen pulled away, slithering sideways along the bench, scraping her thighs across the stone. Clive went after and turned her, tackled her, bringing her down with a soft thud onto the grass, face to face. "Kirsteen," he said. "What's wrong? Is this not what you've been wanting?"

"Please," she sounded like a school kid. "Please."

He pushed a knee between her tight thighs.

"Not now, Clive, I'm frightened. Let's wait."

Both knees insinuated and pushed her legs apart.

"No!" she cried and hit at his chest with her fists.

He took her neck with his teeth. His hands went under her buttocks and raised her hips.

"Stop," she sobbed, head violently turning from side to side, still ineffectively pushing against his chest, trying in vain to kick him off.

Clive positioned himself, pressed against her, but could not break through. He pulled back slightly, and pushed harder. The outer ring of her flesh broke and he was in.

For a second she went absolutely still, mouth wide, back arched. He thrust in as far as he could. It was worth the wait. She was a silken hot wet sheath, tight as hell. He groaned.

Kirsteen took a deep shuddering breath and came alive. She screamed and clawed at his face, grasping the skin of his cheek and his hair. Nothing broke through the pleasure of his body sliding in hers. Until she bit his chin and the sharp teeth cut through to the bone.

He reared back, dark drops sprinkling over her face. He slapped her hard. Her face had become the hideous screaming mask of a harpy. She rolled over, disengaging herself, while he touched his streaming chin. It hurt like blazes, and his vision blurred and pulsed as he watched her crawl away, making pathetic mewling sounds.

Clive's hand came away soaked in blood. His eyes narrowed. The thwarted sex, the challenge of her refusal, the blazing hatred he felt when he looked at her, blubbering and trying to escape, filled him with a raging elation. She stumbled to her feet and made for the gate out the back of the walled garden. Good. Let her. There was nothing beyond but the wild forest.

Thudding footfalls suddenly came close and something hit him full on, knocking him completely off his feet and into the rose bed. He shouted in surprise and annoyance as the thorns cut and came away in his flesh. He scrambled out and slammed into the stranger's midsection, taking him down, crashing against the stone bench. The man relaxed and groaned and rolled over onto the grass, conscious but dazed. He held his head where blood was starting down his face. It was Calum, the love-sick puppy.

Clive barked a laugh and kicked Calum in the belly. Calum doubled up, stopped breathing, gaping like a fish out of water, then began to gasp for breath. Clive looked up to the far gate in time to see it swing open, and the fleeing girl stumble down the forest path.

*

The stones came alive, like friendly cattle, or hovering giants, warmth and light rising from them, or perhaps it was the dancing fire and her increasingly distorted vision. Rosalind opened her arms to the moon and spun around, skipping to the wild cacophony of the fiddle and a chant in Gaelic the women took up, that had a beat like a drum. The moon was the only steady object, washing with silver light all of Scotland.

There was a burst of sparks as somebody threw fresh wood on the fire.

Rosalind felt a soft touch on her arm.

"I'm the Spae Wife," said the stout white-haired woman. "I'll reveal your destiny if you come wi' me."

In an old copper tub beside one of the stones, the Spae Wife stirred the water once, twice, thrice, with a thistle-headed spurtle. "Look deep. See what you can see."

Rosalind knelt beside the tub and watched the little ripples spin, the small whirlpools drawing in the glancing reflections. Spinning down went fire shadow and stars' reflection. Down went her attention with them, pulling her in. She clutched the sides of the tub. In the flashing ripples, a face formed, reflected back at her, not at all distorted by the motion. A face under the water. On the other side of the water. Was this the face of her great grandmother Mairi Ogilvy? No, not her. A reflection of the kindly Spae Wife looking over her shoulder? She glanced up, but there was nobody close by. She studied the face behind the water again, where it faded then reformed, and with a shock realized it was Rosalind herself, maybe thirty years older. Face soft, eyes cheerful, a lovely face, a face that had been carved and etched with time of hardships and passions and courage through its middle age.

She put her hand to her mouth, to see the beautiful old woman that she would be, so powerful a revelation, that she never thought to doubt it.

"Lady," called the witches to Morag, "Tell us what you see!"

"Frithir, tell us," the others called, then fell silent, as Rosalind sat quietly on the soft grass, and let all the turmoil and emotions of the past days fall away into the friendly earth.

*

Aye, the Frith, the augury that stands revealed best on the quarter days from a threshold. And what better threshold anywhere in the world than the portal of the standing stones? Morag stood between the megaliths, facing down the glen. She slowly raised her arms and as they came up her inner sight cracked opened to gather in the visions wanting to manifest for her people gathered.

Two spectral women stood on either side, her mother and her grandmother, the Morag she was named for, hands touching, facing the fiery south, the solstice portal to come, as they had done many times in the decades before. Their extended arms made a link between two stones. Beyond them a ring of folk appeared, in and around the stones; their ancestors, ancient ones, the druids, wearing flattened torcs of gold, or in black veils; and further back a priestess with antlers on her brow, and beyond her the painted people. Spirits flew around the circle's perimeter, like after-images of light as they moved.

And then, Auntie Meg stood among them, her phantom sister and mother reaching to her with shining arms, until her bent and twisted body was ablaze in silver light.

More visions came to Morag, from so long ago, the memory of the Ancestors. An apple tree appeared, with a fantastic bird in its branches, the boar rooting beneath, and a history written in blood and passion between roots and boughs.

"Lady," the voices called again. "The Frith!"

Morag's arms relaxed and lowered from between the stones, and a tentative voice whispered in her ear. "Daughter of the Seers, what do you see for me?" Morag answered, murmuring, unaware of what she spoke or to whom. "Twelve days' time, he will come, and bring with him the answer to your need." To another, "that is not your destiny. Unless you take the other road, it will end badly." And, "it is death, yet from the death will come a new life, all in the same week." They came away, distressed or joyful, eyes turned inward, intent on the revealed message. But some did not ask. Neither did Rosalind nor Helen, both feeling foreigners to this magic, and in any event, enough had transpired to both, and they were content in dealing with what they already knew.

After a time, two women took up a song, a complicated skein of notes that riveted everyone's attention with its beauty. Helen sat down beside Rosalind. Charlotte and David ambled over, arranged their regal cloaks and knelt to join them.

"That's a puirt à beul," Helen said. "Gaelic mouth music."

The music tugged Morag back, a call to return by, her dissolved body knitting back together, and as always, not in the quite the same way as before. High above, the moon's light silvered the mountains, all crevasses and crags smoothed over. Fire-made shadows of the standing stones lifted half-way up the heathery hill, undulating and leaping as vigorously as the dancers had just before.

"Is what you do, different?" Rosalind asked David Gillespie.

"I daresay we focus in more on a liturgical sort of magic. Most often indoors."

"Working in your office, I honestly had no idea," Rosalind kindly lied.

"No, well," said David, "it can mean the end of everything one has worked for, if it gets out."

"Maybe someday it can be out in the open like other religions," Rosalind said.

They both laughed. "Not likely," said Charlotte.

There was a general relaxation after the divination, and the witches distributed plates and bowls of food, and mugs of wine, and were eating and laughing.

"As you can imagine," said David, "I had no idea you would be here, Rosalind, but since fate has brought us together here tonight, it gives me an opportunity to say how pleased I am that you will be staying in Scotland and with our team. It's true we needed you before, but we really will need you now."

"I don't think it would have worked out if you and Clive hadn't welcomed me to the firm."

"Ah, Clive. You'll find things are changing a bit at Gillespie and Company."

Helen drew a deep breath and plucked at the grass. "Clive's made a right mess of it all," she said.

"What do you mean," asked Rosalind.

"Later, later," said Charlotte, assuming her High Priestess authority. "It's always either about money or sex, isn't it?"

"Now then," called one of the young men. "Rise up, rise up and come to the dance!" The bodhran player set up a steady drumbeat as the company got to their feet.

*

Kirsteen's elusive form flitted before him through the forest, the moon so bright it mimicked daylight without color. They sprinted along the bracken and moss, their harsh breathing and soft footfalls on the path the only sound.

"Will you stop!" he shouted. "I only want to talk."

"Leave me alone!" she cried.

He had to talk sense into her or God knew what she'd tell

people. Even as he ran through the forest, gaining on her, he was formulating a plan: either she'd see reason, accept the passion that she invoked in him, admit to the same within herself, and they'd make up and carry on as before. Or, if she were unwilling, he'd easily convince her that it was her doing. Nobody, after seeing them flirting at the castle, would believe she was not inviting his advances. He would explain how foolish it would be to reveal their little misunderstanding to others, how she'd get the blame. And given that he would be in the clear one way or the other, they would finish what they'd started.

She tripped and spilled flat onto her belly, arms windmilling over the leaves, and he was on her in a heartbeat. She gasped and squirmed under him. "Kirsteen," he breathed into her ear. "Be still." He hauled her hips back, found the skirt's waistband, and pulled it violently down her thighs. The pursuit, the tantalizing prize almost in his grasp made him wild.

She twisted around and smashed his nose with her wildly flailing fist. He fell back, face in hands, and she clambered to her feet, tugging desperately at her skirt, stumbled, righted and sprinted away.

He lunged, made a grab for her bare thigh, but too late; she slipped from his raking fingers and was off down the glen, with Clive scrambling after in hot pursuit.

*

Morag lifted her head to the forest path. Something was coming. The haze of the ancient had set over the present, and it was not going to dissipate. Spirits of the Old Ones hovered among the glistening bodies, yet were not as they had been in years past. An expectation stirred them, the same presage, it seemed. Morag shook her head and bent an ear to pierce the depths of the forest. The fire's crackle and shouts and laughter of the revelers made it impossible to separate sounds, and the dancing feet drummed the earth. But something was there. She extended her magical sight out through the trees, but still, the thing was heralded and escorted by such a company in the wakened forest, it was impossible to pick them apart.

Old Auntie Meg, whose one eye missed nothing, sidled up to Morag. "Eh?" she inquired.

Morag frowned and put a hand against a stone. A couple of the older women joined them, offering water to drink, and one who had been attentive to Morag's needs that night tossed a cloak over Morag's shoulders. "What is it?" she asked, brow furrowed as she peered into the forest.

"Aye, aye," Auntie Meg hissed through her gums. "Something's there."

A young witch danced close behind. "By the pricking of my thumbs," she shouted.

The others laughed till they saw Auntie Meg's stern hand raised. "Haud your wheesht!"

"I say," said Helen. "What do you suppose the intoxicating substance is?"

"Which one?" laughed Rosalind.

"I could jolly well get used to this."

The rest could not be held back just to humor the old crone, of whom it must said, enjoyed her little eccentricities. One of the men took the hand of a lithe young woman, who screamed happily as they took a running start, and leapt the fire. Another couple followed. Then another, and another, some individually, literally passing through the flames. The men showed off, jumping sideways and backwards, and one dove in an arc, to tumble in a somersault on the far side. The older witches clasped hands and daintily walked, one on either side of the fire, making an arch over the flames with their arms. On the far side, they each made a formal curtsy to the other.

Helen set her jaw, crouched, and took a purposeful run at the fire's edge. Rosalind reached a hand out to stop her, and missed, mouth open in shock. Helen barely cleared the side of the fire, but succeeded, stumbled, and was caught by David on the far side. Charlotte banged on Helen's skirt to put out a smoldering spark. "Helen, really!"

"Did you see?" she shouted to Rosalind. "Did you see?"

Morag let the premonition go. She slipped the cloak off her shoulders, took Rosalind's hand, and pointed to the fire. Rosalind let out a shriek, and they ran and leapt as one, flames caressing their skin like hot feathers.

Rosalind stumbled to her knees at Auntie Meg's feet.

"Leaping the Samhuinn fire with Herself, are you? Oh ho

ho!" The others danced around the fire like dervishes, while the fiddler and drummer played an ever-escalating reel. Rosalind grabbed Morag's wrists and spun her around, and Helen joined the dance with a remarkable loss of inhibition, waving her hands in the sparkling air, head lolling on her loosened neck, as she skipped like a child. David and Charlotte held hands and danced in a stately little hop and step, then others joined them, laughing, until a circle formed, hands held, kicking and prancing round the fire.

"Gosh, I wish we could get our lot to join in as exuberantly," said Charlotte, out of breath and almost pulled off her feet by the young witches.

"New-fangled rubbish," growled Auntie Meg.

This time the premonition in the forest came more insistently. Morag left them to return to the edge of the circle, all attention in the direction of Carlin Castle, body quivering like a hunting dog riveted on a scent. She glanced behind, then slipped away, into the complete darkness on the far side of the great stones.

Helen was making a go of the divination in the tub, her head circling round and round with the swirling water. "I can't see...oh," she said. "Oh, I'm feeling a little ill."

Rosalind knelt beside her.

"Oh." Helen put a dainty hand to her mouth. "Sorry."

Rosalind pushed back the bangs from Helen's brow. "Your skin is clammy."

"Too much of a good thing I daresay." Helen closed her eyes. "Oh, that's me done. I really don't feel well at all. Rosalind, would you be a dear and take me back?"

Rosalind glanced up but could not locate Morag in the swirl of the dancers. Helen groaned. She was growing pale in the firelight. Rosalind helped her to her unsteady feet, placed Helen's arm over her shoulders, and wobbled with her towards the path to the castle. Charlotte and David offered solicitous aid, but were waved away by Helen. "No, no, won't spoil the party, you lot carry on."

Morag, in the dark of the megalith's shadow, watched them pass, and had an impulse to intercept them. The presentiment of something about to arrive had become so strong, and the presence of the escorting spirits so integrated into it, she could not connect to the mundane world of the two women weaving down the path. The ghosts of the ancients watched and beckoned, and Morag was taken completely into the company of the spirits.

She set out silently on the heels of the two women, their forms wraith-like to Morag's second-sight, as she moved from shadow to tree to stone. The forest closed in around them, immediately shutting them out of sight and sound of the stone circle.

"Oh, dear," Helen said in the flickering moonlight as they stumbled down the path. "I'm so sorry, but I really feel very strange. Not used to bacchanalias I suppose. You could go back, just leave me at the castle where I can lie down."

"I think we left at the right time," said Rosalind. "Let them do their thing. I have a feeling they only just got started."

"But weren't they magnificent? I'll never forget... oh, I must sit for a moment. I'm going to be sick."

Clutching one another, they swerved off the path to cut through the trees to a small boulder dully glowing against a rocky outcrop a few meters away. As Rosalind helped Helen to sit on the stone, something flitted by on the trail, a glimpse of shadow in the flickering moonlight, the faint sound of breathing and muffled footfalls, a passing felt more than seen. It happened too quickly, and at the same time Helen leaned over and vomited on Rosalind's feet.

The runners passed by Morag, she hidden in the tree. It all came clear in an instant. Morag turned and took up the pursuit. The runners were headed for the clearing. The three raced along the moonlit-dappled path. The first runner cried out as the second gained on her, and up ahead the fiddle fell silent. Morag caught up with them just as they burst into the clearing, just as he grabbed the woman by the hair, pulling her down into a tumbling jumble of limbs. To the astonished looks of the witches, Morag was on him. She took him by the jacket on his back and lifted him up, off his feet, to hurl him towards the stones, where he stumbled and half-fell in the fire. His arm banged against a blazing log in a shower of sparks. He howled and rolled away.

The fallen runner gasped for air, clutching her torn clothing around her. Blood speckled her face and breasts, and her bare thighs were scraped where the stockings had been torn.

"Morag," she cried. "Morag!"

The man rose, spun on his heel and ran straight into one

of the women, knocking her down hard, and falling with her. It was Clive.

"Hold him," Morag said, and already a wild elation was rising in her.

Blades flashed in the firelight, as a dozen wild men and women moved among the stones to encircle Clive. He quickly looked around, breathing heavily, found no exit, and paused.

Old Auntie Meg gave her skull staff to one of the others and crouched down by the young woman, to gently draw the damp hair away from her face. "Kirsteen. Are ye hurt my lass?"

Kirsteen, rocked by her heavy breaths, raised her head. "He attacked me," she said to Meg, then to Morag, then to the circle of men and women, as if in disbelief. "He raped me."

There was no sound but for the crackling of the fire. To the mix of bewilderment and rising anger on the faces of the witches, Clive drew himself up. "She's lying."

Kirsteen put her head to her drawn-up knees and wailed.

For a split second the entire group paused as one. Then Morag pulled the broadsword from the earth.

"You raped Kirsteen."

"She's lying I tell you!"

Teeth flashed in a hiss. The spirits, the very mountains seemed to close in.

"Clive Forbes," Morag said. "You were responsible for Catriona's death."

"That's a lie as well!" He backed into a standing stone. "You can't prove anything."

And even now, there was something else. Morag gestured with her head to one of the young women, who ran to the perimeter of the field where the trail entered. She stopped, listened, turned and raised her hand. The company of witches paused in silence as a kilted man suddenly emerged from the forest path, holding his forehead where a black gleam of blood glistened.

"Ah, Morag," he cried. "Is she here?" Then he caught sight of Clive and before anyone could answer, ran at him, and struck him with his fists. "Where is she, you bastard?"

"Calum!" Kirsteen cried.

When he stopped and turned to Kirsteen, Clive saw his chance and sprinted for the trail, but he had to pass by the younger man. Calum tackled him effortlessly. He dragged him back by the leg, to toss him against one of the tall standing stones.

"That's enough of this nonsense," said Clive, switching to play the cool upper classes as he stood and dusted off his sleeves. "Get out of my way. I'm leaving, and you may be sure the authorities will hear about this."

"No, you're not," said Morag.

"Very well, if you let me go now, I won't tell anyone about this... business."

A breath of disbelief filled the circle.

Kirsteen suddenly screamed at Clive, features wild and distorted. He stared, stunned, at the blazing hatred in her face.

"Your destiny," Morag said, "has brought you to this place."

"You incredibly stupid woman," Clive sputtered.

"And," Auntie Meg cackled, "it's Samhuinn."

"How convenient," someone said.

"It's been a very long time," spoke another, thoughtfully.

"It's not often these days," Morag said, "the punishment fits the crime."

Fear began to erase the desperate craftiness in his face. "Ridiculous. As if you can take the law into your own hands. As if anyone would give credence to a bunch of deluded bitches and hags playing at fairy tales."

"Shut up!" Calum shouted. "Shut up, you pompous ass!" He made as if to strike Clive again, but was stopped by a young man's hand on his chest.

Auntie Meg cackled and clapped her arthritic hands together as best she could. "He is mine. He is mine."

"Let me at him!" Calum cried, fists ready to strike.

"Wait." Morag spoke calmly.

Calum stopped. "For Kirsteen," he said to Morag, eyes pleading. "For me!"

"Justice will be served," she said. "Have no fear on that account." She paused and looked around the circle. "Any of you who wish to leave, do so now. You will speak nothing of this to anyone, on sure pain of death. But you may go, and none will think the worst of you for it."

A mix of reactions arose, snarls and shouts of blood lust, to glances of uncertainty. Charlotte and David clutched hands and whispered together. She nodded.

A look of puzzled recognition came over Clive. "David. Thank God you're here. Tell these deluded maniacs to stop playing games."

"I'm sorry Clive. This is no game."

"Have you lost your mind? What are you doing here in that fancy dress?"

"Go, or stay," Morag commanded the group. "But make your decision now!"

A young man spoke. "We are yours, Lady, bound by oath and blood." A cry went up, until everyone joined in, all indecision erased. No-one left the circle.

'So be it," said Morag. "We claim the most ancient of sacrifices on this night."

Clive stared at Morag, eyes wild. "Look, I don't know what nonsense you think you're playing at..." His voice and legs gave way and he slid down the stone.

"Lift him up," she said.

Naked warriors heaved Clive to his feet and pushed him against the stone.

"Calum," Morag instructed. "Make him fast against the stone. Your belt."

After a second's hesitation, Calum unbuckled the wide leather belt of his kilt, and, grasping either end, moved to lower it from behind the top of the stone, to catch Clive by the neck, holding him fast against the rock. Clive pulled at the belt in a panic, but Calum held him easily.

"Take your hands off me," he gasped. "You fucking lunatics."

A young woman standing close reached out and he jumped when she lightly touched his shoulder. "Ha, our Cu Chulainn is here!" Her fingers slid across his chest to the buttons of his shirt. He let go of the belt to strike at her, and she dodged, laughing. Other hands alighted, to unbutton, untie, undo, until his clothing opened to expose chest and belly. He kicked wildly, and thrashed with his arms, but Calum held him fast.

"David," he cried. "Tell them to let me go!"

"I'm afraid I can't do that, Clive."

"You know I'm innocent!"

"Actually, what I do know is that you are guilty of major embezzlement. You would have destroyed me and my family, and brought down the entire firm for your own greed. As far as I'm concerned, you can take what they will deal you, or explain to the authorities."

Morag and the Elders didn't give David's mistaken presumption a second thought. Knives slid from sheaths and flashed in the firelight, and a few of the witches slowly approached, blades held out.

Clive's eyes rolled in fear. "David, for God's sake man, they'll kill me!"

"What is death," said Morag, "but the doorway to new life? Death is nothing."

"David! I'm begging you!"

"What lies on the far side of death is a gift, that I would not have you see. You will sacrifice far more for us."

A knife blade flashed and his trousers slid and bunched at his knees, then his boxer shorts were sliced away on either side, leaving a streak of red where the blade rasped against his skin. Hands slid up his thighs, trailing over his belly and chest. A frown of bewilderment crossed his features, and he barked a laugh of disbelief, when one of the witches plucked a curl of his pubic hair, yanking it out by the roots. He went rigid against the stone, hands moving pathetically between his privates and the leather biting into his neck.

"What will you do?" he asked like a frightened boy. "What will you do?"

"What would you like, dearie?" came the quavering voice of a dark figure across the fire. One witch ran her fingers up his neck, to twist a hand in his hair, to lift his face. To watch his true nightmare tottering towards him on ancient, spindly legs. The Cailleach, a staff with a stag's skull mounted on it in one hand, a fistful of raven feathers in the other. "What would you like me to do?"

*

All the cars were gone from the gravel drive but three; Helen's, that Rosalind had driven, a small Peugeot, and a battered old Land Rover. Rosalind's heart sank.

"A bed," groaned Helen, as they approached the steps to the private castle entrance. "Just a bed will do, any bed. A sofa. A floor. Or, or perhaps the leaves in the forest. Did you know the ancients made mattresses of heather and bracken and animal skins? I should like that very much."

"Come on," said Rosalind. "You can sleep in the guestroom."

Helen twirled her slender fingers in the air. "I shall arise with flowers in my hair and joy in my feeble heart."

With difficulty, Rosalind maneuvered Helen up the uneven steps of the spiral stair, pushing gently from behind, round and round to the top floor, one hand on Helen's back, the other sliding up the central stone column of the stair. She glanced down behind and up ahead, keeping a watch for Angus. Once in the magnificent guestroom, Helen wove her way over the carpet to plunge onto the bed. By the time Rosalind returned from the bathroom with a glass of water, Helen was emitting dainty snores. Rosalind put the glass on the bedside table, took Helen's shoes off, pulled the blankets over her, and quietly left the room.

She descended the treacherous stair, pulled open the heavy door to the main bedroom, and closed it firmly behind her, the heavy latch on its ring of iron clunking easily into place. A little warmth came from the coals in the fireplace, and she sat heavily in the armchair, suddenly exhausted. She searched herself for feelings, for clarity of emotions, then gave up.

"Just go to bed," she said.

Rosalind tossed a couple of logs onto the coals. She shuffled to the bed in a near-stupor, pulled the top of the duvet down on the ridiculous, inviting four-poster, and had just begun to tug her sweater over her head, when a decisive knock sounded. The door opened and Angus looked in. He took in the state of the bed and glanced around the room.

"Angus!" She quickly drew the pullover back down. His unannounced presence in her bedroom made her angry, but concern for his emotional state held her in check.

"I've been looking for you," he said. "Where have you been? Everybody's gone."

"With Helen."

"There's been a massive misunderstanding." He stepped in. "I want to make it right."

"Angus, I'm very tired. Can't we talk later?"

He quietly pulled the door to. "What happened?"

Angus stood between her and the only door. The security of the castle room quickly turned to a perfect prison. But then, it was Angus, only Angus, the man she'd been seeing, the man who loved her, even if she had jilted him. The man to whom she owed some of the happiest times she'd ever had.

"What do you mean?"

"Something obviously happened. It doesn't make any sense otherwise."

"You mean my decision?"

"I pushed you too hard, didn't I? You've been overwhelmed with your Uncle's death, Clive and Helen's difficulties, my suddenly being in the lime-light, and by association, you as well. It's all understandable."

"Well, but..."

"There, you see?" He stepped closer and held out his arms. "All a mistake, easily undone."

His eyes held their old vulnerable, irresistible look, the circle of his arms waited to pull her to the warm protection of his chest. He was offering her a second chance, and doing it with tender affection. In her near-exhaustion, there was nothing she would rather have done than surrender, melt into his embrace, recapture the affection and the promise of an uncomplicated life with a man who doted on her.

"Come," he said gently.

But she knew perfectly well she was not being honest with herself.

"I wish I could, believe me. But nothing's changed, Angus."

His arms dropped. The flash of frustration came instantly. "That's absurd."

She hugged herself and wearily closed her eyes. "Maybe so."

"Then stop this ridiculous game!"

"It's no game."

He grew agitated, unable to stand still. "Do you...are you aware that you led me to believe...?"

"We...we both..."

"No, mine seems a natural progression if you ask me. An obvious conclusion to a certain set of circumstances. What would I not offer you? What would I not give you? What would you possibly lack? Tell me, and I'll obtain it."

"That has nothing to do with it."

"I am at a complete and utter loss to understand you. You pulled an about-face on me. Just when I'd assumed everything was going well. When anyone would have thought as much."

Their friends, their families, the very society on both sides of the Atlantic would rejoice in their fairy tale union if only she'd stop being so obstinate.

"No, I never intended..." She struggled to speak with direct honesty. "I entered into the relationship in good faith. My time with you was one of the most wonderful things that's ever happened to me."

"Then what the hell is the problem?"

"We've talked about all this."

"Oh, right, your independence. I've got news for you, lass, the reality of loneliness will come when all the new-fangled ideals are swept away. We both know opportunities like this don't come along but once in a lifetime."

"I completely agree. Anyone would be lucky to have you."

He made a sound of exasperation and wheeled about on his heel to pace, then stop and fix her with an accusing eye. "What's his name?"

It took a minute to sink in. "You're not serious?"

"You've obviously been with someone." He nodded at the unmade bed.

"Okay, Angus." She put up her hand. "It's time for you to leave."

"He must be something to edge me out, that's all I can say."

"Okay, to hell with this, to hell with everything. I want to know something. Is there anything you need to tell me about the treasure? About that cross you found that you showed me?"

His mouth opened. "How on earth did you hear about that?"

"Oh, my God, Angus, what did you do?"

He leaned against the mantel of the huge stone fireplace. "My God, if you know, that means others know."

Rosalind waited, almost holding her breath.

He looked up at her. "I don't know what happened. I must have misplaced it when I was doing an inventory, I don't know, except that it was suddenly gone, simply gone from the Medieval Department before the display went up. I've been in an agony of fear since then."

"You don't know?"

He stepped back. "You think I took it."

"Did you?"

"This is exactly what I feared would happen. Who told you about this? Helen?"

"What does it matter? I just want to know the truth."

His hand reached blindly to find the top of the chair, and he sat heavily in it, eyes dim. After a moment, he looked up at her. "That's what this is all about."

She shook her head wearily. "No."

"I confess, I thought about it. I seriously thought about it. I even quipped about it to Clive, when he was helping set up the display..." He stopped, brow creased.

"Clive?"

Angus put a finger to his upper lip as he thought. "It never made it to the display, but in the midst of all the madness, I didn't notice until much later. Then it was too late, too incriminating."

"What's going to happen?"

"How could I possibly prove my innocence?"

"Angus, just tell me the truth."

His face was lined with deep anguish. He looked up at her and spoke softly. "Rosalind, how can a pathetic, weak man who doesn't even have the courage to make love to the only woman he's ever loved, have the courage to commit such a crime as this?"

She knelt beside him.

"Angus."

"You smell of smoke. Where have you been? Dare I ask?"

She was in his arms, his breath was hot on her face, and from out of the pain she saw a look dawn of pure slack-jawed desire. And she was astonished at her own desire for him. It was up to her. One word, one touch. One kiss.

She lifted her mouth to his, and they stayed that way for a moment, lips centimeters apart.

"I'm not marrying you," she whispered.

"We'll discuss it later," he said.

Their lips touched and they both surrendered. The kisses came, tumbling over one another, light to rough and fierce, and they did not even stop to remove unnecessary clothing. They backed to the bed, in an embrace of hungry caresses. He lifted her, hands under her thighs, and tossed her up on the high mattress. He climbed up to lie above her. Her legs wrapped around his kilted backside to draw him down and slowly in, where they both stopped and gasped.

"Oh, God," he groaned. "Oh God."

It was as if their bodies had been aching for consummation all along, even as their warring thoughts kept them apart. He moved and she rose and fell in his rhythm, amazed to feel the depths of the passion rising quickly, overtaking her completely. When she climaxed, it tipped him over the edge, and they joined voices, eyes closed, mouths open, astonished at the easy slide into this coupling.

He collapsed and rolled next to her, and they both stared at the wooden carved canopy over the centuries old bed, at faces of grinning Greenmen peering down through ivy and oak leaf.

*

The ancient Cailleach came and stood before him, her one eye tilting her face sideways in its intensity, mouth grinning in a toothless cackle. The skin rippled over the stark ribs down her torso, her flat breasts swung low, and below her slack belly, thin pubic hair crowned spindly legs and knobby knees.

Clive twisted against the belt, hands grasping it on either side of his throat, his feet splayed and digging into the earth. "You won't kill me, you old hag," he said, spittle flying. "You wouldn't dare!"

Meg looked puzzled in the midst of her toothless grin. "Kill you? No, no, stupid fool. Not I, no indeed, not I."

The witches slid more insistent hands over Clive's chest and arms and belly. "Get off me," he shouted, kicking at them, till the leather belt tightened and he gasped. "Don't kill me," Clive whispered to Calum. "Don't let them kill me. I'll give you whatever you want. I could make you rich."

The caresses returned, pinching, pulling, stroking wherever they could reach. His breathing came hard and his penis grew heavier, straining forward in an erection. Charlotte buried her face in her husband's cloak at his shoulder. He held her tight against him.

A young witch turned to wiggle her backside at Clive, pushing against him, and he lifted a foot in an attempt to kick her away, but she was too close. "So you want me? Eh? Come on then!"

"Get off, bitch!"

Kirsteen cried out and put her hands over her face and turned her back on them, bruised shoulders rising and falling with her jagged breath.

The Cailleach handed off the staff and her bony fingers reached to Clive. Some of the young men, fearing for Meg's safety, pinned Clive's arms and legs against the tall stone.

"Is this what you were wanting?" She none too gently pinched the skin around his belly. "Eh?" Trickles of blood beaded and flowed where her jagged nails dug.

His head went back hard against the stone. He gasped and coughed and swore. "You disgusting old hag!" The old woman chuckled, and the young witches took up the lewd teasing in whispers, and the more he gasped and writhed, swollen hard, a string of moisture drifting away from the eye of his penis, the more relaxed became her caresses, until he thrust eagerly into her old hands. Pleading. Cursing. Lost. She stopped again.

"Damn you," he cried.

"Pardon?" she said. "Eh? What's that you say? You want me? You want old Meg?"

When he wept, grinding his head against the smooth rock, she pinched the top of his foreskin in her nails and pulled it mercilessly this way and that.

"Unto me all things come," she cackled, and they laughed.

"Better enjoy it," said one. "It'll be the last time."

With a sob, he ejaculated in throbbing streams, and the Cailleach caught the semen in her hands. She turned away, careful in her handling of it. Calum let the belt go, and Clive slid down the stone, still jerking in spasms.

Morag looked down on him. "Well done, you arrogant fool," she said. "Your very essence is in the Cailleach's hands. Your spirit is ours, and it will be captive, bound to your death. You will never see the light of transformation, but be trapped in the world of the hungry ghosts, forever. You invited my curse, and now you receive it. And for what you have done to my niece, and to Kirsteen, my oath will be met."

"Let me at him!" Calum cried, leather strap grasped between his large fists.

Morag gave an almost dismissive wave of permission. A savage shrill cry arose, and they were on him, whichever way he turned and crawled or stumbled in a stupor, trousers entangled round one ankle. The musicians took up their instruments and began a lively reel. Clive fell to his torn face as if he had not an ounce of strength left in him, and they were on him like wolves on a stag. Calum, teeth flashing in the firelight, snapped the leather again over Clive's head to tighten it around his neck, this time in deadly earnest, strong arm muscles taut. Clive struggled, a clump of hair drifting away on the breeze, to suddenly flare up in the flames, to the sound of grunts and cries and harsh breaths. A bone cracked. The witches bent their heads to savage kisses, and came away with reddened teeth. One of them calmly walked to the bonfire and spat a mouthful of blood into the flames.

Morag and the Cailleach stood over the fire. As Clive's movements slowed, and his blood ran into the earth, Morag pulled and spun the energy of the man, his blood and semen, into a knot, binding all into one, as the Cailleach turned her hand over and opened it, and the white liquid sizzled into the Balefire.

Clive lay still on the thick grass, limbs splayed, and a white haze passed over his open eyes.

The music stopped. All was still. Silence came, but for their breathing and the crackle and quiet roar of the bonfire. The moon still burnished the mountain, but something was gathering in the night.

A wave of energy crashed over them, an explosion of brilliance that burst open in the stone circle, and flooded out in waves of rushing power, and they were taken out of themselves. A shout went up, a weird inhuman ululation. They stood or crouched beside the body, faces savage, roaring in pure blood lust. Some collapsed and lay still, others writhed on the earth, or stood still as statues. Morag raised her head to see. A phantom, a shrieking ghost rose from the circle, then was lost in the night.

Beyond them, beyond the tall stones and fire, up the slopes of the moonlit mountains, heavy tendrils of mist gathered to spill into the glen. Perfect. In perfect accord with the land. The Cailleach Bheur drew her heavy veil over them all, as she received the ancient sacrifice anew.

*

30 November, St Andrew's Day

Dear Ros,

Here, this is the only day you as a woman can enter the hallowed halls of the Royal and Ancient, seeing as how you are not the Queen.

Despite my almost flippant words over the phone, it was a shock to hear about Rabbie and what he'd done. I turned it over in my mind trying to think how I feel about it, and finally I am left with respect and pride, a sort of fierce pride that he did what he wanted despite the doctors and nurses and hospital staff who thought they knew what was best for him. Most folk would be horrified at your decision to let him alone, but I think you did the right thing. It would have been dreadful otherwise.

I must say we are very proud of you. Thanks for sending the newspaper clippings about that business with Lord whatsit and the gallery in Edinburgh. I know nothing about art, as you know fine, but I am grateful that your style is popular. That's the mother in me talking.

I watched and worried on your account and came to understand you were moving beyond what I had wanted for myself. Marriage to your father and a better life through that marriage were all I wanted. Of course it was a jolt – no doubt you understand better now what I mean, leaving Scotland and the family for a new world. Do you know our parents never displayed affection towards Rabbie and myself? I don't remember one hug from my mother when I was a child. Not one! That was just the way everybody acted, and of course we never thought it was unusual, not knowing anything else. And I watched poor wee Rabbie get the belt almost every day of his young life, if not at school, then at home.

Your father took me away, leaving much grumbling and ruffled feathers behind. Rabbie was left without a sister to look after him, and that's what really put him into a forty year pout, if you ask me. Now you've gone back to my first home, and made it your own, whereas if I'd stayed there, I'd probably be a wee wifie soor-face, and my child raised with no hugs or kisses.

Also, the thing itself is a blessing.

Chris and I would be delighted to join you for Christmas. He's already ordered the tickets. Want to know something? He's got a loan – finally! – for the dorm. With both of you out of ma wee hoose, I will be much more comfortable. I'm glad I was here when you needed me, but it's time for both of you to move on. And Chris will be close by if I need anything.

I must say, I'm eager to see the old place, but at the same time thankful that it too has changed. I love you, my darling.

Mum

PS If the weather's mild, do you think we might take a drive to the Cairngorms? You could show us this Laird Comyn's castle. And I'll show you where we stayed for our holidays.

Chapter 26

"Man that is born of woman hath but a short time to live," said the priest, "and is full of misery. He cometh up and is cut down, like a flower; he fleeth as it were a shadow, and never continueth in one stay."

It was impossible not to compare the British with the American service. Henry's funeral in California had taken place in a sterile, immaculately mowed park. The grave itself was hidden, covered by the huge coffin, which they could not afford, but had been cleverly coerced into buying. It rested on a curtained scaffolding of a metal frame and straps. Even the pile of earth was hidden under a green tarpaulin. In the heat of the summer sun, the minister of Henry's church spoke about a primitive and childlike version of heaven. It was an insult, stinging Rosalind to anger, yet the effort to protest required too much, and she knew nothing would be accomplished anyway. Even there, on the edge of sanity, over the coffin of her husband, Rosalind did what was expected or, more to the point, did not act on her feelings. Shock had turned her in, and she could not move out.

"In the midst of life we are in death: of whom may we seek for succour, but of thee, oh Lord, who for our sins art justly displeased?"

Here, on Scotland's east coast, the stark open pit awaited the simple pine box, which at a nod from Helen's priest, the same as had filled in for Niall Paterson at Carlin Castle, was lowered down by four colleagues, including David Gillespie and Angus MacLeod, who let the cradling rope slide slowly and carefully through their hands. The coffin shuddered against the deep earthen sides of the grave, tilting a little awkwardly one way then the other. Rosalind imagined Clive's bare skull nodding within, maybe rolling and bumping the wood, barely separated from the living by a thin plank, in his final descent.

Helen exhibited all propriety in her role as the mourning spouse. She took up a handful of earth, as did Alastair, and Angus.

Rosalind also reached into the loose earth and brought up

a fistful, warmer than the cold air. Something hard, like a flat stone, jabbed her palm. It was a piece of bone, the same color as the skeletons in the Neolithic tomb, a rich tan. The edge of the bone was serrated, like a picture of a river taken from a satellite. A fragment of skull.

"Of course," she whispered. Eight centuries and more of burials around the cathedral, and the bodies did what they were meant to do, decompose back into the earth, transforming from decay and corruption to clean soil.

*

Despite the snows that had already fallen in the early winter, the harsh rock-face had been swept clean by the wind. The Cairngorms demand respect at any time of year, but particularly in the dark half of the Cailleach's reign. It happened that a fervent, some would say foolhardy hillwalker, on the hunt for peregrine falcons and eagles, had spotted what he thought was a dead stag with his binoculars, in a deep corrie cleaving the north face of the mountain that towered above the Carlin Castle estate. Something was odd about the carcass though, in its desiccated hollows and ridges. And when he had scrambled up the strewn boulders to the corrie, it was a man's body he found, wedged head-down in the cleft, like a gruesome breeched birth stillborn in the earth.

A month previously, Clive Forbes had attended Evensong and a party at the castle. Then, he'd completely vanished. Despite extensive enquiries, nobody had offered any information on his whereabouts, and the few castle guests that were questioned hadn't the faintest idea of what had become of him. As luck would have it, nobody had seen him leave the boisterous gathering. The young woman who had driven him to Carlin Castle, confessed to a lover's tiff. He'd been drinking, she said. Thinking he'd jilted her, she'd given up waiting on him to return from his mysterious jaunt, and had offered some friends a lift home in his stead.

The crows, the eagle and the foxes had devoured the meat from his bones, and the elements had washed the withered body clean. The only plausible explanation was that Clive Forbes had, for reasons known only to himself, walked up the hill that bordered the estate, lost his way in the dark, or been too drunk for caution, and fallen over the north cliff in the thick mist that came on suddenly that night. Because he had recently been estranged from his wife, lost his position at Gillespie and Forbes, abandoned his angry girlfriend, and because his only friend, Angus MacLeod, who might have kept up with his plans, had left for Edinburgh that same night, nobody reported his disappearance until a week later, in a bizarre twist of fate.

*

"We commend into thy hands, most merciful Father, the soul of this our brother departed, and we commit his body to the ground, earth to earth, ashes to ashes, dust to dust."

Helen's clod of dirt thudded on her husband's coffin. Angus and the others did the same, some letting the earth sift through their fingers, others getting rid of it quickly. Rosalind tossed in her handful, skull chip and all.

Just behind Clive's grave, the stones in the ancient cathedral wall were subtly defined by light and shadow, the variety of color remarkable, white to black, yellow, ochre, and the ever present lichen along the lower tier. Each stone had weathered in its own way over the centuries. Some were pockmarked and sliced in severe disintegration. Others were sinewy, the weakness in every surface exposed – the elements spared nothing – until each stone fused into wall or tower, the entire cathedral grounds coaxed by the elements into one flowing sculpture.

Visible over the wall where it descended down the hill, the sea sparkled in the setting sun. A fishing boat, headed for the flagged lobster pots, left a dazzling wake behind, and black-headed gulls and fulmars hovered over the boat, catching the sun with their breasts and wings in silvery flashes.

Rosalind smiled at the beauty, already thinking of where she wanted to take her mother and son around the town, to all her favorite places, when they came for a Christmas visit, and a memorial service for Uncle Rab, only a few weeks away. It would be the first time Sheila had returned since she'd emigrated with baby Rosalind more than forty years ago. Angus came to stand behind her, and she let her head fall back to rest on his shoulder. They gazed at each other, and his lips brushed her forehead in a tender kiss.

A crow cawed. Rosalind turned to see Morag standing at the gate to the higher section of the cathedral graveyard. Macha hopped up and back on the stone archway over Morag's dark head. From even that distance, the witch's scowling face conveyed her own agenda, as she watched the proceedings with the patience of a hunter. Kirsteen and Calum appeared just behind.

Alistair also noticed Morag and the young couple standing at the upper wall to the cemetery. He looked at Rosalind and lifted a white eyebrow. He knew, he knew on some uncanny level, what had happened after the Samhuinn gathering at his castle.

*

A crash of wood on the fire instantly woke Rosalind. A dark creature was squatting by the fireplace, reaching for another log and tossing it in, to an explosion of sparks. The creature was naked, a lithe and muscular body decorated in primitive body tattoos, and for a few minutes Rosalind could not tell the species or the sex, or the time, or even recall where she was, until the figure picked up a candle in a brass holder, and turned to face her. Morag, naked but for the torc around her neck, came silently to the bed and drew the sheets away from Rosalind's nude body. She looked with forthright desire, lingering over every detail, until Rosalind sat up in the agony of wanting her touch, and reached out a hand.

The witch in turn extended her arm to Rosalind, adorned with blue tattoos, hand to shoulder, all spirals and lines, and brushed her fingers along the curve of Rosalind's thigh. Rosalind gasped and drew her leg away, with the sudden recollection of the same ghostly arm in Angus's tomb.

Suddenly everything came flooding back, with the castle party, and Angus, and Helen at the stone circle, and…Angus. Who apparently had left after their brief love-making.

Morag bent over, to place the candle on the bedside table, then moved her lips where the fingers had traced, breath hot, until she arrived at Rosalind's throat. Her mouth opened to rake sharp teeth up the neck. Morag paused again, to study

Rosalind's face, then went on hands and knees over her body. It was not human, the look and the movement. Rosalind wondered if this wild witch would smell Angus on her, and had a brief qualm over the unexpected and novel opportunity of taking two lovers in one night. All too easily and without a second thought, Rosalind shed her fear, put Angus out of her mind and welcomed this dark creature. Morag slowly lowered to a kiss. With absolute abandon, Rosalind received her. The kiss was light, yet with all the passion in reserve behind it. Morag remained crouched over her, only their mouths meeting in languorous kisses that grew bolder and insistent, till they paused to draw breath, and then back into a slow slide of lips and teeth and tongue.

Rosalind had been writhing, lifting, before she was aware of it, her hands on Morag's strong upper arms, caressing the hard triceps and shoulder. Morag lowered her body to Rosalind's, and the heat and sinewy movement of it caught Rosalind's breath, and she turned her face away from the kisses to feel the length of their naked bodies moving against each other. Breasts to breasts and belly and thighs between, then she slid her leg up and over Morag's leg and lower back, opening to the slow caressing movement of belly and weight of thigh. The recent memory of Angus returned, and it was impossible not to compare this lover with him, his beard and breath, his masculine scent and the weight of him on her. This was a wonder as overwhelming as that had been, quite different in its pace and eroticism, and she tumbled back into Morag's skillful passion, completely immersed and surrendered to the new sensations.

The only urgency was in the regret of lost opportunities. Now they were together, nothing before or after could intrude, and they let time slide out of all consciousness. Morag embraced Rosalind and rolled them both over so that she lay beneath. Rosalind marveled at the painted body, exploring every part with her hands, and then lips and tongue, tasting the earthy woad and warm skin. All senses became so heightened the dancing flames over the candles were unbearable to look at. Every touch ascended from the previous, to an exquisite pleasure, which they let linger and rise and fall away in abandon, spiraling deeper and deeper into a sensual trance. It ambushed the senses, then consciousness, until they were flying in a calm ocean of bliss.

Orgasm, far from signaling the end, became a punctuation on the way, rising each time in intensity. Hands and arms, feet and shins, lips and eyes, then the entire body lost its sense of solid form, to become a tingling airiness of pure ecstasy.

Rosalind took a deep breath and rolled to her back, and was astonished to realize the lightening of the room came from the tardy November dawn. It illuminated the thick stone of the window casements, as the candle flame leapt and dived into its brass cup, a sudden rise of a thin stream of smoke spiraling up as it extinguished. Exhaustion coaxed them back into their warm animal bodies. Morag lay her head on Rosalind's breast and slept, limbs heavy and breath steady where it feathered over Rosalind's tingling skin. Rosalind stayed awake for a short while, watching the slow dawn bring the world back, amused to see the white sheets crumpled and stained blue with woad, until she too slipped into dreams of fire and dancing spirits. The Scottish countryside dawned quiet but for the rooks and crows waking and attending to the day.

*

A few people crossed themselves at the priest's blessing. He closed his worn prayer book, moved to Helen's side and spoke to her, a signal for others to quietly disperse.

Mrs. Pearse sidled up. "Are you going to heaven?"

"I don't think," Rosalind said to her seriously, "that I can honestly answer you. I suspect the journey on the road to what you call heaven, my bonnie road, is the important thing."

Mrs. Pearse blinked twice. "There is only one way to heaven, and that way through Christ Jesus if you accept him as your personal savior." She held out a pamphlet.

"No thanks," sighed Rosalind.

Morag, Kirsteen, and Calum approached the graveside. They all watched a small avalanche of earth fall onto Clive's coffin as the gravedigger swiftly shoveled the dirt into the pit with a practiced hand. But the intense look in Morag's eyes was quite different from the rest of the company.

"Rosalind." Helen came and embraced her. Tears squeezed from her closed lids. Rosalind held her, feeling the thin, fragile shoulders under her suit.

"I wanted to say," said Helen, "I wanted to say that I'm so glad you're not leaving. Will you come 'round soon?"

"Of course," Rosalind said.

A man excused himself from a small group and came to stand next to Helen, putting a solicitous hand on her back. It was Patrick Buchan, the Medieval Chairman who had hosted Angus's ceilidh at his home. He smiled at Rosalind, and shot a stern look at Angus. There was no real way Angus could protest his innocence with the missing gold cross from the treasure hoard, and the cloud of suspicion would never lift. And yet, Rosalind saw, there was a twinkle in Patrick's eye.

The funeral guests broke into smaller groups to talk. Some drifted away, some stayed to watch the earth being shoveled into the grave. Patrick took Angus aside, leading him to the side of a medieval stone-built well house, the Holy Well, where they could stand on the little lawn in front of the entrance. "Yes, come," Patrick invited Helen and Rosalind to join them.

"What's this about, Patrick?" asked Angus.

"Quite a serious matter. Now," he touched the outside of his dark suit's pocket and nodded. "I have some interesting news. Concerning the missing pectoral cross."

Angus took a deep breath and felt for Rosalind's hand.

"Apparently it was relatively easy to chase down a dealer on the black market when he tried to sell it."

Angus's head snapped up.

"Not only that, he confessed to the police who had sold it to him. No honor among thieves, as they say."

"For God's sake, Patrick, who?" said Angus.

Patrick reached into his pocket and pulled out a rectangular black jewelry box. He gave it to Angus, who carefully opened it and pushed the protective cloth aside. Everyone bent their heads over the box. Angus gasped to see the gold, the ruby, the errant cross that had almost destroyed his career, his life.

"I suppose," Helen said, "it was my delightful husband."

"I'm afraid so," said Patrick.

She laughed. "Don't suppose I'll ever find the money!"

Angus's head was deeply bowed as he closed the box, and handed it back to Patrick. Rosalind slid her arm over his shoulder and drew him into a long, silent embrace.

Helen's family, with the priest in solicitous tow came and

swept her and Patrick away. Following the news of Clive's strange death, Helen had returned to her own home. Her family – sisters, brother, and her elderly mother – had arrived earlier and begun the process of completely clearing out all signs of Clive's presence, with one too many confessions that they never did trust the man, and only wished they'd said something at the time.

Rosalind watched them go out the gate to the Pends, Helen and Patrick walking close side by side. It appeared that Helen would not be lonely any longer.

Angus turned away and fumbled in his sporran to pull out a hanky, which he dabbed his cheeks with, then blew his nose with a honk.

The gravedigger finished his work, and rolled the turf over the bare earth. He gathered up his tools, nodded at them, and quietly left. The cathedral cemetery was empty but for the small circle of friends.

"But I will be a bridegroom in my death, and run into't as to a lover's bed," said Alastair mournfully. "Well!" He broke his reverie and looked around at everyone. "Come along, my dears. Calum has put on a tea for us, if Auntie Meg hasn't scarfed it all."

Angus took Rosalind's arm, somewhere still between shock and relief and joy, and they walked up the gravel path to the upper gate into the cathedral grounds. Rosalind realized that Morag was not with them, and stopped, turning to look back.

Morag stood on Clive's grave, arms folded, head bowed. Then she raised her head, eyes turned inward with a bright ferocity. She slowly lifted her arms over her head in a graceful arc. Her fingers met and spread, like the tips of a stag's antlers.

Rosalind gripped Angus's arm tightly with a sudden foreboding.

One of Morag's feet hovered, toe pointing to the side, and back, then the other, and with a little hop she began to dance a Highland Fling. Slowly at first, her breath hissing, her movements became more and more savage, until her feet pummeled the turf, and her face contorted in savage glee as she spun around on the grave.

"Come, my angels," Alastair said softly. "Sometimes it's best not to look."

The little company trailed quietly along the gravel path.

Familiar distant thunder from pewter-colored skies caused Rosalind to stop when they reached the east tower of the cathedral, well away and beyond the walls from the lower cemetery and Morag's death dance. "I'd like to have a moment alone," she said to the little group, and looked up at Angus. "Do you mind?"

Calum and Kirsteen waved back at her and continued on at a slow pace, his brawny arm keeping Kirsteen close. Angus nodded, squeezed her hands, and followed.

"But of course, my dear," said Alastair. The thunder grew louder as a Leuchars' RAF jet took off. "Per ardua ad astra. That's the RAF motto. Through adversity to the stars."

Rosalind watched his tall figure stride after Angus and the young couple, through the cathedral grounds, his silver-topped cane swinging at each step. She went by the haunted tower and through the small side gate, to the cliffs above the sea. The water was calm, flat, stretching far away into the lighter sky of the horizon. On the rocks emerging from the receding tide, half a dozen tan seals sprawled. The jet roared with renewed vigor. Beyond the castle's silhouette, across the Eden estuary, with Tentsmuir Forest its backdrop, she saw the ball of fire flicker through the trees, then arc up above it all, a single bright flame, going like a star into the sky.

Epilogue

When she looked up again, a shining line had appeared across the bottom of the canvas. It closely matched the silver sky over the subject, the ring of stones at Carlin Castle.

Photographs were pinned to the wall behind the canvas, reminders of the autumn scene as when the painting was begun, on site. It was not satisfactory to rely on film, but she had done enough to need only a few days studio time to finish.

The sound of a lonely pibroch came from the cassette player, a recording of a Gaelic Mod, featuring a piece performed by young Calum Hardie, and a couple of Border Ballads performed by Kirsteen and Morag, which included her favorite, "Thomas Rymer" and his journey along the bonnie road to fair Elfland.

Rosalind worked diligently, sometimes humming or talking herself through rough spots, as a tabby kitten swatted a ball of paper across the skittery floorboards. It bumped into the leg of the old family spinning wheel, and Rosalind reached out a hand to steady the wheel and stop it toppling over. The kitten was a gift from Morag, as was a sprig of mistletoe awaiting placement as Christmas decor. A crystal vase on the small mantel caught the sunlight, a thank you gift from Helen. And in pride of place, perched atop an antique clock, a beautifully carved little seal pup smiled up at Rosalind.

Her lover, Angus MacLeod, would soon be coming over for dinner, and she would take him to the bed she'd been born in, and make love, both journeying with the other into new realms of erotic delights and a deepening companionship made all the better by its respect for her solitude.

The line of silver light broadened in the setting sun's rays coming through the window. It was the solstice, beginning the longest night of the year, herald to the rebirth of a new solar cycle.

To the northwest, in the Highlands, Morag would be in the stone circle, where the weak winter sun was sinking perfectly between the megaliths on either side of the recumbent stone. The collected light would be sent spiraling down its mysterious incised rings and lines and hollows, the sun caught by the stones like a pendulum at the suspension of its arc.

And in Tentsmuir Forest, just over the estuary, the same sun would be shooting beams of white brilliance down the short entrance to the Neolithic cairn, spilling light into the cup-and-ring markings on the stone within, continuing down to illuminate the tomb itself, on this, the only time of year it did so. A tomb excavated, then returned to the dead, the project completed, the brief human interaction barely touching the ancient sleep that lay over it.

The sunlight on the painting reached the stones, as it would the actual stones in the Highland circle, silvering them, highlighting their shadows across the dry wheat colored grass and bracken to the forest's edge. The painting itself changed in the sun's rays, pulling out depths Rosalind had not been aware of, enhancing and distorting her work, so that she stopped and cleaned her brushes, smiling at the little magic happening, and wished Morag well at her solstice celebration.

The kitten crouched by the fire, eyes closing. Rosalind watched the brilliance wash the entire canvas. A shadow flickered, a seagull alighting on the roof across the lane, caught in the last rays. Swiftly the sun sank below the hills, darkening first the lane, drawing a shadow along the bottom of the painting and closing upwards like a theater curtain opening to a new play.

*

Morag's Quair of Light and Shadows
My grandmother passed me in transit. She was leaving, I was coming into this world, my dear mother the midwife of death and birth, her wise hands the bridge at the same mystical passage. Grannie Morag Gilbride kissed me as she passed by, kissed to life a legacy, not only her name to be my name, but her fierceness and gift of magic to be mine, knowing as I could not, how much need of them I would have fifty years later. And best of all, trademark of my kin, she gave me the incomparable ability to manifest divinity in the act of love-making. This, the forgotten legacy of our

ancestors, kept alive yet by a few, by a fortunate few, shared by those courageous enough to embrace us, to die in our arms, to be reborn into the clan of the Shining Ones. The Sidhe of the new millennium.

So. The spell of our lives is cast. The circle of fate is drawn, and we, heirs to the ancient gods, and parents to new-born deities, strive to uncover the magical essence of our true nature from the hurly burly of the profane. It is this in-between time for which I was created.

Find me in the pause where seasons change. Find me behind the spiral lines incised into Neolithic stone. Catch me where the old legends intersect with the birthing of new myths.

I am the quair of divination.
I am the last of the ancient ones.
I am Morag, flower of the children of Bride.

END

Glossary

Sources: (most from Collins, other definitions noted if not)

***Collins Scots Dictionary*, HarperCollins, Glasgow 1996**

***Oxford Dictionary of Celtic Mythology*, Peter B. Ellis, Oxford University Press, Oxford, 1992.**

***The Silver Bough*, Vol. 1; Scottish Folklore and Folk-belief, F. Marian McNeill, Wm Maclellan, Glasgow, 1977**

Glossary of Scots & Gaelic Terms and Phrases

Ainster: Anstruther
Airts: a direction or point of the compass
Arbroath smokie: a small haddock that has been cured by being salted and then smoked over a fire.
Auld: old
Awfy' braw: very lovely
Aye: yes; *adv*: Always, ever, continually, on all occasions
Bairn: a baby or young child
Baith: both
Bane (to the bare bane): bone
Bastartin: a swear word used to indicate dislike or annoyance
Baw Bag: ball bag; testicles
Besom: (**biz**-zum) derogatory term for woman or girl
Birl: to spin or revolve
Bodhran: (bow-rahn) shallow one-sided drum
Boak (gie's me the boak) to boak is to vomit (makes me want to vomit)
Bonnie (Bonny): attractive and pleasant to look at
Brae: hill or hillside
Braw: fine or excellent
Bride/Brìghde: (Bride or **Bree**-ja) 'The Exalted One' a Scottish Goddess

Breastie: breast
Burn: stream or brook
**Cailleach: Old woman; Cailleach Bheur: Blue Hag, Winter Goddess, Scottish creatrix Goddess in myths & place names
Caim: A circle blessing
Cannae gie back: "Cannot give back"
Canny: astute
Cantrips: spell or magic charm
Ceilidh: (**Kale**-ee) social gathering with folk music, singing, dancing, and storytelling
Corrie: hollow on a hill or mountainside
Coorse: rough, course
Couthy: something that is couthy is plain, homely (homey in US) or unsophisticated
Cowrin: cowering
Craw: crow
Cried (as in, 'they cried her'): called
Cu Chulainn: an Irish mythological hero who appears in the stories of the Ulster Cycle, as well as in Scottish and Manx folklore
Daft: a foolish or mentally deficient person
Dae Fash Yoursel': Don't worry about it
Dicht: to wipe something clean
Dirl: to vibrate or shake
Dram: a measure of alcoholic spirits
Dreich: dreary or tedious
Frith: augury, a species of divination enabling the 'frithir,' augurer, to see into the unseen
Gang aboot: go about
Glaur (Ye're a' a glaur!): Soft, sticky mud. "You're a muddy mess."
Girners (to girn): to moan, complain, or grumble
Gloaming: the period of twilight at dusk
Gob: mouth
Guddle: an untidy or messy place or state
Guiser: a person who has put on fancy dress to take part in any various traditional events, notably at Halloween
Hame: home
Harled: to harl the outer walls of a building is to cover them with a mixture of lime and gravel, to roughcast them.
Haud your Wheesht: be quiet
Ken: know

Hoodie Craw: hooded crow
Hoose: house
Jobbie: turd
Keek: to peep or glance at something
Killmoullach: a hobgoblin
Kirk: a Presbyterian church
Lairig Ghru: one of the mountain passes through the Cairngorms of Scotland
Lang Rig: a long strip of cultivated or plowed land
Macha: one of the group of goddess concerned with war, fertility, and prosperity. "Macha the Crow" by 9th C. glossator Cormac
Mind (Do ye mind yon laddie?): to remember
Mod: annual festival of Gaelic language and culture
Noo, or the noo: now
Pibroch: a piece of music for the bagpipes
Piseag Dhubh: little black cat
Plocherin' and Clocherin': Fife description coughing fit
Puirt a Beul: literally "tunes from a mouth" is a traditional form of song native to Scotland;
Quair: book
Reiver: raider
Sain: to make holy
Samhuinn: "Summer's End" Scottish Celtic quarter day Fire Festival
Sassanach: an English person
Selkie: in folklore, a mythical creature which takes on the form of a seal in the sea and a human on land.
Sidhe: Mound or hill. The ancient gods, driven underground below the hills, were relegated in folk memories to fairies, aes sidhe, the people of the hills. Thus the word became the word for 'fairies.' (Oxford Dictionary of Celtic Mythology)
**Sidhe Draoi: dryad 'fairy druid'
Sgian Dhu: short-bladed knife or dagger with a black hilt
Skirl: a loud shrill sound
Slainte: Slainte Mhath, sometimes shortened to slainte, is a Gaelic toast used especially when drinking whisky. It means good health.
Sleekit: sleek
Spae Wife: a woman who can foretell the future
Spurtle: a wooden stick used for stirring porridge
Strathspey: type of dance or music in four-time

Tattie-heid: potato head
Torc: Celtic necklace
Tir Nan Og: Land of the Ever-young, the Otherworld
Trauchled: a work or a task which is tiring, monotonous, and takes a long time to complete.
Tumshee: Neep, turnip
Urisk: a spirit of the forest (McNeill)
Wean: a child
Wee: small or little
Wee Frees: an informal, slightly derogatory, nickname for a member of the Free Church of Scotland
Wee Mary: nickname for timid, plain Scottish woman
Wee Wifie Soor Face: Sour-faced woman
Wheesht: an interjection meaning "be quiet," or "shut up!"
Winnock-bunker: a window recess with a seat in it

Book Club Questions

General Questions:

1. Are there situations and/or characters you can identify with? If so, how?
2. What major emotion(s) did the story evoke in you as a reader?
3. What passages strike you as insightful, even profound?
4. Is the ending satisfying? If so, why? If not, why not...and how would you change it?
5. Has this novel changed you — broadened your perspective? Have you learned something new or been exposed to different ideas about people or a certain part of the world?

Specific Questions:

1. The book opens with Morag's Quair of Light and Shadow. How does this set the scene for the rest of the book?
2. What is Morag's role in the novel?
3. What motivates Clive? How did you feel when you read about his fate? Was it really Morag's curse that brought Clive to the Standing Stones that night, or merely coincidence?
4. Did Ros make the right choice regarding Angus? What decision would you have made? Why?
5. The book is set in Scotland in the late 1970s – what difference would it make to the story if it was set in a different place and time?
6. The themes of fate/destiny and choice are explored closely in The Bonnie Road. Do you think the characters' actions are the result of freedom of choice or of destiny?
7. At the time The Bonnie Road takes place, 'The Wica,' as it was known then, was slowly making inroads from England into Scotland, where it sometimes clashed with the indigenous followers of the 'Auld Ways.' Since then, Wicca and its many variations have spread across the world. More

recently, however, the pendulum has swung back in Scotland to reclaim its distinctive pre-Christian and pre-Wiccan spirituality. The novel explores the first uneasy truce and alliance between the hereditary Scottish witch, Morag, and the High Priestess of an English Wiccan coven. What differences do you see in their spiritual expressions?

8. The two most influential characters that Rosalind interacts with, Angus and Morag, have powerful symbols associated with them. Can you identify the symbols and see how and why they are presented as opportunities for Rosalind's future?

9. Scottish mythology, ballads, and stories weave through the entire novel. Can you find times when characters personify certain roles, such as the terrifying Scottish Goddess, the Cailleach, or the Fairy Queen on her white horse?

10. Three very different spiritual awakenings occur in The Bonnie Road. Do you feel they are legitimate, or subjective? Have you ever experienced anything similar?

11. In the magical realm, Morag conveys these words: "Let us open our eyes to the great mysteries that surround us, Rosalind, my love, for in them is our only true solace in this fleeting world." Do you agree with her?

12. Is Rosalind's frequent bewilderment in the beginning of the novel a result of cultural differences, or are there deeper forces at work?

13. The history of religious persecution in Scotland is presented in a somewhat satirical manner. Could this be a metaphor for current issues in our world today?

14. The author writes with a slightly drawn-in omniscient viewpoint, moving between characters' thoughts in a single scene. How does this affect your reading experience? How would it be different if the point-of-view were entirely first-person, from another character's perspective?

15. Morag sets herself apart from human morality and sees herself as an instrument of fate when she claims that "there is no good or evil in creation but for the thoughts and deeds of men." Is she an enlightened spiritual individual, or self-deluded?

16. What does the 'bonnie road,' as a metaphorical path, mean to you?

More Books From ThunderPoint Publishing Ltd.

Mule Train
by Huw Francis
ISBN: 978-0-9575689-0-7 (kindle)
ISBN: 978-0-9575689-1-4 (Paperback)

Four lives come together in the remote and spectacular mountains bordering Afghanistan and explode in a deadly cocktail of treachery, betrayal and violence.

Written with a deep love of Pakistan and the Pakistani people, Mule Train will sweep you from Karachi in the south to the Shandur Pass in the north, through the dangerous borderland alongside Afghanistan, in an adventure that will keep you gripped throughout.

'Stunningly captures the feel of Pakistan, from Karachi to the hills' – tripfiction.com

A Good Death
by Helen Davis
ISBN: 978-0-9575689-7-6 (eBook)
ISBN: 978-0-9575689-6-9 (Paperback)

'*A good death is better than a bad conscience,*' said Sophie.

1983 – Georgie, Theo, Sophie and Helena, four disparate young Cambridge undergraduates, set out to scale Ausangate, one of the highest and most sacred peaks in the Andes.

Seduced into employing the handsome and enigmatic Wamani as a guide, the four women are initiated into the mystically dangerous side of Peru, Wamani and themselves as they travel from Cuzco to the mountain, a journey that will shape their lives forever.

2013 – though the women are still close, the secrets and betrayals of Ausangate chafe at the friendship.

A girls' weekend at a lonely Fenland farmhouse descends into conflict with the insensitive inclusion of an overbearing young academic toyboy brought along by Theo. Sparked by his unexpected presence, pent up petty jealousies, recriminations and bitterness finally explode the truth of Ausangate, setting the women on a new and dangerous path.

Sharply observant and darkly comic, Helen Davis's début novel is an elegant tale of murder, seduction, vengeance, and the value of a good friendship.

'The prose is crisp, adept, and emotionally evocative' – Lesbrary.com

The Birds That Never Flew
by Margot McCuaig

Shortlisted for the Dundee International Book Prize 2012
Longlisted for the Polari First Book Prize 2014
ISBN: 978-0-9929768-5-9 (eBook)
ISBN: 978-0-9929768-4-2 (Paperback)

'Have you got a light hen? I'm totally gaspin.'

Battered and bruised, Elizabeth has taken her daughter and left her abusive husband Patrick. Again. In the bleak and impersonal Glasgow housing office Elizabeth meets the provocatively intriguing drug addict Sadie, who is desperate to get her own life back on track.

The two women forge a fierce and interdependent relationship as they try to rebuild their shattered lives, but despite their bold, and sometimes illegal attempts it seems impossible to escape from the abuse they have always known, and tragedy strikes.

More than a decade later Elizabeth has started to implement her perfect revenge – until a surreal Glaswegian Virgin Mary steps in with imperfect timing and a less than divine attitude to stick a spoke in the wheel of retribution.

Tragic, darkly funny and irreverent, *The Birds That Never Flew* ushers in a new and vibrant voice in Scottish literature.

'...dark, beautiful and moving, I wholeheartedly recommend' scanoir.co.uk

Toxic
by Jackie McLean
Shortlisted for the Yeovil Book Prize 2011
ISBN: 978-0-9575689-8-3 (eBook)
ISBN: 978-0-9575689-9-0 (Paperback)

The recklessly brilliant DI Donna Davenport, struggling to hide a secret from police colleagues and get over the break-up with her partner, has been suspended from duty for a fiery and inappropriate outburst to the press.

DI Evanton, an old-fashioned, hard-living misogynistic copper has been newly demoted for thumping a suspect, and transferred to Dundee with a final warning ringing in his ears and a reputation that precedes him.

And in the peaceful, rolling Tayside farmland a deadly store of MIC, the toxin that devastated Bhopal, is being illegally stored by a criminal gang smuggling the valuable substance necessary for making cheap pesticides.

An anonymous tip-off starts a desperate search for the MIC that is complicated by the uneasy partnership between Davenport and Evanton and their growing mistrust of each others actions.

Compelling and authentic, Toxic is a tense and fast paced crime thriller.

'...a humdinger of a plot that is as realistic as it is frightening' – crimefictionlover.com

In The Shadow Of The Hill
by Helen Forbes
ISBN: 978-0-9929768-1-1 (eBook)
ISBN: 978-0-9929768-0-4 (Paperback)

An elderly woman is found battered to death in the common stairwell of an Inverness block of flats.

Detective Sergeant Joe Galbraith starts what seems like one more depressing investigation of the untimely death of a poor unfortunate who was in the wrong place, at the wrong time.

As the investigation spreads across Scotland it reaches into a past that Joe has tried to forget, and takes him back to the Hebridean island of Harris, where he spent his childhood.

Among the mountains and the stunning landscape of religiously conservative Harris, in the shadow of Ceapabhal, long buried events and a tragic story are slowly uncovered, and the investigation takes on an altogether more sinister aspect.

In The Shadow Of The Hill skilfully captures the intricacies and malevolence of the underbelly of Highland and Island life, bringing tragedy and vengeance to the magical beauty of the Outer Hebrides.

'...our first real home-grown sample of modern Highland noir' – Roger Hutchison; West Highland Free Press

Over Here
by Jane Taylor
ISBN: 978-0-9929768-3-5 (eBook)
ISBN: 978-0-9929768-2-8 (Paperback)

'It's coming up to twenty-four hours since the boy stepped down from the big passenger liner – it must be, he reckons foggily – because morning has come around once more with the awful irrevocability of time destined to lead nowhere in this worrying new situation. His temporary minder on board – last spotted heading for the bar some while before the lumbering process of docking got underway – seems to have vanished for good. Where does that leave him now? All on his own in a new country: that's where it leaves him. He is just nine years old.'

An eloquently written novel tracing the social transformations of a century where possibilities were opened up by two world wars that saw millions of men move around the world to fight, and mass migration to the new worlds of Canada and Australia by tens of thousands of people looking for a better life.

Through the eyes of three generations of women, the tragic story of the nine year old boy on Liverpool docks is brought to life in saddeningly evocative prose.

'...a sweeping haunting first novel that spans four generations and two continents...' Cristina Odone/Catholic Herald

The House with the Lilac Shutters: And other stories
by Gabrielle Barnby
ISBN: 978-1-910946-02-2 (eBook)
ISBN: 978-0-9929768-8-0 (Paperback)

Irma Lagrasse has taught piano to three generations of villagers, whilst slowly twisting the knife of vengeance; Nico knows a secret; and M. Lenoir has discovered a suppressed and dangerous passion.

Revolving around the Café Rose, opposite The House with the Lilac Shutters, this collection of contemporary short stories link a small town in France with a small town in England, traces the unexpected connections between the people of both places and explores the unpredictable influences that the ripples of the past can have on the present. Characters weave in and out of each other's stories, secrets are concealed and new connections are made.

With a keenly observant eye, Barnby illustrates the everyday tragedies, sorrows, hopes and joys of ordinary people in this vividly understated and unsentimental collection.

Talk of the Toun
by Helen MacKinven
ISBN: 978-1-910946-00-8 (eBook)
ISBN: 978-0-9929768-7-3 (Paperback)

A resonantly emotional black comedy of love, family life and friendship, Talk of the Toun is a coming-of-age tale set in the summer of 1985, in the working class central belt town of Falkirk.

'She was greetin' again. But there's no need for Lorraine to be feart, since the first day of primary school, Angela has always been there to mop up her tears and snotters.'

Lifelong friends Angela and Lorraine are two very different girls. With an increasing divide in their aspirations and ambitions putting their friendship under increasing strain.

Artistically gifted Angela has her sights set on art school, but girls like Angela, from a small town Council scheme, are expected to settle for a nice little secretarial job at the local factory like everyone else. Her only ally is gallus gran, Senga, the pet psychic, who believes that her granddaughter can be whatever she wants.

Best friend Lorraine has very different ambitions in life, and seems intent on finding a man and staying on the scheme just like her mam. But Angie has plans for Lorraine too.

Effortlessly capturing the political, religious and social intricacies of 1980's Scotland, MacKinven will have you laughing and crying in turn as the two girls wrestle with the complications of growing up and exploring who they really are.

'Fresh, fierce and funny...a sharp and poignant study of growing up in 1980s Scotland. You'll laugh, you'll cry...you'll cringe.' – KAREN CAMPBELL

Printed in Great Britain
by Amazon